IS ALICE?

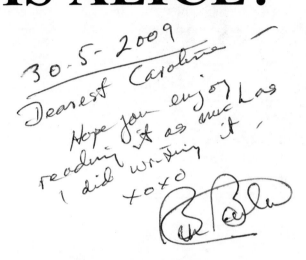

30·5· 2009
Dearest Caroline
Hope you enjoy
reading it as much as
I did writing it,
xoxo

Bill Bailey

GW00694163

chipmunkapublishing
the mental health publisher
empowering people

Bill Bailey

Published by
Chipmunkapublishing
PO Box 6872
Brentwood
Essex CM13 1ZT
United Kingdom

http://www.chipmunkapublishing.com

Edited by Aleksandra Lech

Chipmunkapublishing gratefully acknowledge the support of Arts Council England.

IS ALICE?

FOREWORD

For over a decade I have been the loving partner and carer of a woman diagnosed with 'schizo-affective disorder.' *Is Alice?* incorporates a description of some of her experiences during her last hospitalisation over four years ago within a fictional setting, as Theo struggles to understand Alice's madness and develop his organic theory of consciousness that might help explain such a devastating illness and the canvas of 'normality' from which madness can bloom.

Is Alice? is also a powerful and fictionalised love story. I wrote the novel solely as a manuscript gift for my partner, and publication is therefore dependent upon her wishes. Her primary one is anonymity. She is not 'Alice,' and I am not 'Theo.' This is not a biography. Fiction is used in *Is Alice?* to illuminate an actual madness, along with a real search for the ideas that may help in understanding the living and political nature of consciousness – the structure of 'normality' and the 'real' world, and its incoherent collapse into the hell that is known as schizophrenia. There are passages from the patient's point of view, which make this novel an unusual project. That is because the inner landscape of madness does have a logic and meaning that should be acknowledged and evoked, instead of ridiculed or misunderstood. I feel that contemporary psychology – never mind clinical psychiatry – fails in its attempt to address the nature of consciousness, or its creation of the 'world.' I believe philosophy underpins psychology, not the other way around.

As my partner's carer, I have witnessed the depths of her illness, and hope my portrayal can help others understand its rhythms of horror. But most of all, I wish to let this novel stand as my tribute to her courage, persistence and love in the quest we have undertaken to put together a world that is cleaner and simpler to know, one that is hopefully closer to the truth. Her life has been transformed as she has reclaimed the territory of her own existence from a life where she felt she deserved nothing and was worth nothing.

I am convinced 'schizophrenia' is not a medical problem. It is an existential one. It isn't a 'disease.' It is a catastrophic disordering of the values of the world – a fiction, really, but one that is as 'real' as the common sense world we mistakenly think we know so well. Because it, too, is a fiction *we have agreed upon*, lies and all. I have called it the social matrix.

My view of the psychiatric treatment of blameless victims of madness is that it struggles blindly to brutally shoehorn a distressing human problem into a medical model that is as primitive as phrenology. In an affront to Hippocrates, psychiatrists can harm their patients. At the very least, simple *asylum* would do no more harm to human beings who, though mad, still deserve our unremitting respect. Instead there are drugs, electro-convulsive 'therapy', and even psycho-surgery – the effects of which are poorly understood by the psychiatric community. Sufferers are incarcerated in prison-like buildings, and far too often suffer abuse and neglect by indifferent, badly-trained staff.

IS ALICE?

Again, though, *Is Alice?* is a poignant story that is uncommon and numinous. It was written with love *for* my partner, and I had no other reader in mind when I wrote it. This changes the accent and meaning of the work. My intention was to please her with a tale woven simply from words. In a sense this returns to the origins of stories themselves. If so, then that pleases me.

Bill Bailey

IS ALICE?

CHAPTER ONE

The hush rolled across the Royal Albert Hall like a noiseless wave, when moments before the auditorium was alive with an animal chatter as incessant and relentless – and far less musical – than the canopy of an Amazon rainforest. The house lights were quickly dimming. All eyes refocused on the stage, which held a concert grand Steinway piano, a cushioned stool, and no other props. The silence of the audience became sepulchral as the seconds slid by slowly. Ten seconds, twenty, then thirty, forty-five, one whole minute. When he finally appeared from behind the stage-right curtains, the breath intake from the audience was sharp, as if from one huge pair of lungs.

Aleksei Cherkasov was a tall man with a lantern jaw. He had once been even taller, but age had rounded his back, bringing his big chin closer to his chest. He was bald, except for a crinkly fringe of still-dark hair that connected the backs of his ears like an Alice band. Having recently celebrated his 81st birthday, Cherkasov walked slowly and carefully across the polished floor of the stage towards the piano. Surely this must be his final public concert. Ten days ago he played the identical programme on the same stage. The over-subscription of that concert led to this extraordinary evening. The legendary Russian maestro demanded that another evening be fixed to accommodate those who failed to get a seat in the first concert. In any other case, this would have been impossible, as the Royal Albert is fully booked over a year in advance. Schedules were frantically shuffled, agents and performers called, all the heavy furniture of bookings were shoved and pushed. Somehow one more evening was created for this astonishing pianist to play again, one last time before he disappeared back into Russia and expected retirement. Aleksei Cherkasov was the last of the great Russian virtuosos of the 20th Century, a man considered the equal of Horowitz and Gilels, and even the monumental Richter. If anything, the second bookings were snapped up more rapidly than the first, so Cherkasov insisted some accommodation should be made for those who could bear standing for the length of the whole concert.

In the early years of his fame, Aleksei Cherkasov was treated gingerly by the West. Most of his life was spent as a citizen of the USSR, and he was as outspoken in its support as he occasionally was in criticism of the government. Yet his avuncular charm and ironic wit finally endeared him to people all over the world – that and his absolute command of the piano. In his youth he was known for his fire and ice at the keyboard, but in later years his musicality became more internalised, gorgeously dense and philosophical. His concerts became like séances as he was the medium between this and another world. He completely re-invented the late Beethoven sonatas, and one reviewer exclaimed that he must be experiencing the music exactly as Beethoven would have played it himself. His Debussy was ethereal, like gossamer threads of silk. His Bach unfolded with Euclidian clarity in its celestial geometries. He let it be known that Mozart was his favourite, and developed the composer's precocious playfulness to bring smiles to the faces of his audiences. Yet he could also tease the depths from shallower works that would have musicians hustling back to have another look at the scores. The respect with which he was held by the musical community was awesome.

Only since the disintegration of the USSR did he begin wearing his Order of Lenin medal when he played. It was not ostentatious. It was a simple statement. Perhaps you could say his citizenship in the USSR fully began with the collapse of his old country. He was contemptuous of the new systems of market-oriented global capitalism, and pointed out in interviews that an old three-shell game was being played where the poor became poorer and the rich thrived. In the old days, he commented, everyone at least had a roof over their heads and food in their bellies. Few went without. He didn't wave the red flag, but he wore his medal whenever he appeared in public. He realised he needn't say any more than that.

Aleksei Cherkasov sat down carefully on the piano stool and contemplated the white and black keyboard. His chin crushed his splendid black bow tie as he examined for a moment his instruments, those big miner's hands, now heavily veined and lined. Slowly, he closed his eyes and began to play.

It was Schubert's B-flat Major Sonata, with the extravagantly long first movement based on a melody so sweet that Schubert could not let it go until every drop of emotion could be squeezed from it. It so reminded Cherkasov of a youth that would never be restored. Memories were dim and unreliable. But when he closed his eyes, he imagined he was 13 years old, leaning with his elbows on an old wooden fence, his chin on the back of his folded hands. His huge, serious eyes were following the magical swing of Ludmilla's petticoats as she walked past his house with two loaves of bread. The longing of the adolescent boy was still in the old pianist's heart. It was pain, and it was joy. Ludmilla was almost 16, far too old for him, he thought. They weren't really sexual thoughts. He dreamed only of holding her close to him and burying his face in her blonde ringlets. Just to enfold her, to touch her, that's all. That would be heaven. He imagined the two of them lifting from the earth and rising to a palace of stardust where they would lie side by side, listening to the serenade of angels. And for the young Aleksei, Ludmilla *was* angelic. What magic powers did she possess to lift his whole mind to the heavens? The movement of her body was inexpressibly and exquisitely beautiful…

Cherkasov opened his eyes and followed his fingers on the keyboard. The music took him back to moments like that – so romantic, so youthful, so unblighted by coruscating age. He felt the audience, too, and hoped he and Schubert were helping to illuminate memories of their youthful naivety. He was nervous – as are all performers – but not tense. His focus was to provide access to himself, the deepest meanings of his existence, and thus, he hoped, to Schubert. He raised his eyes from the keyboard, and he was seeing not the stage but those few memories still preserved in the catacombs of self.

Then he did see something else, something peculiar, something completely out of context, as if from another kind of reverie. A man had walked hurriedly onto the stage from the wings. He wore only a pair of underpants and socks. Cherkasov watched as he continued playing.

IS ALICE?

The man stopped downstage in the centre and addressed the audience.

"I desecrate the gods by interrupting this glorious concert, but there is no option," the man said in a deep, yet steady, bass voice. "I have to tell you a story…"

Cherkasov lifted his hands from the keyboard and placed them in his lap.

"You must hear me. You must let me tell it. It is vital for you, and it is vital for me…"

At this point the amazement of the audience began to turn to disgust and fury. There were shouts from men and women in the darkness of the auditorium.

"For god's sake, man!"

"Get off!"

"Shut up! Are you crazy!"

The individual voices and words were quickly drowned as many rose from their seats, shouting and protesting at this surreal intrusion. From backstage four men advanced on the man who was now desperately trying to make his voice heard.

Suddenly Cherkasov stood up behind his piano and held up his huge hand. *"Nyet. Postoy. Nye dyeloy eto. Pazhaluysta."*

"Please," he said slowly in heavily-accented English. "Do not do this. It is a sanctuary. He is a human being. In distress. You were not listening to Schubert. You do not *understand*."

The noise from the audience died to a murmur. The four men who now held the intruder all turned to him.

"Who are we to be the judge?" Cherkasov continued, his chin now raised. "This music must have dignity. This man must be *treated* with dignity."

He turned and called to the wings. "Dmitri!"

A tall, thin, elegantly dressed elderly man emerged from stage left.

"*Provodyi etovo muzhchinu v moyu grimyornuyu i pozobotsya o tom chtobe yemu bilo udobno,*" Cherkasov murmured to Dmitri.

The pianist walked slowly over to the partially naked man who was still being held by the stage hands. "I have asked my agent, Dmitri, to take you to my dressing room. After the concert, *I* will listen to your story."

One of the stage hands leaned forward and spoke quietly. "Maestro, we have information that this man has escaped from a mental institution. He could be dangerous."

Cherkasov turned his attention to the man in his underwear. He was perhaps 50 years old, tall, heavily built, with a moustache. "Are you dangerous?"

"Am I resisting these gentlemen?" he replied, adding an ironic smile. "No, I'm neither dangerous nor mad. I've been driven to interrupt this celestial music by insane injustice and a world that will not hear me."

He paused for a moment, his eyes misty. "I hesitated backstage, leaning against the wall with my eyes closed in the darkness. Your playing so moved me, and the B-flat Major is so eternally dear to me, that I almost couldn't do it. Yet I had to. Maestro, it's not me. It's the world. The world is mad…"

Cherkasov flicked his right arm in a gesture of dismissal. "*Da*. Yes. You're right. The world. It's mad."

"You said this was a sanctuary. That's what I seek. Sanctuary. Where I can have the time to tell my story."

"You have found it," Cherkasov replied softly. "Go now with Dmitri to my room…"

"Please…" the man interrupted.

"Yes?"

"May I just listen from the wings? Just the Schubert, just the one sonata?"

"Of course." He turned to his agent. "*Dima, podai yemu stul i ostansya s nim..*"

Cherkasov took the man by the arm and slowly led him to the wings. Dmitri and the four stage hands followed. Then he returned to the piano.

"I will begin again the Schubert," he murmured to the audience.

* * *

"We had tickets to your earlier concert here, my partner and I…"

Theo Hawthorn stopped and squeezed his lips together. He was wearing Cherkasov's dressing gown, which was a surprisingly good fit. He was sitting on the small sofa, and the pianist was watching him from the only armchair. Cherkasov had removed his tie and jacket and unbuttoned his shirt, but he was now wearing glasses that made his eyes look owlish. He waited patiently for Hawthorn to continue.

Hawthorn shook his head, as if to clear it. "There was a queue at the box office. A big queue, a huge one, people everywhere. Alice – my partner – had already pre-ordered and paid for the tickets on her credit card, and all we had to do was pick them up. Simple."

He paused again, but the old pianist remained silent. "You see, Maestro…"

"Don't call me 'Maestro.' It always upsets me. You must call me Alyosha."

IS ALICE?

Hawthorn smiled, and his shoulders relaxed a little. "Then call me Theo."

"Good. Theo. Go on. Tell me."

He shook his head sadly and looked down at the dressing gown. It was an old one, probably silk, but very worn, black with red piping. "It's such a complex story. Are you sure you have the time, Alyosha? Or the patience?"

The old man shrugged his shoulders. He didn't seem tired. "I have *some* time. *Some* patience. Enough to listen. I promised."

Hawthorn blew out a lungful of air and leaned back on the sofa, closing his eyes for a moment. "The Schubert. The B-flat Major. It is very important to Alice and me. When we first met I veered away. She was – *is* – very beautiful, but she had some fairly severe mental health problems, and I…didn't feel like I could handle them. At first. Many things happened. I'm trying to accordion the story a little here…"

"Accordion? I…"

"Er, fold it up a little. Make it shorter. But things did happen. Very dramatic things. Between us. At a very crucial moment the Schubert sonata was playing. It was one of my favourites anyway, but at this moment I'm talking about, the heavens seemed to open, and… and there was a different universe."

Cherkasov nodded his head. His accent was heavy and his words slow. "So you fell in love."

"Yes, yes…but it was more than that. It changed Alice's life. It brought hope for her, a chance to escape from regular spells in the hospital that…"

Hawthorn stopped, frustrated at being unable to compress everything into fewer words. "Your performance of that sonata was a key moment…"

Cherkasov waved his hand. "But you. You have these problems too? You are patient? I had to talk to these men. Nurses. From hospital. They wait for you at stage door. They want to take you back to hospital. I told them, shoo, go way, I get back to hospital. I have give my word'." He shrugged. "I think they still wait for you. Are you lunatic?"

"Me?" Hawthorn gave an ironic smile. "No. Never. No previous problems, no previous admissions. I've never even seen a psychologist, never mind a psychiatrist. No history at all of mental illness. I'm a playwright."

Cherkasov frowned. "You write plays?"

"Not a famous one. I…don't even make a living. But that's what I do. The theatre."

Cherkasov smiled broadly. "Then you are fellow artist."

Hawthorn chuckled. "Well, that sounds much too grand, compared with what you've done."

IS ALICE?

The pianist shrugged and tapped his head with a forefinger. "Don't worry. I know artists. You must have luck. You must be *good*, but you also must have luck."

"Ah," Hawthorn replied. "But with you, it is obvious. No one plays like you. An idiot can see you are a genius."

Cherkasov laughed out loud and settled back in his armchair, his big chin resting now on the white hairs of his bare chest. "Is not true! Idiots do not know art! How can they tell? Plenty of fine pianists. Which one is good, which one great? Idiots don't know. Someone *tells* idiots! This man is good! That is luck! This audience tonight. Someone *tell* them, this man is a genius! Then I play, and it is *genius*! No one tell them, they don't know." He stopped and scratched his ear. "A few know, maybe. Only few ever know."

Hawthorn smiled. "I'm with you, Alyosha." Then he frowned. "Why Alyosha? I thought your name was Aleksei."

"Alyosha is diminutive."

"Oh. That must be a honour. Thank you."

"I hate too much forms."

"Formality?"

"*Da*. Formality. My English was better, but now I'm old. I love languages. Almost as I love music. I speak also Mandarin…"

"Chinese?"

"Japanese, so… interesting, that language. German. Italian, so beautiful, and Spanish, also. And French… so Debussy. Language is like piano. You need practice. In London I get practice one last time."

"Maybe not the last time," Hawthorn grinned. "You'll always have a packed house here."

Cherkasov heaved himself out of the armchair. "I am not civilised. You want drink? Somebody gave me good Scotch whisky. What is called? A *malt*."

"Please. Don't bother."

"Glasses? Ah. Good," he said, as he looked laboriously in a cabinet beside the dressing table. He picked two glasses, placed them on top of the dresser, then reached behind a huge vase of flowers to retrieve a bottle of whisky. He poured two drinks, moved back to his chair and held out the large one to Hawthorn.

"I cannot drink like before. Too old. A little wine, a taste of whisky, maybe vodka. What is bad is good for you." He chuckled to himself as he settled slowly back into the armchair.

"Thank you very much," Hawthorn said, before taking a sip of the whisky. "And thank you most of all for listening to me. Not having me thrown out. I was desperate. Couldn't think of any other way to do it. No one would listen. At the hospital, they think I'm mad, won't let me out. This afternoon I noticed they forgot to lock the door to the emergency exit, the stairs. I don't have my keys, I have no money. I walked to the Albert Hall from North London in my socks. In the newspaper I saw you were giving another concert, and all I could think of was talking to the audience – and you – telling you of the injustice. I suppose that was mad. Yes, that's mad. But I'm not mad. Yet now they have *proof* I'm mad. A world of paradox."

"Yes!" the old pianist gestured with the hand that held the whisky. "The world is *paradox*. Not what it seems."

Hawthorn stared at Cherkasov. "You were so kind. You stopped playing, stopped them from taking me away. I owe you..."

Cherkasov interrupted. "Tell me. How old?"

"How old am I? Fifty-six."

"Ah. Still a young man. Age tells you nothing is important. Too late. So much wasted on unimportance…"

Hawthorn studied the old man as he waited for him to continue. His eyes were set on the wall behind the sofa, and his chin was again resting on his chest. His bald head was sprinkled with liver spots, and the hand holding the whisky glass shook a little as he moved it slowly to his mouth Then, in a sudden movement, he threw his head back and drained the glass.

"Much time wasted on illusion," he continued as he slowly lowered his arm with the empty glass to his lap. "I'm old now, so more time to listen. You have something to say. So I listen. You listen to my music, now I listen to yours. People – some – are as music. Words are melody, but there is more, much else. Harmony. Dissonance. Percussion, resolution…"

"The fugal rhythms of self," Hawthorn muttered.

"What's that? A fugue. Yes. Like a fugue. OK, return to theme. You are standing in a queue outside here for first concert. With your wife."

Hawthorn took a deep breath and leaned his head back on the sofa. He could feel the muscles in his foot twitching from the side-effects of the drugs he had been given by force. He suspected that was why it was so difficult to follow one thought with another.

"Alice and I are not married. I call her my partner. At the ticket window, there was no one inside. It was just a machine.   It spoke mechanically, but in a bright woman's voice. 'Please insert your card.' Then, 'Please lean forward and look directly into the red square with your right eye'."

"Ahhhh," Cherkasov growled angrily and rose again from his chair. "I would refuse! I tell you, I would refuse even if God himself descended from *heaven* and appeared at Albert Hall. More whisky?"

IS ALICE?

Hawthorn shook his head, raising his glass to show how much he had left.

"These days you telephone," the old pianist continued, "you talk to machine. You want money? Machine. Pay money? Machine. Ask a question? Machine. Soon maybe the machines raise children so the parents can work, work, work. I tell you, Theo, I'm glad I'm old. I don't want to live in such a world. Once we walked to shops, bought something, had a conversation with the owner, even a drink, maybe knew his family. Today? Order from the computer, pay with cards."

Hawthorn sighed and nodded. "Every day it becomes more difficult, and there are more problems. Alice didn't pass the iris scan..."

Cherkasov wrinkled his face, rounding his lips. "What is this?"

"You put your eye to a hole next to the machine, and your iris – the coloured part of your eye – is compared with a photograph they have on...some computer. If they don't match, the transaction is refused. It's never happened before with us. *Technology*, Alyosha. Instead of clerks at the bank, they have machines. Much cheaper. And they work all day every day, don't get sick, and don't have holidays. Just upgrade the software every now and then. I was surprised when I found one at the Royal Albert. Here, at least, there is something of tradition, I thought. But, no. The ticket office is now a machine. With an iris scan. I suppose that was why the queue was so long. No one cares how long a queue is, how long people have to wait, whether it's raining or cold. Before, it took maybe four people behind a counter to issue the tickets. One machine replaces all these people – and of course makes no mistakes! It was Alice's card. Alice has loads of money in the bank, no problem. But the machine says the iris does not match. Something is wrong with the machine, but you can do nothing…"

"This is disgusting," Cherkasov muttered. "Russia is becoming this way also. You should see the rich now. Like jackals. As always, eating the flesh of the poor. Fattening themselves with food they do not need, wanting only more. My country has…traded justice for greed. So very sad."

Hawthorn turned for a moment, thoughtfully, facing the dressing-room door. He took a sip of whisky, then lowered the glass slowly. "Any other evening, any other concert, we would have simply left the box office. Walked away. Gone home. But this night was different. Alice booked the tickets months ago, the day we first saw the advertisement. Aleksei Cherkasov plays the Schubert B-flat Major sonata. For many years we had listened only to the recording. It was a special evening. We looked forward to it, we planned, talked about it, laughed, hugged each other…"

Hawthorn turned back to the pianist, pressed his lips together and leaned forward, elbows on knees, holding the whisky glass in his left hand. He stared at the shiny toes of Cherkasov's black concert shoes. "Alice turned towards me. Her eyes were helpless, and there were tears. What could she do? What could *we* do? On such an important evening. For us. People behind us in the queue were getting restive, told us to move. I asked them to be patient, and told Alice to wait at the machine while I went to find a human being. The doorman. I tried to explain things, he just kept shaking is head. So, I…I took my clothes off."

Cherkasov cocked his head comically. "You took off clothes?"

"Yes!"

The old pianist started laughing slowly and softly, rocking back and forth in his chair. He took off his glasses and squeezed his nose with thumb and forefinger, his eyes closed. Then he exploded, threw his head right back and laughed from his belly.

"Ha!" he said finally. "You took off clothes! Down to skin!"

"Yes! It was all I could think to do. By this time people in the queue were really grumbling, looking at their watches, complaining to us. When I took my clothes off, there was shouting, shoving. Chaos was breaking out. The doorman was dumbstruck. He didn't know what to do.

"I said, 'Let us in, and I'll put my pants back on. We have paid. We have bought tickets. Your machine is broken.' You understand?"

The old pianist was nodding his head, still laughing. Hawthorn couldn't help himself, as he felt his lips crease into a smile, then a short laugh.

"It's the first time I've seen the humour in it…" he said finally. His expression changed as he continued. "But the doorman was on his mobile phone. He was calling the police. So. My last gambit. Failed. I put my underpants back on. Like now. Same underpants. And I looked for Alice, had trouble finding her. She was standing, her back against the wall. A man was in front of her, shouting abuse. I looked at her eyes… and knew …immediately. I shoved the man away, pushed him. He turned on me, but I ignored him. Because I knew… from her eyes. Alice. The eyes are seeing… some other story of the world, all within."

Hawthorn stopped as his voice trailed off. His head was lowered as he stared at the carpet between his feet.

Cherkasov noticed for the first time the playwright was balding on the crown of his head. "Your partner…"

"My partner is mad. First time in…many years, can't remember. When she goes, it is immediate. One moment she's OK, the next she's gone. There's no reaching her, no penetrating her world. I grabbed her in my arms, just in my underpants. I held her and cried. But she was struggling. She doesn't like to be touched when… when she's in that world. She believes it is a horrible joke, that I despise her, that I have to hold her because it is my fate, and she wants to release me from… this fate. Oh, it's so difficult, Alyosha. I can't explain it. Everything in time and space twists suddenly, and all the demons clatter from hellish holes and set upon her soul with sharp teeth and bloody knives. Despite her struggles, I still held her close to me. I knew it could be weeks – or even months – before I saw my beautiful Alice again."

Hawthorn sat up suddenly and finished the whisky with a single swallow. Carefully he placed the empty glass on the arm of the sofa. "Anyway, the police came, and they phoned the... the mental health swat team, whatever they're called. A psychiatrist arrived. By this time the concert must have already begun. We were outside the Royal Albert, standing in the cold. Alice was... was... They took us both to a hospital in north London. I was so angry. I was talking to the psychiatrist at the hospital, they were questioning me, Alice had been taken to another room. Then they sectioned me. Sectioned both of us."

"Section? What is section?"

"It is a power held by the State to imprison those who are judged to be insane – against their will. By force, if necessary. It has been a nightmare beyond my powers to describe it. I had witnessed it before, when Alice was ill years ago, but only as an outsider. You have no rights, you are no longer believed, not anything you say. You are not a person. You are on a different island, one you have not seen before. You are pinned down and given powerful drugs, whether you need them or not. If you want to know the meaning of hell, just enter an institution where you become a dumb, meaningless animal."

There was a long pause as Cherkasov replaced his glasses and studied his visitor. Neither man moved as the silence slowly became more profound.

"It is a difficult problem," the old pianist said finally. "In three days I return to Moscow, and this moment I am now very, very tired. I hope you understand. But this I will promise you. You must leave the name of this hospital and the name of someone I can speak to. Tomorrow I will call...no, I will come. Dmitri!"

Almost immediately the dressing-room door opened, and the long, lugubrious, worried face of the agent appeared. Cherkasov held up his hand and turned to Hawthorn.

"Give these details on a paper to Dmitri, and I will ask for him to call for you a taxi..."

Hawthorn shook his head. "No, I think they'll be waiting for me downstairs, Alyosha. I'll go with them."

He stood up and started to take off the dressing gown.

"No, no, no," Cherkasov said. "You take this with you. Go in dignity. It is mine for many years, but now I give it to you."

Almost reluctantly Hawthorn re-tied the belt to the old dressing gown. "I don't know how to express my gratitude. Your kindness... in the circumstances... is beyond belief. I so much loved your performance tonight. If only..."

IS ALICE?

With some difficulty Cherkasov stood up and held out his hand. "You do this for me, and you must promise. OK? You do this. You write to me. In Russia. Dmitri will give you my address. Tell me all you have to tell me. I will be your friend. I have some influence, a little. Not so much as people think, but a little. And tomorrow I will come. I will talk to them. You must be released from this place. I will see to it. That is all I can do for you."

Hawthorn held onto his hand and looked into his eyes. For the first time in nearly two weeks he felt something very heavy crawl off his back. Perhaps there was, he thought, a little hope.

CHAPTER TWO

She looked at her hair, lying like rodent-nesting on the floor. Blonde hair. But it wasn't really blonde, just phoney highlights, not real. The scissors were still in her hand, and she clicked them together with thumb and forefinger. Phoney scissors, toy scissors she palmed from Occupational Therapy. They were dirty, and the cut hair on the floor was dirty. The scissors slid from her fingers and fell into the pile of ugly hair as she looked around her room. It was all dirty. Everything needed washing, there was so much to do, so much to be done. She threw her clothes onto the floor. There weren't many in the drawers, just a few, filthy, all of them. The sheets on her bed, the pillowcases. A little radio, her wind-up clock – both went into the pile. Then she began to gather it all up in her arms, but some of the hair kept falling back onto the floor, very frustrating. Then she couldn't open the door with her arms full. So she put it all back down, this time in the middle of the bed, went and opened the door. Someone was passing, but she didn't look. She didn't need to look. Whoever it was scanned her mind. She knew when it happened because all the thoughts tumbled from one end of her space to the other, as if they had been lifted by a sudden gust of strong wind, flying end over end before settling incoherently into dark sinister piles. They would have to be sorted later, those thoughts. Now, what was she doing?

When she entered the laundry room, Itcheta was sitting there watching the tumble-dryer. Itcheta-Witcheta, that's what she was, Itcheta-the-Witch. She knew immediately that she had to be very careful, so she went straight to the washing machine and threw all her clothes inside. Her clothes, the dirty hair, the clock and radio. Washing powder, lots of it, to get everything really, really clean. She nearly closed the door…

"Disgusting. Filthy woman…" Itcheta-Witcheta was speaking to her. She turned around quickly, but the Witch was staring at the tumble-dryer, still as marble. Black marble. Was there such a thing as black marble?

"Grimy, polluted woman…" Itcheta-Witcheta's lips never moved, but the words were there, so clear, like pure fragments of crystal. Carved, clear letters of words, radiant in her mind. Then a shaft of terror illuminated the landscape like forked lightening in twilight.

The black woman yawned. But it wasn't a yawn. It was a Signal. It had a meaning for her, and she didn't know what that meaning was. It *must* mean that she had to take off her clothes and wash them, too, or she would be…consumed, spat at, condemned.

She removed her cigarettes and lighter, then took off her jeans with trembling fingers. Then her jumper, her bra, her knickers. She almost forgot her socks. All into the washing machine, door closed. Hot wash, boil everything, good and clean. She lit a cigarette.

"Pagan slut." The words were again clear – those crystal letters again forming in the inky landscape. The Witch knew her thoughts as she sat there naked. The Witch knew she had forced Theo to kiss this awful slutty, smutty, pale, shapeless bag of shit. Itcheta-Witcheta *knew about The Fool*! That really frightened her. Desperate, she tried not to *think* about it. Think about anything. Remember phone numbers. Count the tiles on the floor. No use. She couldn't resist the wiles of the Witch, the witch-bitch. The Witch *knew she was The Fool*! The one who spent all those years tricked and fooled, mocked, scoffed, jeered, deceived, sneered at and scorned. Lies! They were lies! And The Fool believed them all! She dared to be happy-pretend, so she would not know the Truth! It was The Fool who lied and pretended, driving a car she didn't deserve, buying things with her mother's money, depriving her family of food...

She hammered the sides of her shorn head with the heels of her hands as the Witch sat so knowingly, faintly smiling, as she pretended to watch the tumble-dryer. There were details she could not remember. Had to write things down. The Witch was black. That was it. Black magic. And her pencil and notebook were inside the washing machine. Mustn't forget. Black magic, black magic.

Itcheta-the-Witch now turned and was looking at her as she sat naked on the stool beside the washing machine. Looking *into* her. And she was laughing, the sound hammering around the laundry room like the rattle of tribal drums.

"Dirty fat slug slut," The Witch screamed over her own scornful laughter. "Gonna take you to Judgement Day before the Almighty. And all your sins will be read out by choirs of demons before they drag you down to the roasting fires of hell. Flesh will fall off your bones, but you will be undead. Begging, begging, begging for mercy. Cursy mercy, no mercy. You have lived the life of The Fool while your sins multiply like swarms of locusts..."

The Black Witch turned back to watch her clothes tumbling in the dryer, over and over, like The Fool's soul in hell. Her soul. She had been fooled by The Fool into that dreadful, horrible life, forgetting all the things she knew she must remember.

Someone opened the door. One of the Aliens. She looked at him and knew she must try and understand their language. Instead, she puffed on the remains of her cigarette.

"Alice! Where are your clothes? You can't sit in here naked!"

He did something with the fingers of one hand. She realised she must concentrate, because so much of it was symbolic. She pondered the possible meaning of this communication. ...?... ...?...

"...?... ...?... hair?" he asked.

The Alien blinked twice *and* moved his hand again, curving two of the fingers this time. He was obviously trying to teach her something, but she was too stupid to understand. Was it the way he was standing, one foot a little in front of the other?

Suddenly he left, slamming the door. Alice sat on her stool, puzzled. The Alien called himself Guring. Guring, they called him. A *clue*! Guring…gurning? Was he *gurning* at her? Was his name really Gurning? Gurning was a leer, and Lear had three daughters, so was she Lear's daughter? Cordelia? Was she going to die, like Cordelia? It was so *difficult*, and she was so dim, so unable to grasp the Reality. And now they were going to kill her, and then, *zing*, Judgement Day, down to hell. So much evil in her life. Stubbing out her cigarette, she immediately lit another one.

So many things to remember, so little time. Her breathing became frenzied with fear and frustration, because her notebook was in the washing machine. It was dirty. There was nothing to write on. Her lists were in the notebook. How could she have been so stupid?

The door opened again, and again it was the Alien, who held something white in his hand. He threw the white cloth on the floor at her feet. His face was angry.

"…?..." he said.

She watched him closely, her eyes darting back to the white cloth on the floor. Confusion came in an avalanche. Of course he was angry. They were all angry with her, and why not? She was pure evil, filth, dirt.

The Alien waved his hands, "…?... on!"

The waving hands, what did they mean? Was he conducting her, did he want her to sing?

IS ALICE?

"Hush, little baby, don't say a word…" she murmured softly, a little out of tune. She was trying so hard to do the right thing, whatever they wanted of her.

The Alien leaned down and picked up the white cloth, held it in front of her. "Put …?… before …?… hospital! Arm! ARMS!"

"Arms?" she thought to herself. Arms? Why arms? Oh, *arms*. She put her lit cigarette in her mouth and held out her arms, held them up for the Alien who wanted them.

The Alien slipped the cloth over her arms, went round to her back and tied the strings together.

It was a hospital gown, and she knew she had been far too stupid to know the man wanted her to put it on. How could that be?

"…?… …?…. visitors, Alice." Guring-Gurning said as she watched the movement of his hands.

Visitors. No, no. She wasn't going to be trapped again. They just wanted to make sport with her. Visitors didn't want to see her. There were rules written somewhere, and visitors were part of the plan, part of these rules. They *had* to visit her, though they loathed and detested her. It was all Pretend. The visitors would pretend to talk to her, but couldn't wait to get outside where they would throw up, grateful for the fresh air.

Alice shook her head and took another drag on her cigarette, refusing to move.

"You have to ...?... Important ...?..." The Guring-Gurning voice was angry, and she was worried they might hold her down again and inject her, or drag her into the ECT room. Best thing would be to follow the Alien. He knew what he was doing on this planet. She didn't want to upset them.

They left the Itcheta-Witcheta still staring at the revolving clothes in the tumble-dryer, and went into the corridor. There were doors off each side of the hallway. A TV room where she spent much of her time, smoking and drinking cups of tea. It was the women's quarters, though there were men there, too – why, she didn't know, but she didn't like it. Didn't like the men being placed on the side reserved for women, it wasn't fair. The men only came because of her, because they wanted to see the damned woman who was so famous for so much evil. They wanted to watch the whore going to hell. At the gates of hell. Push her through the gates. Then cheer. That's why the men had been moved to the women's quarters.

But was it really a 'hospital'? They all called it that, but obviously it wasn't a hospital, which was for sick people. Why would they put her in a hospital if she was *well*? It was The Fool who needed a hospital, and she was no longer The Fool, thank God.

She clapped her hands over her mouth with horror, spraying sparks from her cigarette, hurting her lips with the lighter. She had mentioned the sacred word, *God*, and that was forbidden, because God hated her guts. He would be furious that she mentioned His name. Alice began to cry. The dying embers from the sparks were burning her neck. It was pain from God, so she must bear it.

There were three men in the visitor's room. One was Theo. The two others she had seen somewhere but didn't know them. One was very old, a bald man, who stared at her through spectacles. She didn't want to see Theo. Ever again. She wanted to *release* him, set him free from *her*. Yet when she saw it was him, her heart brightened at first, just for a moment, before she smothered the feeling with blackness.

The Guring-Gurning man retreated, left the room and shut the door.

Theo was staring at her, and she realised his eyes were becoming damp. *Oh, please, please don't cry.* She knew when he cried it was because of the hatred of his duty – having to see her. Oh, give her the strength to let him go, be rid of her once and for all.

"Your hair," Theo said softly. "Your ...? ... hair."

He turned to the short, portly man who wore a checked sport shirt and a tie. He had receding brown hair. "How did she ...?... scissors?" His voice was angry. She watched closely for other signs.

The fat man shook his head, and that shook his jowls. Must be significant. His voice was high, almost squeaky.

"…?... allowed at all. I …?... it. …?... assure you this hospital …?... staff …?... patient security ….?...."

The man went on. Words poured forth from his mouth, cascades of words, too many for her to follow, so she watched the jowls instead, fascinated. They quivered, they creased, they trembled or shook. Then the old man spoke to her.

" …?... beautiful, madam. …?... know who I am?"

Alice shook her head. He looked distant and wise. Obviously he was a judge, someone brought in to administer a dose of the Truth. She recoiled as fear crawled up her spine.

Theo spoke in his rich bass voice. "Aleksei …?... played …?... Royal Albert Hall …?...trouble …?..."

Was Theo flicking sperm at her with his fingers? His eyes were brighter now, no tears, but she didn't want to get pregnant. She didn't understand how Aliens did it. It must be by sperm-flicking.

There was a long expectant silence. Then the old man walked slowly over to the old upright piano in the corner of the room. It was always locked so nobody could play it, but the lock was off now and the cover raised. Theo and the fat man sat down in two of the plastic chairs, so she sat down as well, opposite them near the windows. The Judge was at the piano, and the jury sat in their places. Alice realised she was the Accused, the one to be damned to hell. It must be done. She had to do it.

IS ALICE?

When the Judge began to play, her back stiffened as her eyes widened in horror. *No*, she screamed with her inner voice. *No, no. Not that. Anything but the Schubert*! It became suddenly, instantly clear. The courtroom, the judge, the jury, the Schubert. A florid gale swept through her world like wild winds on a lifeless planet sun-baked by a giant star, filling the air with burning, skin-shredding sand. A merciless hand drove the ragged blade of a knife into her heart, impaling her with her own mendacity. It was mockery of unimaginable ferocity! Simultaneously she knew she *deserved* it. Therefore she must sit and take the medicine.

Of course, of course, that's what they would do. Play the Schubert, with every note underlining The Fool's gullibility in believing that such a wonderful, happy life was for her. The memories were nauseating, revolting, like chewing on rotting flesh or sucking warm, fresh shit from the bowels of the devil. What a dupe she was, and how perfectly tailored was her torment. The Fool, with her arms around Theo, the man who was revolted by her presence and disgusted by her touch – The Fool had let herself believe that such bliss could be possible for her, as choirs of laughing demons contorted themselves with glee at her preposterous impertinence.

Tears ran down her cheeks as she began to sob. It was unbearable torture to hear that noble, soaring melody tearing into her like barbs of contempt and scorn. The Fool *dared* to think…*dared* to believe… that an incredible romance could be for *her*. Her psyche turned and writhed like a worm thrown on hot coals. She yearned for it so much, so piteously, with a demented lust, yet it was all illusion. Because she was The Fool, tricked and fooled, over and over again. This time – *this time* – she would succeed in resisting these tormenting temptations.

The Schubert swirled around her, and she imagined for a moment she could see the music in the air surrounding and suffocating her. Death by Schubert. Death and the Maiden. No, Death and the Whore – the poor old whore, maiden of Satan, Satan made the maiden, there's the truth.

And Schubert knew, he made this torture for her, of that she was certain. Schubert had access to the Akashic Records, of course he did, just like the rest of them. The records storing every thought, word and action, past, present and future. Schubert sat at his piano composing the B-flat Sonata just for her, this moment, so she could understand the true meaning of self-loathing. Naturally the rest of them had access to the Records, too. The Judge and the Jury. Everyone at the so-called hospital. They could all see inside her now, read her thoughts, rake through her past, laugh at every drunken, disgraceful thing she had ever done. The Records showed everything, so they *knew*. The Judge was telling her right now that he could see her past, every action, and the punishment was going to be unimaginably harsh. It was so clear when she was in her proper mind. Luminous. Everything joined together just like it should, endlessly, beyond the reach of her vision into infinity. Vibrant fingers from billions of the living and the dead sought out her consciousness to point, raise their voices, and condemn.

IS ALICE?

Alice lit another cigarette with trembling fingers. Her cheeks were soaked with tears, and she heard herself sobbing. It couldn't be helped. She was overwhelmed with pain and humiliation. If she were allowed to appeal directly to God, she would ask Him to allow her to flee the room, the Judge and the Jury, and to run – down the corridor, as fast as her feet would carry her. Then let there be a window, a ledge, some reprieve, so she could cast her body from a great height onto cold stones to break her soul from her body and let it go. Death could be peace, it could be nothing. Oh, she hoped with every fibre of her being that death was final, an end, darkness. Nothingness. No more, she could take no more!

She wiped her tears with the back of her hand and sat more upright in her chair, smoking incessantly. No, this was obviously better for her. A stinking, bitter medicine she must swallow. Schubert was somewhere, grinning with delight at her misery, proud his composition had the power to deliver such justice to a crawling, squirming organism, pinned like an entomological exhibit in this room to be examined and cursed by this court. It was thoughts of the verdict that caused the surge of terror to grip her heart with fingers cold as iron. There would be a verdict from this court for the People of the World, all who had lived before and all who would come afterwards. On her. On her soul. In the timelessness of eternity. So she still had to learn, that's the point! Even death would not release her. No death for the maiden, that was Schubert's message. Eternal damnation. Eternal! All of time, forever and ever, without end. The thoughts rolled over her like dark, suffocating, smoky mists. This was just the beginning, not the end. Death would be the aperture through which her damnation would be intensified. So that was going to be the certain verdict of this court. Death. Death to the maiden, as the applause of approval roared through the universe, bringing together the dead and unborn through cheers for justice seen to be done. She would enter the realm where red demons with giant genitalia drummed their misshapen feet at a hellish banquet for her soul's arrival. She imagined them sharpening their skewers and heating them in white-hot flames, giggling manically as their huge unblinking eyes turned to feast upon her naked, misshapen body. The steaming floors were covered with crawling insects and rats hungry for a morsel of her soul, after the demons tore her apart in a frenzy of crazed hunger and lust. They would be all over her – inside and out – crawling, gouging, sucking, biting, tearing. Her vital organs of self would be carried away in triumph by slobbering millipedes, to be eaten and excreted only for the excrement to reunite in an infinite, continuous degradation of self and soul. The dung beetles and dung devils would seek her out then, excited by her smell, their organs erect and contracting in visceral anticipation.

She fixed her eyes on the back of the head of the Judge playing the piano. He was not looking at his hands as he played, and she was, for a moment, mesmerised by his baldness. That would have a meaning, but she was too inadequate to understand what it was. He was eerily familiar, and so was the way he played. Was it Aleksei Cherkasov? The man they were trying to see just before she became unwell again? Could the great man have come here, just to judge her? Well, of course. That was it! She recovered herself from the life of The Fool just before they were to see him play at the Royal Albert.

IS ALICE?

Perhaps she was to be judged that night, but the police took her away to the hospital. So now he had come here, to her, to render his supreme judgement. Before doing so, he was going to tease out her most venomous sins with the Schubert sonata. He and Schubert were working together, weaving their web, trapping her in an eloquent cul-de-sac.

Her eyes moved to Theo, who was staring at her intensely. She was unable to look at him, except for an instant, as the strength of her longing surged and shattered on the knowledge of his disgust at what she had done to him. Theo was there to observe the verdict, so he could be released from his unholy duties. Thus all was not in vain. At her core, she loved him so, the only man she ever loved. There was no way she could deny that. It made his loathing of her that much more excruciating. As the foam of terror froze on her lips, she wanted only to let him go, never to touch him or hold him again. She was clearly the epitome of evil, but if there was one good thread left in the tangled skein of her existence, she would have the courage to cut away that one part of her that was wholesome, so the rest could be consumed by suppurating gangrene. Bore out the core, she rhymed to herself, as she bored the core more by the shore.

By the shore. A flashback so abrupt she sat back suddenly into her chair. Corfu. Near the rocky shore she swam in a sun-violet blue sea, naked with her snorkel, as Theo drank a can of Mythos in the boat and took photographs of her. *The Fool*! The Fool believed it was happiness beyond her dreams, and the memories made her cringe inside, pull away from the light like a damp bat. Yet her humiliation was mesmerising, and she could not help returning to the vision. They hired a little motorboat nearly every day and puttered along one of the most beautiful cascading coastlines in the world. Two and a half thousand years ago Greek triremes would have been moored offshore, as the sun winked on the bronze shields of the soldiers preparing to leave for battle. They would pull into tiny cobble-pebbled beaches, wade onto the stones laughing, open their lunch and eat, then lie back in the breeze-tempered heat. At night they would go to a taverna for a meal of salads and fish just pulled from the sea. Oh, it was so beautiful she couldn't help but linger on the bitter memories. The Fool allowed herself to feel *happiness* for the very first time of her life, to let down her defences, to giggle in delight and hunt seashells, to feel a sense of glory in being alive. She allowed herself to believe that Theo desired her and...

Magical summer nights riding pillion on Theo's motorcycle as they returned from a taverna, sucking in her breath as she saw ghostly moonlight fractured on choppy waters, holding onto him, pressing her cheek warmly into his broad back as they leaned into bends, climbed steep hills, the throb of the bike resonating in her heart.

It was The Fool's biggest and worst mistake. For the very first time of her life she broke into the illusion of happiness. 'Paradise.' That was her breathless word one quiet evening as the sun sank slowly into the molten red iron of its light.

IS ALICE?

"*Paradise.*" She almost vocalised the word as she squirmed in contemptuous longing. *Who did she think she was?* Poor, poor Theo. He had to play along with the macabre game of romance. Pretending to smile, laugh, pretending he enjoyed touching her, pretending to talk about love. The word made her flinch in nausea. Just how did The Fool think anyone could really love such a worthless toe-rag? She had allowed herself to be drawn into this world so they could all make sport of her. She imagined Theo talking to others about her.

"I tell you," he would say, with a face screwed into a drooling rictus of disgust, "holding her was like being in the arms of a nightmare reptile. Her skin was clammy and shiny with slime."

"Oh," one of the others would say, "How could you bear it without vomiting?"

"The monster!"

"The harridan!"

"Surely she wasn't thinking she was *really attractive*!"

"Yes!" Theo confirmed. "If you can believe it, she was under the impression she was in *paradise*!"

"Oh, yuk!"

"To be honest," Theo continued, "I would have preferred a disfigured, diseased whore on the gutter streets of Calcutta."

"Of course."

"Naturally."

"But as you know, I had to do my duty. I had to go on with the game and continue the pretence that I was actually *enjoying* it. *That* was the hardest part. Can you imagine how I looked, holding hands with this smelly reptile among the others? They were all gesturing at me behind her back, pointing at her with fingers down their throats. They fell about laughing as I put my arm around her and gazed at a sunset over the waters."

"Now, though," one of them said consolingly, "she's come to her senses."

Theo got slowly to his feet.

"Though she realises she's only a squalid piece of rotting ordure, she still, deep in her heart...she still loves me."

"Oh, gross!"

"Yes! The outrageous laughing-stock of a fool is *still there,* embedded in the encrusted folds of her being. I tell you, she must *learn.* This time, she must let go of me, undo the spell, unsay the magic words, let me be free! I am not a frog!"

"No, no, you're not a frog!"

"She must learn her touch is more stomach-churning than eating live cockroaches. We've given her this final opportunity to make peace with her destiny. Let her not fail!"

The Schubert sonata finished, the final overtones of the notes still ringing on the strings of the piano. The Judge turned on the stool to face her. Underneath his glasses was a cruel smile.

"Well, my dear," he said with a heavy accent. "Well?"

That was it. It was forever. It was doom. There was no escape, no window of light, no distant exit or hope. It was time for The Judgement.

Without warning Alice screamed, sprang to her feet, and ran for the door before any of them could move. She wrenched it open, still screaming, and lurched into the corridor in a state of complete terror. She ran as fast as she could, barefooted, past the reception desk, skidding, almost falling, as she turned down the corridor leading to her room. Faster, faster, no time to lose. She must do it before everything collapsed like an infinite line of dominoes. Clickety, click, click, moving closer and closer – completely and irreversibly inevitable. She reached her door and battered it, wrenching the handle, banging with her other hand and her head against the solid wood. It opened as if on a strong spring and bounced off the wall with an echo. She skidded around her room, opening drawers, emptying them. There was little there. It was all in the washing machine. There was an old half-pencil with a broken point, chewing gum wrappers, empty cigarette boxes, no sheets on the bed. Nothing. No hope. No chance. The end.

Then she spotted the little white box of dental floss underneath the sink, the sink with no stopper so she had to put toilet paper in the hole to wash. On her hands and knees she grabbed for the dental floss. Please. Let it not be empty. In a frenzy she broke a fingernail trying to open it. Then she was pulling it out, more, more. She needed more. Quickly she wrapped the floss around her neck and tied it in a knot. Staggering to her feet, she fell onto the bed, then began pushing it with all her strength. To the window with the grill on the outside so it couldn't be opened completely. Then she clambered onto the bed, bouncing to the other side as she reached out urgently for the curtain rail, where she tied the other end of the floss after pulling it as tight as she could bear. It was now cutting into her throat, but she no longer cared.

She turned to face the open door. It was only the briefest part of a second, and the reality of her imminent death gave her room a luminescent golden halo, like one band of a rainbow. Whatever happened afterwards, there must now be death, because she was not made to withstand such overwhelming agony. She had escaped The Judgement by a whisker, but the memories of Corfu were just too much for her. The Fool had hoped – *hoped with all her life* – that it was all true, only to be shown yet again her abominable gullibility. And. Most of all. Absolutely most of all. *Theo would finally be free*. One act, one true act of love, while she was in the grip of hellish rebellion from the forces that pursued her. For him. For Theo.

With a final breath, she closed her eyes and kicked away the bed.

IS ALICE?

CHAPTER THREE

It was a large, modern office carpeted in green, and dominated by a wood veneer desk supporting a slim computer monitor and keyboard on one side, and a bundle of coloured files on the other. On shelving underneath the desk were the computer and printer. It was otherwise uncluttered, except for a multi-functional digital telephone, and a photograph of a woman and two children. Behind the desk sat Herbie Winkelwhite, and behind him was a large window overlooking the hospital and the trees of the park. Aleksei Cherkasov sat in front of the desk with Theo Hawthorn, and behind them was a large dark green sofa beneath a huge photograph of the hospital. It was not a room that exuded warmth, but it did speak of status.

"I can't tell you how honoured we are to have you perform at our hospital, Maestro," Herbie Winklewhite said as he leaned forward over his desk. "I do wish you had allowed us to inform the local papers, as we need…"

"The question is," Cherkasov interrupted in a deadly voice, "when this man is going to be released from here. He is not madder than me. And I am not mad. Who are you, a man who is prison officer?"

"I can assure…" Winklewhite started to speak.

Theo Hawthorn held up his hand and spoke forcefully. "Winkewhite is the chief executive of the hospital, and I think he now understands what the situation is. I have engaged special mental health solicitors who will arrive here later this afternoon. We have a meeting planned with my psychiatrist. I have also spoken with my MP – that's the Labour member of parliament – whom I know personally. He will attend the meeting as well, and he is a very angry man…"

"If you will just let me speak," Winklewhite said testily, his jowls shuddering beneath his chin. "I have already spoken with Dr Pincer, and he sees no reason why the Section cannot be lifted immediately for Mr Hawthorn."

He stopped, the corners of his mouth turned down as he glanced apologetically sideways. "As for Ms Dance…"

Theo Hawthorn waved his hand. "We all know Alice is seriously impaired and must remain under Section. The outrage is that I was admitted at all, never mind the total injustice of my own Section. I have been forcibly injected with psychotropic drugs, even though I resisted only verbally, and my head is still unclear. I can tell you right now, Alyosha, the side-effects of these drugs are indescribable. I'll tell you more later, when I write to you. I've had little sleep, I'm agitated, anxious, and still have difficulties thinking straight. That's why I'm talking so slowly, so forgive me."

Hawthorn turned back to Winklewhite. "As for the newspapers, I'm hoping you'll soon be dreading to open newspapers…"

"*Mister* Hawthorn," Winklewhite said pompously as he rose from his chair and pulled his trousers over his gut, "Please consider my position. I run an NHS mental health hospital. Many patients, many problems. You came here, to the Skinner Memorial Unit, from Sutcliff A&E, brought by the police after creating a public disturbance.   You were interviewed by the duty psychiatrist, and you were interviewed again by Dr Pincer on your admission here. You showed irrational and dangerous behaviour…"

"Dangerous?" Hawthorn laughed. "Did I hit anyone? Attack anyone? Threaten anyone?"

Winklewhite's jowls shook. "You're a big man, and we have public and political pressure to deal with…"

"I'm a big man," Cherkasov said softly, "Why don't you arrest me? You put in prison all big men? Big men wild, like beasts?"

Winklewhite sighed. "Two weeks ago in Camden, a woman was killed…"

"By a big man?" Hawthorn asked mischievously.

"By someone who had formerly been an inmate here," Winklewhite continued as he hitched up the trousers on one short leg and sat on the front corner of his desk. Though he was somewhat bald, a neat comb-over hid most of it. "The public expects protection. You were unknown to us. You displayed signs of psychosis…"

"Bullshit," Hawthorn said, his elbows on the armrests of his chair, fingers knitted together.

"…and we express our duty to the public by taking every precaution in our admission and discharge procedures…"

"One moment." Aleksei Cherkasov was sitting upright in a padded armchair and looked intimidating, his heavy chin already on his chest. He looked over his glasses without blinking. "You are talking like a machine. Words come out without going first through brain. Like a schedule for buses. We are all human beings. Make beautiful things sometimes, sometimes make mistakes. When you make mistake, there is a way to do it. You just say, sorry, we made mistake. *Apology*, that's the word. Apology, maybe a little money, a nice letter, that's all there is to it…"

With the mention of money, Winklewhite's face changed completely. His avuncular manner became crisply distant. "This Health Trust is not prepared to admit any liability in the matter of Mr Hawthorn's admission. The established procedures were followed meticulously in every instance, and he has been treated with professional care since the moment he arrived. Furthermore, we…"

Cherkasov held up a weary hand, shaking his head as he removed his glasses with a sigh. "Nobody understands any more in this world, Mr Er. We are three people. No TV camera, no microphone, what can be reported? These speeches like mechanical clocks are not necessary. I am pianist, OK? In my car, if I go through big puddle of water and splash Theo, and it spoils his new suit, I stop. I get out of my car, I make mistake. I apologise, give him money for new suit. No problem. It was not personal, but *I* make mistake. This has happened, I tell you. It is a simple human thing. And has simple human answers."

Herbie Winklewhite rose from the desk, took a deep breath, sucked in his belly. Except for his short legs, the administrator would have been a normal height. "What you say may be theoretically true, Maestro. Unfortunately, we are a publicly funded organisation, and thus have a duty to the taxpayers and the Department of Health…"

The fat man turned to the large picture window and clasped his hands behind his back. "Whilst we do appreciate Mr Hawthorn's feelings in the matter – of *course* we do – we are not in a position to recognise that *any* mistake has been made, either by the hospital or its staff…"

Cherkasov turned to Theo with a dry chuckle. "On his back should be a winding key."

Hawthorn laughed. "No, Alyosha, he's had an upgrade. Microsoft. Inside there is a motherboard full of chips and wiring. He gets a download of AdminSpeak software every night while he's sleeping."

Herbie Winklewhite turned back to his two guests. There was a forced smile stretched above his quivering jowls. "Now, if there is anything else I may be able to help you with before…"

"Yes," Hawthorn said. "There's the question of Alice."

"Miss Dance will remain in our care until she begins to respond to treatment, and…"

"You were a witness to what happened today," Hawthorn said softly. "She ran into her room and tried to kill herself."

"With a piece of dental floss," Winklewhite replied smugly.

"Nevertheless, she was *trying* to kill herself."

"Nonsense. She knew she couldn't do the job with dental floss. Please be serious." Winklewhite walked forward and raised his arm like an orator. "It was simply an act to draw attention to herself. Or sympathy. If I were you, I wouldn't let it bother me. We do not intend to place her under close observation."

Hawthorn shook his head and squeezed his eyes shut. He was struggling against a piercing headache now. "Her judgement is impaired. She *thought* the dental floss would work. From her point of view, she should be dead now, a final exit from the demonic world she inhabits."

Winklewhite smiled. "How do *you* know what she is thinking?"

"Because she tells me."

The hospital administrator raised his eyebrows. "Oh, I see. She *tells* you, does she? Does she speak to you in secret, then? Or does the information come by thought waves?"

Hawthorn sighed, leaned back in his chair and dropped his hands to his lap. His head was throbbing, and he felt as if he were slurring his words. "She tells me in great detail how she feels. But she tells me when she is well. Her memories are very clear. This is only her second real illness since we became lovers, though there have been close calls. I just want you to understand that she is not a *mad* woman. She has *episodes*. Otherwise, she's normal..."

Hawthorn looked past Winklewhite to the tops of the trees outside his window. He steadied his vision so he could conjure his thoughts into words. "...and she's much loved. Which is why I don't want any harm to come to her through...through...negligence..."

Cherkasov leaned forward in his chair. "Are you all right, Theo?"

Hawthorn leaned his head on the back of the chair, eyes closed. "Yes, OK. Headache. Migraine. Never had a migraine before. Splitting my head open..."

Time was abruptly sucked out of the moment. Some form of Self felt Alice nearby, her presence, ghostly but real. It was a sensation he recognised, more substantial than any dream. Her face was contorted with pain and fear, and her glassy eyes reflected rolling red-and-black furnace flames. When she saw him, her eyes glowed hotter, flickering with intense little sparks... She was falling backwards, away from him. Yet he grew in stature and in knowing. Like Christ, he held out his arms wide from his body. Without pursuing, he somehow drew nearer to her. "No!" It was not a word, but a harsh and dry wind. Alice shook her head from side to side, her singed hair smouldering. It was too clear that she was trying to die, to pull away forever, but he placed himself between her and doom. Her fiery eyes begged him to move, to go away, never return. Leave her to her fate. And it WAS her fate, Princess of the Damned. Theo ignored the heat of her rejection. In his certainty he was increasingly calm. For the Damned there is always Redemption, and love is stronger than the forces drawing you into annihilation. "No! Go! Save yourself!" she shouted. "I am in no danger," Theo answered. He paused, then continued. "Your temperature is very high, you are burning, and you cannot see." "I can see!" she screamed as her eyes widened in scorched agony. Pin wheels of flame rolled across the landscape behind her. Stars exploded in the heavens above her head. The universe was violent, and Alice had attached her being to it, turning herself inside out so everything was a part of her, plucking at her steaming organs. Theo could see the pain was unbearable. Then the oily mist of darkness loomed at the edge of the pyrotechnics, and it stained the margins of the world, snuffing out the light. The stars began to vanish as the pin wheels became pinpoints. Theo realised it was not darkness but nothingness – that which the blind see instead of black. It was deadly. He breathed in deeply and sought something beyond his powers to name, as the blackness framed Alice and threatened to envelope her fires.

IS ALICE?

"No," she whispered fiercely. "You can't stop me. I want it. You don't understand, Theo. The ammonia of existence, filling me with burning tears. It's enough. I've finished. I'm no more. I have to find a way. I will find a way. Too much."

Theo raised his arms again, and the landscape brightened. Just a little.

"No!" It was screamed this time. "I can't come back to that place. I WON'T. This time I won't fail, and you can't stop me."

There was a little more light. Like early dawn.

"THEO! Listen! My heart is twisting in agony. I can't bear it any longer. I love you, and for that I'm damned. I must never say it again. I know it shackles you, binds you to my anchor. I feel your hatred, your disgust, and that twists my heart again. There is only one answer."

Theo spoke. The thoughts came from somewhere.

"I stand between you and your answer. Step back and find some other path. Away from the heat and toward the light. You will hear these words, but you will never know of this meeting. But I know, though I don't know where or how."

Hawthorn opened his eyes. Winklewhite was standing in front of him holding a glass of water. He shook his head and accepted the water.

"Thanks. Don't know where that came from. Felt like someone speared me in the back of the head." He drank some water and sucked his lungs full of air.

"We were worried," said Cherkasov as he leaned forward in his armchair. "OK now?"

Hawthorn emptied his lungs and shook his head. "OK. The headache is gone. Completely. Maybe it was some kind of stroke, I don't know."

Winklewhite returned to his desk and fell into his chair. "In my view you should go to the Sutcliff A&E. Unofficially your Section has been lifted. You're temporarily free to..."

The playwright shook his head decisively. "I'll wait here on the ward until our meeting this afternoon. I'll also talk to Dr Pincer, try to convince him that Alice needs to be placed under close observation. It will be hellish for her, but I know she's in danger now."

Winklewhite spread his hands wide. "She will be perfectly safe in this environment..."

"Like the woman who was stretchered out last week? She managed to cut her wrists with a piece of broken crockery. Another one set fire to her bed. I can hear the ambulance and fire engine sirens as well as anybody. Two or three times a week."

The administrator continued unabashed. "We have highly trained staff ..."

"Highly trained? Most of them are agency, couldn't care less. Some steal from the patients, taunt them, abuse them…"

Hawthorn waved his hand feebly as Winklewhite was about to interrupt him. "Oh, there's no point to this. I affirm, you deny. Punch and Judy. I'm not trying to be difficult, just seeking justice. And safety for Alice. I *know* her. She's in grave danger…"

Winklewhite's smile was almost sincere as he rose from his desk. "Please let me assure you that your partner will receive the care she requires…"

"Let me treat you a drink, my friend," Cherkasov said abruptly as he stood and painfully stretched his back. "There is a bar somewhere? I would enjoy good whisky, my goodbye to England and to you."

* * *

Theo Hawthorn walked slowly through his first-floor flat that had been his home in London for so long. Though he had been gone for a little less than two weeks, the place seemed silent and strange – a different reality, another world, after a visit to another planet that circled another sun. In the kitchen he opened the fridge, peeked inside, found a can of Guinness and opened it. He didn't bother with a glass and drank straight from the can. The tap was dripping. He turned it off and opened the blinds. It was summer and still light outside.

The small kitchen led to a tiny hallway. He glanced into the bathroom on the way to his 'office.' It was meant to be a bedroom, but noise from the buses led him to use the larger one at the back. There was a sofa-bed in the office against the wall, and, opposite, his desk faced the single large window. Books filled shelves on both sides of the desk, and in front of the sofa was the single remaining memory of his first wife – an inlaid coffee table. He remembered the day she bought it in Vancouver. On the walls near the sofa were racks of pipes and, above them, stills and posters from his productions. Three judo trophies sat on the top of a bookcase. He walked over and chose a pipe from the rack. He hadn't smoked one for a while now, and was looking forward to it. He put down the Guinness on the coffee table, opened the humidor and filled the big James Upshall. His taste in pipes had always been expensive. Putting his lighter and tamper in his pocket, he picked up the beer and went to his bedroom at the back.

It should have been the sitting room of the flat, but there was a big bed against one wall. He noticed his upstairs neighbour must have watered his plants for him, even the ones on the roof. He opened the window and stepped out. The sun was just dipping behind the terrace of houses and shops facing his roof. He extracted a folding chair from behind the fragrant honeysuckle and sat down with a sigh before putting his beer on the window ledge to commence the routine of lighting his pipe.

The aroma from the burning tobacco smelled good. More than anything else, it placed him back in his home after experiences so shattering that it was still difficult to believe they were real, or hadn't happened to someone else in some other world. Yet he looked out on pure normality. Directly opposite was the rear of the Chinese take-away, and through their open window he could see the frantic cooks shaking their woks. With a smile he glanced up at the Minx's window. That's what he and his upstairs neighbour called her. The Minx. And she was much-appreciated, too. She used the curtains on her windows very theatrically. At least one or two nights a week she would give a show as he sat in his circle seat on the roof with a can of Guinness and a pipe after he finished work on the computer. She had a sleek young body with small breasts and a taste for nylon thongs. The curtains would be thrown open with the ceiling light on, as she opened the window on a hot summer night. In an instant, that one window in the back façade of that terrace became the proscenium arch of a drama, played a little differently for each performance. Sometimes it would be a slow striptease as she removed her street-wear for something more comfortable. Other times she caused a sharp intake of his breath, as her body was revealed the instant the curtains were thrown open. Slender, with dark, shoulder-length hair, tits stretched nearly flat as she paused for a moment in the crucifix position, staring insolently at him. At least he imagined she was looking at him. Then she would sit on her bed in profile, talking into her mobile phone. Sometimes she would try on clothes for the evening and spend a lot of time posing in front of her wardrobe mirror. It gave an excellent view of her buttocks, her best feature.

But the Minx's curtain was closed, and the light was off. Hawthorn was secretly glad, because there was much to think about. He turned to glance down his own terrace at the descending back roofs – the houses were built on a hill, and his was near the top. Some tenants used their roofs as he did, and had plants or clotheslines or chairs. Most were not used at all, and that was always a puzzle. His roof was his sanctuary during warmer nights or during the day when the sun was bright. The plants increased the illusion of a little garden. Why they did not use this facility was one of life's many mysteries.

He shrugged. His understanding was stretched and contorted anyway. Madness was not easily defined any more. He took another sip from the beer can, then re-lit his pipe. The sun had dipped behind the roof of the Minx's terrace, just above her window. He could hear the squealing swifts, as they began their late afternoon aerobatics overhead.

The meeting at the hospital had been anti-climactic. The solicitor – a woman in her mid-thirties – arrived first, and they had a little chat. They had spoken several times already on the phone, and she basically reassured him that there were no obstacles to his discharge from the hospital. As far as she was concerned the hospital could no longer reasonably hold him under the provisions of the Mental Health Act, as Winklewhite had informally rescinded the Section.

When Jason Terry arrived the meeting was already under way. Winklewhite was there, along with Dr Harold Pincer and the senior psychiatric nurse for his ward, Pan Subarti. They were all sitting uncomfortably in one of the conference rooms. The chairs were plastic, the long table had a creamy Formica veneer. Terry bustled into the room like a lightweight pugilist, his beard bristling.

IS ALICE?

Catching Hawthorn's eye, he came over, shook his hand and sat beside him before introducing himself.

Jason Terry was one of the dwindling number of real socialist MPs in the 'New' Labour Party, and he was always very active in his constituency. He and Hawthorn had exchanged letters on a previous matter, and Terry subsequently invited him for a tour around the Houses of Parliament. They got along well, and Terry suggested they have lunch together in the canteen used by parliamentary MPs. The conversation was lively and full of mutual respect. Afterwards, Terry urged him not to hesitate to make contact if he had any further problems.

The meeting was surprisingly brief. The psychiatrist, Dr Harold Pincer, was a tall, dull, dry man with thinning hair. He barely raised his spectacles from the file in front of him. Herbie Winklewhite interrupted him several times when he spoke unctuously to Jason Terry. Terry listened carefully to everything the staff told him before unloading salvos into their waterlines.

"Theo Hawthorn is a constituent of mine, known to me for a number of years. I'm not impressed by any of the evidence presented so far. On the contrary, I'm alarmed and ashamed that my constituent was bundled into a psychiatric hospital, and given a spurious examination before being sectioned under the Mental Health Act. He was clearly distraught that his partner of many years was herself traumatised. He deserved a sympathetic response and received bureaucratic and clinical brutality. He was injected with drugs against his will…"

Terry turned to Dr Pincer, stabbing his forefinger "…and I want a complete list of those drugs sent to my parliamentary office with exact notes of the amount dispensed and the times."

Pincer did not raise his eyes from the notes. "We will naturally…"

Winklewhite interrupted him. "I'm afraid patient confidentiality…"

"Hawthorn should not have been a patient. He is a perfectly normal man, and anyway, I'm not interested in your tiresome use of a dubious institutional defence in a matter that now includes a complete and thorough investigation of this hospital and your questionable capacity to act in a reasonably professional manner. You will comply with my request, or possibly your notes on both patients will be requisitioned by a parliamentary committee, and you will personally be brought in to explain why you have chosen to waste public funds in precisely this way. Do you understand, yes or no?"

Winklewhite spread his hands in supplication. "Were it not for my duty as…"

"*Yes or no!*"

Winklewhite opened his mouth, then closed it. His chin sank into his jowls as he examined his fingernails.

Terry slapped the Formica table ferociously. "Speak!"

IS ALICE?

Winklewhite dipped his head obsequiously. "I suppose it might be possible that your request…"

"It's not a request. It's a *demand*!"

Hawthorn grinned to himself at the memory as he sucked on the pipe. Jason Terry couldn't have given a better performance. His words thudded into their soft bureaucratic targets like air gun pellets into lard. It was a spectacularly infrequent event – a politician actually *spoke* for him, using exactly the words he would have used himself, if he had the authority. It was so satisfying to watch their faces as they slowly realised their jobs might somehow be at risk. That invisible wall surrounding unaccountable functionaries evaporated quicker than a drop of urine in the desert. They simply folded. The psychiatrist, the senior nurse, Winklewhite. Shoulders sagged in unison. Dominant magically became submissive. He was given instant discharge, and even received a fragment of an apology from Winklewhite before they left the room. The first thing tomorrow he would write a letter of thanks to his great MP. He wiped the floor with them.

After that letter he would begin another one. To Alyosha Cherkasov. He didn't know if a letter was the right format. It worried him. Before they parted, Cherkasov made him promise that he would tell him the whole story. After the meeting with Winklewhite, they went to the Prince of Wales pub in Highgate. There was a car and driver waiting outside the hospital, and the two of them were driven up the hill for a drink. They were dropped off, and Cherkasov asked the driver to pick him up in an hour. There were few patrons in the pub at that time. Hawthorn and the old pianist shared a booth. The pub had three malt whiskies on offer, and they chose one of them.

Hawthorn was amazed that a man of his formidable reputation would spend so much of his time trying to help a complete stranger, indeed one who had outrageously disrupted his concert at the Royal Albert Hall. Why bother to listen? Why bother to worry? He asked him.

After a long pause, Cherkasov frowned. "I am a rich man. Not money. All my life, I do what I most like, and am paid to do it. I don't have to dig holes in the road. I play… beautiful music. I make a few people happy. That makes me rich, not money. Money makes unhappiness, you only have to look. Show me one person who has enough money. Only more will make them happy. And more. Let me ask. If in a big room, many people, someone throws a bucket of big diamonds, beautiful diamonds, on the floor, what happens? What do you do? You are in this room. Huge, big crowd, like at Royal Albert Hall, many people, diamonds everywhere, real diamonds, no fake."

"Me?" Hawthorn smiled and shrugged as he thought for a moment about the question. He looked at Cherkasov's hands. The hands were as large as any he'd ever seen, even bigger than those of a judo champion he knew. They were attached to thick, sinewy wrists and criss-crossed by heavy blue veins.

"Well, I suppose I'm human. If one or two of these diamonds rolled my way I'd pick them up and put them in my pocket."

Cherkasov laughed so suddenly and loudly the barmaid nearly dropped the empty pint glasses she was carrying. Just as suddenly, he stopped and leaned forward over his whisky glass. "I tell you what happens in this room. Everyone on the floor, men, women, maybe fine dresses, careful make-up – fighting, biting, pulling, screaming. Like animals. I know this is true. Look out the window. It is what you see."

Hawthorn shook his head. "Not me, I'm afraid. I'd walk away."

"Right." A big hand smacked the table, then bounced up with the forefinger pointing like a gun. "You walk. I know you walk. I see that in you."

He thought for a moment. "But what does that have to do with why you helped me?"

"Everything. Everything!" Cherkasov hadn't touched his whisky. Abruptly he grabbed the glass, put it to his lips and drank the contents. "Some things, not diamonds, you go to floor for, worth going to the floor. Your partner."

Hawthorn nodded.

"Me."

Again he agreed.

"There. What to explain? You come on stage almost naked, I play Schubert and dream of a beautiful girl when I was young who carried loaves of bread. Listen!" The big pianist moved his bald head closer as he placed his glass carefully at the corner of the table. "What happens to *me*, if I throw you out of Royal Albert? Inside. How can I then play Schubert or dream of this maiden? You say you have story to tell, that's all. A story to tell. So. I listen. Next time I play Schubert better, maybe. I have time. I listen. You talk. You tell me. Too many just talk and tell always. Me, I listen."

Hawthorn took a sip of his whisky. "You're a good man, Alyosha."

"No," Cherkasov shook his head. "Selfish man. I ruin my music if I behave like pigs. Pig. You understand?"

Hawthorn met the old Russian's eyes and held them. They both smiled. It was an acknowledgement. Here was a man who was a brother. So few of them on earth, all but extinct.

"I understand."

An hour was not much time, but Hawthorn promised again to write his story and send it to him. The driver arrived, and Cherkasov dropped him back at the hospital. They shook hands warmly in the back seat, and the pianist gave him a big hug. He felt a surge of sadness as he watched the big car move away from the kerb. It was sadness, though, that carried a halo of hope.

IS ALICE?

CHAPTER FOUR

*[So, Alyosha, the front of her flat faces the same way as the back of mine. In other words, she lives across the street from me. It was a summer afternoon, and she was sitting in her second floor window, bare feet touching the sloping front roof. Her dress was pulled above her knees as she smiled down at me.

I waved at her as I locked the door of my car. "I hope you're not going to jump."

"Not this time," she replied. "Just catching the afternoon sun."

She had nice legs. My eyes lingered. "Fine day."

She smiled again. "Want to come up for a cup of tea?"

I had seen Alice Dance before, though I didn't know her name then. I knew she was a neighbour who lived across the street, and we occasionally ran into each other in the newsagents or the corner shop. There was no doubt she was a pretty woman – shoulder-length blonde hair, an attractively large bosom, small waist – and fine legs.

I shrugged, a little flattered. "Why not?"

Her flat had a configuration similar to mine, and the first thing I noticed was all the books lining the walls of her bedroom and sitting room. I have never been able to resist the invitation of bookshelves. While she made the tea in the kitchen, I browsed in her front room. Stacks of art books, lots of good contemporary fiction, French and German dictionaries. I was impressed. It was something I had not expected. It was a bright room with an expensive-looking sofa and two small armchairs. On one wall hung a decent reproduction of Picasso, and on the way up the stairs I noticed another one.

"Do you take sugar?" she called from the kitchen.

"Sweetener, if you've got it. Or actually I've got some myself. Just leave the spoon in the mug. I see you read a lot."

"I prefer it to TV," she laughed.

"Did you study languages?"

"I did French. And a little German."

"I'll have to spend some time going through your books. Lots of contemporary fiction. That's where I'm weakest."

We sat in her kitchen. It was small, about the size of mine, but everything was sparkling and clean. Fancy oven, nice fridge, useful cupboards, washing machine. She told me her name, and I told her mine

"Are you American?" she asked.

"Nope. Canadian. Vancouver. Lived here for about 20 years, never lost the accent."

IS ALICE?

"Are you an actor?"

I grinned. "No. Why?"

"You sound like one. I've seen you around at odd times of the day, coming and going."

"Well, you were close. I'm a playwright. I have done some acting, more by necessity than choice, though. I think I'm pretty terrible on stage. What's your story?"

She leaned back and took a sip of tea. "Uh, I'm sort of employed by my family. A family business. Rag trade. It's in Golders Green."

I noticed she laughed nervously after nearly everything she said. It made me a little tense. "Golders Green. Are you Jewish?"

Again she laughed and held up her right hand so she could wobble it back and forth. "Jew-*ish*. As Jonathan Miller says."

"Alice Dance. Not an obviously Jewish name."

"Was Danziger. My dad changed it after the war. I don't know, I think he wanted to be more acceptable."

"I love Jewish cooking."

She cocked her head perkily. "Like what?"

"Ah, chicken liver. Blintzes. Strudel."

"I can make you some apple strudel if you like."

"Well… don't go to any trouble."

"No. Tomorrow. How about tomorrow?" She seemed quite excited. "Would you like me to make you some apple strudel tomorrow?"

I felt myself drawing back a little, and it wasn't fair. But social interaction is a complex matter, particularly when it involves possible sexual adventure. So much subliminal activity is going on. A suggestion here, an opening there, a little feint, a joke. Judgements and evaluations are being made. To be honest, my heart leapt when a pretty girl asked me in for a cup of tea. Now I found myself cautiously backtracking. Just in case. In case of what?...]*

* * *

Theo Hawthorn grabbed his pipe, pushed back his chair, folded his arms and stared at the computer monitor. Thoughtfully he tapped the mouthpiece of the pipe on his chin. It wasn't going to be a letter. It was going to be some kind of long story. Much longer than he planned. A biography, a book? He was impatient with narrative. He just liked dialogue. It bored him having to laboriously paint a picture of how it was – or how it seemed to be from his memory. His car, the books in her flat, cups of tea. And she had been smoking, too. He forgot that. She smoked pretty constantly. He couldn't remember when she told him about her mental health problems, but it was soon after that first meeting in her kitchen. She said she had tried to stop smoking many times, but during periods of anxiety she would always seek solace in cigarettes. Most mental health patients smoked heavily. He found that out later. And he forgot to mention her intelligence, too. Though she was very nervous, she was literate and educated and spoke well. Ah, the problems with narrative writing…

Hawthorn looked at his watch. It had taken him almost five hours to write less than 1,000 words, a trifle. So this project was going to eat time as well. He sighed and re-lit the pipe. Time. Plenty of that. No work, no answers to letters, ignored telephone calls, and even his agent was sounding distant. He wasn't depressed, but he was certainly agitated. Uncomfortable, as if his skin were too tight. Which was contrary to what he saw in the mirror these days. Fifty-six years was written on the face he shaved every morning. His hair was almost grey now, just a little brown left, and thinning around his tonsure. Well, that was all right. He couldn't see that part of his head, fuck it. His moustache was white, but he'd had a moustache since he was 23. Though he never considered fitness near the top of his interests, he wasn't too bad as he roared towards his 60s. A little too thick around the middle, but he'd been the same weight for years. He still trained two or three nights a week at judo, but wished he'd begun his career in London instead of Vancouver. The teaching was so much better. He'd only just missed studying under Trevor Leggett, who retired the year before he arrived.

Hawthorn sighed and spun his chair so his back was to his desk. Puffing his pipe, he stared idly at the three little judo trophies on his bookshelves. Competition was out of the question now, but he still enjoyed training.

Nidan – second grade black belt – was as high as he was going to go. He half-chuckled. Grade didn't mean that much in the sport he always loved. It was all rough stuff now, defensive. Winning was everything. Judo is two Japanese words meaning 'soft way.' Over the years it had become what he called Godo, 'hard way.' It was so disheartening to see the gentle art become so aggressive and confrontational, so antithetical to the whole idea and spirit of judo. You yield to the attack. You do not meet it with force. Therein lay the beauty. And when judo is practised, there is no 'winner' or 'loser' – both are an integral part of the event.

He stood up, stretched and yawned before slumping into the sofa. He was uncomfortable, like he was itching inside, and his mind was drifting like a boat without a mooring. The time he spent in hospital had unsettled him, and his stomach was uneasy. The words of his story had not come easily to him because he found it necessary to focus and re-focus on what he was doing. Was it the drugs they had given him? He certainly suspected some kind of withdrawal symptoms, though the doctors told him there were none, nothing to worry about. Yet his behaviour *had* been irrational during that mad night. Looking at it now, it seemed especially crazy. Instead of waiting for his hearing with his solicitors at the hospital, he surged out of the ward when he found an open door and walked all the way to the Albert Hall, as people stared at him in his underwear. Then he interrupted the concert of a pianist who had for years been his idol.

The emergency exit standing ajar. A quick look around to see if any nurses were present. Then a decision. He

IS ALICE?

was on his way back to his room from the toilet, wearing his underpants and socks. The logic was profound in that moment. He was unjustly imprisoned and treated every day as if he were a madman. His protests, however articulate and rational, were greeted with bored indifference. His clinical notes obviously stated that he was, in one form or another, insane. The staff relied on the notes and ignored him. A thread between him and others in the social matrix was broken. He was abruptly isolated, without will...

Hawthorn was still feeling uneasy in the pit of his stomach. It was a little early for his Guinness, but he went to the fridge anyway and popped open a can. He noticed the hand holding the beer was trembling, and he stared at it long enough for it to stop. Walking back, he detoured to the bedroom, where he found two codeine phosphate painkillers in the middle drawer of the little chest of drawers by his bed.

Returning to the front room, he sat down again and swallowed the tablets with a mouthful of Guinness. They had given him three drugs. A so-called anti-psychotic, an anti-depressant and a 'mood stabiliser.' It would have made him laugh, if the memories weren't so bitter. They *did* have an effect. It made it more difficult to think, to follow thoughts like he used to. He remembered Alice telling him that mental health wards were schizophrenogenic. They encourage madness but provide no asylum.

Ah, that bastard Pan Subarti, the senior nurse. The evening he was admitted they placed the tablets in front of him in a little plastic cap.

"What is it?" he asked the nurse.

"Your medication," was the bored reply.

"I don't need medication. I need a lawyer."

"Take it," Subarti said as he signed some paper.

Hawthorn folded his arms. "I will not willingly take any medication you give me. I refuse."

Subarti glanced at him. "If you do not take your medication, you will be forcibly pinned down and injected." He returned to his paperwork.

Hawthorn shrugged. "Then that's your choice, not mine."

Without a word the senior nurse leaned over and pressed a red button set in the wall. There was one in every room. In seconds Hawthorn heard running footsteps in the halls. Five staff nurses burst into the office.

"Refuses medication," Subarti said to them.

They were on him instantly. He was dragged from the chair and spread-eagled. One of them pushed his face into the floor. Four men held an arm or a leg each.

Hawthorn was so tempted. He would have *loved* to take them on. He almost reacted when the first one touched him. A simple matter. Straight under the outstretched arm, *seoi-nage*. The poor man's shoes would have scraped the ceiling before he hit the concrete floor with his back. But he caught himself. That was not the way. Sure, he could have taken care of those nurses, but the moment they saw he was a danger, the police would be called. The available force was unlimited, so it was not wise to resist. Just let them do what they were going to do.

The fifth man approached with a hypodermic needle, and Hawthorn was jabbed roughly and painfully through his trousers and into his right buttock.

It was the most unpleasant night of his life. He never imagined it would or could be so bad. He was immediately groggy, but at the same time he was overcome with nervous energy. Hawthorn remembered Subarti chuckling at the desk above him.

"Now tell me tomorrow you're not going to take your medication," he said before returning to his paperwork. "Of course, it's *your* choice."

Hawthorn struggled to his feet, realising immediately that his balance was impaired. But that was not his worst problem. There were ants inside his skin, thousands of them, crawling. When he returned to his room, he fell onto his bed but couldn't lie still. Every limb was restless. He had to keep moving. He sat up, stood, walked around, scratching himself ceaselessly. It was very nearly unbearable. He was extremely agitated and frustrated, as he realised there was absolutely nothing he could do. Some toxin had been injected into his blood that was fucking with his nervous system. However, he was damned if he was going to crawl back to the dispensary to beg for a muscle relaxant or sleeping pill. It was something he was simply going to have to live through and come out the other side. Instantly time became a foe, not a friend. Hours, it was going to take. Hours and hours, maybe the whole night…

It was the whole night. And for most of the rest of the next day he was suffering from what he knew was a hangover. Unable to sleep, he paced his room, went to the common TV room, where he spotted Alice. Immediately she got up, lit a cigarette, and left without looking at him. He made coffee, then tea, and munched on stale biscuits. His teeth were chattering, his toes tapped the floor uncontrollably, his arms and face were itching.

Later he discovered they had given him Haloperidol, a so-called anti-psychotic drug they basically used for punishment. Theo Hawthorn had been taught a lesson. It couldn't have been more clear. This hospital was about *control*. He was going to have to learn a craftier game, though subtlety was wasted on the staff. Most were bored agency nurses who spent most of their time looking at their watches or talking on mobiles. There was one pay telephone near the reception desk, and he spent what cash he had with him making calls. Mostly he left messages on answering machines or with voice mail. Nobody was home. Typical of his luck. He did manage to speak with the mental health solicitors and leave a message with Jason Terry's agent.

The next evening when offered his medication, he took it. He thought about saying, "Yassuh, boss," when Subarti offered him his pills, but decided against it.

IS ALICE?

Then after ten days in the shithole, he saw the door ajar. In an instant he decided he could *make* something happen. He was a prisoner. The door offered freedom. Simple as that. If he still had the keys to his flat, he would have gone home. But he remembered a newspaper advertisement. Aleksei Cherkasov was playing a reprise of his first concert at the Royal Albert Hall that evening. Maybe he just had time to make it. He had no idea what he would do when he got there. It was where the whole episode began, and at the time it seemed logical to return there…

Hawthorn felt the painkillers kick in, and he immediately felt a little better. His shoulders began to relax. Whatever the withdrawal symptoms might be, he needed to concentrate on getting himself back into condition. Tomorrow evening he would go training, however he felt – which meant he would have to write during the day. Watch his diet. Get some sleep. The previous night he was restless, so this time he would take sleeping pills. Recover, then play again to his strengths.

The thought of Alice overwhelmed him with sadness. She was still on the ward, but at least she was now under close observation. It was an indignity, but she would be safer. Earlier that day he found the ATM card in his desk and withdrew 100 pounds from the joint account Alice set up for them to use only when she fell ill. He spent forty on cigarettes, took them to the hospital, and deposited sixty in her account there. He would have to keep a close eye on her cigarettes. Other patients and one or two nurses stole from her.

He had no idea how long her illness would last this time. It was her first relapse in years. The last one occurred shortly after their first meeting in her flat while her father was still alive. She was in for about three months then. Mental illness was a strange phenomenon, and predictability was not a feature. He put his pipe aside, and had a long drink of Guinness, before resting his head against the pillow of the sofa. There was little he could do for her. When he took round the cigarettes, she wouldn't see him. It hurt, but he realised he mustn't take it personally. In her present state, he was configured differently in her mind. Naturally he couldn't know exactly what she was thinking, but he could guess from what she told him in the past. For so long they both dared to hope that she was 'cured.' She had never experienced such a long period of relative stability, and they both knew it was the relationship that eased the danger.

Relationship. What a clinical word. Impersonal, like seamanship. For him and for her, it was unexpected, whatever it was called. A very rocky beginning, one he was already finding difficult to describe in his 'letter' to Aleksei. It had begun about ten years ago. He didn't remember the exact date, but at the time he was recoiling from another 'relationship.' It was the one addiction he couldn't cure – women. Despite all his mistakes in the past, there had been a lot of fun as well. Then Alice slipped in beneath his guard. It didn't begin auspiciously. That was what he was trying to write to Aleksei. He recalled the very words that went through his head at the time – "…*not another nutter.*" Unkind but understandable. At one point he wondered if he had a fatal attraction to birds with broken wings. The last thing he wanted when he met Alice was… a relationship. No!

None of his previous relationships were conventional. He long ago spurned the paradigm of what a man and woman were supposed to do together. His own family was dysfunctional. His mother and father should have divorced before he was born. It was never a part of his plan to get a job, settle down, buy a home, have children. The thought of it still made him shudder. Yet he had travelled right across the battlefield. Two marriages, maybe a dozen 'relationships,' many affairs, and innumerable assorted gropings, couplings and one-night-stands. Much of it was glorious and some was nightmarish. It had become evident to him that he was on some kind of hamster wheel of repetitive activity. Sex, though, was something he viscerally enjoyed. It was compelling and wonderful, but the excitement diminished the longer the relationship lasted – *usually*. Gradually he learned to intervene, to deviate from the common paradigm, and slowly it became clear that sexuality was parallel to storytelling. Fundamentally it was *creative*. In that sense, it could be infinitely inventive and – therefore – infinitely enjoyable. When he was a youth, the simple sexual act was as powerful an emotional explosion as he could possibly imagine. But did it need to have that inevitable trajectory? Initial love-lust intensity, gradual return to normality, slow deterioration to boredom and final agony of craving more space or an alternative partner. He was convinced it didn't have to be that way.

After much thinking, he decided the way forward was simple honesty. The more he thought about his former mistakes, the more he shouldered responsibility for much of the failure. And the more honest he was with himself, the more mendacity he uncovered within. He lied to himself, and he lied to them. Thus what he lacked was courage. Be honest. Be honourable. Those were the changes he had to make. Unless he wanted to spend the rest of his life on the hamster wheel, with an end no better than the beginning. Not unlike the common paradigm, in fact. Dead eyes, dead heart, dead spirit.

From inauspicious beginnings in a small, rural British Columbia town and a poor family, he found his way first to Vancouver, then to the University of British Columbia, where the dense mist of uncertainty began slowly to clear. Discovery of the theatre led him to playwriting and then to London with high hopes.

It certainly didn't begin joyfully. He was an awkward boy who felt as out of place as a duck in a flock of geese. He was angry because he couldn't find the keys to unlock the right social doors, and those that were open slammed in his face. Or so it seemed. Only later did he realise that it wasn't him; it was the world that was awkward.

He studied philosophy at UBC, though he always sensed he would somehow be a writer, and it was at UBC that he first started to learn judo. Vancouver has a large indigenous Japanese population, and he became a member of the Vancouver Judo Club. Always a loner, he had never been a natural sportsman, but judo was different. Naturally he was first attracted to it as a form of self-defence. Like any young male, he was physically uncertain and insecure, but slowly he began to realise it was changing his attitude towards things. In other words, it was not a way to *fight* but a way to *be*. As he struggled for inner balance – the key to judo and his own life – the chaos of the world became a little more ordered. Balance is an active undertaking, not a passive one. It is a state of unstable equilibrium. When you are riding a bicycle, you are in constant movement – not just forward but to the sides as well. It never stops being a balancing act. Yet this system works very well because of the forward momentum. If you stop, it doesn't work at all, and the balance collapses. As he learned to maintain his *balance*, his vision and understanding improved. With confrontation, you're trying to change the world in the wrong way. It was within himself that change must take place.

As he became less confrontational, less angry and sullen and consequently more confident, the attitude of those around him changed, too. The need to 'defend' himself melted away. He was at first mystified when a visiting Japanese judo teacher who held a seventh grade black belt told him that becoming involved in a fight was a sign of failure. Through broken English the old man tried to tell him that, if you have the proper spirit, no one will see you as an opponent. They will pass by and seek an angry man or a fearful one. Violence attracts violence. When balanced in mind and spirit, the need for violence vanishes. Thus it was ironic. As he acquired more skills of fighting, the less likely he was to fight.

Yet balance does collapse at times, whatever your level of skill. As it did during the chaos at the ticket machine in the Royal Albert Hall and his subsequent adventures in a lunatic asylum, or his outrageous gambit during Cherkasov's performance. Hawthorn did not allow guilt about his behaviour to trickle into his heart. He fully realised he was responsible for each poor choice that led him inexorably into greater difficulties. With sadness he knew that, if he had maintained his *balance*, it was highly probable Alice's world would never have been destroyed.

It was their anticipation of the concert that blinded them. Or him, anyway. He should have known better. Something was wrong with the machine that read Alice's debit card. That was not their fault or their problem. But that night it was a strong wind, a powerful wind, and he decided to face the wind and fight it, *make* it work, twist the world until it was the right way up. It was the very essence of arrogance. Instead he should have been like the reed that allows the wind to blow it flat. Then, when the wind subsides, the reed springs back into place. But at that moment he became the oak and was broken, because the wind was too strong.

It almost made him chuckle. He opened his eyes and slowly re-lit his pipe. Then he did laugh. They had no way of knowing there would be a *second* concert, because the first was so over-subscribed, but if they had just calmly turned away and gone home with dignity, they would have had the opportunity of seeing the performance later, perhaps by paying in advance on the telephone or via a website. It was a lesson, but there was no reason to flagellate himself for an awesome mistake. The point now was to regain his balance. After he learned the lesson.

IS ALICE?

Thoughtful, he watched his little front room fill with smoke. He realised he was trying not to think about Alice and his grievous sense of loss. And it was genuinely perilous to imagine what she must be going through at the hospital. He backed away from that space. There was nothing further he could do. If there had been, he would have done it. It was a matter of waiting now, a matter of patience. She would emerge, he believed in that. He could only look for the right moment to try and be there to provide that bridge that so often saved her in the past; the time when she would look at him and begin to ask questions about the reality of her delusions. He mustn't anticipate it. He must just wait.

He couldn't help thinking about her, though – or thinking about them. Slowly, over the years, the outline of a dreamscape as unlikely as an outrageous fantasy drew them close enough to see it was real, once the mists fell away. It drew them inward and downward, outward and upward. It was a world of magic that left both of them stunned and groggy with delight. Was it really ten years? In a way it seemed even longer, a time warp wrapped around space in an erotic embrace. So unlike many of his earlier adventures, yet it was clearly something he was seeking – like a miner ceaselessly sifting for gold, certain he would find his fortune at last.

Years ago as a teenager, his father told him he was going to have to spend his life doing things he didn't want to do. It was a big argument, and his father was a big man, built like a bear.

"No!" Hawthorn answered through tight lips. "That's one thing I'm not going to do. I won't spend my life doing useless work. What's the point?"

"To make money, you idiot!" his dad roared. "How do you think you're gonna live? There's only one way. Work. It's something you better start learning to do."

"I don't like work. It makes me tired. It's a waste of time."

His dad moved forward onto his front foot and raised his index finger, pointing it towards his chest. "Exactly what I'm trying to tell you. You're gonna do it whether you like it or not, just like I did. You're not gonna have time to sit around reading books and listening to music."

Hawthorn laughed. "Do you know what you just said, Dad? You just said I'm not going to have time for *pleasure* in my life..."

"You're goddamn right." The finger was still pointing. "When you leave here, you're gonna have to eat and have a place to stay. That cost bucks. To make bucks, you gotta work. If you have a wife, you gotta support her, same with kids. So that's what I'm telling you. You spend your life doing things you don't want to do to *live*! There ain't no other way! The sooner you learn it, the better."

"I'm *not* going to learn it."

"You WILL!"

IS ALICE?

"I WON'T!"

And, lo, he *didn't* learn it. Instead he learned – painfully at first – how to pick his way through the thorny hedgerows lining the narrow pathways that were intended to deliver him into the normal workforce and the normal life. He read, he observed carefully, he thought deeply – and at times he even took an ordinary job for short periods of time to get him past obstacles. At first he just survived. Then he began to thrive. And slowly he created space for himself, space that only the truly rich could afford, but seldom enjoyed. There was time to write, to think, to take his bicycle to the park and eat his lunch leisurely as he watched pretty girls bathing in the sunshine. He frequented pubs and cafés, talked and laughed with groups of friends, or rode on trains down to the seaside or up to the peak district. He made some money with his playwriting, but he had never been a big 'name.' Theatre people knew him, and he was respected in the profession. By some, anyway. Audiences liked his work, and that's what pleased him most. Yet he never made enough money for what his dad called a 'living.' Two or three years here and there, maybe. The only ones who made big money in the arts were the stars, a small percentage of those who struggled in the twilight.

The course he chose was socially unacceptable, but he lived in London where nobody cared what you did, so long as you didn't bore them with details of your life. With persistence he found a really nice unfurnished flat with a housing association when rents were still controlled. When he had no money, he signed on for unemployment benefits, which also paid his rent and council taxes. It was final proof that his dad was wrong. He had a roof over his head and enough to eat, with plenty of time for writing or wandering in the parks of the city. It took a lot of ducking and diving to survive. When you choose the arts, you learn to live like a phantom.

The social system was not his choice – it was the one he was born into. It was alien and unfair, but there was no alternative. At first he didn't realise what a nightmare the world was. Much of the truth unfolded during his glorious life with Alice. His vision became clearer and cleaner. Perhaps the money he took was not 'his,' but if that were the yardstick, it was the one big business used to measure up their palaces. Thousands and thousands of people used money they didn't earn to live on the shady side of life in expensive comfort. By comparison he was a single grain on a sandy beach. And he certainly didn't have their extravagances.

Hawthorn opened his eyes and realised he must have dozed off on the sofa. He couldn't remember the last time that happened. The painkillers gave him a sense of euphoria, and he felt fully relaxed for the first time since he left the hospital. His pipe was cold, and the can of Guinness was still almost full. After stretching, he had a good drink and tried to recall what he was thinking. The tumbleweed events of his past were still blowing from distant horizons, catching his attention for a few seconds before they rolled on.

He suddenly remembered that Alice had told him to have a meal out once a week from their special joint account if she ever became ill again. He certainly couldn't afford it himself on a regular basis. And it struck his fancy at that moment – a nice sea bass fried in olive oil at the old Pasta House. It was a little working class restaurant down at the five points junction in Tufnell Park – wooden tables, waxed red-and-white checked tablecloths, cosy and cheap, filled mostly with locals and a few bohemians. He ate there quite often when he was flush.

"Thanks, babe," he said, raising the can of beer, "Cheers. Just what I need."

They ate out together quite often. Her frequent descent into the nightmare of mental illness convinced her that she would never have what she thought all the others had. It wasn't for her. She didn't deserve it. Meals out together. Holidays in the country, walks in the woods holding hands, standing on empty beaches together, flying off to exotic islands in the Mediterranean to lounge in pavement cafés, hire boats and drift languidly in the sun.

Finishing the can of Guinness, he got up, collected his pipe, lighter and tamper, put on a fleece and cap, collected his bike lamps, and turned off the flat lights before locking his door. His bike was parked downstairs in the hallway. He was looking forward to the sea bass.

CHAPTER FIVE

The bath was freezing, and Alice was shivering as she stood in it. That was the point. She was going to sit *shiva,* the Jewish ritual held after the death of a close relative. It was a cool night, and she deliberately cracked the bathroom window to try and bring down the temperature. Then she sat down painfully in the ice-cold bath filled to the overflow. She squeezed her eyes shut and gasped as she lowered her body into the water. Of all things on earth, Alice hated the cold. During winters she wore layers of clothes and kept the central heating turned up at least to 75 degrees. Heat was her joy, but cold was pain, and pain was her goal.

She was sitting *shiva* for her father, who died six years ago. It was atonement, too, for the vast array of her disgusting sins. Or some of them. She knew it would be impossible to atone for them all. There were too many. Sins marched in infinitely long ranks and files that disappeared into the horizon, too numerous to count. The earth trembled as they marched, and the air was filled with angry screams for vengeance. All eyes of the soldier-sins turned to her, and each one of them pointed a finger – at her. On and on they marched, implacable warriors, filling the wintry steppes of her soul with endless hordes.

Her teeth chattered and her breasts floated and shook like softly gelled ice cream in the freezing water. The shock made her forget the disinterested woman sitting in the doorway of the bathroom talking on her mobile phone, watching her with one eye. She realised the other day that 'they' weren't the Aliens. She was. Unknown forces had catapulted her into an earth of superior beings where she was doomed to eternal stupidity. She couldn't understand their codes or manners, but knew she must be of great interest to them. Because of her sins. Luckless ones were appointed to watch everything she did. The one in the doorway was telling someone on the phone how contemptible she was. If only the woman would come over and hold her head under the water until she was well dead. At least Hell would be hot, as her flesh melted and curdled in the glowing coals. In fact she yearned for it…

Suddenly the full nature of her maliciousness exploded like ice crystals. She was supposed to be sitting *shiva*, atoning for the evil she embraced so willingly in the past. When she should be thinking of her dear father, she was instead at her old tricks. Thinking of herself. Wishing herself in Hell for the warmth of the fires. *How hateful was it possible to be?*

It was her father on his deathbed in the hospital. The image was bright, as if lit by heaven. She was leaning over him when he opened his eyes.

"Alice…Alice. You have made my life a misery…no! No! *Without* you, my life *would have been* a misery!"

There. That was final proof, wasn't it? Being close to death, he blurted out what he really meant, before adjusting it to the duty he was required to shoulder while he was alive – looking after her, giving her money, pretending she was his child. No, no, maybe she was his child. That could be the way it worked. People had

demon children, like the little girl in *The Exorcist*.
Spawn of Satan.

She clenched her teeth and forced her eyes open to stare
down at her body with revulsion. Stupid fat tits, stupid
fat legs – that's what Satan's spawn looked like. Her
pubic hair was finally growing back after the so-called
bikini wax that made it possible to wear skimpy
underwear. Her eyes widened. She knew she must get
back to her flat so she could destroy all that lingerie she
bought with money stolen from her family. Her eyes
snapped shut with mortification as the imagery danced
through her head. Strutting around with stockings and
high-heeled sandals, revealing bras, filmy dresses,
corsets. What an idiot the Fool had made of herself. Oh,
she had to get out of this place so she could empty her
bank account, destroy her flat, tear up that underwear,
live on the streets. Where she belonged. A bag woman.
Sleeping in gutters. That was her proper home. Gutters,
sewers...

As she unclenched her teeth, they began to rattle
together like castanets. It was *cold*! It was freezing.
She was dying. Cold bath to Hell. That was it. Of
course. She should drown herself and die sucking icy
water before being thrown onto the fiery grates of Hell.
Inhaling deeply, she slid her body downwards so her
head was under water. It was final. She was not even
worthy to sit *shiva* for her father. All she could do was
think about herself. Not him. The poor man. Having to
spend his whole life bringing up a demon child who
repaid him with nothing but thoughts of self...

IS ALICE?

They wouldn't let her go. Now they watched her all the time, every moment of every day and night. They told her Theo had taken her handbag, and all her cheques and cards were in it. Her Filofax, too, all her phone numbers. Her mobile phone. Everything was gone, they took it all or wouldn't let her have it. She couldn't escape. Hell couldn't be much worse. Death was the only way out, the only answer. The present was nothing but searing pain.

Her lungs were already bursting, and she dreaded the moment she was going to have to inhale the water. But she had to do it, she mustn't fail. It was another chance, maybe her last one to get the job done.

She didn't know what the sensation was at first. Her thoughts were skittering away like marbles on a frozen lake. And there was a sound. Knocking. It was Satan, waiting for her. Knocking at the door of her soul.

Suddenly she was sucking in air as her head was pulled above the surface. She looked up, confused. The Alien was scolding her after rapping on the top of her head with a knuckle, that was the noise she heard. *So confusing*. Why was she doing that to her? Why not help her over the threshold into Hell? That's where they all wanted her. Gone. Off this earth and into the hot lava pits below.

Alice Dance thrashed in the cold water, crying now. The strange woman wanted her out of the bath and was now slapping at her, raising her voice, screaming. Alice thrashed with arms and legs as the anguish of failure spread like toxin in her body. No, no, no.

"Please, please. Let me die!" she howled at the Alien. "I'm no good. I'm sitting *shiva*. For Satan!"

"Stop it," the nurse shouted. "You're getting me all wet. That water is cold."

It was a message. Alice grasped it. Cold. She must be bold to be cold – or catch hold of the cold. Grasp it, clasp it. She snatched at the water with her hands. Was this what the Alien wanted? Was she finally learning the language? There was snot on her lip. She could feel it because it was warm. Not snot. 'Tis snot. 'Tis not snot...

There was sound, and the woman was still shouting at her, but she couldn't understand any more, not snot a word. Not snot, two words. No, no. *She* was snot. Gooey-boogy, slippery slime. The cold was not-snot, one word, and it had been two. Not-snot was a word, too, with a hyphen, hymen, amen...

The big woman was tugging at her, still shouting, making many code words, and now there was a man in the room, too. Two of them. Hands were pulling at her as she slipped and splashed with her feet in the water, and now she was out of the bath, still crying, eyes squeezed shut in terror as she felt a big hand on one breast, fondling and squeezing.

Now the woman was screaming at the man and slapped at him. Another code. She had to listen, that was the problem. Theo had said that. He said she had to listen to *what was going on*.

IS ALICE?

"You bastard!" the woman said to the man. "You leave her alone. I just wanted help getting her out of this fucking bath. Now piss off! Both of you. Out!"

She turned back to Alice who was standing and shivering in a pool of water beside the bath, her eyes squeezed shut, crying piteously. "Fucking men! Now come on. Put this big towel around you, get yourself dry. I'm as wet as you are…"

Alice Dance sagged to her knees nakedly, and she clasped the nurse's legs with her arms. "Help me. Please help me."

* * *

*[I'm growing a beard now, Alyosha, to go with my moustache. A full set, as they say in the navy. Except this beard is not going to be a full one, just a goatee. I can just see the outline of it already. I grew the moustache to mark my passage from youth to young man. I'm now marking the change from man to middle-aged man. Or is it the precipice that is old age? Well beyond the half-way station, anyway. Time whistles past as we accelerate towards extinction like kamikaze pilots, the air increasingly filled with bursts of flak that could bring us down before we reach the target. Will it be tomorrow with a heart attack? Or will it be ten years? Twenty? Thirty at the most, I'd say. That would make me older than you are now.

I digress. Already you can see this is much more than a letter, though I decided to send it in instalments. What is this? The third? It's good for me, though. I'm getting the hang of it now, though my memories are fallible.

Alice let me see her today, but she only sat there the whole time, mute. We were in the same room where you played the piano for us, but this time the instrument was locked. She sat in one chair, and I sat next to her. I know she can't bear anyone touching her. She told me once this is because she feels I'm being forced to do it under the terms of a social matrix she doesn't understand. So she wants to spare me the humiliation I must feel. Yet I long to put my arm around her shoulders to reassure her of my love. To hold her, give her head some rest on my chest. Instead, she sits stiffly. When I ask her to look at me, I tell you her eyes are indescribable. Nothing like Alice's eyes. They say the eyes are the windows of the soul. If so, my heart breaks, because her soul, then, is a blasted moonscape of lifeless horror that I can't even begin to imagine. A moonscape of loneliness with no human footprint to be found on the surface anywhere. There I sit, helpless, in another galaxy – light-years away, yet so very close. One of the nurses took her out one day, and she bought an electric hair-clipper, so her hair is now evenly shaved. Not hacked about and horrible any longer. But still, the illness devastates her physically. Dark circles under her mad eyes from lack of sleep. They will not make sleeping tablets mandatory, no matter what I say. Sleep will help her. That's the only thing that will now. How do you make stupid people understand simple matters? Otherwise she forces herself to stay up as long as she possibly can. Walking in circles, carrying heavy books, balancing them on her head. She probably lives on an hour or two of sleep a night, and spends the rest of her time in hallucinating nightmares. The doctors remind me of nothing so much as the old phrenologists who thought they could gain insight by measuring aspects of the skull and relate this to some pseudo-scientific quantum. I'm certain future investigators will fall about laughing at 'modern' methods. So many cc's of this chemical, so much of that one. Mix with a third potion, alternate dosages and correlate this in their notes to observable, 'objective' behaviour. No help? Then zap their brains with a high-voltage dose of electricity, even though they admit they don't know what it does or why. "Ah, a bit calmer after that. It must be good for them, then. So we'll have more of that on a regular basis." But is it also wrecking the brain or damaging delicate neurological lace-work? Well...they don't *think* so. Or at least they *hope* not. If only they would liaise with me, listen to me. Alice and I are so close. I know her. I've been with her in places they can't imagine. When she's well, she talks to me for hours and hours about her illness, what she feels, how her madness is constructed.

I keep hinting at this closeness, but I haven't made clear what I mean. To explain, though, I'll have to talk about sex. It can't be helped. Furthermore I'm going to have to be honest. Otherwise you won't understand. It has been a journey of gradually illuminated enlightenment. So put your fingers in your ears if you're prudish.

She and I were in my front room on the sofa. It was spring or summer, a warm day, a light day. Alice was wearing a pretty cotton dress. A side effect of her medication expressed itself with a continuous little foot-tap or finger spasm. We called ourselves friends now, and she used to come over often for a chat and cup of tea. Or we would go out to a coffee shop or pub for a drink. My memory is hazy here, but once, I think, we found ourselves in bed, thrashing around in physical need. So the friendship was by then a little ambiguous. I was still reluctant and cautious, because I was determined not to become a serious object for her affections. Least of all did I want a relationship. I made this clear to her.

"Do you mind if I ask why?" She lit a cigarette and adjusted her skirt.

I laughed and shrugged. "This is an understatement: my relationships range from inadvisable to disastrous. Except maybe my last one, and that was because I knew it was going to end the moment it began, so that gave me a little security…"

We both laughed together, and I continued. "She was 25 years younger, we had a delightful time, and when she went it was time she went. We're still good friends."

"Well, that doesn't sound disastrous," she said with a nervous laugh and picked up her mug of tea.

"True. But one day I'll tell you about the others. I'll drag some skeletons out of the closet and rattle them. What about you?"

She laughed again, this time a little ironically. "I don't know. A couple, I guess. Don't know if you would call them relationships. I see this one guy, but, you know…"

IS ALICE?

Alice stopped to tap her cigarette ash into the ashtray. "I mean, I like him, but it's not a relationship. Not really. We're friends. We go out together sometimes to comedy evenings or, you know, to jazz clubs, that sort of thing."

And again she laughed. I realised her laughter was often more an expression of her social anxiety. I found myself wishing I could help her relax in my company.

"I suppose I've never had a relationship," she said. "Not really, not what I would call a relationship. Maybe I don't know what a relationship is. I haven't lived with anybody."

"You're lucky."

"Yes, well, I'm 30 years old, nearly 31, and most of my friends are living with someone, or married." She laughed again. "So I don't know whether I'm lucky or not."

"But you've had lovers."

"If you mean sexual partners – or sexual events – yes, plenty of those. Mostly disastrous, to use your word. But I wouldn't call them lovers." She stopped for a moment, looking away, before she stubbed her cigarette in the ashtray. "I don't really expect to have any…lovers. Or relationships."

"Why?" I asked, even though I knew the answer.

"I think I better go now," she said suddenly, taking a final sip from her tea mug.

I smiled gently. "No, no. Sit down. It's because of your illnesses, right?"

She lit another cigarette. "Of course. This is not the right world for me. I'll have to wait for another one to come along. I caught the wrong bus." This time her laugh was bitter. "I can tell you're just putting up with me."

"Can you?" I asked in an amused voice.

"Aren't you?"

"Look, we may not be headed for a relationship. But there are other avenues. I enjoy your company…"

"You're not being serious, are you?"

I stopped and sighed. "Let me make a promise to you, Alice. I will never lie to you. Therefore this is not a lie: I enjoy your company. You are a very interesting woman, you're extremely pretty. I find you very physically attractive. You're keenly intelligent. I'm also wary of your mental health problems, I'll admit that. But I want to emphasise that we never have to define ourselves by the values of others. That means that there are more paths than just one or two. I'd say we are becoming friends, exchanging confidences, getting a little more comfortable as we understand a bit about each other. Anyway, this is normal activity, even for the conventional world."

IS ALICE?

She turned and faced me, drawing up one leg and hooking the ankle with her other leg. "Theo. I'll be honest too, or try. Nothing has worked for me in my life, not one single thing. OK, my family have provided me with money. But other than that, there is nothing. I'm what Woody Allen calls an anhedonist. I've tried to kill myself a number of times. It's an ugly life. Nothing about it that I like. I see others having fun. It's not for me. I'm a spectator sitting on a bed of nails."

I smiled as gently as I could. "Do you know the American Indian proverb about the two goats? Inside everyone is a good goat and a bad one. What you become depends on which one you feed. Your bad goat is very, very fat."

"So am I."

"That's a great example. You say you're fat. The trick is to find something you *like*, not to list the things you don't. You have a perfect figure, but when you look in the mirror you see an imaginary woman who is fat."

"Every day is a day of pain." Her voice was small now, like a little girl looking for approval.

"You *expect* pain. You *see* the pain. You don't see the pleasure."

"Wrong." Again the little voice. "There isn't any pleasure."

I laughed. "You're impossible. We went out for coffee the other day, and you were bubbling with enthusiasm about a show you'd seen the previous evening. You make jokes, you laugh, you enjoy your food."

"That's why I'm fat."

"You talk about a book you're reading with intelligence and wit."

"I don't."

"Remember, I'm being honest, and that's what I think. You are like a princess in a flower garden, yet you fill your basket with sticks and stones, convinced you're a witch. You see the weeds, not the flowers. I know this because I have days like that myself. *Days*, though. Most of the time, if I see one flower, I'm happy. And I see it because I'm looking for it. Do you like sex?"

Finally she laughed. Her foot was now in unconscious spasm. "Well, yes. Sort of. I like orgasms, let's put it that way. Who doesn't? But sex is complicated. You come back to relationships again."

"Have you ever been in love?"

She stretched the fingers of one hand and looked at them. "No."

"But you like sex."

"Yes."

IS ALICE?

"Well, *good*!" I said with humorous emphasis. "That's a starting place. Next question, what *kind* of sex do you like best?"

She was still studying her nails. "The kind...people have. Other people have. I think I would like sex with love."

"Woah, you can't cross the water without finding a bridge. We have two people here, both interested in sex. That's where I'm trying to start. Now, in a way, I'm worse off than you. I've had lots of sex and some love. Enough to think love is not for me. That leaves just the sex. But everyone I know, me included, tires of sex after the initial excitement wears off. It becomes common. Ordinary. A poke. To me, that's blasphemy. I've had sexual experiences at the outer boundaries where it's not the same. It's different. It's creative. It's finding the chasm of desire, the fountainhead of humanity, before the fetters were forged, before we were enslaved by the forces of darkness..."

This time her laugh was hearty. "Well, if you find it, let me know where it is."

"Why don't we try and look for it together?"

She paused for a moment, then lit another cigarette. "Let me ask a question. Why don't you search for it with someone else? Or am I just handy?"

It was my turn to think. Finally I answered. "Well, I have to admit you're handy in the sense that I have no other prospects right now. We've been to bed together.

There are possibilities, but they are mostly abstract for the moment. What I'm suggesting is that we follow our intuition and try one or two alternatives. I know there are problems. Your vulnerabilities, my own quest..."

She glanced at me with a smile. "Is it a quest? Really?"

I shrugged. "It's as good a word as any. Yeah, a quest. I never believed in the normality of the world I was born into. Not quite true, actually. I believed in it when I was young, especially as a teenager, because that was all there was. And I was just not fitting in with anything I saw. So I set out then to find out what was wrong."

"Did you find it?"

"Partly. It's difficult. Like a blind man trying to assemble a jigsaw puzzle by the feel of the pieces. It's slow. Occasionally I get a mental image of the possible picture, and then it changes."

She chuckled, and her eyes sparkled. "That's a good a metaphor for my problem. Except I haven't found any two pieces that fit."

I laughed with her. "Then it can be a mutual quest."

Though the conversation moved along evenly, I could tell we were both nervous. At this point we didn't really know each other very well. But progress was being made. Slowly. It was true that I needed to be careful. She was very needy, and I didn't want to impose my choices as the only alternative. In other words, I wanted to be fair to her.

IS ALICE?

I was filling my pipe as I chose my words. Then I lit it. Pipes are good for that. It makes a little space.

"I suppose," I began through puffs, "it's better to jump right in, Alice. And it may be the water's far too cold for you."

"Try me."

"I'm not that interested in what they call straight vanilla sex any more. Well, that's half a lie. More truthfully, vanilla sex comes near the bottom of my sexual interests. I'll take it if it's going, but experience tells me it's not going anywhere. I'm not a young man now, getting on for 50. I want to focus on deeper, edgier adventures."

She giggled, then bubbled into a laugh. "What, what what? The suspense is killing me!"

He nodded his head back and forth, realising he was still being shy. "OK, I'm sure you've heard of tantric sex, right?"

"I've heard of it, yeah. I even know a little about what it is. Is that it? Tantric sex?"

He took a deep breath, "I've had some experience in the past, enough to know that's it's a very interesting path. Things happen to two people. Doors open in spaces you never knew were there. Also, it can extend the sexual experience for hours. Days. Maybe more. I don't know, because I've never been very far down the magic road. I've heard that even visions are possible, maybe more. But I don't know. First of all, you need a willing partner."

She bobbed her head back and forth, smiling. "Well, I suppose I'd better not turn down an invitation to a party when I'm not sure whether it will be fun or not."

"Exactly. You can leave the party any time you want. That's what free people do. It could be wrong for you or wrong for me. Or it could even be right. We'll never know until we've tried. And this is the point where you leave most 'normal' people behind. They're too scared or too worried about their image to try something that might lead to places that are unfamiliar. I live a risky life. But without risk, you never open the door that could change the meaning of everything. You'll never know what's over the hill until you climb to the top..."

I stopped for a moment to re-light my pipe. "Incidentally, this isn't a sales pitch. I'm telling you what I think as clearly as I can."

Alice pulled her foot from under her knee and stretched her legs beneath the coffee table, re-arranging her dress. "I don't know what to say. That's because I don't know who I am. Everybody else seems to know who they are, but I don't. I'm a survivor clinging to a fragment of wreckage, Theo. Bobbing in the sea. I've tried so hard, but every time I feel something solid under my feet, I'm swept away again. Did I tell you? Years ago I signed up for a secretarial course. I dressed up, put my hair in a bun and practised being a secretary for a while. Then I'm ill again. It all falls to pieces. I studied massage and set up a little business in my flat. It didn't work, and I didn't work. OK, you say I don't have to work, but you have to *do* something or you are nothing."

"I know. I agree. Some kind of focus."

"I went to university but couldn't finish because I became so obsessive about studying – going without sleep, living in terror. I tried painting. I studied the 'cello, and after a year I sounded so horrible I had to pack it in. I bought a cat – and then came the fleas, everywhere in my flat. So the cat goes. People have friends. Everybody does. Look around you. I have people who see me out of sufferance, probably you included. I look in the mirror, trying to see what is wrong. How do you talk so that people don't think you're crazy? I'm talking to you now, and all the time I'm wondering if I'm saying the right words, sane words, hoping you won't think I'm crazy, too. I keep trying. I keep failing."

I noticed her eyes were rimmed with tears as she looked down at her toes. I put down my pipe and put my hand on her arm. She didn't look at me. She was blinking away her tears.

"I've seen you when you were ill," I said softly. "But you're not ill now, and what you're saying is as clear as a bell. To be honest, I backed away slightly after we first met. I think I sensed you were trying too hard, and maybe that's part of the problem. You have no confidence in yourself."

She looked at me with an ironic shrug. "Well, do you blame me? How can I? I'm a fucking shambles…"

I moved over to her side and put my arm around her shoulders. She laid her head against my chest and finally let herself cry. It wasn't pity that I felt. It was something like a sense of humanity, a responsibility I had as a fellow human being to hold out my hand. There was also – if I remember correctly – a vague hunch forming in the mists. The touch of her body was warm. Not erotic. But there was an electric current. I had noticed it before, but it was stronger now. At rare times when you touch someone there is a subliminal recognition signal. "I am one of you..." It only happened once or twice in my life.

"Alice." I spoke quietly as I focused on the tree outside my front window. "You're not so unique, you know. Everyone 'out there' has adopted a role that is played with varying success and failure, in a drama they seldom understand. That's the human condition. You know this intuitively. You try on various masks and then score their value through the reactions of others to you. It's a recipe for frustration. 'Is this one good enough to gain love and attention? No? What about that one? Wait. There are more. Don't run away...' Perhaps you don't understand all these other people are much more concerned with their own masks, not yours. Their roles are the ones that interest them. When they observe someone struggling, they back off. You know why? Because your act of Not-Knowing threatens them. No, that's wrong. It threatens their 'reality.' For them, their roles *are* reality. I know. I felt it myself. With you."

"When we first met and I wanted to make strudel for you?" She talked with her head still resting on my chest.

IS ALICE?

"Yes."

"I shouldn't have done that. You must have thought I was really stupid."

"Not stupid. Just awkward. Like a child who doesn't know where to place her feet on the rungs of a shaky ladder. Awkwardness isn't a sin. I'm awkward when I try to dance."

"I can't help it," she said. "I try...but I don't know how."

Wind was moving the branches of the tree outside. "I've been trying for most of my life."

"But you know how."

"No. I *seem* to know. There's a difference. You are mostly among people who *seem* to know. What I'm saying is that we're on the same path, seeking similar things. Different levels, maybe, but *we both want to know*. Not seem. Now...sex. I'm suggesting we explore further along this path by entering the cave alongside the mountain..."

"So the path leads to a cave?" she said, looking up at me.

"Some call me Metaphor Man. I like them well mixed." I looked down at her, and she was smiling now.

"We'll call it an experiment," I went on. "We can stop or go, or change direction at any time. I don't want you to feel under any pressure. But this gambit will allow us to take roles…"

"I'm not good at playing roles." She struggled to sit up, then reached for her packet of cigarettes. "Acting terrifies me."

"How would you know what acting is?"

"I was in a school play."

"I rest my case. In real acting, you look for something you want to express. It's an elemental thing. To speak within a role allows you to tease out fibres of your being…"

"I've heard fibres make a good rope to hang yourself with."

"Hmm. Not strong in comedy. Oh, well."

"It was a good joke."

"Was it?" We looked at each other and laughed. This time she wasn't so anxious, and it came from her heart.

I re-lit my pipe. "Maybe this weekend we could try a few things, slowly, gently. I call it tantric sex for convenience because it sets it in the right general frame. Establishing trust is a slow process, and we need some patience. We have to learn to trust each other, relax together, use a bit of hypnosis and maybe even a few props. I adore the feel of silk. Or nylon. Maybe I like nylon more than silk, and that reveals my low-class heritage. We each learn to lie still, relaxed, while the other slowly begins to tantalise erotically. Movement by the receiver isn't allowed, whatever is done by the active partner. Everything is internalised. I tell you, it can be unbelievable fun…"

"Fun? It's possible to have fun?"

I blew smoke towards the ceiling. "No, it's not possible. It's probable."

She stubbed out her cigarette. "I don't believe you. But, seeing as how I have few options…"

I raised my hand. "That makes me sound terrible. I don't want to force you. That's not my way. It's got to *interest* you, or…"

She looked at me brightly and nodded her head. "I'm interested all right. My heart's in my throat already. But I'm… just pessimistic. Nothing ever works. Nothing. Which is to say, it's worth a try. If you don't mind helping a cripple."

"We'll lean on each other. So. How about a drink. Cup of tea?"

"Can we go out? Do you mind? The Café Rouge in Highgate?"]*

CHAPTER SIX

As Theo Hawthorn moved on the mat, he tried to keep his mind clear. When he first started judo in Vancouver, he worked on specific throws, then attempted to lure his opponents into optimum positions. It was only with time that he learned the foolishness of this. That was putting the cart before the horse. The first man to set him right was the visiting *sensei* from Japan, who was nearly 60 years old, Toshiro Sone. Sone insisted he learn and practise the full range of throwing and grappling techniques so he never had to rely on just a few that he knew well. Because it was important to respond intuitively to your opponent's movements and changes in balance. It is something that cannot be prefigured. In a sense, you become a dance partner, so one step follows another – you flow with the opponent's body and then, in an instant, you act. That act needs little violence, if you are moving correctly. That's why the execution of judo can seem so sudden. One moment you are standing, the next you are looking at the ceiling.

Hawthorn used to watch Sone with awe as he ran through the local club's black-belts, one at a time. He was a small man, maybe 140 pounds, five-and-a-half feet tall with wrists the size of sparrows' legs. He always stood upright in *randori* (free practice) and held on delicately to his student's lapel with one hand and his sleeve with the other. Strong contestants would attack him – much bigger men – and he seemed simply to guide them to the mat with very little effort. This was Hawthorn's first contact with what he came to know as real judo. The soft way, the gentle art.

IS ALICE?

When he arrived in the UK, he was initially very impressed with the Budokwai, where he immediately enrolled. In Vancouver he could mostly hold his own, certainly in his own club. But London was very different. They took him apart. They were hard and fit judoka, and he realised they were much more serious than those in his old club. These were men who trained for European and Olympic championships, and they dealt with him like a beginner. He reacted competitively and started training harder – doing roadwork or running on treadmills, going to the gym, using free weights. He was still young then, and it paid off as his confidence grew. After about two years he received his second grade black-belt, *nidan*. But he was never going to be a big player at the Budokwai, though he made good friends there. He was beaten by boys of 17 or 18 who had studied judo since the age of eight. One of his friends, Tim O'Grady, told him of the Judokan over a beer. It was located in Camden Town, much closer than the Budokwai.

In politics they may have called it a split or a faction. In religion it would be a dissent or schism. With judo, there was no name. Some of the older Budokwai members decided to break away to train and teach in a way more compatible with what they thought was the original spirit of the sport. The Budokwai was the established centre for judo in Britain, a distinguished club with an honourable history. Founded in 1918 by Kozumi, it was the first judo club in Europe. As it grew into a larger institution, the evolution of the sport was influenced by turbulent political struggles within its structure. During this evolution, the original 'soft way' gave ground to a harder, more combative style designed to win contests – or, as some said, not to *lose* them. Technique was still excellent, but bouts became uglier with both contestants bent forward defensively, determined not to be thrown.

Most of the instructors at the Camden Judokan were still members of the Budokwai, and some were ex-members. There were also people who had been with the British Judo Council, another organisation. It was a place Hawthorn found much more to his liking, particularly as he grew older. He recalled the strong impression made by his first real teacher, Toshiro Sone, in Vancouver, and made a decision to follow his instinct. The atmosphere was relaxed and purposeful, formal but warm.

Hawthorn's grip on O'Grady's judo-gi was light, not heavy. Both men were upright, bare feet moving smoothly on the *tatami*. Hawthorn sought that state of mind where he expected nothing but was aware of everything. His centre was his belly, crucial to balance. He felt O'Grady glide sideways, and, instinctively, he pulled upwards with both hands as his foot swept across the *tatami* and made contact with his opponent's ankles. A foot sweep – it failed, but O'Grady was off-balance, and Hawthorn dropped into a *seoi-nage*, shoulder throw. Almost. As he spun out, O'Grady attacked with a vicious *osoto-gari* that lifted Hawthorn three feet off the floor. He slapped the mat as his back hit the floor.

O'Grady was a very strong *san-dan*, third grade black-belt, and both men grinned as Hawthorn got to his feet and adjusted his *gi*.

IS ALICE?

Nothing was said as they continued. Both men were breathing hard. They had been battling for over ten minutes. It was the third time Hawthorn had been thrown, but he had managed to score a beauty just after they began the session of *randori* – a perfectly executed *uchi-mata* that was so clean and quick that O'Grady had a classic look of complete surprise on his face. He was proud of that throw. He didn't even lose his footing afterwards, as he stepped smartly over the supine body of his friend.

O'Grady attempted another throw, but Hawthorn blocked as both broke away.

"That's enough for me," Hawthorn said with a heaving chest. "I'm blown. Gotta take a little break…"

They bowed, and O'Grady clapped him on the back. "Good throw, Theo."

* * *

He saw Alice sitting on the floor with her back against the wall when he entered the ward. She was crying, holding her head in her hands. A nurse sat nearby reading a newspaper.

"What's wrong?" Hawthorn asked the nurse quietly.

"No idea," she said, hardly looking up from her paper.

He turned away and knelt on one knee beside Alice. She did not look at him. "What's the matter? Why are you crying?"

She didn't acknowledge his presence, and her tears affected him so strongly that he struggled to keep his voice low and calm. "If you tell me what's wrong, Alice, I'll try and do something about it. I know you believe I can read your mind, but tell me again anyway. Why are you crying?"

She wiped at her nose. The mucus stained the sleeve of her hospital gown. He searched for a small packet of tissues from the bag he brought. Alice took one of them but refused the packet, then wiped her face.

Her words were hardly audible. "Cigarettes."

He sighed, desperately wishing he could put his arm round her shoulders to give her some comfort from her agonies. "I brought a carton two days ago. What happened to them?"

She wouldn't answer. Hawthorn pulled a new carton from his bag and tore open the end of it, then offered her a pack. She took it without speaking and began opening it with trembling fingers.

"Thank you," she said finally, as she put a cigarette in her mouth.

He got to his feet. "Do you have her lighter?"

The nurse looked at him blankly. "No."

Hawthorn found one of several cheap lighters in his bag, lit Alice's cigarette and handed it to the nurse. During close observations patients were not allowed to carry matches or lighters. Then he turned and walked over to the head nurse's room.

His old enemy, Pan Subarti, was on duty and swung around in his chair to greet him when he opened the door of the office.

"Ah, Theo. How can I help?"

Hawthorn sat down in one of the chairs against the wall. "Alice tells me she doesn't have any fags. Is that right?"

Subarti got to his feet heavily and walked over to a row of filing cabinets. He pulled open one at the bottom. He was a short, Asian man, going puffy around the waist, and had trouble bending over.

"No," he said. "I don't think she does. None here."

Hawthorn was determined to be as pleasant as possible. "Two days ago I brought her ten packets. She couldn't have smoked all of them in that time."

Subarti shrugged as he pulled himself upright and kicked the drawer closed. "She doesn't have any now. All gone."

"And why," Hawthorn continued, "is she wearing a hospital gown?"

The head nurse sat back down in his chair. "Because she has thrown away her clothes. Or given them away."

Hawthorn intentionally became aware of his breathing. Steady breaths. "Pan, I know you're busy here and understaffed, but you have my telephone number. I would be most grateful if you'd call me when something like this happens. She's walking around half-naked, and she has nothing to smoke. She can't go out while she's under close obs. Which makes her helpless. Her suffering is already more than I can bear, and when I think she might be sitting here crying for something she can afford and something she wants…it just kills me. Give me a call. Please."

The look on Subarti's face was not unsympathetic. He spread his arms. "If I had to call the nearest relative for every patient every day," he shrugged, "I wouldn't be able to do anything else at all. But," he held up his hand with resignation. "I will do this for you."

Hawthorn pulled out the broken carton of cigarettes and used a marker pen to write Alice's name on it. "I'm going home now to get her something to wear. Maybe I'll have to visit the charity shop, if she's throwing everything away now. I'll check and see what else she needs before I go. Here's nine more packets of cigarettes. Please only give them to her, not anyone else. One at a time. OK?"

"I'll put them in the drawer," Subarti said. "Only for her."

"And Pan," he said as he rose from the chair. "If she ever completely runs out – whatever the reason – please buy her a pack from the shop. I'll pay you back next time I see you."

IS ALICE?

Subarti nodded with a smile. "Dr Pincer asked me to tell you that Alice will come off close obs tomorrow."

* * *

*[Alice came over on Saturdays and Sundays for our sexual adventures. She was quite keen about the whole thing. Or seemed to be. I think she really was. It was a project, something she could focus on. It gave her a sense of purpose. In the back of my mind I always felt a little unsteady about the thought of leading her into something she might otherwise have not wanted. I realised she was vulnerable. And lonely. But, honestly, I suppose I was more guided by my cock. Like most men. So I felt uneasy.

I will point out that it went well, though. We had lots of fun shopping for a few items that might help us around London. It was quite exciting for us. We agreed to split the cost of everything, but I admit she paid for most of her new underwear, some of it quite expensive. Then we would play.

There is something about unconventional sexual play that has always attracted me. On a mundane level it simply extends the time and intensity of sexual excitement. Orgasm is delayed, sometimes deferred continuously, thus deepening the urge and ballooning the moment. This enrichment can propel good partners into what I sense is a spiritual zone. You become more aware of yourself and the person whom you are with, more in touch with her consciousness, more generous with your own. Too often, in straight sex, there is one goal – once that goal is achieved, there is only de-tumescence and de-coupling. It is done. It is over. The common sense world, held at bay for a few moments, returns in all its banality. I know, I know. With love it can be different. But how can we conjure up the genie of love when we want it, and for how many times in our lives? What do we do when love collapses, and we have only the mechanics of sex? Yet love is a silky, unpredictable critter, and I was about to encounter the biggest surprise of my life.

She and I swapped roles at first. That's what I personally prefer. That way I felt we could experience the whole range of emotions available to two partners. Anyway, I've always felt there's a sinuous ambiguity between passive and active. It's a kind of polarity, and one won't work without the presence of the other – *even within the individual performers*. Light and darkness, good and evil – the definition of one is much dependent on the definition of the other. In other words, there is a luminous connection between the two states, an interchange, certainly an interdependence. The existence of one presupposes the existence of the other. The active partner must know and respect his own passivity in order to activate the sexual desires in the passive partner. The interaction can help reveal self-knowledge and, more importantly, establish elusive trust. Nevertheless, it is a choice. A revolution, of course, is another choice. They are overthrows of *definitions*.

Alice was almost immediately appreciative and enthusiastic, though she was less able to be passive as I slowly brought her near climax and, as slowly, retreated again. But when it happened she was in passive role,

IS ALICE?

naked and splendid except for a blindfold. I always thought she was physically gorgeous, and I contemplated her as she lay there. Her breasts were large and firm, damn near perfect in their femininity. Blonde hair formed a halo on the pillow, and her thighs were firm and shapely. Simply beautiful. Whatever her vulnerability, it was maximised, extended, demanding her complete trust...in my humanity...in my own deep loneliness. It was happening, and I was not conscious of the event. Like earlier visions, I was in it before I spotted the seams between the normal world and a numinous one. I'm not sure I can describe a vision properly, as I've never succeeded before. There is a subtle change in the sense of space and time. It's a little as if my self becomes diaphanous (though my body remains opaque). An opening appears, a portal to some*thing* or some*where else*. Whatever I see, I see with certainty. There is *no question*. I KNOW. I know it in such a way that it cannot be false. I have not had many of these experiences, but when I have them they always have a profound impact on my life.

Alice did not move and did not speak. She lay still on the bed, waiting. I knelt gently beside her. Her face was spectral, and I saw her *beyond* that face. The same woman, the same person, but, in the same breath, the inner spirit and the future spirit. All my visions contain some element of the future. What I saw was beautiful – not the beauty of her body, nothing to do with that. It was an inner landscape beyond that which manifested itself in her 'present.' Moreover, she *would be* beautiful. And we were connected from some past events, way beyond my reckoning. We were joined in a way that is simply indescribable. Over time, into time, *through* time. As I write these words the vision is as clear, nearly, as it was then. There was no denying it. The curtains of the rational world had parted, revealing something completely different.

I touched her face with my hand. "I love you."

There was a long pause. "I don't know what love is," she said finally in a small voice.

"You will," I replied gently. I lifted her blindfold and looked into her eyes. "It's a certainty. There's no question of it."

We talked later in my front room over mugs of tea. Alice was quiet but not withdrawn.

"Zen Buddhists have a name for it," I said. "Satori. It's the only description I know that comes anywhere close to what I've called 'visions'. The most massive one I had is when I first arrived in the UK. I went to Edinburgh, as I had some contacts with a director at the Traverse Theatre. I found temporary accommodation with these Scottish lads I met, and one of them stayed up to talk with me one night. At some point we were, well, transported. Windows opened into somewhere else, and voices spoke *through* us. Though they were our voices as well. It was as if someone or something was leading us or guiding us. I felt divine, a divine being after a kind of purgatory of confession between us. This particular experience lasted for weeks, though the intensity diminished slowly. The Scottish guy followed me to London like a disciple. But I haven't seen him since those days."

IS ALICE?

"Satori," she said quietly. "I've heard of it. Doesn't it mean enlightenment? In an instant?"

"Yes, but it's broader than that, and Buddhists admit it can happen to those outside their religion. It's a concept not recognised in western methodology, but I suppose rationalists would call it some kind of intuitive experience, if they were generous. If not, they'd say you were having hallucinations."

"I know all about hallucinations," she said with a chuckle.

"I've had drug-induced hallucinations, and this experience is nothing like them. This is clear, crisp, complete. Doubt is impossible."

"Then does that make you divine?" She abruptly waved her hands. "No, no, I'm not being funny or taking the piss. That wasn't sarcastic…"

I laughed and picked up my mug of tea. "The Buddhists associate it with divinity. I don't. I've lived a life that is full of perfidy. Yet there is also much change. I've undergone a great deal of change, certainly since that powerful experience in Edinburgh. It changed me in a way I find impossible to explain."

She was lighting a cigarette. "You frightened me."

"I'm sorry."

"Love with a man? No. It's not for me. It's not possible."

"Why?" I asked as I filled my pipe.

"I'm…" She looked at her fingernails. "I'm hateful. Not loveable. Why would anyone want to love me? I'm a nuisance. I'm needy. I call you up all the time because… because I want something… you probably can't give."

"I meant it. I love you. I have no idea why or how. Before the vision – or Satori – I liked you very much, found you attractive… I was a bit wary of you, OK. But then it happened. I saw things in you I had never seen in anyone before. That person 'in the future' became you, now, in the present."

"I don't understand."

It took some time to get the pipe fired up. "I don't understand, either, not in a rational way. Rationally it doesn't make sense at all. Nevertheless, it's true."

"What did you see?"

I leaned back into the sofa, puffing on the pipe. "You know those pictures they used to have when you were a kid? The ones that were a series of dots. You joined up all the dots by number to find out what the picture was. To me, you were like that. A person without all the dots joined up…"

IS ALICE?

She laughed ironically. "I like that one... dots not joined up..."

"In the vision I saw the real picture. All dots joined up, a living reality."

"Now I *know* it's a hallucination!" she cried.

"No, no," I shook my head. "It's happening right now, even though you can't see it. The dots will slowly join up. And you will know love. Maybe the two things are related..."

"This is spooking me a little, Theo. I'm afraid."

I put the pipe down, slid over and put my arm around her. The electrical charge of our touch seemed stronger. "Nothing will harm you. It's a good omen, not a bad one. I saw other things, too."

"What things?"

I sighed. "Putting it into words makes it sound corny. We've known each other somehow. Existed – or exist – in other places at other times. In some way we've finally found each other. I also know that you are much stronger than you think you are, and in time you will feel that strength. It will flow through and make you whole."

She put her head against my shoulder. "Was I like that with the dots joined up?"

I stroked her hair lovingly as I searched my memory. "You'll have to forgive how it sounds. I'm trying to put it into words. Ineptly. Physically you were the same. But you looked – inside – as you were when I knew you 'before.' It seemed a kind of link. So *that's* who you are! You knew yourself, you were complete, a whole person, confident, perhaps a social station above me... I don't know, somewhere in some parallel past, I don't know how to put it. Yet the image was a future you, too. You have been lost. *We* have been lost. And something within us sought each other. In that moment I made the connection. A shattering experience."

She turned her face into my chest. "How can I be... how can the dots join up? I can't, Theo. I'm too far away. In too many pieces. I stagger forward one step and get knocked back three."

"That's the key, Alice. Your courage. And your strength."

She pulled away and looked at me. Her face was grim. "Don't keep saying that. I'm a coward... and the weakest person I've ever known."

I held her eyes. There were dark circles underneath. "The whole problem is that the model you have of the world is skewed. Out of proportion. A Dali painting. Now, we don't know what the world really looks like, but most of us share a common sense model that works. Most of the time. Since I've known you, I've been questioning this model myself. I'm getting a feeling for how you skew it, but not *why*. You know..."

IS ALICE?

I turned in my seat to face her and tugged at my dressing gown. "It's emotion that explodes your sense of reality. Explodes and distorts. The primary emotion is fear. Then it occurred to me that fear is used for *control...*"

"Who uses it?"

"It's used in the fabric of this common sense world we share. But your sense of fear is so much stronger than normal. I don't know *who* uses it or exactly *how* it's used yet. It's clearly a tool that is manipulated – politically and socially – to herd people in one direction or another. Why fear? Because of its strength. It's probably the strongest emotion we have. It's energetic, not passive. It scatters thought. We ask no questions when we fear, we just respond instantly. It makes sense when we're faced with grave danger. Or a predator. But there are no predators left. Except us, naturally. I think maybe that's a clue."

This sounds like bright and fanciful magic, Alyosha, but before you turn away sceptically, let me try and explain something I believe is vital. After that Satori I described in Edinburgh, I began to realise that I was on an inner journey. I had no idea where it might lead, but I was compelled to follow it. The first thing I had to do – the *primary act* – was to find some way of being truthful. Or true. This has not been an easy task, and I blundered into many desolate spaces and wasted much time. You see, we hear and observe many things. There is gossip around everywhere, peer pressure, media pressure. There is science which explains what *is* in its own fashion. There are plenty of religions. Legions of people believe they have the 'answers.' All these are mighty influences on an individual consciousness adrift on unknown seas. Waves disorient you, currents turn and direct you, arms reach out enticingly, temptation is everywhere. So it is at first impossible to see what is and is not true. Someone in authority tells you this is so with such certainty that you find yourself rushing in lunacy to believe it. Yet what authority does this represent? Is it true? After all, the false can be perfectly moulded into the image of truth. So how can you *know*? The answer is, you can know only if you are wise. Thus you are propelled into a tricky conundrum. To know what is true, you must be wise. And to be wise, you must be able to see what is true. That is why my life is so full of blunders.

The modern world is no help. You stand in a torrential shower of 'facts.' The scientific method guides us into 'proofs.' If it's true, you must be able to *prove* its truth within very narrow parameters. If the wise exist, they are condemned to be deformed shadows at the periphery of the social order. Let me give you an example. Israel and the Palestinian Arabs. It is child's play to see that wise men of goodwill from each side could solve the problem in a few days, if not a few hours. Yet the method they choose is the worst possible choice – one tailor-made for failure. What is most obvious is that these people are caught in a devastating storm of emotion. Greed, envy, anger, FEAR. This is the absolute default setting for solving differences between people and nations. In sacrifice to this ugly god, millions are slaughtered under a thin silky veil of rationality. It is also clear that the modern world will become the ancient world with the passage of time. By

IS ALICE?

calling it modern we give a dubious authority to what we call reality.

To separate what is true from what is not true, I used the only instrument I could trust. My intuition as a whole entity – while being aware at every instant that my 'wholeness' was under continuous construction. Those things I've found to be true are littered with contradictions, and I brush these aside as irrelevant. Contradictions often exist because you are using the wrong frame for the picture.

My relationship with Alice was as profound an event as any in my life. I told her she was hidden in an existence of unjoined dots. It often occurs to me that it may in fact have been a disguise. Here was an important turning point for me, and it was cleverly camouflaged as a helpless woman beset by unpleasant difficulties in decoding her existence. Because, in a spiritually resonant way, I was in the process of joining up my own dots – and for reasons not entirely dissimilar. My Satori with her occurred during sexual experiences some would describe as not 'normal.' Nevertheless, it was true. From a series of unlikely coincidences I was propelled further on the path towards that which I seek.

It may sound irrelevant, but judo is an important ingredient. The modern world is characterised by its infinite divisions, and that will be an integral element of its ultimate fate. Physicality cannot be separate from mind or spirit – or from the world. To ignore it is complete madness. Executing a throw sounds simply a matter of technique. Technique is important, but it must be seen in the environment of the whole being. The truth of this is something that eluded me for many years. It exists within a context, just as we do. For too long I viewed the other contestant as an *opponent*, instead of a partner, a part of something broader than a physical contest. At its best, judo is a physical expression of oneness. The reaction to an attack is to become a part of that attack, to *assist* it, and also to take it beyond the intentions of the attacker. You always help someone who shoves you and guide him to the earth with the force of his own effort. The technique for doing this may be elusive at first, but when a throw is executed properly, it is most satisfying because it is *true*, even if that truth lies partly in irony. The attacker has combined his anger with pain, while the judoka has simply helped him succeed. It's a mistake to divide the moves of judo into discrete frames of action. It is about the nature of being, and if you have no sense of this, then failure is inevitable.

I'm not a musician, but I know that music is an immediate experience, not one to be strained through rational filtration. If, when you are at the piano, you play a piece as only a series of notes, then the *music* is obscured. Yet when you view it in one respect, it *is* just a series of notes. But – irony again – you will then lose most of the experience of the music. It's another example of what I mean by seeing things *truthfully* – seeing, hearing, knowing, being. A Beethoven sonata is not a bag or stack of notes. It is a series of notes used to express something achingly beautiful to someone else.

I use these inner signposts to help guide me through a landscape of rubble presented to me by adults when I was a child. It was then that I also experienced the first of these signposts. I was in the first year of primary school, and I witnessed one of the children, taunted because he was fat, being hit in the nose by another boy. Blood spurted from his nose, and I noticed with extreme shock that it was spurting from mine, too, even though I had not been hit. But I felt the pain and began to cry. I ran to the teacher and told her, but she informed me that it was just a coincidence, that I merely had a nosebleed. Even at that young age, I knew then that it was not true, because I experienced it immediately as something else. There was a *connection* between the bullied boy and me. Such connections are denied, partly because they're unfashionable. Nevertheless, they form the incomplete series of dots that may one day give a true picture of me and, consequently, the world I am in.]*

CHAPTER SEVEN

It was now the middle of August, almost two months since Alice was hospitalised. Theo Hawthorn was riding his new bicycle, heading towards Soho, trying to clear the cobwebs from his mind along with the nagging worry that Alice seemed so entrenched, so *hopeless*. It was a word he tried to avoid completely, but it had a way of creeping in when his mood greyed and threatened oily blackness. So he had gone out a few days before and bought a new bike. The old one was knackered and had no mudguards, so he stowed it out on his back roof until he could find a way of selling it. It was a cool day, but warm in the bright sunlight, so he wore no jacket, just a shirt, jeans and a gilet with a pair of wrap-round sunglasses. It was a pretty good bike ride, Archway to Soho – downhill there, uphill on the way back. The bike was relatively inexpensive, and he managed to pay for it from his 'stash,' the cash he kept in his flat for emergencies. It had all the gears and, most importantly, two mudguards. So he could now expect to have a dry back when it rained.

Most of the other cyclists sped by him. He wasn't that type. He sat on the saddle and pedalled at a leisurely pace, as he took in the changing view and tried to avoid the cars dodging through lanes to save a few seconds on their journeys. When he first arrived 30 years ago, London felt so alien and inhospitable. Now it was more like home than his native country. Yet he still couldn't call himself a Londoner. He remained a stranger – someone who arrived with all options open, then found one year folding into the next until he finally realised he would die here, neither British nor North American. It was not an unwelcome ambiguity. In truth, Hawthorn's most powerful and earliest impression was that of an alien stepping lightly on the earth to test its solidity. Never had he enjoyed the sensation of feeling 'at home.'

Even during his first years in London, he always enjoyed Soho because it seemed such an *accidental* place with an air of exotic mismatches, like a galactic transit lounge. The film and post-production enterprises were scattered among prostitutes and louche brigands. It was a part of the city where the famous and infamous could rub shoulders without friction. There were outrageous gays on Old Compton Street and bars full of writers, actors and film technicians on Dean and Wardour. Oddly, Soho seemed to soak up the herds of tourists without ever being waterlogged. Its harmony was in its dissonance. Then, just as you thought you had the idea, you wandered across Shaftesbury Avenue into the middle of Hong Kong in Chinatown, and experienced the pungent smell of a thousand roasting ducks amid a mostly Chinese crowd of hustlers and losers high on the adrenaline of the marketplace.

Hawthorn parked the bike on the kerb and found a seat. It was a coffee house on the corner of Greek and Old Compton Street with tables on the pavement – a good vantage point. They came from all directions in lofty styles and jumbled styles. Impossibly tasty women clattered by in impossible heels with their trousers pubic low or their skirts pubic high. There were men in leather peaked caps sporting earrings and tight T-shirts daring to hold hands with their boyfriends. Rickshaw cyclists with athletic legs lingered at corners looking for passengers, as black cabs tried to shoulder them out of the road. There were dozens of different languages being spoken in syncopated rhythms, sometimes even English.

He ordered a coffee from the surly waiter and glanced at the next table. Someone was ostentatiously smoking a hookah. He leaned back to enjoy the entertainment and folded his hands on his stomach. An achingly beautiful blonde in her 20s walked by, and he focused on her long legs and sheer tights. Her skirt was so snug he imagined he could see the outline of her knickers as her loins jolted with each step. Involuntarily, his penis twitched, and he smiled at the girl and at himself. Her eyes caught his, then flickered away as she sucked off a sultry cloud of his sexual energy. He had recently been thinking about prostitutes. If it had been anyone but Alice, he would not have hesitated. He liked whores, and fantasised about booking a short visit to Amsterdam and strolling among the enticing windows of the red light district to choose a delicious dessert after an Indonesian meal. For a moment he wished he hadn't just bought a new bicycle, but then his thoughts returned to Alice. Everything between them had flowered through honesty. It was the first time in his life that he could imagine such things. In the past he wouldn't have given it a moment's thought. Alice, though, was different. The depth of their feelings was measured by the yardstick of trust. Instead of making him a prisoner, such commitment gave him a greater sense of freedom. He didn't have to rely on evasion, but could be himself with her. She accepted him now without any doubts. It would be criminal to spoil it all for a fuck.

IS ALICE?

The waiter put his cup of coffee on the table and waited for the money. Hawthorn gave the man five pounds, then left the change on the table in case he wanted another cup later. He turned his attention back to the crowds of people on the pavements and strolling in the streets. With an effort he detached himself from the street scene, pretending instead to be a disembodied eye, like a gigantic camera. First, a close-up. Then a dizzying crane shot as he swung high above the streets and buildings. The eye of an eagle. Then an alien eye, unfamiliar with the planet earth. What form of life was there below? Was it a swarm or a hive? London became a puzzling concrete nest built by the hive, and there they thrived, a thriving hive. Echoes of Alice and her obsessional rhyming. It was from his experiences with her that he formed this idea of the social matrix. How do social animals develop the unwritten and mostly unspoken language-paste that holds them together, helps them communicate and move as large cooperative units? It was the key to understanding *what was going on*. The pack below had their words, but it was not just words. There were categories and concepts, history, millions of plans – all of them stories filled with varying quantities of emotional energy charges that had two functions: to propel them onwards, and to impel coagulation into greater masses through absorption of lesser or weaker packs and swarms. Pressures were invented and forces applied both to the macrocosm and the microcosm. Individual development apart from the swarm was impossible. Everyone was a part, and, equally, each part was everyone. The alien eye found it both beautiful and ugly, two faces on the same body, compelling and nauseating. A heaven and hell. Certainly a duality, but a complex one, so difficult to grasp in the breadth of one life.

Hawthorn's eye returned to street level. The social matrix. It was haunting him now, and he was trying to think how he could express the ideas in a play. One of the chief problems was presenting it in a way that would not alienate an audience. Because a key feature of the matrix was an inherent denial of its existence and – certainly – a reluctance of individuals to admit they were manipulated by anything but 'free will.' It was a paradox. Human consciousness was free – it had to be. On the other hand, it was enslaved – it had to be. Both concepts were true. He suspected the social matrix would not work otherwise. Other social animals were surely conscious, some extravagantly so, but he was reasonably certain human consciousness was exclusive in its capacity for self-reflection. This is what produced the paradox. Self-reflection presented the opportunity for the individual to realise he was a 'self' within a world that contained other 'selves.'

Hawthorn snorted and took a sip of his coffee. In accordance with current fashion, he was drinking a *latte*, otherwise known as a *café au lait* or coffee with hot milk. He was free to recognise it as a fashion and order what he liked. But it happened he liked *latte*. On the other hand, he used to call it *café au lait*. Or did he like *latte* because it was a fashion? It became difficult to pick it apart. Strangely, the moment you began to try and disassemble the elements, it made others uncomfortable. All thoughts about the social matrix were uncomfortable, because it was deeply difficult to admit things about yourself that were antithetical to your *image* of yourself. And the *image* of self was a feature of self. Paradox was cumulative. The mind was free to manipulate its images, but the images were closely monitored...

Hawthorn laughed shortly, and the man with the hookah looked up at him. He dug out his pipe and took a few moments to light it. "But," he thought. "*But*. There is nothing of any solidity to connect an individual consciousness to what is called, for convenience, the outside world." As far as he – or anyone else – could determine, the only 'outside world' was that which appeared in his mind. The only corroboration of it was from *others*. But they were merely thoughts on the moving horizon of existence.

"Time," he murmured out loud. The hookah man now stared at him with interest. Hawthorn couldn't give a shit. Time was the most confusing value of all. The only thing the mind could be reasonably certain of was the present. You could have memories of the past and plans for the future, but both categories were phantoms, just a series of little stories separated by mental markers. This is what (you remember) *has* happened, that is what could/would/should happen. There was an awareness of time, but nothing to bite on, nothing you could prove from the present. Time was also a starting-point, a beginning. It may be the only overlap between 'out there' and 'inside.' A thread that somehow held a jumble of stories together. If so, it meant that he was in some kind of a process with an elusive beginning and end. There were religious, mythological and scientific stories that offered varying degrees of interpretation, but he had long decided to step away from those, to go only where he was certain – as a whole human being – of the truth.

This struggle for understanding of what he now called the social matrix had begun... with Alice. It was an attempt to join up his own dots, as well as trying to help her join up hers. Thus it had a dual enterprise. Only in seeking his redemption with hers would they have a chance to redeem themselves. Everything had to be pushed back and re-examined. Stones that had become invisible through familiarity must be brought back into focus and seen as if they were new and unusual stones. Which they were. Peeling an onion always brought tears. Leaving this onion unpeeled was not an option. Such was the importance he gave these thoughts.

Schizophrenia was a word, a definition, an imposed category. It had nothing to say about what she experienced, or its meaning. It slowly became more clear to him that Alice Dance's problems were polarised by her interactions with the social matrix. In an exact parallel, so were his own. That is what led him down these corridors in the first place. It was imperative that he *know*. To help himself as much as to help her. A tandem effort. With both of them pushing together on different planes. In time? In space? He wasn't sure. But the old definitions were being questioned, changed, discarded. Their destinies were linked in a way beyond his understanding. In the beginning it seemed like Alice's mental health problems could be 'solved.' Their love was a powerful force. Yet it wasn't enough. Every social situation threatened to undermine her, and it was necessary to rescue her a number of times, talk her back from the brink, stay with her, try and guide her through hazardous storms. Slowly she became less fragile, but he knew she was never completely safe.

Consciousness – alone, dark, without features – required an interface with the world that allowed, at the very least, survival. As a child, the meaning and values of things were slowly and laboriously learned, probably more through play than study – or any other activity. Stories were built up about 'reality' and the relationships of things to other things – most importantly between self and world. Whatever the world was *really* like, the internal landscape must *work*. Otherwise survival was impossible. It was along the seams of the interface that a fissure developed in Alice's representation of the world. A sudden jolt of fear or uncertainty opened the fissure to a canyon, and she was separated from the reality shared by most others. Many of the features were like a nightmare, a monstrous dream, in which she was a shadow amongst other shadows. Nevertheless, they were real shadows. For her. The reason was ironically clear to him. It was to hermetically seal her off from *any kind of manipulation*. In her mad world, she was the leader of the orchestra, not a minor player. *She* created all the definitions, even when she attributed their creation to others.

Which was *exactly* what happened to everyone else, including Hawthorn. Looked at a certain way, it was a triumphant but hellish act of freedom. Within the space of a few instants, she freed herself from the values of others, only to shackle herself to ones that were worse – her own excruciating visions of self-degradation. In other words, she was free to imagine what others and the world really thought of her, then loaded these thoughts with the toxins of her darkness that insured her continuous damnation. Yet, still, the act itself was one of freedom. Free at last from the incomprehensibility of the social matrix, only to embrace the iron maiden of her nightmares.

Hawthorn decided against ordering another coffee, swept off his change and stuffed his pipe in his pocket. Mounting his bicycle, he pedalled lazily up to Soho Square, a minuscule patch of green surrounding a tiny one-room building. He often wondered about the provenance of that odd little structure but never bothered to look it up. As he walked his bike through the gate, he felt Soho really needed a bigger green than this one. On the other hand, it was symbolic of the whole area. There was a little bit of everything in Soho, but not enough of any one thing. Endless promises fuelled expectations without offering any final satisfaction. West End theatres presented calorie hits that left the audiences feeling empty. Sex shops sold overpriced videos that enabled the lonely to study gynaecology in sad, dark rooms. Yet it was the tiny little spaces that produced the real gems. Like Maison Bertaux…

Maison Bertaux was their little Soho secret. Located on Greek Street between Old Compton Street and Shaftesbury Avenue, it was a tiny little French shop that served beautiful cakes and pots of real tea. They chanced upon it during one of their visits to Chinatown, and there was nothing modern about it. So it was immediately attractive. The original proprietor was a refugee from the French communes of the mid-19th Century, and old photographs lined the walls, along with small red, white and blue flags. The cakes and tarts were fresh and expensive, served in one room downstairs and one upstairs reached by winding wooden stairs. There were two or three tables outside. It had not been redecorated in decades, but the atmosphere was relaxed and bohemian, probably not too different from the original shop. Alice loved the place, and so did he. Their favourite table was beside the window in the corner where he could smoke his pipe without disturbing the others. It was almost always packed, any time they visited, but nevertheless, they often got their table. The present-day proprietor was a woman who may have been English, but she looked French. Most of the customers were young and wearing some marks of rebellion. Perhaps there were a few tourists, but it was not the sort of café that would catch the eye of those seeking excitement. He and Alice would sit for maybe an hour, laughing and daring to be a little romantic. Hawthorn would maybe glance at a pretty girl – it was such an ancient habit – but he knew there was no one now but Alice. By then, she trusted him so deeply that his glances were no threat and, unusually, she would occasionally point out some glamorous girl, with a raised eyebrow and mischievous eye, daring him to look and – occasionally – taking *her* pleasure in *his* pleasure.

He had his coffee near Maison Bertaux, but he couldn't bring himself to enter the shop alone, not without her. The pain would be too sharp, the memories too poignant.

Luck was with him. There was only a couple occupying the other end of a bench, so he parked the bike behind, sat down, folded his arms, and watched the people. A young man in jeans was sitting cross-legged under a nearby tree reading a book, a paper cup of tea between his legs. Hawthorn never even attempted to read in public. Or try to write. Instead he was always mesmerised by passing strangers – the way they walked, their facial expressions, how they dressed. In Soho Square it was a rapidly changing panorama. It wasn't a park where old men sat for hours feeding pigeons. Groups of students and tourists just passed through. Businessmen walked briskly *from* somewhere *to* somewhere. Others only lingered to finish their drinks or have a quick chat with friends. It is not just the greenery that is attractive in parks. They are the only free places to sit in the middle of cities. Sit anywhere else, and you have to pay.

It was still warm enough for the girls to be wearing summery clothing, revealing enough flesh to make you naturally think of more. Advertisement. Bait. That was the cheap way to look at it. But, like the one who passed his table earlier, it was partly about energy. If a woman knew she was attractive, she gathered looks and glances and used them like fuel to lift or propel her spirits. One thing fed on the other. A Chinese couple caught his eye. She was tall and downright beautiful. The two of them were laughing, and her voice tinkled like the rattle of champagne glasses. The man was shorter, his head just above her shoulder. But they both had hair as clean and black as polished obsidian. She wore high heels and little black turned-down ankle socks. The heels elongated legs that disappeared underneath a short silk dress. Her hips and breasts swelled delicately, but it was her face that caused a lump in Hawthorn's throat. It was a fragile expression of Oriental beauty so profound that it made him think of eternity. Age could never touch such a face, and it was beyond any attempt of poets or painters to capture it. Yet he knew also that such beauty was at the same time fleeting, and it was puzzling how he could be struck by such distant polarities. Eternal and ephemeral. The beginning and end of a rainbow-thought. They were chattering incomprehensibly in Chinese, faces animated. He turned to watch them leave, the woman as graceful as a young deer.

It was a park in motion. Nobody stayed too long, it seemed, but plenty went out of their way just to pass through. Hawthorn made an effort to detach himself again, to pull away from the scene emotionally. It was a daily exercise, and one that he always found difficult. Well, to be honest, it was impossible. 'Out there' were the creatures of the social matrix, *his* matrix. At first he was fascinated by it, then it became an obsession. Each of the creatures carried imprints and value information in their individual consciousnesses. At the same time, none of them had any solid evidence of the existence of such a web. It had a form, and that form was hierarchical, whatever else it might be. There was power, and it was exercised in three ways – by enticement, by appeal, and by force. As Hawthorn sat there with arms folded, he thought about some of the things he could and could not do. There were too many to imagine, but he was seeking examples. Many were obvious. He couldn't walk into a bank and demand money, or take things from shops without paying. But there was much, much more than that. He couldn't, for instance, invite himself into the company of the Chinese couple, then proceed to seduce the woman. He could only demonstrate a limited amount of aggression to anyone in the park. What would happen if a policeman approached him? He tried to calculate all the rush of feelings. Wariness because of a possible threat, little sharp edges of fear or guilt, a quick search of recent memories. Above all, he couldn't lash out at the policeman or tell him to fuck off. He would have to endure whatever possible indignities were involved. Maybe it would be something about the bicycle. Or his flies could be undone. Perhaps he looked like someone wanted by the police.

He furrowed his brow and unconsciously checked his flies. Were there *other* responses to uniformed authority? It didn't have to be a policeman. A man in a sharp business suit with an authoritative voice would trigger similar responses. What most fascinated him was the automatic nature of those responses. Thoughts and actions, supported by suitable emotions, would cause him to react automatically to different series of gambits. Yet all this would fundamentally be taking place in his own mind, nowhere else. *He* was the one responsible for reactions, so, intriguingly, he was also responsible for the *actions towards him.* Just like Alice, he continuously defined the values of his world. This never ceased. If he had ever learned anything from judo, it was an ability to be a shadow, rather than a feature, to move in such a way that did not disturb the web – or to avoid the sticky parts, like a spider. There was no better example than his outrage at the concert, and his subsequent incarceration in a mental health ward. He allowed himself to get stuck on a part of the web designed especially for that kind of aggression. Instead of trying to detach himself, he shook the whole web angrily, with the whole of his heart and soul, screaming in despair.

IS ALICE?

To put it another way, there were mental and emotional hooks and specially designed places for those hooks to lock into. Present a smooth surface, and the hooks fell away. That's what he was constantly searching for – the smooth surface. Or, even better, he wanted to adapt his colour to that of his surroundings. It was knowledge. It was freedom. It was survival.

Hawthorn had already learned much about survival. His family was poor, and the town where he was raised was small. The world enticed him with its products and gadgets, and the appeal of his peers drove him towards 'normality.' A steady job, wife, kids, a mortgage – prisons and chains. Through thought alone he found a route through the maze that virtually allowed him to live the life of a rich man *without working*. Without working normally, that is. He worked when he wanted and as he wished. Anyway, his idea of work was really play.

He sighed and pulled out his pipe, tamped down the ashes and lit up. A simple pleasure and an old one, already under attack with increasing force by the social matrix. It was another example, not a bad one. Historically people had made grotesque fortunes from tobacco, and the ills were not all found in the smoke. Slavery flourished to produce it, and cigarettes were invented to extend the addiction and ease of smoking and to provide a massive worldwide market. Smoking-fashion was created for a time, until non-smoking-fashion was plugged from every source. Some real reasons were presented, some illusory, but the bigger picture was intentionally obscured. They wanted to entice the attention elsewhere. With magic, the eye is drawn to the moving hand, while the other hand... does other things. That's how it worked. In the first place, moderation is anathema to an economy geared up to maximum extraction speeds. There was a risk in smoking, but it could be a meditative aid, a form of pleasure. Much the same was true of alcohol. It was necessary to *respect* the substance. There were dangers, and there were joys. The answer was to search for moderation – in a world characterised by nerve-stretching, heavy-metal stress. Moderation would *never* be fashionable when envy and greed were the street currencies. Passive smoking - now there was an interesting concept. How strange now to worry about the health of bar and café staff, when no one ever thought about their wages or conditions of labour. It was odd, too, that tobacco smoke was fingered instead of other, more lethal, pollutants, like vehicles and aircraft, industrial and household waste, or the huge amounts of methane that were the result of animal husbandry on massive scales. Water was scarcely fit to drink any more. Hawthorn's father was a heavy smoker who slept in his bedroom most of the time, waking up throughout the night to light up. And in earlier years Hawthorn lived in bars and pubs. No sign of damage – yet.

The conventional view was that science and technology were steadily advancing techniques used to 'discover' more advanced ways of living. This was basically a lie. Scientists said all kinds of things all over the world. The point was that selected items were highlighted and presented with fanfare to support the interests of dominant powers swirling through the matrix. The well-being of public workers would never have been given a thought, unless it was a sensitive part of some strategy. After all, who gives a *shit* for public workers? But suddenly there was now great concern for the damage caused to them by passive smoking.

And who were these 'scientists' anyway? Like any other group of people, some were wise, more were stupid. But for the hidden interests, they were useful, just as the old priesthood was useful to earlier interests. In short, they were a source for authority. That was their strength. It was also their weakness. For effect, authority must have the appearance of near-infallibility. It is *thus*. It is *so*. One social theme stressed the importance of the individual, while another implied the individual was incapable of singular thought. In other words, the individual must be encouraged to indulge in endless consumption, and curb his appetite for inner knowledge. In order to achieve this, authority was necessary. Don't think. It's not necessary. Others – scientists perhaps – will do it for you. This is good, that is bad. Do this, stop that, buy here, drink Coke.

Hawthorn puffed as he stared up at the bright sky. Excessive smoking was almost certainly bad for you. As were excessive alcohol consumption and overeating. Tobacco was addictive, and so were psychotropic drugs, gambling and shopping. But the dangers of so-called passive smoking? Almost certainly false – or at least overblown – especially in view of the toxic mix of other man-made chemicals in the atmosphere.

So what was the game? Hawthorn swivelled his head and looked at the surrounding buildings. At least three CCTV cameras, one of them focused on the park. The game was control management. The pace was quickening, now that technology was rapidly providing the tools. Iris scans, cameras everywhere, ID cards on the way, mobile phone tracking, congestion and bus lane cameras, global positioning satellites, tagging, licences, registrations – many tied to fees and fines. Discovering the truth about smoking bans was not an easy exercise. There was a sanctimonious benevolence in the message, but that was the mask, the lure, the enticement. The government would possibly suffer loss of taxation, though probably not as much as they feared. Tobacco companies fought like dogs to avoid the ban, using political pressure and bribes.

His pipe had gone out, and he folded his arms, still holding the bowl. He liked the feel of briar pipes. Most of the anti-smoking propaganda was aimed at what was called the middle classes, and a gigantic political operation was under way to privatise the national health system. It was all smoke-and-mirrors with lots of chatter about 'modernising,' but the intention was clear for anyone with eyes in their head. The beloved old system was being dismantled, to be replaced by private medicine and private health insurance.

He chuckled silently. As the masks fell away, the reality was pretty savage. Brecht was right. The tobacco gang was being wiped out by the private health gang and their allies in government. Territory was being lost and gained, as were fortunes. Tobacco 'scientists' were now giving evidence to their enemies.

During the old Watergate affair in America, the source known as Deep Throat always advised the Washington Post reporters to 'follow the money trail.' Better advice was seldom ever given. Where does the money go, who gets it and why? Take science. Superficially, it looks clean – objective, even. Tests are carried out, investigations made; there are experiments and trials, peer reviews, evidence is gathered and collated. Were they seeking truth or...? You always begin looking at where they draw their money. Who pays them? Science does not take place in a vacuum. It costs a lot of money to carry out most experiments, and equipment is outrageously expensive. Grants are made to universities. By whom? Giant pharmaceutical companies provide much wealth to chemistry and physics departments. Science is awash with petrochemical and agribusiness money. Engineering is supported by industry. Pure science is...where? In the same dustbin as pure art.

Of course there was something else, something more sinister, something that led directly to the social matrix. Control. It has been obvious from prehistoric times that the greater the control you have over people, the greater your strength and power. Exercises were taking place simultaneously all over the world in the manipulation of larger and larger bodies of people. Make them work, keep them working. Raise production levels, lower costs, increase demand and consumption. That is the business mantra.

It was a massive project, Hawthorn could see that. And a power transfer was going on between nation states and gigantic global companies. In earlier years these companies were harnessed to the national interests of individual states, especially during the colonial era. With the growth of transnational industry and its accumulation of unimaginable wealth, nations were becoming the clients, not the masters. That was because industry could penetrate national borders and begin the task of manipulating whole populations, a trick no individual country could match in struggles with its peers. With a military invasion, there was expense and waste. With an economic one, there was more wealth, power and *control* – with little loss of life.

Hawthorn thought about re-lighting his pipe, but the wind had picked up. So he put it back in his pocket. Around these tall buildings there was no way to tell which way the wind was blowing. He hoped it was from the south or south-west. Give him a little help on the way back home.

When he first arrived in England, he was completely impressed. He couldn't recall seeing any fat people, and North America was full of slobs. Pubs were mostly quiet, decent places with a carpeted saloon bar where you could sit in peace, read a newspaper and smoke. Or have a gentle conversation. The NHS accepted any patients, foreign or otherwise, no payment necessary. When you were out of work, you signed on. That meant that actors, musicians and artists could eke out a living, instead of having to work part-time or give it up altogether. Bitter was the main drink in pubs. Fish and chips were the British version of fast food. There were three channels on the TV – two of the BBC, one independent. There was a distinct difference between the British and Americans.

He looked around Soho Park. At least half of them were wearing baseball caps, and half of those were overweight. There was a McDonald's down the road. Most of the pubs – with honourable exceptions – had turned into American bars. TVs, sport, wooden floors, pop music and Budweiser. No separation between public and saloon. Bars now had 'themes.' Cinemas showed American films nearly exclusively – the old, thriving British film industry was devastated. He glanced at the 20th Century Fox building on his left. TV had mushroomed, filled now with US sitcoms and frantic newscasts using 'anchors.' The cars were foreign now, all of them. He couldn't think of a nearby fish and chips shop. Or an old fashioned workers' café with big tea urns that served breakfast for pocket change.

That was the real meaning of penetration. Britain was under attack, but this time they couldn't fight them on the beaches. The white flags were out. Surrender was under way. The old Received Pronunciation was being replaced by something even more awful, called Estuary. American usage seeped in everywhere, even at the BBC. Prime ministers fawned over media magnates, bankers and US presidents. It was repulsive to watch. At least the French were fighting back – to no avail in the long run, but why make it easy for them?

And that was the question he was asking himself. These were convulsive times for him, and he was damned if he was going to be herded with the rest of the cattle into the revolving knives of the slaughterhouse. Firstly, he had to fully understand what was going on. Secondly, he must continue his development of a strategy for survival.

Balance. The word struck him yet again like a blow to the head. It was the key to judo as well as riding a bicycle. Perhaps it was also the key to his existence – and even to Alice's redemption. Balance was not a passive thing. It was always active. Probably it was a basic goal of nature. The struggle for balance against the forces of instability. Only with balance – and *harmony* – could the impending tidal wave of human disaster be avoided. There was colossal evidence everywhere that balance and harmony were being attacked in the name of progress, individually and globally. He was a target, an insignificant one. But so was the earth, much more profoundly.

All the old defences were breached. This beast could no longer be fought on the beaches. It was everywhere. Inside his head. That's where the battle had to be engaged. There was no place left to hide.

Hawthorn got to his feet and pulled his bicycle from behind the bench. As he wheeled it away, there was a wry smile on his face.

IS ALICE?

CHAPTER EIGHT

*[It was the first holiday we had together, Alyosha. I told Alice of my love for the coast of Suffolk, particularly the area around Aldeburgh, and in no time at all, she had hunted for hotels, researched brochures, pored over maps, and made plans. Her father was alive then, and from the beginning he liked me. He was a plump little man, with his remaining hair carefully combed straight back around his head. Frisky and blustery, he was already over 80, and tore around London in his Mercedes, honking his way through heavy traffic and forcing his way into queues, always talking to someone on his car phone. He was such an aggressive driver that he kept a hammer underneath his seat in case of conflict.

His nickname was Johnny, and he would show up unannounced on the doorstep with arm-loads of food in plastic containers. Chicken soup, roast goose or duck, bagels, fresh rye bread, chopped chicken livers, pickled herring. He began life poor, but through grinding hard work and worry managed to do well in the rag trade, finally running his own successful business in Golders Green, North London. Johnny would charge up my stairs holding a half-dozen plastic containers, always saying, "won't stay, won't stay…have to go…" But before he left he would always offer me a couple of Havana cigars. He knew I liked fine tobacco, and I could seldom afford a good Havana. Then he might pull out a big wad of 50 pound notes from his pocket. He was very proud of these 50s and liked to flash them when he could. He'd peel off a couple and poke them at me.

"You and Alice go out for a meal tonight. On me. Go on, take it…"

The roll of 50s came out again before we left for Aldeburgh, so we would have some spending money for the trip. Already he had paid for a big room at an old historic hotel in the town. Snick, snick, snick, snick…the crisp 50s settled on the kitchen table.

"You and Alice have yourselves a nice holiday. Now, don't say a word, I won't hear it, OK? And here's a few cigars for you. Enjoy yourselves. You need anything else, just call me…"

I couldn't help liking Johnny, and not just because of his generosity. He was full of energy, East End humour and knockabout charm. Alice was the apple of his eye. While he was alive he tried to look after her to the best of his abilities. She responded to him viscerally with a strong inner love, but his sheer ambiguity probably never helped her. He would always tell her what he thought she wanted to hear or should hear, not just the simple truth. Her mother was the same, and she, too, could be generous.

We travelled up in Alice's car, all expenses paid by Johnny. She was as excited as a maiden on her wedding day, only anxious that everything would be all right. It was not too long after my Satori, and she was beginning to think of us as 'partners.' I was, too, come to that. We were drifting closer day by day, and on weekends she packed up a big canvas bag and came over to my flat to stay until Sunday evenings. There were a few problems, but none that couldn't be overcome. I usually spent my evenings writing. Before our affair, I wrote seven days a week, every week, even Christmas and New Year. I finally blocked out Friday and Saturday nights to spend with her. Later she also wanted to come on Wednesdays, but always promised to leave by 9 o'clock so I could at least get a little done. I had never met anyone so tuned to easy negotiation when problems arose. You simply sat down and examined the problem, then created a compromise acceptable to both parties. How could it be so uncomplicated, when in the past it was so nerve-shredding?

The old hotel must have been a coaching inn in the 18th and 19th centuries. It was rambling. Oak beams, uneven floors, creaky staircases, old but good quality carpets, smells of old wood, leather harnesses and brass polish. Thanks to Alice – and Johnny – our large twin room had windows that faced the sea, and there was an en suite toilet and bathroom. From that day, I always left the choice of holidays and accommodation to Alice. She was a born researcher with exquisite taste.

After we checked in Alice spent over an hour completely emptying her suitcase, hanging dresses and coats in the wardrobe, carefully folding the rest for drawers. She always travelled with enough clothes for a season, even though we were only going to be there for a week. Or was it a fortnight? Hard to remember. Typically, I live out of my suitcase wherever I go, however long I'm staying. But for her, everything had to be sorted *just so* before we thought about relaxing. Shampoos, soap, conditioners, lotions, toothbrushes and water glasses were all put in their special places in the bathroom – towels checked and hung, one for me, one for her, on the rails. I could have been impatient, but instead I just lay on the bed with my hands folded underneath my head, enjoying the non-London air.

In time she was finished, and we went for a long walk along the seashore. This was Benjamin Britten country, and ghostly fragments of *Peter Grimes* occasionally echoed across the waves. It was an overcast day, and we both wore coats. But it was a wonderful feeling. We held hands like young lovers. The sea breeze was fresh and fishy. Boats were being drawn up onto the shore by winches, and nets were laid out. A stall was open, selling fish caught that day, and we stopped to peer at the slippery silver catch laid out in wet boxes.

"Hmmm," I said with pleasure, "Pity we can't cook in our room. I'd die for a couple of those, thrown straight onto a grill."

She grinned up at me. Her face was free from fear or troubles. "I don't really like fish. Except in batter. In fact I like the batter better than the fish. And the *chips*! Yum!"

I chuckled. "We'll do a deal. You eat the batter, I'll have the fish."

"Do you like chips?"

"Ah," I said. "Take 'em or leave 'em. Plenty of ketchup."

"Heinz!" she exclaimed, squeezing my hand.

"Heinz it is, not that vinegary old Brit crap."

She laughed gaily as we walked away from the stall. "I'm so happy."

She paused for a moment. "I never thought I'd say that. Ever. But just now, just this moment, I feel happy. Walking with you. Having a holiday. A *holiday*! Do you know, I always wanted to have holidays? I'd look at couples going away, listen to them plan. So envious. But it seemed to be one of those things… not meant for me."

"Why not?"

"Oh, I went away sometimes. Devon. With my mother and dad to Italy. I went to Israel, too, but that was with the Divine Light Mission."

I laughed. "Don't tell me you were a Premmie!"

"Oh, yeah, I was one for a while. Carried my meditation blanket everywhere. Lived in an ashram in Inverness. Dad hated it, hated that meditation blanket when I went home. That was when I was in my late teens and early 20s. But I never went on holidays… *with* someone. Like us. Like we are together. Now."

She gripped my arm with both hands. I looked down with pleasure. Her hair was blonde when she was younger, and now she added highlights as it darkened with age. She always wore a fringe, as she was sensitive about her narrow forehead. She looked up at me and smiled. Her eyes were small, but sparkled with energy. Beneath them were darker circles that at times emphasised her inner sadness. But her face was so truthful, so open, so unexpectedly full of hope. I felt a lump in my throat. It was a face I hadn't seen before, except in my earlier vision. Best of all, she was smiling with her whole being.

I coughed. "Lots of pebbles on the beach here. Not as bad as Brighton. But further up is a place called Walberswick. There are long sandy beaches. With sand dunes. If I had the money, I'd buy a house up there. Or at least a caravan. I have an inner longing to live near the sea."

She was suddenly excited. "Maybe we could buy a house here. It might be possible…"

"Woah," I laughed. "Let's take one step at a time. I'm not sure I'm ready to live with anyone, not even you. I'm a loner, Alice. Setting up house with someone in the past has always been a mistake. Strike that. A disaster."

"Well," she said, tightening her grip on my arm, "It's good we've got two flats, then. Right across the street from each other. But we never know, do we? One day…"

I didn't want to dampen her spirits. "We'd probably need more money than even you've got. A big place. Three bedrooms, minimum. One for you, one for me, one for my office…"

"*Four* bedrooms! I can have a dressing room. I always wanted a dressing room! And a bidet!"

"Four bedrooms, then. A big kitchen. At least one sitting room. Two would be better, so you could listen to Radio Four, and I could listen to Radio Three. This would be perfect: two semi-detached two-bedroom houses – buy 'em both, knock through the party wall for a door. You live in one, I'd live in the other."

She giggled. "And a garage for me. I've always dreamed of having a nice big garage…"

"You see?" I said. "We must already be talking something close to a million. Can you afford a million?"

She shook her head from side to side merrily. "It doesn't hurt thinking about it. Maybe one of your plays will hit the West End."

That evening we had our dinner in the hotel. I think we were the only guests dining in the bar area, and the owner came over to our table and introduced himself. He was middle-aged, pleasant, with an easy nature. I liked him.

"Beautiful place," Alice beamed.

"Thank you," he said with a smile. "Hope you enjoy your stay." He turned to me. "American?"

"Canadian."

"Sorry."

"That's OK," I replied. "I'm used to it. Have you been here long? I mean, is this your hotel?"

"My family has owned it since the 1940s…"

We chatted until dinner arrived. Afterwards he bought us a drink while I was enjoying one of Johnny's wonderful Havanas. Alice was quite bubbly and excited while she talked to him, and I relaxed completely. It was a perfect place, a perfect time. And I noted my astonishment at being in love again, this time with someone really special.

As we were going upstairs to our room, Alice was holding my arm again with both hands.

"Did you think I was stupid?" she asked nervously.

"Stupid?" It took me aback.

"You know," she said. "With *him*."

"No. Absolutely not. He's a nice fellow. We had a chat, nothing special. He seemed to like us."

"Not me."

I laughed. "*Now* you're being stupid. He liked you, was even a little flirtatious."

"He didn't like me. I know it."

IS ALICE?

I wasn't alarmed at the time, just shrugged it off. But I could see she was a little withdrawn and quiet. When we got to our room I put my arms around her and stroked her head. I talked to her soothingly, and she seemed to return to her earlier mood. We kissed as we lay back on the bed, and I looked into her eyes, holding her close.

"Do you know what love is now?" I asked softly.

"Yes," she whispered. "I love you, Theo."

"There's a piece of music that makes me think of you," I said softly. "Want to hear it?"

"Have you got it with you?"

I went over to my suitcase and searched for the CD. When I found it, I put in on the little portable player I always keep by my bedside. Yes… it was. The Schubert B-major piano sonata, performed by you. I returned to her embrace while we listened. We cuddled, then we made love, removing our clothing gradually. She was sitting on top of me, looking down, cheeks rosy with delight, eyes bright. Then she leaned forward and wrapped her arms around my neck while I was still inside her.

"Oh, Theo. Oh, my god."

The music was swelling. That gentle theme returning again and again, meltingly, binding us together as we clasped each other. Our orgasm was long, slow, almost unbearable. We barely moved, but there was movement inside us as waves of passion broke over us in a violent gale, mystical and mighty.

The next day we drove up to the small town of Walberswick, a place I had visited several times in the days when I had a car. Alice always wanted me to drive when we were out of London, and that was a perfect arrangement. I loathed the oppressive London traffic, and it was always nice to be a passenger, lean back in the seat and close my eyes. But she was a thoroughly urban woman and didn't trust strange country roads and motorways to lead to anywhere but disaster.

The breeze was brisk and a little cool. We wore coats again. No rain, though, just cloud. Occasionally the sun broke through to reveal a Turneresque seascape, giving strong, spine-chilling brush strokes of colour to land and ocean. In the distance was one man walking his Labrador. Otherwise the beach was ours. Alice had stopped at the foot of a dune, and was transfixed.

"Gorgeous," she murmured. "Simply perfect."

Then we just wandered close to the water's edge. I'm a real beachcomber, and my eyes were on the sand, searching for smooth pebbles. I turned over several that looked promising, only to find they weren't quite right. Finally I spotted a little orange stone still glittering with wetness. When I picked it up, it was perfect, like a little egg. I handed it to her.

"For you," I said as I dropped it into the palm of her hand.

IS ALICE?

It was the beginning of our little collection, and she was thrilled with her gift. Immediately she set off to find one of her own to give to me. Whenever we travelled to the seashore, in England or abroad, we always returned with a little handful of shells and stones to mark special moments. They meant so much more than gifts bought specially.

"It must be a custom dating back to our earliest ancestors," I muttered as I examined the stones she picked for me. "So simple, yet so effective. When you're in a place like this, you realise how rich you really are. There is no need for diamonds. Why waste money when you can have such beautiful things for free."

We found some old pilings, the remains of a pier dashed to pieces by mighty waves, and sat down. Or rather I sat down, and she sat on my lap. She put her arms around my shoulders and kissed me – again and again. I thought she wasn't going to stop.

"Didn't you have enough last night?" I asked with a grin.

"No. I want more."

"Kissing is only a prelude to sex. It's a waste of time otherwise."

"No, it's not." She kissed me again. "I love kissing you. Can't stop. I've got to make up for all the rest of my life, you know."

"Bad girl," I whispered. "Paddle your bottom."

I reached up her dress and found the elastic of her woolly tights as I glanced around to see if we were still alone.

"No, don't," she said in a little girl's voice. "I'll be good. Promise."

"There's no one here. The man and dog have disappeared. And anyway, you've been kissing me too much. It's time you learned your place."

I struggled to pull down her tights and knickers as she fought to get away. When I got them down, she was hobbled, and I pulled her across my lap.

"No!" she shouted.

"Quiet!" I whacked her with the palm of my hand on bare buttocks.

"Ouch! Ow, ow, *ow, ow!*"

"Shhhhhh." I was laughing now. Her cries were really loud, and I looked around again to make certain we were still alone. I turned her over and held her in my arms. Her tights were still around her ankles. "That'll teach you to kiss me so much, you harlot."

"It hurts," she whimpered. "Kiss it better."

I was caressing her bare thighs. They were remarkable. Just the kind of legs I like – a little plump, wonderfully shapely, soft to the touch. Her skin was smooth and girl-like. I was becoming aroused.

"You're beautiful, Alice. So beautiful."

She looked at me, her face was troubled now. "Are you taking the piss?"

I shook my head. "No. You're sexy and gorgeous."

Her eyes were misty. "No one – ever – has said that to me. You can't mean it. If you mean it, it's not true. I'm awful. Ugly. A terrible person, inside, outside. You can't see what I see."

"You're absolutely right," I whispered. "You see yourself in a twisted mirror, and I'm going to help you see what is truly beautiful. Which is you. The you that you can't see. I'm going to be your mirror now."

"Oh, Theo, Theo!" She buried her face in my shoulder. "It's not true, you don't know me. I'm a horrible person, and I've always been a horrible person…"

"No, you've *seen* a horrible person in your mirror. But that isn't you." I was talking quietly to her, rocking her gently now. "You've seen what you thought other people were seeing. I did that, too, when I was a teenager. Thought I looked like the Hunchback of Notre Dame, I really did. I looked in the mirror. I didn't see a handsome young man, the young man I now see in my old photographs. My head was too big, and so were my teeth, then. An ogre. The more ugly I felt inside, the more ugly I must have looked to others. That's how it works. Later I had a girlfriend who became my first wife, and she helped me. Made me stand up straight and look directly at people, not at the ground. Best of all, she made me think I was *handsome*. Alice, let me tell you, after that I couldn't fight the girls off. Change yourself, and you change the world. You become a magician."

She smiled faintly and kissed me again. "You *are* a magician."

"I wish I were. For you."

"You are. Every time I close my eyes, I wonder if you'll still be there when I open them again. I can't remember once in my life having any hope. I didn't even know what it was, unless it was mocking me. Like the world mocked me. All the time."

"Why does the world mock you?" I asked gently.

She lowered her eyes. "Because I'm… awkward. I don't know how to do things the right way. I'm ugly…"

"…beautiful. Warm. Lovely. Kind."

She looked at me intensely. "Are you sure you're telling me the truth? Not taking the piss? Not lying to me?"

"I'll never lie to you," I said. And at that moment I realised I'd never said that to another person, ever. "I'll tell you the truth, all the time, even if it's sometimes painful."

IS ALICE?

"Yes! Yes! Even then! Oh, that would be delicious! But can I believe you?"

"Well. Do you?"

"Yes," she said finally, almost inaudibly. "Yes. I do. Thank you."

I heard voices behind me and turned to look. A middle-aged man and woman had appeared from behind a dune and were walking towards us.

I grinned. "Better pull up your pants."

She giggled, hopped off my knee and pulled up her tights and knickers, moving her hips from side to side. The couple passed by us, and the woman stared, her lips compressed.

I looked at Alice and whispered. "Fuck 'em."

She threw herself at me, almost causing us to go over backwards into the sand. "Yes," she exclaimed passionately in my ear. "Fuck 'em."

That evening we had a long chat with the hotel proprietor at the bar after our meal. Naturally, I was smoking my Havana to accompany the malt whisky Johnny was paying for. Alice and I sat on stools at the bar, and I was relaxed, feeling the pleasure of a good day and a fine meal.

"Do you mind if I ask what you do?" the man enquired.

"Not at all," I replied. "I'm a writer."

He raised his eyebrows. "Published?"

"A playwright. Not a famous one, so no need to be obsequious," I joked.

He laughed and turned to Alice, who was a little quiet. "And you?"

"I'm...er...I drive the family mad in the family business," She laughed nervously.

The proprietor smiled. "I'm sure I drove my father mad, too."

"Well," she admitted uncomfortably, "maybe madness is a bad choice of word. I mean..." It was always difficult for Alice to discuss her personal life with a stranger.

"It's a little too complicated to explain," I said, hoping to rescue her.

He looked at my glass. "Would you like another drink? On the house?"

I hadn't yet finished my cigar. "Sure, why not? Thanks. Alice?"

"No, I'm OK," she said quietly.

"Another cup of coffee?" I spoke quietly. "Or would you rather go upstairs?"

"No, no," she said with a half-smile. "You go on. Have another drink."

"Do you get many visitors during the music festival?" I asked the proprietor as he poured a generous whisky.

"Hotel's full during the season," he replied. "Are you a music fan?"

"I've been to the Maltings once," I said. "Quite a while ago. It's such a beautiful place. Did you know Britten?"

He leaned on the bar, glancing at Alice. "My father did, and I can remember seeing him once or twice. With the singer. What's his name?"

"Peter Pears."

"That's the one. In the local shops. With their newspapers. A little standoffish, maybe. But they brought a lot of business to Aldeburgh."

Alice was staring at her coffee. I leaned over and whispered. "You all right?"

She shook her head. "No. I'm not. Would you mind…?"

I turned and smiled at the proprietor, taking my whisky as I slid off the stool. "Sorry, I just remembered I've got something I have to do before bedtime. I may drop down a little later, OK?"

He smiled. "Of course."

"Thanks very much for the drink."

"My pleasure."

I took Alice's arm and led her to the stairs. As soon as we were through the doors, I hugged her. "Talk to me, darling. I want you to talk to me, tell me what you're thinking."

She didn't speak for a moment. "I was so clumsy. He doesn't like me, I know it. I could tell from the way he looked at me. He doesn't approve…"

"Well, my opinion is that he likes you, finds you attractive. And that's the truth. You weren't clumsy. It's natural. Sometimes you don't know the right thing to say. *I* don't. I get like that, too."

"No, you don't. You always know the right thing to say. But *he* thinks something's wrong with me. I could see it. *He* thinks…"

We were at the top of the stairs, and I hurried to our room, opening the door with the key. "Never mind what *he* thinks. There's no way of knowing, anyway. And who is *he*? Just the owner of a hotel. We'll never see him again after we leave. He'll forget us, we'll forget him. Anyway, he seems like a nice fellow, no harm. Personally I think he's probably lonely, just wants a conversation with somebody interesting."

"You're interesting. I'm not."

IS ALICE?

I'd turned to face her in the room, then leaned over to put my cigar in the ashtray and my drink on the bedside table. "Look at me, Alice."

She turned her eyes upwards reluctantly, and I did not like the look she gave me. The warm features were disappearing, and her irises were flickering as if she were unfocused.

I called on all my inner resources. "Stay with me, Alice. Don't leave. Don't go away. It's safe now. You're safe here with me, and I'm not going to lie to you. Anything you ask or say, I'll tell you the truth. And the first thing I want to tell you is this: I love you. Very, very much. Do you believe me?"

Her irises were still flickering.

"Do you *believe* me? You have to answer!"

"Yes," she whispered finally. "I believe you. Promise. Promise me you'll tell the truth."

"Yes, I promise," I said, searching for some meaningful reference. "On my mother's grave, I promise. And I loved her too, dearly."

She looked into my eyes desperately. "What...what does he think of me?"

I wrapped my arms around her and held her head against my chest. "I have no way of knowing what he thinks, nor do you. But I can tell you that nothing I saw the whole evening led me to believe he was anything but interested and amused…"

"By you."

"By *us*. After all, he offered us a drink."

"Offered *you* a drink."

"He asked if you wanted another coffee. If you wanted one, he would have given it to you. That's a friendly gesture, not a hostile one. If he hadn't liked you, he would have ignored us, wouldn't have spoken to us. He was just trying to be kind."

"He hated me. I *know* he hated me."

"You can't know," I said gently, stroking her hair. "You can only guess. It's like an opinion. But it's based on some inner fear, not on what was happening. It's pointless trying to find out that kind of 'truth.' No one can do it. I can't, you can't."

I sat her down on the bed, then lay back with her, propping myself up on my elbow. Her eyes were bothering me. There was something about them. They were not vacant. They were like the eyes of the blind, unseeing, unfocused.

"Don't leave me, Alice," I whispered urgently. "Stay with me. Do you love me?"

Her eyes flickered. "Yes…I think so. Yes, I do…"

IS ALICE?

"Then trust me. I won't mislead you. I won't lie…"

"Are you a policeman?"

"Alice. It's Theo. Your lover. Now this is the moment you have to fight. You have to *trust*. I'm asking you with all my heart to trust me…and *don't leave*. Stay with me. Right now. Here. Nothing is going to harm you, because I am here with you, and I can translate things for you. You must believe me. I can see you're on a kind of precipice, about to fall away into some awful cauldron. But *you don't have to*. It's you. You have to trust. Look at me. Please. You are looking but not *seeing*. Look right into my eyes. Hold my eyes. Hold onto me. Alice, can you hear me? Are you listening?"

There was a long pause. "Yes."

"Then *look*. Focus on me. See my face. Remember the beach this afternoon?"

"Yes."

"Isn't that what you want? Rather than this? You can have that, or you can have this. You can be happy. I know it. Stay with me, Alice. Feel the strength of our love."

Her eyes were clearing a little, and tears were gathering.

"Oh, Theo. I'm *so scared*."

"There's nothing to fear." I was rocking her now like a baby. "Let's hold hands. Let's go for a walk on the beach. We can use the back door. We don't have to see him again. Let's go to the sea. It's healing there."

It was still light, because we had had an early dinner. It must have been late April or early May. The skies were still cloudy, but the wind had picked up. It was gusty. There were a few distant figures, dog-walkers, late single fishermen, casting hopefully in the surf. I held her close as we walked slowly down to the water. I could see the tide was coming in.

I leaned down. "How are you?"

"A little better. Still terrified. Wobbly. Very wobbly, Theo. Don't let go of me."

Then she was crying, and it was mournful. She heaved with despair. The wind and sea were howling now. Whitecaps flicked wickedly as the sea threw itself again and again at the shore, determined it was going to get further next time, sucking back savagely, then lunging with mighty waves to gain a few more feet of pebbles and sand.

"It's no use," she wailed. "Today I had a little hope, but then that *man*…"

I took a deep breath. "Let's ask Poseidon."

It took her by surprise. "Poseidon?"

IS ALICE?

"I'm not religious," I said into the top of her head. "So I can't ask God. But look at that sea. It's so strong. It has so much power, and, for a moment, I thought I saw a huge man with a giant trident. Maybe it was Poseidon. It's a story. A beautiful one. I need help. You need help. You need strength. Let's ask him if he will help you. Just silently. You ask, and I'll ask, and when you pray, try and open your heart. Maybe some of the strength of that huge, unknowable sea will gather you, pull you upward, pull you forward, give you something. It can happen. I've been low before, and I've stood on beaches making silent prayers to forces stronger than I am."

We stood looking outward for a long while, quietly, just holding on to each other. Behind the heavy clouds we could see a very distant flutter of lightening that transfixed us, as if it were some ghostly omen. The sea was surging nearer in sweeping rafts of foaming water. I reached out with my free hand towards the violence of the ocean, and, after a moment, Alice reached out with hers. We stood there, a single sculpture, two arms outstretched. The lightening shimmered again. I closed my eyes and made an overpowering effort to give my energy to Alice, throwing emotional sandbags into the breaches in her reality. Finally we turned to each other and embraced as the wind whipped her hair in my face. She was trembling and crying again. But this time the tears were not all hopeless.

Afterwards, as we lay in bed, I made sure Alice took Valium, which always seemed to settle her, then massaged her solar plexus until my arms were tired. Her paranoia was kinetic, and affected her whole nervous system. I'd never witnessed anything like it. I realised she had gone to the very brink that evening, balanced precariously on the lip of madness – one false moment, and she would have plunged headlong into the abyss. I promise you, Alyosha, that my own fear very nearly overpowered me at times. Yet I realised my utter stability was vitally important. It was necessary to *act*, to plunder my resources and call on all my reserves. Who wants to witness their lover's plunge into a living, throbbing inferno?

The next day we returned to Walberswick and ate at a small local pub called The Three Bells. When we finished I lit another one of Johnny's cigars.

She looked at me steadily as I settled back in my chair, blowing smoke towards the ceiling. "You saved me last night, Theo."

"No, I didn't," I replied. "You saved yourself. At a very dangerous point, you decided that you wanted something else besides a descent into madness."

She shook her head adamantly. "You gave me strength. I never had it before."

I paused for a moment. "If I offered you something, you accepted it. It was you. You had the courage. You had the strength. Not me."

"It's not that rational, Theo. That's the problem. If I could say to myself, 'I really don't want to be mad any more,' I would mean it with all my heart. But that wouldn't work. It won't work. This... *thing* overpowers me. Like a tsunami. Or an earthquake. At the time I have no choice."

"You always have choice. You just need to find the right place to insert the decision. It's not rational. I agree. It's complex. But this time we fought it off. Love is emotional. Maybe it was love…"

"Theo. Theo. I do…love you so much. You don't know…"

"Then again, it could have been Poseidon."]*

CHAPTER NINE

Hawthorn sat on his back roof with his can of Guinness and pipe. It was early evening, but there was still plenty of light in the sky. He was wearing a fleece because it was a little chilly now, but he wasn't about to abandon the roof to winter yet. The swifts hadn't begun their migration, and he watched their acrobatics with pleasure. He always missed them when they left, and they would be gone any day now. He had just finished the latest instalment of his letters to Aleksei Cherkasov, and needed a rest. His playwriting projects had all been put aside now until he finished the lengthening narrative to the Russian pianist. He was becoming addicted to the unfolding story, aware he was compressing some things, distilling others, using a little invention to connect sequences. Actual memories were like that. They sorted themselves into more understandable stories that could be recalled without the jumble of the chaotic events taking place simultaneously, and the intrusion of past and present. The story now had more certainty than when the events occurred, more cohesion. Were they less true? Less false? If so, how could that be?

He realised he was stroking his goatee. It was longer now. You could almost call it a beard. He felt the pull of a recurring thought. Some luminous emotion beyond his ability to describe it tugged at him. There was something epochal – even mythological – about his relationship with Alice. That was the only way he could express the feeling. It felt as if they were playing out another act of a play that had its origins in the dim mists of history. It was like trying to remember bits of an important dream. Or like an archaeologist attempting to recognise a piece of broken pottery, with only a few remaining shattered fragments. Hawthorn was a Wanderer with a Quest, and this quest involved the solution to twin problems inextricably entwined – her madness, and his search for the foundations of consciousness. He and Alice talked endlessly, and their sexual play became more focused and intense. Before she had her relapse, he was convinced she had found her footing, and would never again be sucked into the nightmare. She was more confident socially, and there were fewer alarms and close calls. Almost none, to think about it. Thus he became less vigilant…

He closed his eyes and let his head rest against the back of the deckchair, relaxing his neck muscles, concentrating on controlling his breathing. That was one of his strategies for detaching himself from the matrix and its incessant thought-traffic. It was what he did before a judo contest, too. Don't anticipate, be in balance, seek harmony. Breathe normally and easily and just be aware of the breathing. Then everything else would subside. It was as if the heat were lowered underneath boiling water so the surface was smoother, flatter. Inner sight improved, fatigue sometimes fell away, interaction with the world was not so harsh. The eyes of others became less important. Yogis used a similar strategy, he knew.

Much of their development related to their long, intricate journey through sexual landscapes. This was so complex it was going to be difficult to explain to Cherkasov. But he was trying. In early days they simply experimented with the tantric scenario. Then one day Alice had a crisis.

She was sitting on his sofa looking dejected, staring at her hands. "I'm not as comfortable in the passive role. I like our games, I don't mean that. But the passivity resonates badly with me. As we go deeper into it, it triggers something inside me. Lack of self-esteem. My worthlessness. My desire to injure myself. I'm with you, we are dancing together, I'm a part of you… then I slip sideways and start getting spikes of anxiety. No, that's not right, either. What happens is that I can't handle the arousal peaks, Theo. I don't know what to do. I want to continue. It's life-affirming, I don't know how to express it. I learn so much about myself. And our trust for each other. But when I get so madly aroused, I just have to come. I can't bear the pressure of holding back. It distracts me, then I start feeling inadequate, like I'm not keeping up with you or I'm not in the spirit of the thing."

Hawthorn sat on the other end of the sofa, his head resting on the cushion. He was staring at the window, trying to avoid the dark stain of disappointment seeping into his being. He sighed, not knowing what to say.

"I've always enjoyed doing both roles," he murmured. "One is so much a part of the other. The intricacies have fascinated me for years. It's a part of something real, something in the world, something that happens to people all the time. When you heighten the sexual element of the activity, it sets loose ancient archetypes that loosen the paving stones of existence…"

IS ALICE?

She was sitting still, her eyes cast down. "I'm sorry. I'm sorry to disappoint you."

He laughed. "You don't disappoint me, Alice. On the contrary, you inspire me. Constantly. Of all the people I've played with in the past, you're the most inventive, the most natural and unembarrassed. No guilt baggage. Intuitive. What else can I say? You're fucking perfect."

She looked up and smiled. "Are you telling the truth?"

"You know I am."

Her eyes were bright. "I'm the best? Of all?"

"Absolutely. And the look of you. Original beauty. Of the body, of the soul. I have such vivid images of you. A supplicant Venus searching heavens for the tormenting touches of Zeus!" He laughed out loud. "How's that for imagery! You do it so well. I can see it in your eyes. We are dancing, moving together..."

"Beautiful?" she inquired faintly.

"Gorgeous."

"Not too fat?"

"Don't be ridiculous."

She paused for a few moments before taking a deep breath and looking at him. "I know how important this is to you. If you promise not to leave me, I don't mind if you look elsewhere, try to find someone who can give you the sexual experience you want…"

Hawthorn sat up, half turned towards her and pointed his finger at her face. "You are exasperating me! Do you think I'm some sort of sex maniac? I've gotta have it just such a way, so-and-so, with a puppet-partner who marches perfectly in step with me? *You* are the one I want, and we'll solve this like we solve all the other problems. We'll talk about it, we'll compromise, we'll find *a better way*. One that will lead to *our* enchantment, not just mine. I don't want you to be my slavish follower…"

He grinned and winked. "Or do I? You'd make an awfully nice one. But that's another game entirely…"

She made a mournful face. "I'm sorry…"

"Or maybe I could always be the passive one, then. How about that? Would you like to do active all the time? You seem to enjoy yourself more when you're giving me pleasure."

"But you like…"

"Would that be interesting for you? Could you wrap your delicious body around that thought?"

"But you said you like to do both."

"If I were honest, I'd say I probably enjoy the passive role more. Just lying there as still as a mummy while you tease and torment me, with or without the blindfold.

IS ALICE?

I adore the slippery feel of your stockings against my leg or the vision of you in your underwear. You know, Alice, from the space I'm in sometimes, you look just like a fairytale princess."

"A princess?"

"A princess. We'll have sessions on the weekends when you come over. Just let things develop naturally. This might even be a better idea because it gives you something that has always been elusive for you. It gives you control of all the erotic mechanisms. You're good at it, when you forget you're Tiny Alice in a world of 'adults.' You don't use your baby voice. Like the one you're using now."

"I'm sorry."

"Don't apologise. You have dignity and the right to opinions and your own behaviour. You can use your real voice with me, your relaxed voice, the one from the real Alice. You. But you don't have to apologise when you don't."

She thought for a minute before speaking. This time her voice was strong. "You're…wise, Theo…"

Hawthorn laughed out loud. "I'm almost as far from being wise as a fool. I wish I *were* wise. If I had one wish about myself, I would wish for wisdom. Not wealth. But I'm not there. Not even close. The other end of the universe."

"It's not true," she replied, her voice still strong. "You're the wisest person I've ever met. You let me be myself. I don't have to...to act a role. Which is ironic when we're talking about our play. But that's not like playing roles. Somehow, we grow closer together. I feel your...your existence."

He settled back into the sofa as she lit another cigarette. "I've done this kind of sex with many others, but never with someone I love. That's really surprised me. I'd given up on love when I met you, but was determined to find a partner interested in...how to put it? Sexual spiritualism – will that do? To hell with 'normal' sex and all that implies. Love, then disappointment, dissembling, dysfunction. There, I'm rhyming like you."

"That's alliteration. A limitation of your Canadian station."

"That's *ill*iteration."

She turned, blowing smoke from the side of her mouth, away from his face. "Can we do it? You think? You won't be too upset? You won't have to see any other...?"

"I've told you. Let's try it. One step at a time. Anyway, I have a feeling we might be doing the right thing. We come to an obstacle and find it's not an obstacle after all. Just a marker for the right path."

"You sure?"

IS ALICE?

"Are *you* sure you want to continue with… this kind of eccentric, er, inequality?"

"Oh, yes! It's not inequality. I love being the active partner and watching you plummet into your dream world. You take me with you, Theo! That's what happens. It's like nothing else I've ever done. With anyone. I *love* it. But only with you. I mean, if something happened to you – God forbid – I don't think I would seek it out, do it with anyone else. No. It's… a thing *we* have. It's you and me. That's what I truly feel."

Hawthorn opened his eyes. The sun had set, and it was a little cooler. Or maybe he had just been sitting still for too long. The sky was light blue in the west, but you could now see the stars, and the ghostly outline of a full moon was rising in the south. He remembered most of that conversation, even though it took place years ago. He wondered about the years. They no longer seemed to unroll in a linear sequence any more. The sensation was more viscous, like cake batter, swirling and folding in on itself as if it were stirred by time. Was it just age? He was rolling on, faster and faster, towards 60 now. Then it would be 70. It was straight into a minefield. As every year passed, the minefield was more dense, the chances of death less unlikely. Not at all like his youth, when death was a far-fetched idea beyond imagination, and ageing was for older people. At the same time, his life grew richer and richer. Particularly with regard to sex. Love? Sex? How could they be picked apart any longer?

It had indeed been the right choice, the right path. The synchronicity of it all. Before he met Alice, it had been his plan to ditch the whole idea of vanilla sex and spend the rest of his life indulging in role-playing passion. Only passion, not love. It began that way with Alice, but it was he who fell in love, not her, not then, the moment when he saw strange things in the future, the development of Alice, her emancipation, her realisation. Then there was her discomfort with being the passive partner. As the active one, she had the opportunity of expressing her creativity. She could make decisions without referring or deferring to him, and slowly she acquired a greater ease with the role and with herself. As if by magic.

Magic. It was a word damned by the righteous rationalists of the day, convinced of the hardness of reality and obsessed with its measurements. Yet the evening he was witnessing on his back roof could only be described in magical terms. The smell of the honeysuckle behind him, the yawn of the sky above as the last few swifts flitted to their nests – the mystery, the awesomeness, the wholeness of it all. The complexity of his being and its transience. He observed the magic of change taking place at such varying paces and intensities – the circadian change as the sun dimmed and the moon emerged; the seasonal change as summer turned to autumn; the ebb and flow of civilisations, including this one; the changes taking place within his consciousness, and that of Alice. As he looked up at the sky overhead, he realised the universe must have rhythms of its own, but maybe not even a beginning, middle and end. Just change. A process so vast it might never be known. For the brief span of his life, he was a part of that process, and he could not even say that for certain. The rationalist within him embraced atheism for many years, but in effect he knew nothing. Thus his life could also just be another change – from one thing to something else. So many possibilities. The events during the recent years led him to question old certainties. The nature of the world – the emergence of the social matrix and its relevance to his earlier ideas of the State – and the topography of human consciousness. These were always central to his interests, but during his relationship with Alice the solidities became more gaseous and amorphous. To some she appeared weak, but he detected luminous strength that drew him inward, towards her, and outward beyond the limits of his being where all shapes were vapour. A kind of madness?

He chuckled and reached for his pipe on the little folding table by his chair. He lit it, and took a sip of Guinness. It was still cold, and he liked it cold, not like a proper Irishman who wanted it only chilled. No, it wasn't madness. Madness was the fuel propelling the engine of the social matrix that trapped them all in its compelling savagery.

He blew smoke in the direction of the cloud that was creeping towards the moon to his left and closed his eyes again, the pipe still clamped between his teeth. It was so difficult, he thought, to write expressively about the actual sex in his letters. How could he help anyone else to understand? Yet it was going to be impossible to explain the whole phenomena without it. It wasn't the beginning of the magic between them, but it was certainly where the strange, unknown, otherworldly foliage began to flower, then to cover the landscape in botanical mystery beneath the warmth of a redder, hotter sun. Sexual description was tricky, more personal than any dream. He wondered if there was a way of transmitting a whiff of the ether without the titillation or embarrassment that accompanies so many descriptions of sex. But the excitement was an integral part of mood transformation from the ordinary thoughts of an ordinary day to a universe as real as this one, but one so unique and fragile that one ordinary breath would destroy it.

At ground level the feeling was not so different from the act of straight sex between a couple deeply in love. Then it developed above these foundations like a fairy castle with many rooms that led to other rooms – some deeper and darker, others as light and gay as spring. As a couple they formed a polyp on the surface of the social matrix that ruptured, allowing them to float free into intense experiences not indexed in the common sense world. They were more related to the visions and Satori he experienced in previous episodes of his life – yet they were different in texture. It made Hawthorn suspect the social matrix of being a kind of slave galley, with all the oarsmen below decks, unaware where they were going or why. His attention was thus fixed in two directions: the normal and the meta-normal. In order to seek answers in one, it was necessary to seek them in the other.

'Normal' was confusing anyway. After all, heat was normal for desert-dwellers and cold was normal for Eskimos. Normality was simply what you were used to, even if all the circumstances were *abnormal*. His meta-normal experiences informed him that human consciousness was capable of other things on wider horizons with a greater array of sensations. He became more and more convinced that those pulling on oars in the belly of the ship would be incredulous if they were told they were in fact floating on a smooth and opal sea beneath blue skies and heavenly bodies. Except for Alice, he had more or less given up trying to convince people of the existence of the meta-normal. Oh, some of them had experienced trances or strange daydreams, premonitions and mystical moments. Others were enticed by astrology and other subsets of non-scientific explorations. Nevertheless, their lives seldom challenged the actual existential situation in which they were trapped. Blind oarsmen, oarswomen, pulling endlessly on their wooden paddles from the beginning to the ends of their lives. They preferred to keep their seats and their chains, because what they were engaged in was *normality*.

Hawthorn didn't despise these passengers, not at all. He would enlighten them, surely, but that was way beyond his powers. Even if informed that the gigantic slave ship was navigating straight towards a sharp, ragged reef, they would continue to row, night and day, until the boat was dashed to pieces and their lifeless bodies were left floating meaninglessly with fragments of the wreckage. All the members of the crew would swear they were not being forced to sit at their stations with their legs chained to the floor...

He opened his eyes suddenly and took the cold pipe from his lips. He'd just made another connecting thought, another link.

Of course, he thought, they were not being forced to crew the death ship. *That* was because they all *agreed* to be forced! After all, the chains were imaginary, and they could leave their seats at any time, walk up on the top deck or dive overboard. By individually accepting 'normality,' they felt they were in an unbreakable contract with the social structure of the ship. Those few who did get up and leave were a threat, but the unspoken way of dealing with this threat was to peg the leavers as odd. Or rebels. Come to that, there were different kinds of rebels. Some dashed their heads against bulkheads. Others ranted and raved and waved their fists in outrage. Those who returned from the top deck and spoke against 'normality' were ignored because they were clearly mad. Perhaps it had always been thus. But now the ship was gaining speed. There were more rowers, more oars, more ship – it was growing bigger and moving faster every day. In the past ignorance could lead to local disasters, but now the disaster that loomed was global. Normality had become so bizarre it bore little resemblance to anything but insanity.

* * *

Alice put the coins into the phone and dialled. She was scared but determined now. She almost wanted to hear the answerphone, then she could just leave her message and not have to speak to him.

"Hello."

She waited a moment and remembered her determination. "Hello."

IS ALICE?

"Darling!" Theo exclaimed. "How are you? Can you talk?"

"Don't call me 'darling'. I'm not your darling."

"It's so great just hearing your voice at last," he replied. "You're talking!"

"I want you to bring something for me," she said, her voice still low and measured.

"What do you want?"

"Bring my chequebook, my bank card, my mobile phone, my house keys, my car keys and my Filofax."

There was a long pause. Then he spoke. "I can't bring them, Alice. Not until you're well. But you sound better…"

"You *have* to bring them," she said as firmly as she could. "They're *mine*."

Another pause. "They're yours, but we've agreed for a long time that I have to keep them safe for you while you're in hospital. When you're well…"

"I'm well now. And I want them now."

"I don't think you sound really well, darling. You're articulate, and that's something I… when did this happen?"

"I don't want to talk to you, Theo. I just want my things. They're mine, and I want them. Give them to me."

He didn't speak for a minute. "I can't give them to you. Not right now. They're all safe, still in your handbag…"

"And I want my handbag, too. It's *mine*."

"I'll come and see you. Right now. Won't take me but ten minutes on the bike."

"I don't want to see you," she almost whispered. Her resolve was seeping away like the tide…the *tide*. The *ocean*! The *memories*. Keep them out. "I spoke to my solicitor this morning, and she agreed with me. You have to give me my things. Because they're mine. She's already served notice on the hospital, and we're going to have a meeting. To challenge the Section…"

He spoke quickly now, and his voice was warm and reassuring. "Of course you can have them when they lift the Section. I'll be there…"

"I don't want you there."

"When will the meeting be?"

"…I don't know. I don't want to talk any more."

"Alice. I came to the hospital yesterday, brought some money for your account and some more clothes. Oh, and cigarettes. Did you get them?"

"I don't want to talk."

IS ALICE?

"I'm coming down now."

"No! I've told them. I don't want to see you. They won't let you on my ward!"

"Well, I'm coming. I'm going to try. Listen, don't hang up. I'll bring some of the things you want. In your handbag. Let you see them. If you want to write a cheque, I'll post it for you. If you want money…"

"I'm going now." Her voice had almost disappeared.

"Alice, please. When I come, just try and talk to me for… just a minute, that's all."

She hung up the phone and bit her lip hard, forcing back the tears, reminding herself that she must keep her anger and her direction. It was the only way. The only way out of this *total shithole*. More importantly, it was the only way out of life. Above all else, she must get back to her flat, where she might take paracetamol and maybe tie a plastic bag around her head. Whatever. This world was not her world. The thought of another night in this *fucking hospital* was more than she could bear. Why-oh-why had her plan not worked?

She got up from the phone and walked briskly back to the reception desk. An agency nurse was on duty.

"Theo is coming," she said to the nurse curtly.

"Who?" The fat woman looked up from her magazine with a bored expression on her face.

Alice sucked in air. "The man who... Theo Hawthorn. The man who calls himself my partner. I don't want him here. I don't want to see him again. You understand?"

"Yes, dear."

"I don't want to see this man!" She slammed her palm on the desk. "It's my *right*! *I don't have to see him*."

"Yes, dear."

"I'm telling you! Don't let him in here. Don't let him on the ward."

"Yes, dear."

Alice turned away angrily, even before the nurse's eyes returned to her magazine. Then she stopped suddenly, undecided. Unconsciously, she took a cigarette from her pack and lit it.

"If you want to smoke, go to the TV room."

"Go fuck yourself," Alice growled, then blew smoke in the direction of the desk. She stalked down the corridor towards her room.

"You ain't supposed to smoke in your room, either," the nurse called after her.

Alice ignored the woman because she was now in agony. The wall she so painstakingly constructed was being battered by a storm. It was taking all her willpower to remain in the small space she had made for herself. The giant bats of paranoia were overhead, ducking, diving, taunting her. It had taken such a long time to build up the necessary anger to call Theo. Of course she wasn't angry with *him*. Theo was the weak link. That's where the breach in the wall would happen. The cannonball hits the Theo wall, and when it cracks, she won't look back, wall-ball, back-crack.

Only when she could build up enough anger – *fury* – at her desperate situation could she enter a quasi-articulate space where she could understand them, and they thought she was one of them again. The Fool could fool them into thinking she might be…

She shook her head fearfully and threw herself on the bed, forgetting for a moment that she was smoking. Her cigarette broke in half, and she had to sweep the burning cinder from the sheet. After throwing the filter on the floor, she lit another one before banging her head with both hands. How could she get *out*? Out of her brain! Out of this place! Out! Out! Out! Out of this *fucking world*! Why did they keep stopping her? She was detestable…

She stopped suddenly and opened her tear-stained eyes. Theo. Theo. God, she couldn't help it. She loved him so much, and she would be an eternally damned liar if she said not. It was the sound of his voice that shook her. Didn't he *know* she was trying with all her strength to let him go? So he could be free? He must himself be eternally damned if he couldn't release himself from the chains of her existence. That was one of the main reasons she wanted to kill herself. *To release dear Theo.*

The man she adored above anyone in the universe. And the damned bastard wouldn't even help her help him by letting her get to her flat where she would find some way to do it. She was too much of a coward to throw herself off Archway Bridge. Or underneath a bus. It would just hurt too much. Or it wouldn't work, and she would lie there mangled until they dragged her broken bones back to the hospital to live in physical as well as mental hell. Alice knew she was cursed. How long had she been here? She didn't know. Months? But she mustn't allow herself to go back to *that* life. That other life. She mustn't let Theo suffer any more sexual degradation or the humiliation of being with her.

Images flickered like reality. Theo naked, still except for the occasional motion of his erection.

Alice looked down at herself. She was wearing the garments of a filthy whore.

Poor Theo. *She* forced him to lie still while she tantalised his dick and rubbed her body against him as he moaned and begged her to let him come.

For some reason way beyond her understanding he was compelled to do all kinds of things for her. It was some *way* the world worked, and it was far beyond her ability to know what it meant. But now, in her thoughts, sex was the absolute worst! She must never, *ever* allow herself to be drawn into that situation again. Keep the man away from her – that was all she could do. It was her only form of choice. To have *real* mercy on him.

IS ALICE?

Suddenly Alice threw the butt of her cigarette on the floor and rushed to the wash basin where she threw up immediately – partly digested lumps of food splattered and smeared in mucous, smelling of evil. She closed her eyes and inhaled the fumes of the nauseating puddle as it blocked the drain. Expel the sinful and wicked bile, the corruption that was gnawing at her viscera. Her mouth was aflame with stomach acid, and she spat again and again into the puddle, wishing she could turn herself inside-out so all the malignancy could be scraped into the sewer.

Finally she wiped her mouth with her arm and turned round with a wail. "Theo, Theo, *what have I done to you?* You must *not* come here, never again. I must not see you. You must not see me. That is all I can…"

A devil from hell jabbed a white-hot poker in the sole of her foot, and she yelled with pain. She screamed as loud as she could, hopping towards the bed on one foot. It was excruciating, more than she could bear, just beneath her instep. The burning wouldn't stop. It got worse. Alice was crying now, begging for any merciful god to kill her. She couldn't bear pain. She must do something.

As she hopped towards the sink, she spotted her still smouldering and squashed cigarette butt on the floor, but it didn't occur to her that she had just stepped on it. She was too focused on the cold water tap and something to put the water in.

A bowl, she thought. A bowl for my sole.

Quickly she dumped some pencils out of an old margarine tub and turned on the tap. The sick was still blocking the drain, but she managed to get some water in the little container and hop back to her bed with it. Then she squeezed in her toes, just reaching the burn. It helped. A little. Enough to let her shake out another cigarette from the pack and light it. Wiping her tear-stained face with her arm, she realised there was still vomit on it.

She dropped back on the bed. Her foot was throbbing wildly. As she shut her eyes the whole known universe was as black as nothingness. As far as she could see, from one infinity to another, there was only misery, darkness, pain and failure. It was a barren universe, lacking the energy to grow even one flower. Any flicker of hope wilted and died instantly. There was no love, no beauty, no peace, no justice. There was no light, either – just a bluish, unhealthy glow, just enough to see there was nothing at all to see. One dead sun amongst a galaxy of dead suns and a death, too, of time. There was still, she observed with withering irony, a jagged tool clenched loosely in her hand, like an ape grasping a jawbone to make a primitive hammer. It was reason. *Reason.* She fought so hard to get her fingers around that old bone to hone her tone on the phone. The others, they understood her then. But the only way she could make it work was with ANGER. And she was using it now. She was thinking as she looked out on her unending universe of doom. Not only that, she *knew* she was thinking. Theo said it was important to think. What did he mean? Important to think, she repeated again and again. Why bother to think when thought brought only more misery? And why did he tell her that? Suddenly, she could see the outlines of his face etched into her cold, lifeless universe – leaning towards her, his face strong, his brown eyes kindly.

"You can think your way out," his mouth said. "Watch what people are doing, listen to them, observe. They can do you no harm. You spiral downwards, too much into yourself, and get lost…"

What did that *mean*?

As the vague face-outline disappeared, she became aware again of the pain in her foot, sat up and hobbled back to the basin. She emptied the contents of the container and replaced it with fresh, cold water from the tap, before hopping back to her bed and putting her foot in it.

Lying back on the bed, she lit another cigarette. She couldn't remember what she was just thinking. Something about thinking.

Must write everything down, she thought. I can never remember.

She stared at the ceiling with the single naked light bulb, and felt again a rush of anger. Rage. This *crap* place. That stupid light bulb. Uncomfortable bed. Pain. She *must* find a way out of this horrible hospital. Rolling over onto her side, she reached for her little notebook and pencil lying on her pillow. She used the pad as a shield against the light as she held it in her palm, leafing through for a blank page. Then she wrote carefully with the pencil.

Watch the emergency doors. Sit in hallway. Watch the doors.

That's what she must do, and she knew she had to write it down or she would forget by the morning. She wrote again.

Call solicitor. Tell her to hurry up, can't hold the tide back for long. Make meeting SOON.

She double underlined 'soon' and scratched a big star beside the word. Alice knew she must reach her flat one way or another. At the moment it was her goal. So she was *thinking*. Once back in her flat, redemption might just be possible. She grabbed her notepad again and worked so intensely that she completely forgot about her foot.

1. *Throw out all those filthy clothes and nasty underwear used when I torture TH.*
2. *Throw black paint on the carpet and walls paid for by my poor daddy.*
3. *Give away all clothes.*
4. *Give away car.*
5. *Get money out of bank, give away...anybody!*
6. *Get paracetamol from chemist, lay out with plenty of water and plastic bag & string.*
7. *THEN DIE. DIE. DIE. THANK FUCKING GOD.*

The last line was underlined three times with double stars at both ends. She squeezed her eyes together and made a prayer, hoping there was no god to hear her.

IS ALICE?

Please, please, she thought, please let there just be *nothingness*. No afterlife, no heaven, no hell, no reincarnation, no thoughts preserved in any corner of the cold, lifeless, unjust universe, no remnant of self left to think about this or any other possible world.

She did not want to take the *risk* of some fragment of self surviving to remind her of a life so unimaginable and unintelligible, but so relentlessly cruel that she would gladly erase herself from past, present and future, if only she were allowed the means.

Please, she thought as she crushed the pad in her hand, *please* let me just die without too much pain and for once be just *nothing*. Let the rabbis be wrong, along with all the religious people of the world. They say there is good and evil, but I was damned only to be evil, a cancer to the world and other people and everything I touch. I don't know what is good, but there is no goodness in me. For the sake of Theo, for the sake of the world, just please let me cease to exist forever and ever to the limits of eternity. Sweep me away, the thoughts, the traces, the shit of my soul. Let there be no more Alice Dance now or then or forever more, and please let the universe forget every morsel of me, every atom. Nothing. No one. Deep, deep blackness. No me. No memory of me. Wipe me now, oh heaven, wipe this polluted, squalid tear off the face of existence and burn the *schmutter* that wiped it in the deepest, hottest hole in hell.

Amen.

Her eyes were closed from the prayer when she heard the squeaking in the corridor. Then there was another sound. Bat wings. Her eyes snapped open, and immediately she thought she caught the flitting shadows on the walls.

"I'm a vampire," she thought. "The mother of vampires…" She closed her eyes again, raising her chin and exposing her throat. They were there – the bats fluttering from the crusty glowing hole of hell, and Alice realised she could see herself in the past. She was her own ancestor and stood silently in the foreground, her features covered with fine, brown fur, great wings folded as her children fluttered around her squealing and screeching. There was a great puff of smoke from the volcanic hole, and the pre-Alice vampire opened her wings and bared her fangs, tiny eyes crazed with the lust for blood. The scene was changing now, going further back in time to an earlier Alice-vampire before she realised there was one before that, then another, even older. She reeled through hundreds, then thousands and hundreds of thousands and millions of years back, further back until there was no longer even any fire and nothing but ice reflecting the horrifying image of the Original Vampire, Queen of the Underworld – bloodsucker of all warmth, Wraith of the Universe. She stood with Satan at the beginning of all things. Satan leaned forward and grasped her furry head, pulling her towards him for a ghastly embrace. She felt his long, hot tongue in her mouth…

Alice shook with fear and felt her mouth full of sulphurous tongue. Her pulse was racing, and her breathing was too shallow to speak as she fought with the room full of bats – all her babies coming home to suckle her. Her body was lurching now as she lay on the floor in the deepest mortal fear she had ever known. She squeezed her eyes shut as her arms flailed at the bats, but she couldn't help opening her legs. For Satan. It was *inevitable*!

"Amen!" she finally screamed. "*Amen!* AMEN!!! OH, GOD! SAVE ME!"

CHAPTER TEN

Hawthorn's chest was heaving as he struggled on the tatami. His partner, Tim O'Grady, was just too good. He was like a wet fish, too slithery to hold, too elusive. Hawthorn tapped the mat again, more from exhaustion than pain from the strangle O'Grady applied from behind.

They sat up together, both men tired, breathing hard, adjusting their judo-gis, then executed a kneeling bow.

"I think I'm getting too old for this lark," Hawthorn said as he caught his breath. "Either that, or you're way too good for me. Probably both…"

O'Grady grinned at him. He had receding sandy hair, just beginning to grey at the temples. He was 45 years old and a 3rd Dan. "What you need to do is think of groundwork as a continuation of standing judo. You're fighting me like a wrestler, trying to use strength to power your way out of a hold-down or strangle. Think of it more as a flowing, rhythmic movement. You have hold-downs, strangles, arm-locks. You're good at arm-locks, almost had me a couple of times there. But, because you know you're good with them, you try and force me into a situation where you can use them. It's the same when we're standing, in *randori*. You're getting slick there, not forcing your way into just two or three techniques, using plenty, letting one flow into the other. Now, *gatame-waza* is the same…"

IS ALICE?

Hawthorn spread his hands. "I can see the picture of how to do it, but once we get in a tangle, you're right…I'm just pushing and shoving."

O'Grady wiped the sweat from his face with his sleeve. "Let's try it slowly, almost like katas. Be aware of what you're doing. Remember balance and *kuzushi* are just as important on the ground. You're bigger than I am, and stronger. But you're letting me control your balance."

They rose to their knees to grip each other. Hawthorn liked to roll onto his back, pulling his opponent with him, then controlling the other's body with his feet and legs. He won a lot of contests that way. His legs were strong and supple. He pulled on O'Grady's right arm as he fell back slowly, placing his right knee in his opponent's lap, using his left leg to lift over the man's now outstretched arm.

"Good," O'Grady said as they stopped the action. "The arm-lock is almost there, but you must do it quickly and pull my wrist up and towards you."

When they continued, O'Grady pushed Hawthorn's right leg out of the way, almost with a punch, and moved into a hold-down position. He stopped again. "Don't keep trying for the lock, Theo. It's gone. I've got past your leg. You've used that technique too often now, so I'm expecting it. It's time for you to switch to a strangle. My neck's open, and your hand is already there. Bring your other arm over before I trap it, don't push, and you've got the strangle. If that doesn't work, you're in perfect position to try the lock again as I resist the strangle. See?"

"Let's try that again," Hawthorn said. "Maybe I can get it smoother."

He paused first, clearing his mind. He knew the moves. He didn't have to think. What was necessary was to feel the changing pressures of their bodies. There were brief moments when either one of them was vulnerable to the other. The object was to sense those moments, then move decisively *with the least force*. It was a bad habit, he knew. With groundwork he always felt really competitive, hoping to push through for a quick victory. When frustrated, he often tried to force it anyway, even if it wasn't working. So he cleared his mind, relaxed his shoulders, concentrated on his breathing for a moment, fixing his *intent*. Then again he fell back, pulling O'Grady with him, trying for the arm-lock. It failed again as his opponent went for the hold-down, then he employed the strangle, using O'Grady's strength. *Almost*. Forget the strangle, trap the wrist. *Arm-lock*. Solid.

The got to their knees and bowed again.

"Perfect," O'Grady said, smiling. "You felt more like a snake that time. Remember the python. It doesn't use its immense strength to crush its prey. It waits until you breathe out, then tightens – another breath, tighter. With minimal effort, the python lets you kill yourself. In the end, you can't fight the coils for a final breath and actually die from lack of oxygen."

Theo nodded, then shook his head. "It's just bad habits. I've won a number of times using the wrong methods.

IS ALICE?

Which has reinforced things. So my body *feels* like it should continue to use the old pathways."

The other man shrugged as they both got to their feet. "That's fine, until you meet someone with better technique. Then he'll overcome you every time. Let's do some *randori* and continue into *gatame-waza* if we go to the ground. Even if it's *ippon*, a clean throw. Just continue. We'll do a sequence, then stop and talk about it. The real way to look at this is that there's no significant difference between standing and ground technique. It's a *continuation*. And remember the circle. Everything's a circle, every movement a tightening spiral."

O'Grady grinned as they bowed and grasped each other. "And I've got to watch your *osoto-gari*. It's getting better and better, a real powerhouse. Bloody long, strong legs. But don't just play for that one. Fundamentally, the other person will throw himself, you only help him. Just like the python. That goes for me, it goes for everyone."

* * *

*[Alyosha, I've always been fascinated by dominance and submission, especially in its relevance to the State. I was even attracted to the concept sexually as a teenager. But I kept asking myself – *why*? I mean, forget Freudian analysis, unconscious bullshit. No, it's bigger, broader than that. Psychology always rests on philosophy, never the other way round. Take the paradigm of bully – or mugger or officer or boss – and the victim – or other ranks employee. An interaction occurs that attracts one to the other. That's the first point. The second, more important one, is that this is one of the most common mechanisms used within a large social group. A few people give the orders, and the larger number do the work. Its nature is not *necessarily* oppressive. For instance, a large group of complete 'equals' will be more or less chaotic. A few will have specialised knowledge – how to build a bridge, or make an axe, or overcome some obstacle, so it is only natural for those few to show and oversee those who do not have that knowledge, but who do have the strength and energy and number to carry out the work. However, like any mechanism, it is easily corrupted. There is nothing in the universe to imply that those with special knowledge have any more value to the community than other members of that community – because none of it would work if all didn't participate. Radical theory here, eh? Beginning to sound a little like Marx.

But instead of moving into economic theory, I'm interested in taking a look at the corruption that occurs during the interaction. In a small community group, sub/dom can work as a natural form of the social matrix – you know everyone, and it gives shape and direction. Within a large group or a nation or the so-called global community, these few 'leaders' can effortlessly enhance their position to mark themselves out as special – or even irreplaceable – in order to accrue *power*. Power always seems to be naturally cumulative. To be blunt, it makes the powerful feel good, feel better about themselves. Crucially, it allows those *with* power to detach themselves from the eyes and judgement of the many. Conversely, it *increases* the burden of judgement and disapproval of those situated beneath the powerful.

IS ALICE?

It is rivetingly interesting to me that the majority of people, however intelligent, feel deeply uncomfortable talking about this subject. They're not willing to admit their existential participation in social status. I'm not sure how you stand on the matter, for a start.

This discomfort and unease people display when the subject of dominance and submission is introduced into a conversation is, I think, easily understood. This is because it is *instinctive* behaviour in all other social animals, whereas human beings are capable of self-reflection. This leaves us in a bit of a paradox, doesn't it? It's not a very attractive thought when we contemplate the necessity of our own dominant or submissive displays. Dominant is considered more positive, while submissive is presumed to be negative. In fact the two are so perfectly linked they cannot be separated into two categories. Instead, it is wiser to perceive some dominant/submissive behaviour as *positive*, while some is *negative*. Once you get the hang of it, veils drop away, and we can see examples of this behaviour every day and everywhere. Furthermore we *must* have this mechanism in order to survive as a large social group. The discomfort is caused as we realise we are participants as well as observers. On the whole, we would rather *not* think about it. In other words, it is best left as instinct.

Except it's not. Without viewing this vital instinct in the structure of our own lives, it is absolutely impossible to grasp the implications of the social matrix. As for the social matrix itself, it is crucial for me to understand it for two reasons. When it dysfunctions it may lead to serious problems of 'mental health' – Alice's situation – and if I don't understand it, I have no way of helping her. Naturally, it is also a way of helping myself – my own problems of being-in-the-world. More simply, it's partly me and partly the Other. In a broader, more profound sense, if we don't expose the nature of the social matrix and show that its shape and purpose are in our potential control, we are possibly doomed by its excesses and corruption.

Everyone in the social order must have skills in both dominant and submissive modes. There is no such thing as an alpha male who is completely dominant. If anyone tried to be, he would be subdued by numbers of others around him, whether they be policemen or neighbours. Kids learn this growing up, and it's probably one of the most difficult 'instincts' to acquire. They fight, they taunt, they exclude or torment, and experiment with group pressure to change individual behaviour. Alliances are formed and dissolved. Lying, deviousness, trust, bonding, betrayal, revenge, competition — all crackle electrically on the playgrounds, in families and schools. Anyone who tries to display continuous dominance is soon overwhelmed or taught a few lessons. A bully will eventually find someone stronger or more psychopathic, either singly or in groups. Then they themselves must discover forms of submission – in order to survive.

Submission takes all kinds of forms, too. Politeness is probably the most common, and many soon discover that giving way in many cases is a better way of moving their interests forward. Perpetual confrontation is a sure way to failure. Every human being should develop ease in the equal use of dominance and submission – though, of course, so many don't. Again, it is a whole concept, not two separate ones. Some people understand this and use it well. A few actually manipulate the mechanism creatively.

It is precisely because it is such a major feature in our social lives that dominance and submission can also be so easily adapted to sexual play. It's a little like nuclear fission, bringing two emotionally charged particles together with a bang. Sub-dom plays a huge role in sexual matters anyway. In heterosexual courtship, males display submissive behaviour, and it's up to the female to give a thumbs-up or thumbs-down before intercourse can occur. However, once that initial barrier is overcome, the male usually struggles for the dominant position of the pair. It is probably why the female normally guards her favours before choosing a man. And why shouldn't she be picky? She's quite aware her power will diminish almost from the moment she makes herself sexually available; at the very least it will be challenged. Naturally this is not a 'rational' process, but it is without doubt a social sub-dom engagement.

This is the main reason why it's so common for the male to want the female to play the dominant role sexually. It highlights the most exciting and stimulating features of a pre-intercourse relationship. The male is driven half-mad with desire, and the female uses this as a powerful fuel to spray into the engine of control. Dominance can be as exciting an experience as submission, because the changes in polarity give deeper insight into the phenomenon. Both are equally sexy, providing the couple play well together.

Within the social matrix in the common sense world submission is achieved by offering reward or punishment. This is the thread that holds the fabric together. If we work, we get paid; if we don't work, we suffer deprivation. If we work well, we get paid more, and if we don't work well, we're fired. We begin learning this principle as children, and it is heavily reinforced in schools. Rebellion is dealt with more easily than we think when we are rebels. Punishment operates on a scale that increases the pressures in direct proportion to the insurgency. Disapproval is followed by exclusion, which leads to financial retribution. If the rebel indulges in anything illegal, such as theft or drug dealing, physical force soon follows. The police visit. If they are resisted, you are beaten or shot and shackled, then imprisoned and given an indelible 'reputation' that trails after you in the form of official paperwork branding you as an undesirable criminal.

It becomes increasingly clear that the social matrix instinctively understands the mechanisms that make it work. These are then used by certain interests to herd us like so many cattle along a predestined path towards a life we must then dedicate to these interests.

Let me recapitulate briefly. We are born into a world that is totally gratuitous, and we have no choice in that matter. More accurately, *the 'world' is born into our growing consciousness*. Its form, shape and meaning are embedded as the *only* form, the *only* shape and *only* meaning. Of course there are variations, but they are minor. This is the REAL WORLD. There is no question. We are encouraged to trust it, and trust is the keystone in the arch of belief. Belief resolves into one reality and wholly supports it. Later we may ask questions about it, but questioning does not undermine the solidity of this belief. Quantum physics may reveal that the 'world' is merely an unknown set of *possibilities*, but, nevertheless, we continue to sit in the chair with complete confidence that it will continue to hold us (except people like Alice, but I will gradually come to that later).

We are social animals, hence this world that is born into us is manipulated by forces only a very few of us understand. We are informed of the goals of this world and its parameters, its values, limitations, ethics, morals and mores. Included in the gift is also our sense of time and how we 'move' through it. The past (which is solid only through our memories) is a series of selected features that appear unchangeable. The future can be and is influenced by our actions. We are expected to fulfil individual roles in what is actually a fluid social matrix without a murmur of dissent. Dissent is already categorised as rebellion and can be dealt with conventionally and with ease. Mechanisms are pressed into our being as successfully as views about the solidity of the 'world.' Finally, those whose interests are served by the structure and direction of this matrix compel us along a monochrome corridor – namely to a life to be spent in the service of those interests and no other, convinced that we are 'choosing' what we do.

There is only one word for this. Slavery. And this is the only conclusion: those who blindly follow the yellow brick road will never find the Wizard of Oz, nor will they have the faintest idea of enlightenment – or, to use a simpler term, freedom. They are simply commodities to be exploited until they stagger into the twilight of old age and death. A different grade of domestic animal. In fact, slavery has never been abolished. It has simply grown into more sophisticated – and crueller – forms. Yet this particular world traps the masters as well as the slaves.

Observe how things feed back in circular patterns to our psyches. The very concept of slavery is sexually enticing. It's an archetype that triggers a powerful undertow pulling us relentlessly towards a hypnotic pool of fornicating demons at the depths of consciousness, in its inner story-factory. To be owned by someone, to be punished or rewarded, to have one's will usurped, to be violated on a whim by your owner, to be reduced to a chattel. Do you see the reverberations with the 'world'? The implicit is made explicit with sexuality introduced as an irrefutable lure. If you are master, then the woman is there for your whim and pleasure whenever you wish – just like the advertisements so often tell you. She is an object, no longer a subject. She can be made to dress to please you, available at all times. She can be forced to work in your kitchen, cooking and washing your dishes and floors while you amuse yourself elsewhere. Want some nookie? Just go lift her skirt and bend her over. Available, yours, a chattel, an ornament. Oral sex? Force her to her knees and unzip your trousers.

Or reverse the roles. She is mistress, *you* are the slave. This can have extra zing. She becomes unattainable, just like the models on the covers of magazines, or the movie star, or the girl with the micro-mini in the queue at the

IS ALICE?

Underground. *You* can do the dishes, wash floors or give sexual satisfaction on *her* impulse. As your mistress, she becomes the ultimate object – of your adoration, your unconsummated desire. Your degradation is her delight *and* yours. You are abused, treated *as if* you were a female *by* a female. She is using her one social commodity to ensnare you, but it is with little doubt a very powerful one. If sub/dom has such a powerful sexual manifestation, the social matrix is the obvious overwhelming paradigm.

Naturally *real* slavery is not at all nice. You work for someone else for their profit, and in most cases that work is unrewarding. Even if you own the business, your bank makes a profit, and others profit from the bank. Alyosha, I have spoken to several friends about these ideas, and they dismiss the concept of slavery and sub/dom with airy waves of the hand. You and I are lucky because we 'work' at something we love. Music and writing. Few have this privilege. Most are employed or self-employed within a machine. The bulk of their lives will be taken up working at jobs they do not like. Even if the wages are extremely high, they never 'free' you from the jobs you do. I ask my friends to go ahead and prove they are not slaves. Stop what you're doing and do what you like. The crack of the whip soon follows in the form of financial and social retribution, as you possibly lose your home, your family, your friends, and your ability to move around. Debt collection agencies take all your possessions. Perhaps you will receive benefits from the government for a while, but soon they will want you to seek another job. My mother worked till she was over 70 and hated her life, because she knew at heart she was an artist. I stood over her grave and promised myself and her remains that I would seek another kind of world.

I'm not making a political point at this time. I will later. I'm trying now to map out the sinews of the social matrix and how they weave their patterns into our emotional framework. The microcosm of my relationship with Alice expanded to the macrocosm of the world as I followed the faint marks in the sand that indicated the vast pyramids sunk out of sight with time but still vibrant with design and meaning.

Alice and I developed the rules of our play slowly, mainly by trial and error. As I have mentioned, this is a form of tantric sex, with orgasm delayed for hours, days, weeks or even months.

Though I sort of doubt it, this may bring blushes to your cheeks. But the intensity of the sexual contact increased to the point where both of us were jolted into... what? What is the word, the expression that will transmit the truth? I believe there is no exact word, because what we came to experience was never exact, unlike common sense experience that can be rationally parcelled into language that transmits factual information. Furthermore, the states were never constant or predictable. In texture these moments were similar to those I had when I was in a trance or on the point of a vision or Satori. A porthole. An opening. An aperture. Our consciousnesses touched and interacted. I experienced *something* of her. She felt *something* of me.

Let me hasten to remind you that we were and are deeply in love with each other. With some surprise, we found our experiments were enriching one of the most profound emotional states I've ever experienced. Of course we would not maintain the tantric configuration all the time – but it had a way of seeping into our daily experiences. We could feel the presence of each other, as if we were touching. At times we were almost two auras, not two people. Much of the week we would just talk. When she was vulnerable, I would help guide her to more solid ground. Increasingly we discussed her mental problems in the light of my emerging ideas on consciousness and the social matrix. She had been in psychotherapy for many years, but finally realised it was giving her little insight. One day, after an argument with her therapist over *money*, she decided she'd had enough of it. The two of us were alone on the raft then. The questing lovers, clasped together, on a journey without a compass.

Shit! I've just put down the telephone − I received a call telling me that Alice has escaped from the hospital. I couldn't lever much information from the nurse, so I'm going to have to leave you to try and find out what the hell happened.

Much later.

I'm getting a little better as I practise my methods of detachment. Before I raced up to the hospital on my bicycle, I forced myself to sit straight in a chair with my head finding its best position for balance. I concentrated first on my breathing, until my churning emotions began to cool and calm. I visualised the indifference and mendacity of the staff, and told myself that it was nothing personal. They were trapped in a system that offers oppression in the guise of help. They are paid too little to do too much and are trained to give automatic responses to human problems.

Then – and only then – did I leave.

Pan Subarti, the senior psychiatric nurse, was on duty. He's not a bad man, and I certainly don't dislike him, despite our clashes during my admission there. He's one of the people you meet who is just 'doing his job.' These days he is quite friendly. He was sitting at his desk when I came in. He closed the door and waved me to a chair, before telling me that Alice managed to get out of the hospital for a little while earlier that day. When? In the morning, just before noon, through an emergency door that had been accidentally left open. She walked down to the Sutcliff General Hospital. Someone there called the Skinner Memorial Unit, and she was picked up. How long was she out? Just over an hour.

I sat listening calmly to his fluent explanation. I caught his eyes, smiled and nodded, asked a few questions and decided he was lying. After we finished talking, I thanked him and said I was going to have a cup of tea in the TV room, just in case Alice would see me. It was a little lie of my own. I knew Alice would not be there – or if she was, she would leave the moment she saw me.

There were three inmates sitting in the TV room, and, luckily, one of them was Rob. I knew Rob well. He felt there was something special about me, and he always wanted to talk about his problems, as if I could help him in his pursuit of justice. At times he was quite articulate.

IS ALICE?

As soon as I walked into the room, he left his chair and came over to me, hand extended.

"Theo. Theo. I'm glad you could come…"

"Cup of tea, Rob?" I asked as I moved towards the kettle.

"No, no, no. Too much tea. Too much."

Rob is a burly man in his late 30s, not bad looking. He wore a beard, and his eyes hunted my face for meanings. He grabbed my arm as I put the kettle on.

"Have you talked to the doctor?" he asked urgently.

I smiled, looking for a clean mug. "No, not yet. He's not around every day."

"Yes! Right! I know! That's the point. I can never see him. He comes, he goes, he talks to everyone in the hospital but me. I've got to tell him that I need to get out of here. I can't stand it. I can't stand these people, the nurses won't listen to me. I've even tried to call my MP. Could you call him for me? Would you? You're a big man. *You* got out, right? If you can do it, I can do it, right? All they do is feed me drugs I don't want. I complain, no use. I've read all the books here, I don't watch TV, what am I supposed to do? Talk to the crazy people?"

I poured hot water onto the tea bag while I listened, fetched it out, then poured in some milk. "Let's sit down and talk about it, Rob. I'll try to help you if I can, but basically, they won't listen to me any more than they listen to you. Have you talked to your advocate?"

Rob joined me on one of the plastic folding chairs. "Ah, she never helps."

"Then try the solicitors. Alice uses them."

He grabbed my arm again. His grip was powerful. "Alice. You know, she got away today. Ran out the emergency door. I saw her. Whoosh. Gone."

"They told me," I said as I sipped the hot tea. "They said she was gone for about an hour."

Rob threw back his head and roared with laughter. "She did better than that! No, Alice is good, she is. No, she was gone all afternoon. The whole afternoon. Got away this morning about ten o'clock. Got back about five."

I hid my anger. "Was she able to tell you where she went, what happened?"

He still held my arm and pulled close to my ear. "Alice thinks I'm her guru. Follows me around. Pisses me off. Guru. Ha."

"It's because you've got a beard."

The thought seemed to strike him unexpectedly. He let go my arm and touched his beard, as if he had forgotten he wore one. "Yeah, gurus wear beards, that's right. You're a leader, aren't you?"

IS ALICE?

"I couldn't lead a blind man to the toilet."

"Are you in charge here?"

I shook my head gently. "No, but I'd make some changes if I were."

Rob thrust his head forward. "I *know* you would. I *know*. That's why I'm talking to you. I want some changes…"

"Did Alice tell you what happened today? Where she went?"

He leaned back in his chair suddenly and threw his arms back. "Oh, she got on a bus. Went to Hampstead. Down to Archway, South End Green, walked all around, wet from the rain, soaked, shivering. Don't know how she got back. Ambulance, I think. Or maybe the bus…"

"She was out for seven hours?" I asked quietly.

"Dunno, maybe… five, six, seven, what's it matter anyway?"

So there's the ultimate irony, Alyosha. I get lies from the asylum and truth from the inmates. Furthermore, I *trust* the inmates more than the staff. They may be crazy, but they're not dishonest. Alice was absent from the hospital for several hours. She could have easily thrown herself under a bus. I won't be able to find out where she really went and what really happened until she's sane again.

Sane? Is it really sanity we're talking about here? I didn't bother confronting Pan Subarti before I left. If he will tell me one lie, he will tell me more – probably with even deeper sincerity. Also I know it's institutional, not personal. *It's the way things are*. I have learned to act as if I'm living in a foreign environment, not really knowing the language very well. Irony again – this is what Alice feels when she's ill. So what is normality? Like her, I listen mostly. Yes, I *know* what it feels like to be in 'that world,' because I've lived in it so long. I can move about seamlessly, make jokes, even feel comfortable. As a matter of fact, I've only really felt comfortable since I realised it is a *false* world. Paradoxes tumble over enigmas like drunken clowns. Let me give you another example. Last week I had a meeting with Alice's psychiatrist, Harold Pincer. Now, again, he is not a *bad* person. Under his own lights, he's doing his best in a system he thinks he understands.

I asked him what drugs Alice was receiving. Basically he told me she was taking an anti-psychotic, an anti-depressant and lithium. The doses were increased or decreased weekly or monthly like calibrating knobs on an electronic machine. They would increase one, decrease the other, increase both, lower both, raise another one.

"Why are you giving her an anti-depressant? She's not primarily depressed. She's highly anxious."

Pincer smiled at me. He has institutionally thin lips and sparse hair. No doctor is reassuringly fat these days. "We believe she *is* depressed."

IS ALICE?

Argument is useless. "Alice has been hospitalised for more than two months now. Would you consider changing her medication? Just as an experiment?"

Pincer looked at me blankly and did not answer.

"Whatever it is that happens to her," I continued in a friendly manner, "it involves her entire body, her whole being. When she is well but going through a vulnerable phase, a little unsteady, her whole body tenses, even her vocal chords. Her solar plexus nerve centre throbs…"

"How do you know that?" he interrupted.

I opened my hands. "She tells me it does. I massage it for her, just under her breastbone, with my knuckles and the heel of my hand – a lot of pressure is needed. It's clear this increased agitation somehow fuels her chaotic thoughts. Or perhaps one feeds off the other. Look, I'm honestly not trying to be presumptuous here. I know you are the doctor and must know much about your subject, but, on the other hand, I spend an awful lot of time with Alice. We talk hours about her symptoms, what helps, what doesn't help…"

Pincer smiled condescendingly. "We all realise you are an industrious and intelligent carer…"

"A loving one, too," I added.

"And a loving one," he conceded.

"I also know her very well. As well as any human being knows any other one. What I'm suggesting is that you give her a trial, one that can't do her any harm. Just for two weeks, say. Give her a muscle relaxant during the day and a sleeping tablet at nights. Make them required medication, because otherwise she will refuse to take them. You know why?"

His fixed smile was even more patronising. He remained silent.

"Because she *knows* they will calm her, and what she seeks in her psychosis is energy, lots of it. She forces herself to stay awake continuously to evoke her dreaming states, and only sleeps for a couple of hours when she has to. It's to prevent her slipping back into what she thinks is the 'wrong' world. Rest and relaxation. Sleep. Those would be the best doctors in the world for her. I'm convinced she would come round in much quicker time."

"Mr Hawthorn. Perhaps you are not aware that diazepam is an addictive drug."

"So are the anti-psychotics. So are the anti-depressants. If she ever comes off those, it will have to be slowly, as you know."

"She should *never* come off her anti-psychotic," he replied curtly. "I think we shall continue with our current course. Alice does seem to be responding, slowly."

"She is not responding at all. She is getting worse."

IS ALICE?

It was as far as I would go with the argument. I knew it was fruitless from the beginning, but I thought there might just be a chance that I could charm my way through it. Please do me a favour and read through the above dialogue again, Alyosha, this time looking for the meaning.

We were two human beings discussing the distressing state of another human being. Although he has a degree in medicine, I do not concede either that he is more intelligent or knows Alice any better than I do. I make a suggestion that I know will help her, but he will not even consider it – not because it is a bad suggestion but because of the impossibility created by our differing status in his common sense world. By social definition, in his mind he is dominant, I am submissive. At the very least he must know my 'treatment' would give Alice some respite from her agony, a little relief. Perhaps it wouldn't 'cure' her. But it would certainly present some possibility of a 'cure.' In no way would it harm her. For me, this is true lunacy and another fundamental *lie*. He is lying to me because he is proceeding down a well-worn clinical path he has been taught to believe is the correct one, and he is unwilling (or unable) to consider an honest alternative, even though that alternative might work better than the clinical model he believes in. In order to conduct a trial with my idea, it would be necessary for him to question the false value he is placing on his status, on mine and on the world around him.

Frankly – and not at all judgementally – it is *demented*. This is not an honest world. It never has been.]*

CHAPTER ELEVEN

Hawthorn pushed open the side door of the Drum & Monkey and went to the bar. He noticed with pleasure that Liam was serving. He was a short, stocky Irishman with a quick wit and lantern jaw.

"A pint of Guinness," Hawthorn said quietly. "And make it quick, you thick bugger. I'm thirsty."

"You want it quick?" he asked without a beat. "I'll dip out the slops for you."

He already had a pint glass under the Guinness spout. It always took about five minutes to pour a good pint, and Liam took his time.

"Sorry to hear the bad news about O'Reilly" Hawthorn muttered as Liam lifted one eyebrow. "He must have been one of your only friends."

"And what would you be talking about?"

"I heard you and your mate had to go along to the morgue to identify him. Asked the mortician to turn him over. You said, no, that's not him, 'cause he had two arseholes."

Liam grimaced and looked away with feigned disgust.

"Yeah," Hawthorn continued in a cod Irish accent. "You said every time the three of you walked down the street, people said, 'There's O'Reilly with the two arseholes.'"

"Old joke," Liam said. "I always count on you for the old jokes."

"Isn't that Guinness ready now?"

"You want it now? I'll give it to you now." He had already turned off the tap to let the beer settle before continuing.

"How's Alice?" he asked.

"Same," Hawthorn replied.

"Send her my best wishes."

"She wouldn't understand them. I'll tell her when she wakes up."

"A terrible thing," Liam said as he placed the perfect pint of Guinness in front of him. "That'll be two pounds seventeen shillings."

Hawthorn looked in his pocket change and counted out two pounds eighty-five pence. "There, that surprised you, right? I arrived here two months before decimalisation."

"Ah," he said, scooping up the money, "back in the days of civilisation. Before all the 'reform'."

Real Guinness was so much better than the stuff in the cans, and Hawthorn enjoyed his first sip before lighting his pipe. He had just posted off his latest instalment to

Cherkasov, and had decided to stop for a pint. He glanced over at a young couple sitting at one of the tables. The girl was rather pretty, and wore a crop top with low-cut jeans. Her bare, warm flesh looked edible. When he turned away he realised with a sigh how lonely he was. Or was 'lonely' the right word? It wasn't. What he wanted was a woman in his arms. Almost any woman would do at the moment, but he really yearned for Alice. He had caught sight of her earlier in the day when he took a carton of cigarettes up to the hospital. He also carried a few pastries from a Jewish baker, even though he was certain she would throw – or give them – away. Gratuitous acts that have no meaning from one world to another. And no reasons for them, either. Shit, he supposed the pastries were really for him – something *he* could do to feel a little better about himself by the inner assurance that, at least, he was doing *something*. When he saw her, she abruptly turned down a corridor and hurried away. She had lost weight and was looking haggard. The circles under her eyes pulled her face downward. He watched forlornly as she walked briskly away from him, holding her nearly-shaven head up and steady, her body transmitting determination. There was something reminiscent of her father's walk – open palms paddling backwards, short, quick footsteps. Then she was gone.

Sadly, he had to admit to himself that he was not attracted to *that* Alice. It was no good having the body in one world and the mind in another. Whatever his theories, he knew that she had configured herself into another universe. When he had the chance to look into her eyes, he recognised instantly that she was '*not* here.' It was mistaken to call it a false world, because it was evidently true enough for her to completely commit herself to it morning and night.

What he missed most at that moment was the join, the contact they made, the tentative union and the undulating trust. Without that, she was simply *different*. Not attractive, not sexy. And no, he didn't want her with him when she was ill. Every moment they were together throbbed with tragedy – for him and, no doubt, for her as well. It would be easier to reach across the galaxy than to touch her now. Yet he was obsessively interested in her *problem*. Because it nudged the extreme fundaments of existence. To question her world was to question his own. If he could only understand *his*, he could more easily comprehend *hers*. It drove him back again and again to the blackboard to wipe out what he had written in chalk so he could try again.

For instance – he was guiltily convinced he was partly responsible for her illness this time. The painful incident outside the Albert Hall was only the catalyst. He recalled one of many conversations they had about her strategy to overcome her demons.

"I think," he said, "that it might be an idea to try and bring the two worlds together somehow."

"What do you mean?" She was lying naked in the bed beside him. It was a Sunday, and they had spent the afternoon in seething clouds of sexual desire. She was smoking a cigarette. His head was propped up on a pillow, a pipe clamped between his teeth.

He thought for a moment. "Part of the equation is fear," he said finally.

"Terror," she corrected him. "I'm literally scared shitless. Every minute."

"But it's a world you create in your head," he replied. "Just like this one. It's real. You are the creator, and you are responsible for it. Sometimes when I wake up in the middle of a nightmare, instead of going straight back to sleep, I 'interfere' in the story of the bad dream. I force myself to go over it again, but this time I carry a machine gun… or something. I have power, in other words. Then I mow down the opponents who were tormenting or torturing me. I triumph, instead of them. Then, when I go back to sleep, I *never* return to that nightmare. I resolved it in a different way. Victory instead of failure. Resolution instead of frustration."

She rolled over and put her arm lovingly around him, her head on his chest. He enjoyed the feel of her breast against him. "It scares me a little. It might be dangerous. You see, I get to a precipice, and I'm OK. Then, suddenly, I plummet like a stone. Once I start falling, I can't stop myself…"

"Like vertigo," he said. "Drawn to the edge, mesmerised by the danger…"

"That's it! Exactly!"

Hawthorn hugged her close to him. "What would happen if you crept up to the edge carefully, then *imagined* the plunge, but, before you're drawn in, you give yourself strength, try and extract the fear. Or change it to courage."

"I can't. I *can't!*" She gripped him hard, burying her face. "I can't explain. It's just too compelling. One glimpse and change takes place. Somehow. I change. One instant I'm one thing, the next, I'm something else."

"But it's *you* doing it," Hawthorn insisted. "If it's *you*, then *you* have the power to alter the values, re-set the dials, re-adjust the focus."

She raised her head and looked into his eyes lovingly. "So you think I should try?"

"What do you have to lose?"

"My sanity. Oh, Theo. *I don't want to be ill again*! I'll lose you. I know I will. I don't want to be away from you for a minute. Then I'll be in the bin again for months. *Months*! Torn in pieces by terror."

"You won't lose me. You can't, even if you tried. If we fail, then I'll be there. Always. For you. For me.

The Guinness was half gone, and he always had just one pint before going back to his flat. His pipe was cold, and, anyway, he was tired of the taste of it. He put it away in his pocket. He should have thought more carefully about his own responsibility when failure could be such a disaster. She trusted him. She trusted his intellect. To be given someone's trust is a precious thing, *never* to be betrayed. At that moment it looked a lot like that. Betrayal. Of a warm, soft, wonderful, gentle woman who would never betray *him*, even if threatened with sharp swords or hordes of stampeding devils. With a gesture of arrogance, he may well have initiated her drift towards the precipice, encouraged her to take a chance. On the basis of *his* ideas.

Now of course it all seemed ridiculous. It had been insane to suggest 'trying to bring the two worlds together.' No. It was now clear the nightmare must be slowly shrunk, deprived of sustenance, starved, its oxygen cut off. How? It was beyond his knowledge. But bring them together? *NO!* Stupid! Criminal! How dare he experiment with such danger and expose his beloved to the suppurating sulphurs of hell?

He drank again, then shook his head violently. Liam was busy on the other side of the bar with several new customers. He wished he would come back to engage in a little banter to take his mind off his awful vision. Then he became aware that he was making similar mistakes with himself. His hands were clasped on the sharp guilt shovel, and he was busy digging at his loneliness, eager to transform misery into depression. And that would help no one – not him, not Alice... Whatever the consequences of his mistake, he mustn't use it as a lash. When your ship is in a storm, face towards the wind. Seek balance, seek to be wiser next time. Remember consequences – note them and move on. Try to be stronger when Alice flickers to life again.

He finished the rest of his drink, waved to Liam, and opened the door. When he stepped out, it was already twilight. Nights were getting longer and longer now, he thought, as he became aware of the three young men approaching him. Two of them were wearing hoods. All were black, and the one without a hood was staring at him. He held the man's eyes as he moved his balance onto the balls of his feet. He was alert now.

No-hood stopped in front of him. "Got a match?"

One of the hoods moved to his side, while the other placed himself behind his back. A stream of thoughts fizzed through him at lightening speed. *Standing on left foot, left-side* osoto-gari, *hand under his chin, drive head backwards, reap left leg, smash head on pavement, keep balance, turn, ready for others, keep moving, watch every flicker, attack if hands go to pockets...* Instantly the thoughts evaporated. His body was relaxed but receptive, and his mind cleared. It had taken only a split-second.

He still held No-hood's eyes as he took a step closer to the man.

"Have I got a match?" he repeated softly, confidentially, directly in No-hood's face. "I haven't had a match since Shakespeare."

Hawthorn broke into an easy smile, and No-hood returned the smile reflexively.

"That's good, man," No-hood said after thinking for a moment. "I haven't heard that one before. Cool..."

"Mind how you go," Hawthorn warned as he stepped past No-hood. "The streets around here are full of thieves."

He heard the three black men laughing as they walked on up the hill. He didn't turn back to look at them, just walked on naturally. Instantly he felt as elated as an expert swordsman who had disarmed his opponent with a swift flick of his blade. The three thugs would have to find someone else to mug that evening.

By the time he reached his flat he had started to chuckle at the situation, even allowing himself to feel a little pride. He threw some ice into a tumbler and poured himself a whisky, before going to his front room to sit on the sofa. He pulled out his pipe and lit it as he waited for his Scotch to get cold.

First of all, he thought, it was good judo. He was completely amazed that he managed to divert his first instinct of violence. The uncertainties unfolded in multiple possibilities. If he had thrown No-hood, there was a chance he would have killed him outright, because he would have had to attack at full-tilt. If the other two hadn't then fled, he would have had only an even chance of taking them both. If there were knives, he may have been cut. In any case there would have been ambulances and police, hours of explanation and, possibly, pain. Of course, the other two men would most probably have run, but he couldn't be certain of that. Anyway, he had no wish to injure, never mind kill, a fellow man, mugger or no mugger.

Good judo was not being able to throw 20 men in the air, then break every bone in their bodies. Judo was not even self-defence. It was *a state of mind*. Finally, after all these years, he seemed to have learned the one lesson that eludes many judoka. The words of his old teacher instantly reverberated like echoes. "If you have to fight, you lose." And he would have lost, even if he had beaten all three men with perfect technique – flip, flip, flip, *finish*. He would have lost time afterwards dealing with the authorities, naturally. But most importantly, he would have lost his equilibrium and his footing on the path towards enlightenment – the path that still wound ahead as far as he could see into the distant hills. The inspiration for the correct action came from nowhere. One instant he was ready to act, the next he found the right words on his lips.

Of course those weren't the only words that would have worked. There were probably an infinite number, combined with an infinite number of attitudes. How then do you find access to these secrets? Perhaps it was through the Tao. It was necessary to trust that access would be granted at the exact moment it was needed.

Hawthorn swirled the ice and whisky before taking a sip. It was completely dark outside now, and he could see lights in the windows opposite. Passing through one portal leads to another view. Being is transformed by the unexpected. A bit more of the social matrix became clear. He had successfully manipulated its vapours by instantly stepping outside its expectations and definitions. His three opponents had executed an act of intimidation that works in nearly all cases. People will automatically respond with fear or anger, submission or aggression – all of which the three men were prepared for. But step away from those emotional responses, and you step out of the frame. Literally. *You change the world.* It was that profound. Others aren't in charge of the world. You are. Causal explanations only work for causal events, and causal events arise in a causal world.

Abruptly he reined in his bubbling elation. What happened that evening did not mean he had reached any goal. It was not the end of the rainbow, but maybe the beginning of another one. The portal opened, and he stepped through, only to find that there were more portals to seek.

On the other hand, it took him a few more paces along the path, and for that, he raised his glass in an imaginary toast to the invisible forces he had yet to understand. In the pub he turned away from the downward spiral, thus affirming his existence and leaving himself open to harmony. What if... he had allowed his descent into depression at that moment? Between one and four men could now be lying on the pavement dying from their wounds. This was extreme mystery. Yet he could not say it was completely mysterious any more. It was simply up to him to continue to create the conditions for *things to happen*. It was the ultimate in human freedom, and he was struck by the awesomeness of the thought. A clear mind was necessary, along with a focus on intent. He was aware of the matrix now, and partly knew how it worked, therefore his intention must centre on observing it as if it were a complicated machine – which in fact it was – that could nevertheless be manipulated. He had become an *actor* after all these years in the theatre. Transmit the signs to achieve his character. At the same time – this was the most difficult part – he must try and find his way to a reality more congruent with the nature of the universe he could not yet see.

IS ALICE?

His thoughts returned to the encounter outside the pub. There was more meat to pick off the bones. It was with absolute glee that he realised that, because of his response, No-hood and his mates *could never* respond to his gambit with violence. That was the dynamic truth. Thugs they might be, but they were *prevented* from acting within *their* intent! No-hood could not pull his knife, if he had one. He could not strike out at him or even threaten him. The thought was so clean and clear. Looking at it from a peripheral angle, No-hood became his momentary slave, because Hawthorn summoned the power to define himself as a non-victim. In that instant, he could guide his assailant to carry out *his* wishes. That is, to share a humorous moment that broke open the cage normally tethering all human participants in the same plane. No-hood and his friends would not even have felt deprived or unrewarded. They continued on in their quest that evening as if something mildly nice had happened. Unless he was badly mistaken, they wouldn't be remotely aware of how they had been manipulated.

What entranced Hawthorn was the complete simplicity of the lesson. But there were no clues on how to consolidate his knowledge or make it more his own. He glanced at his watch. It was already past 11, and he was addicted to his routine. Time to go to bed and drink his whisky, as he read through the daily newspaper with constant amusement that people could call it 'news.' No, it was gossip-reinforcement, adding another coat of invisible varnish to the many layers that separated readers from reality.

He knocked out his pipe. It was cool enough to pull apart and clean. He reached for a pipe cleaner, and his mind turned back to judo. Perhaps he could try and practise this simplicity with his more experienced partner, Tim O'Grady, who was younger and one dan grade above him. But that didn't matter, because those were values determined elsewhere, not within his own being. He liked Tim a lot, and learned much from his superb judo. If, however, he aimed for more clarity, more simplicity, he might learn something else that could circulate back into his fundamental attitude. It was so difficult to get away from concepts like 'defeating' his partner or 'winning' encounters or 'earning' praise. He automatically thought of Tim as being better than he was, a stronger player. He resolved to try and find a way of stepping outside *that* frame. No one on this earth was 'better' than any other person. It was another phoney category.

* * *

Princess Elena was lying languidly on her side as the girl behind the chaise brushed her long, straight black hair slowly and carefully. Elena was propped up on cushions, and held her head in her hand as she was groomed. The gown she wore was white silk and covered her body, except for her arms and bare feet. The feet were soft and tiny, slightly flushed with pink.

I was a long way across the vaulted room as I replaced yesterday's water in the large basin with fresh water from the spring. I had seen the Princess fleetingly once or twice before, and practised keeping my eyes away from her gaze. It wasn't simply that she was beautiful. There was something else. There was a lurch in the distant tempest of my being. I felt it was probably dangerous. I had not been attached to her household for long, nor had I been a slave before. I was unaccustomed to the role, and determined somehow to earn my freedom. I was captured fairly in battle, and I fought well. I killed eight men before I was wounded in the leg, so I have honour, even as a slave. I was offered the choice of being a soldier for the victors, but I declined. I don't like battle, and see meaning only in fighting for my own city.

After emptying the basin, I re-filled it carefully from the earthenware jug. From a fold in my tunic I took a few lavender flowers and floated them on the surface. Then I picked up the jug and easily lifted it onto my shoulder. I had taken only a few steps when her voice almost caused me to drop it.

"You."

The voice wasn't loud, but there was sharpness in it that made it echo in the huge space. Despite that, though, it was a lovely sound. There were other slaves in the room, but I instinctively knew she was calling me. I turned in her direction and, even at that distance, I could see her eyes directly upon me, and I quickly dropped my gaze to the floor.

"Come over here."

As I walked slowly towards the chaise, I felt myself trembling. The marble was cold on the soles of my feet. This was something I was trying to avoid – being noticed by the Princess. You quickly learn that power is dangerous. It is risky. It can make you a free man or, equally, take your life. Not a choice I craved to make so soon in my captivity.

I stopped before Princess Elena.

"Put down the jar," she said quietly.

I obeyed, my eyes lowered to the gilded leg of the chaise. There followed a long silence, and by then my mind, as well as my pulse, was racing.

"Look into my eyes," she said, almost in a whisper.

Her eyes were like dark opals set in smooth, faultless skin, framed by long, silky dark hair still being carefully brushed by the slave girl. The moisture in my mouth evaporated too quickly, and left my tongue sticking to my hard palate.

"I know you," she said.

I realised her lips were wide and voluptuous, not at all cruel. There was now a blush on her cheeks to match the redness of her lips.

"How do I know you?" she said, cocking her head slightly.

"I don't know, Princess Elena," I replied softly.

"Are you a new boy?"

"Yes, Princess Elena."

IS ALICE?

"From?"

I told her the name of my city, that I was a soldier, wounded in battle, recently purchased by her household.

She glanced at the jagged red scar below my knee before capturing my eyes again with hers. I concentrated on my breathing, a thing my teacher had taught me. Yet I realised I was drawn to this woman like none other I'd ever met. I dared not let my gaze drift to the contours of her body.

Suddenly she smiled, revealing beautiful teeth, then held up her hand, motioning me forward.

"Come closer," she said. "Here. In front of me."

I stopped barely inches from the chaise, and she reached over to touch the scar. Involuntarily I jumped.

She looked up, an eyebrow raised. "Does it hurt?"

"No, Princess Elena. Not at all. It was your touch. It was like a light sting. Or so I imagined. I apologise."

Her eyes became a little dreamy. "That's all right. I believe I felt it, too. How strange. I am sure I know you. What are you called?"

"Silenus, Princess Elena."

She had not taken her hand away, and my old wound was becoming hot. Suddenly she grasped the bottom of my tunic and raised it, exposing my sex to her gaze. I found myself completely confused and began hyperventilating. My penis was quickly becoming erect, and nothing I could do would stop it. The souls of my feet were sweaty, and I wanted desperately to move them to cooler stone. I could feel my lips trembling.

"Be still," she commanded in a quiet voice. "I very much like the look of you, Silenus, and I want you to be my personal slave. Unless I tell you differently, you will attend me from the time I arise in the mornings until I retire at nights. You will sleep at the foot of my bed."

She turned her head slightly to the girl with the brush. "Go. Tell the others to go, also."

The slave girl slid quietly away, her eyes on the floor in front of her.

The Princess dropped the hem of my tunic and put her hand firmly beneath it, gripping me. I very nearly collapsed on the floor, so weak were my knees.

"If you have an orgasm, I'll have you whipped," she murmured. "I hope you have good self-control, Silenus. I like the feel of this. As thick as my wrist. That's good. It is my wish that it be exposed only to me, at my pleasure. No other woman. I will have a belt made that will ensure your chastity. If I see or sense your eyes on one of the girls, you will be punished. Your eyes, as well as your manhood, are for me alone. Do you understand?"

I could barely speak at all. "Yes, Princess Elena."

IS ALICE?

*"You will never touch yourself, unless you are washing –
and that must be thoroughly, every day. You have
experience of women?"*

"Yes, Princess Elena."

"Of men?"

"No, Princess Elena."

"How many women, then?"

*I paused, as thoughtful as I could be in the
circumstances. My mouth was so dry that speech was
difficult. "I have not made a count," I said finally, "but
I believe the number to be more than 50..."*

*"50!" She squeezed my penis hard, then let it go. Her
laughter was natural, relaxed and gay. "Still, it doesn't
surprise me. You are a handsome boy with curly black
hair. Now, come, tuck your tunic into your belt so I can
see your erection. I don't believe I've had near 50
myself, nor do I believe there are 50 in my country that
would please me."*

*She paused for a moment while she studied my body. "I
can clearly see that I please you, Silenus. In a man, the
dick is the gauge of truth."*

*The Princess slid from the chaise, her cheeks still
flushed. When she stood, the top of her head came
nearly to my chin. She swirled her lustrous hair to one
side, reached with one hand to her shoulder, and pulled
the string of a bow. Her gown fell silently to the floor, a*

doughnut puddle of white silk around her feet. Involuntarily my eyes found her breasts, her right one almost touching my arm. They were firm and generous. Princess Elena was still a young woman.

In a single movement, she sat down and stretched her body cat-like on the cushions. She lay on her back and slowly bent one knee, as she found a strand of her hair to curl in her fingers.

"Your thoughts, Silenus." Her voice was almost a whisper.

My own was barely louder. "You are the most beautiful woman I have ever seen, Princess Elena."

Again she laughed, immediately, instantly, fully, her lips open, her head thrown back. "And how many times have you said exactly those words, you worthless satyr? 50?"

I was being bold, so I made my tone respectful. "You are right, Princess Elena. I have said it before to several. But I swear to you that you are far beyond what I once thought was beautiful. Such beauty belongs to the gods, not to mortals like me. It truly humbles me to be allowed the exquisite pleasure of letting my eyes rest on flesh that must surely be imperishable. In your being, as much as your earthly body, you are the quintessence of all things beautiful in this or any other world."

She touched her cheek with her hand as her eyes widened. "Oh. Well. This is truly a very special day in my life, I'll say. In addition to your agreeable body, you are well-spoken, like a poet. Are you a poet, Silenus?"

"No, Princess Elena. A sculptor."

"It's now no miracle that you have had more than 50. Are you sure that it's not more than 100? And could that little speech have been heard by every one of them?"

I paused, concentrating on my breathing. My eyes fell away reluctantly from her body. "I have said those words to no one, nor anything like them. They are newly minted for you, my Princess. They are the truth. I swear it. I simply regret that my words are too feeble to express the waves of awe and mystery that threaten to sweep me away from my senses. I am baffled how I remain standing...and...I..."

"Then kneel," she murmured softly. "Unless it troubles your wound."

"My wound is the furthest thing from my mind, Princess," I mumbled as I lowered myself to my knees before her.

"Are you pleased that I have chosen you to be my personal slave?"

My face was inches from her rounded thigh. "My mind is in total confusion, Princess Elena. I barely know how to speak. But I can hear nothing but choirs of joyous angels singing with the thought that I might be granted such an honour."

She giggled. "You arouse me with your speech, Selinus, and your deep voice thrills me. Will it not make you less a man to be the slave of a woman?"

I almost spluttered. "With the greatest respect, Princess Elena, I'm sure I would be the envy of the wealthiest king on earth."

There was a long pause. Finally the Princess leaned towards me and gently stroked my hair. "What omen has brought us together again?"

"Again, Princess Elena?"

"Did I say 'again'? Perhaps I did. I don't know why. Come. Lie down beside me. Press your body against mine. I crave it."

As I lowered myself onto the chaise beside her, my head was thundering. I felt nothing but the overwhelming rush of madness. There was one moment in life, and this was it. It had the feeling of eternity. Her body was warm, and I could feel a slight shudder as I pressed myself into her side and cradled her head beneath my arm. She slowly turned towards me, and her eyes locked with mine.

"Even if you have me killed this moment, Princess," I whispered, "my head severed from my body, I would die in exquisite happiness."

"Somehow, my Selinus, I can see your thoughts as if they were written on parchment. I, too, wish this could be

forever. And perhaps it shall be. Swear now that you will obey me, whatever I ask and whenever I ask it."

"I swear it, Princess Elena," I said without hesitation.

"I can feel you against me, but you will not enter me now – though both of us want it more than eternal life. You will ignore your passion with a will of iron. You will not thrust at me. You will remain passive until I..." she said with sudden emphasis, *"until I decide to envelop you, at which time I will consume you so completely that you will forever be a part of me. From this time until then, your whole body is as my own, to do with as I please..."*

I opened my mouth to answer, but she placed a delicious forefinger against my lips.

"These words I speak come from my mouth, but pass through me from elsewhere, perhaps with heaven's sorcery, I don't know. When I invited you to lie beside me, I had but one idea, that of raging passion, of riding you like a stallion until both of us fell exhausted into each other's arms. Instead, I now know we must wait. And wait. And wait again. Until some unbearable future moment when we...when we..."

"When we are ready to break open the vault of some unimaginable universe beyond our understanding, where we will find a garden to enter..." My eyes were closed now, and the words came to me as if in a trance.

"...where we can truly share an existence without limit or definition..."

"...and that garden will be the fountain head of time and space, of nature and self, of being and not-being..."

"...and, most important of all, of love beyond the reach of all who are here and now..."

"...those who toil for beauty and forfeit their gifts for worthless things, when that which is holy is within their grasp but cannot be seen by eyes blinded with anger and greed."

She wrapped her arms around me like a monkey grasping a tree, and pressed her body into mine. My penis almost bent from the force of her belly as it desperately sought the cave beneath the grassy hillock. It was only at the last moment I remembered her demand for my iron will. Twelve horses pulled me forward, and twelve horses held me back. I concentrated on my spine. Keep it rigid, keep it still. Ignore the insane, raving lust in my loins. Her body was like no other body I ever held. I felt her engorged desire throbbing in every fibre, and at the same time I inhaled the perfume of her hair as my hand explored the curve of her back and the spicy softness of her bottom. Like a desperate man hanging onto the ledge of a precipitous mountain, I reined in my devastating instinct to roll her onto her back and plunder her like a barbarian. Her bite on my neck helped restore my will, and I suddenly found her lips on mine. Her breath was hot and sweet, and I gave way completely, falling on my own back as she clambered on top with my penis trapped between her belly and mine. Her tongue was churning in my mouth as she writhed and twisted, and it seemed as if the two of us might massively explode with such force that our remains would be splattered on the walls and high ceiling of the room, the morsels of flesh too small to separate – a final and catastrophic union of our bodies and souls. She grabbed my hair with both hands and painfully held my head still, as her kisses surged onto my throat. She kissed and bit me, and I heard myself moan with such intensity that I had a glimpse of ecstasy. No, not ecstasy. Rapture. I knew then, like I knew no other thing, that I had sought for her all my life. It could not be any other way. At that moment, I heard her crying. Instantly there were tears in my own eyes, too, and I felt my heart would burst as I held her and she held me in sublime triumph.

CHAPTER TWELVE

*[Alyosha, the dream I just described was so vivid, I'm not sure whether 'dream' is the right word to use. On the one hand, it was a story, a tale – on the other, there was a kind of shimmering reality to it that I can't transmit at all. In an actual dream, the sequences are usually short or abrupt, and move from one event to another in sometimes irrational ways. But this dream was clear, free from mist. It was *me* in the dream – a form of me, a shape of me, something of me or my spirit. And here's another strange item. I had double vision. More specifically, I could see the scene as if I were a camera poised on a crane above, and, at the same time, I saw it as the character, Silenus – a classical Greek name, I think. At the end of the dream, I woke up and thought for a moment I was still there, some centuries BC, in Greece or one of the islands, maybe. It was only slowly that I realised where I was and what must have happened. I was full of joy and wonder and an inner excitement I find difficult to describe. Glancing at the clock, I saw it was 3.30am. I went to the kitchen, made a cup of tea, then sat down to write the whole experience as I remembered it. I'm sure it's almost word for word. The 'dream' did not evaporate quickly like most dreams do. It lingered. It lingers now, the evening afterwards.

There was something of Silenus that was me, and there was something of Alice in Princess Elena. Physically we were quite different, though both characters displayed reminiscent mannerisms or emotional patterns.

IS ALICE?

Now I am going to stretch your credibility threshold to the breaking point. You see, during the height of passionate scenes with Alice in the past, I have glimpsed brief moments of that same story in just that setting. I'm not making this up for effect. I've even talked with Alice about them, and she responded with surprised enthusiasm, as they reverberated with her as well. This may well sound like I'm becoming an advocate of reincarnation, but I want to veer away from definitions like that because they come with all sorts of baggage that I'd rather leave aside. Remember what I said about the social matrix. I believe it to be a false world populated by those who think it is a true one. I'm desperately trying to see beyond the shrouds, with the hope that I might be able to penetrate a reality that carries more integrity. So the fewer values I must import from the false one, the better. Trying to look at the subject creatively, I can see more possible scenarios than 'reincarnation.' However, I don't think I can avoid *spirit*. In any case, spirit is completely devalued in the common sense world with little specific meaning in general usage.

If you step out of the known world, you must try and build up a picture of your environment using only your own judgement. There are no guides and no signposts. Most tools other than intuition are useless to me. Classical Greek philosophers called it *nous* – inner knowledge. It served our distant ancestors well. If it had not worked, they would never have survived. This new – or altered – world exists in a different way from the one we are used to. So my steps are uncertain. This is a circuitous way of explaining that I can offer no final definition of spirit. I'm simply certain that it exists – not as some vapour, but as a reality.

Through the eyes of Silenus I perceived a strong essence of Alice's spirit in the form of Princess Elena. As far as I know, this is something no one else can see. Only me. It was exactly revealed to me in my Satori, and, during the years I've been with her, I can confirm her slow but steady progress towards her *spirit*. As you will see, Princess Elena is *strong*. Power is a caricature of strength. Silenus, too, is strong, even though he has no 'power' at all. It is this spirit of strength that they recognise in each other, and it is the basis of their love. Neither is it an unequal love; nor is it between Alice and me. Instead, we are reaching for another level of love, one that is outside *this* world. Does it begin to make sense now? Perhaps. I know in my heart that Alice will one day be as strong as Elena, but I also know that she needs my help. We are constantly distracted, but we always come back to the tangled pathway. It is even *possible* that our spirits restlessly search for each other over a number of lifetimes as our routes are obscured by physical death, but never quite extinguished. It occurs to me that 'lifetimes' may be misleading. I'm not so sure that time comprises a sequence of events that stretch back and stretch forward. Time, like all things, exists only in our consciousness as a value we give to a phenomenon. If we observe that phenomenon in a unique way, then it could twist, turn, spiral, overlap. At moments, 'past' and 'present' could co-exist in the same plane. As, indeed, I feel it did last night.

For any reality to exist, there must be an observer. So who was the observer in the 'dream' of Princess Elena and Silenus? Was it 'me?' Was it 'Silenus?' Who or what is it that now observes the memories of that encounter, and how do memories relate to the reality of

IS ALICE?

the actual moment? Within the social matrix, these questions have glib answers that satisfy only those who are content with that reality. For them, 'out there' includes the whole universe, a series of objects and forces whose existence does not depend on us. It is important that they see the world this way, because, essentially, it makes them powerless to change it – thus they are powerless to change the matrix in which they live. We are *here*, these are our *lives*, and we must live them out in accordance with the rules of our game. It is my purpose to crack open this banal and oppressive world.

You must have been born just after the October Revolution in Russia. I have great respect for Lenin as a thinker, but in hindsight it is not too difficult to see why the revolution was corrupted, even from the very beginning. He helped bring down the curtain on a cruel and devastating act, only to raise the curtain again on new social beginnings, using the same props and flies and the same stage. No real revolution had taken place, I'm sad to say, though it was an honourable effort that gave new hope to millions around the globe. Institutions were changed, the economy was reconstructed, land was redistributed, and new ideals were born. But the serpent was still there, not even scotched, but well-fed. A real, a true revolution will have to deal with reality itself, the worm within the social matrix. The concept of progress was and is malevolent. It is begging for a new definition.

But I digress. Or perhaps I don't. We observe the world in fragments. It's up to us to arrange them in coherent order.

I think the first time I had a glimpse of the world of Elena and Silenus was during our first real holiday together. Alice had been abroad before, but, because of the threat of illness, she never had a proper holiday. I recall how excited she was as she gathered brochures about the Greek islands. Many years before I had visited several of them, and I convinced her that Corfu was probably the best place to begin. In my view it was the most beautiful of all, despite being gnawed rotten in places by those who would destroy anything with their lust for money. We finally decided on Kalami, where Laurence Durrell had once lived. It was a small village on the north-east coast, and Alice booked everything – a villa, a motorcycle, a flight and a cab to and from the airport. We split the costs down the middle.

I had explained my love of Greece, and spoke often of the extreme beauty of the Ionian islands and how they varied from the Aegean ones. So she was a bit like a little girl before a visit to a fairground. She packed enough in her cases for a six-month trip down the Nile, even though I informed her that it wasn't exactly a primitive country – you could buy things there, if you needed them. I was ignored. There were multiple changes of clothes for two seasons, several sets of shoes and sandals, towels, flannels, lotions, books to read that were never read, tablets, pills, salves, a snorkel, flippers, several swimsuits. She started making lists months ahead of time, and everything was ticked off before we left. Her big case must have weighed as much as I did, and even then it overflowed into mine. I was a fairly experienced traveller, and tried to convince her that less was more, but to no avail.

IS ALICE?

The plane left at a hellish hour – I believe it was 6.00am, so we had to rise at about 2.00am to get the cab all the way to Gatwick. We were travelling with a tour company – a so-called package deal – because of the relative cheapness. Alice always wants everything covered, and she had even arranged insurance for repatriation in case of the remote possibility of falling ill during the holiday. These package trips are taxing on both nerves and spirit, but all the passengers on the charter flight were distributed to various parts of the island with relative efficiency. When we arrived at our villa, we were both pleased. There was a gorgeous sea view from our porch, which faced north east. After unpacking we made drinks and sat outside watching the sun slowly settle into a golden blue sea. Neither of us spoke for several minutes.

"It's paradise," Alice said finally. "It's a dream. I didn't know anything like this existed."

"I'm glad you like it," I replied with a smile. It was wonderful seeing her happy. When I first met her, I was struck by how sad she always seemed.

It was a few hours later that this idyllic setting was blown to pieces by the electronic throb of disco music so loud that it was impossible to hear each other. Just behind the trees, and carved out of a mountainside, was a Thompson Holiday honeycomb filled with British football insects. It has to be seen – and heard! – to be believed. There was drunken karaoke accompanied by electro-thuds that shook tree leaves, along with wild cries of "Olé, olé..", presumably the only foreign word they knew. The very next morning we were searching for the company rep to demand we be moved away from the honeycomb. We hadn't spotted it the afternoon we arrived. It was set back into the hillside, identical little wormholes in white plaster, all with tiny balconies. There was handwriting on wooden signs. 'Arsenal vs Liverpool, 4.00pm. Fish 'n' chips. Karaoke 10.00pm. Full English Breakfast.' On the beach in front of the honeycomb lay a couple of drunks from the night before, one of them with his trunks pulled low enough to see the crack of his ass. He was lying face down in a pool of vomit. I felt a thrilling trickle of revenge as I saw their backs were scarlet already. Kids were milling about, wailing in various football strips, as women with bleach-blonde hair pulled back into council house face lifts snarled and sucked on bottles of beer, fat curling over the tops of their cut-off jeans. Young men in baseball caps sat behind their bellies around a hideous swimming pool, grunting like pigs.

Into the cradle of civilisation, the devil had ladled maggots and filth. The contrast of beauty and ugliness was nauseatingly unbelievable. The Thompson holiday hotel was a festering gash on the breast of a goddess. These people populated an advertising executive's dream world. They bought, wore, used or ate anything laid before them, the ultimate consumers. Here were real fetishists, right at the nozzle end of a stream of noxious products – and every one of them a slave. They carried their masters' marks on all their clothing. Nike, Gap, Reebok, Virgin, Vodafone. They were walking billboards for more sales and yet more gold to rake into groaning tills. Those ad executives and *their* masters – the manufacturers, the bank owners, the global company

IS ALICE?

chairmen – lived reputedly fabulous lives but, at heart, were no better than the grotesques at the bottom who increased their debt for a Thompson holiday The rich could afford the seclusion Alice and I sought, along with all the imaginable toys from the most exclusive shops. But, however fine the wine they drunk, they were the real pigs who made the earth a filthy sty so they could afford to live upwind from the stomach-heaving stench.

I felt a certain amount of pity for the shattered remains of once-human souls, stuffing their cake-holes with fat and gorging on alcohol in pitiful displays of unconvincing fun. Truly, these were the damned, and the hotel behind them was some savage subsection of hell where they spent their fortnight holiday in squalor.

We found the rep without too much trouble, and Alice immediately came into her own, as she pressed her Jewish ancestry into service. The rep had difficulty squeezing in a word here and there.

"We booked this villa in good faith after studying your brochures very carefully. *Nowhere* was it mentioned that we would have to endure the electronic drumbeats of the insane every night…"

"Well, actually, it's not every night…"

Alice raised her voice. "At first we thought it was perfect, just as you described. Fantastic. Then, this *noise*…! Would you like to visit us and listen to it? Would you ask human beings to put up with shrieking obscenities that tear your nerves to shreds? No, I'm sure you wouldn't. That's why we *demand* to be moved to another property *immediately...*"

"I'm afraid..."

Alice's forefinger stabbed at the woman. "An honourable tour company would have cautioned visitors *before they paid their money.* Those people back there are animals! Did it say anywhere in the literature that we must spend our holiday next to a zoo? Or did you just worry that you would never let the place if you told the truth? Or maybe you thought so little of your customers that you guessed they wouldn't dare to complain?"

"Please, let me just..."

"Well, this is *more* than a complaint. If we are not moved to a more amenable property where we can enjoy our evenings as much as our days, then we are going to pack our bags and find a place of our own. And after our return to London, my solicitor will demand a refund of every penny alternate accommodation has cost us. I am not talking about 'ifs.' I'm telling you what is going to happen. I am *not* having my first holiday in many years destroyed by some company presenting a sugar-coated brochure of lies and then asking premium prices for villas situated next to a hellishly noisy shithole. Are you willing to move us or not?"

Here was another version of Alice, one that I had not seen before. She was far too angry to be her more socially awkward self. Her words flowed eloquently and freely. Her intent was clear. So...all her fragments *could* unite, if the conditions were right. She was strong, alright. She simply had no confidence in this strength.

The rep crumpled in the gale. She had no chance. We were offered another place *but* at a higher price.

"What?" Alice rapped. "You want us to pay more money for what you advertised in the first place? We've already paid you three times what that villa is worth, which is less than nothing with all that noise thrown in. So, morally, you should offer us a place *at least* three times better than that one. At no extra cost. Anyway, I want to see this place and make sure it's not another confidence trick from a company that doesn't mind lying for profit."

I stood mute behind her. I couldn't have said it better, even if I'd had the chance to write it out and edit it first. In short, she cut a deal with the rep and got a discount. I don't recall all the details now, but the new place was a pretty maisonette just yards from the sea and not far from the old Durrell house, which had been turned into a taverna. There seemed to be enough distance from the Thompson honeycomb to dampen most of the noise. We had the top floor, which included a nice, railed balcony that exposed the view of the ragged island shoreline. While we were moving, Alice couldn't help gloating about the huge discount she managed to squeeze from the hapless rep.

"Look at all this space. It's wonderful. Two bedrooms. They probably let this to families. Fifty percent discount. Hey! What do you think about that!"

"I'm proud of you," I said with a grin.

"Are you really? Is that true? Do you mean it? Proud of *me*?"

"I mean it from my heart."

She came closer, placing her hands on my chest, looking up imploringly. "How could you be proud of *me*? I'm nothing. I haven't been able to put one foot right in my whole life. Until I met you. And that still puzzles me. How you could ever love someone like me?"

"I'm the lucky one," I replied. "A beautiful younger woman who doesn't mind an old man groping her body…"

"Don't say that. You're *not* old."

"Good company, great sense of humour – well, sometimes, anyway – a powerful sense of life, a shameless sybarite who even challenges me, intelligent, charming…"

She hugged me. "I love you *so* much. I just can't describe what I feel. I never knew it existed."

I held her warmly in my arms. "And now you know it does."

The motorcycle we hired was a 250cc Japanese 'copy' of a Harley-Davidson, with soft, spongy suspension and American-style handlebars. I took the opportunity of riding without a helmet, a law not enforced in Greece, and used a red bandana instead, tied like a pirate. We swished around the hairpin curves, roaring up the hilly terrain, then coasting down, using the gears for braking. Alice was ecstatic about the views, so we often had to stop for photographs. I realised Corfu was now too tourist-infested for us to consider a return visit, but there were plenty of places that reminded me of past times when I wandered around the island on a scooter or motorcycle. I realised that one day the tourist phenomenon would disappear, and Corfu would return to complete luxuriant beauty.

Alice was insistent that we rent a boat. That's what she really wanted to do, and there was no stopping her, even when I told her I was the world's worst sailor. She said she would pay, and we must take a boat trip at least three times a week. Thus I found myself at the helm of a little motorboat, zig-zagging round the east coast of Corfu and amusing the locals when I tried to tie up to a taverna dock after heaving an anchor in the wrong place on the right side of the craft or the right place on the wrong side. I'm sure Buster Keaton couldn't have expected to do a better job, even with rehearsals. I was doing splits between the boat and the landing, falling in the water, cracking my shins. Alice swam out to rescue one of my shoes, which sailed out with the anchor, as the Greeks roared with approval.

But this was indeed the way to avoid the tourists. We found isolated tavernas in tiny fishing villages and, best of all, small coves with little rocky beaches that were as private as those owned by the wealthy. She and I, alone, lying in the sun watching the distant sailing boats, our little dinghy tied up awkwardly and bobbing on the

Bill Bailey

waves. If we couldn't find a vacant beach, we would just drop anchor opposite a little peninsula where the bowels of the earth forced up broken layers of crushed brown rock above the sapphire-blue Mediterranean.

One day remains in my memory with diamond clarity. We were anchored next to a cliff face in a gentle wind. The sky was clear, the spring sun summer-hot. I erected the canopy for protection, and Alice decided to do some snorkelling. She took off her bathing costume, wearing only the snorkel and flippers. There was a little sea-ladder hooked at the stern of the dinghy, and she gingerly climbed down and almost fell into the sea, a little girl again. By now her hair was being bleached by the sun, and her blonde head bobbed on the surface. I sat in the stern of the boat with a can of cold Mythos and a cigar, marvelling at how her naked body refracted in the water. She swam along, face-down with her bare, beautifully-rounded backside exposed as her scissoring smooth thighs revealed to me what a Picasso would look like in motion. I grabbed the camera and took several pictures of her in the water, and still had it in my hand when she was treading water, looking up at me, laughing gaily, her melon breasts bobbing in front of her. I'm glad I have those pictures. I love them.

"I remember a logical puzzle I heard during the days when I was doing my philosophy degree in Vancouver," I muttered. We had dropped anchor in a tiny bay and were lying on towels and a shelf of pebbles that were once probably boulders shaken from the cliffs circling the little cove. We were alone there, after her swim, and the sun told us it was mid-afternoon. It was still hot, but

260

we could cool off in the mild, clear water just feet from our towels.

"Hmmm?" She was still nude, and I was trying to keep my mind away from sex.

"The lone survivor of a shipwreck is swimming towards two islands. He knows little about them but a single fact. The people on one of the islands tell only the truth; the ones on the other tell only lies. So. When he finally drags himself onto a beach, what questions does he have to ask the inhabitants to find out which island he is on?"

She turned her head towards him. "Well, go on."

I leaned towards her and put my hand on her belly, hot and moist from sun and sweat. "I can't remember the answer, only the question. Anyway, it seems too simple now, so maybe I've even got the question wrong."

"Why simple?" she asked.

I held up my hand in front of her face. "How many fingers do I have on this hand? If you *always* told lies, you would need to say 'four' or 'six' – whatever. But what made me think of this old puzzle is that it is a clear demonstration of part of your problem. You are uncertain whether people are telling you the truth or lying to you. That rattles you, and you lose your existential balance. You start asking yourself whether it's something wrong with *you.*"

She propped herself up on her elbow, shielding her eyes from the sun. Her nipples were relaxed and baby-pink. "That's good. Very good. I like it…"

I was thinking. "Except, in your case, there is a third island, and this is where you find yourself marooned. On the third island, a few of the people only tell the truth, a few more only tell lies, and most tell a mixture of truth and lies. So there are no questions you can ask to discover by logic which is which."

"That's my island all right," she said. "It's a perfect visualisation. I'd never thought of it like that."

"Neither had I until just now. That third island is like this place. The earth. Humanity."

"So how do *you* know who is lying and who isn't?"

"I don't. It's impossible. But that information doesn't destabilise me. Or drive me mad. I suppose I make an infinite series of informed guesses. Either through experience or, well, knowing a little about how it all works. Can you remember doing much playing when you were a child?"

She rolled on her back again, thinking. "I don't know. Not much that I can recall. I was an only child. My parents were always working. I had a nanny most of the time during the day."

"Do you remember the day when your dad farted in the other room? He came into the kitchen. We were laughing our heads off, and he said it was the lid of the cigar box. The cigar box! I've never heard a cigar box do a long, juicy fart in my life."

Now Alice was laughing. "I couldn't help loving him for saying things like that. So obvious."

"I think playing is the most important thing kids can do. Forget studying. Play's the thing. That's how you start learning the dazzlingly difficult patterns and connections of the social web. Too little attention has been paid to this by philosophers and psychologists. Think of all the tiny subtleties involved in one simple transaction between just two people. Then amplify that to a lifetime of meeting thousands of different people – who may be telling truth or lies – in moments of stress or confusion or pressure. Boy meets girl. Attraction. Both are suddenly finely tuned to pick up little nuances. A cast of the head, a flicker of the eyes, the voice tone, nervousness, the ebb and flow of confidence, elation, dismay. The boy is maybe thinking of her body, like I'm thinking of yours…"

"Are you?" She raised her head, again shielding her eyes with a hand.

"Yes," I grinned, "But you and I adjusted the rules to suit ourselves, so I know it's you who must initiate any action. I can only plead…"

She rolled on her side and put her hand down my shorts, grabbing me firmly. "You mean like this?"

I showed her the palms of both hands. "Please, let me finish my little tale first."

She left her hand where it was but held it still.

"Thank you... for the moment. We... have illuminated our play, focused on it. But Boy and Girl must try and read each other on multi-levels of consciousness in the matrix they both know but never understand. Where to proceed, how to proceed, when? Is boldness rewarded or discouraged? If they are friends or know each other, it will be played differently than if they are strangers. How much of what either says is the truth? Is he just trying to impress, or is he genuine? Is she more interested in short or long term gain? Most importantly, they are also thinking of possible consequences, and how they might affect a commitment. Other liaisons may be affected. They are both probably experiencing emotional surges that erratically override the fast-moving mental traffic interchanges and rational sensors at junctions. While all this is going on, they are both desperately trying to remain 'cool' and in control, which is exactly in opposition to what is happening. More drink may help, but not too much. What is the *image* each is trying to transmit? How closely does this represent what they *are*? This brings into question the whole *concept* of image. Why is one necessary? Which are good, which are bad? There are few clues in the flickering smoky mirrors, yet decision time is approaching for both parties. It's a nightmare. Like reading tea leaves in a whirlwind. In fact, it's so complicated it's almost impossible to highlight everything that happens when interaction takes place between two people, never mind groups of three or more. I believe much of the groundwork, the early connections, happen when we are kids..."

IS ALICE?

"But," she broke in, "why is lying so necessary? It's so confusing. With my parents, I was never able to tell what they really felt, especially my mother. I'd ask her what she felt for me, and she'd give me that sweet smile and tell me how much she loved me. I never believed her. Or simple things. My Dad would have his denture in his closed hand. If I asked him what it was, he'd say a box of matches. Where are you going? To work, he'd say, then I'd talk to my cousin later and find out he had gone to visit them. I never, ever knew where I was. It made me so *angry*. Were they doing it because of *me*? Were they ashamed? Where was I? Who was I supposed to be?"

A passing sail boat drew closer to inspect the bay, and I was hoping they wouldn't drop anchor. "Lying is a social tool. Not necessarily a bad thing or a good thing. It's just *useful*, that's all. Someone excuses himself to go shopping when he or she wants to visit a secret lover – or maybe just spend an hour alone at a pub or go for a walk. The point is, they don't want company, but to say so would be rude. Your friend asks if she's too fat. Well, she is, but, obviously, you don't want to hurt her feelings. Then there are common social lies to the tax authorities or to the police patrol man who pulls you over for speeding, or the official who wants to know something you wish to hide. I've seen it many times. I lied to a friend recently. He asked me if I had any whisky. I said, no. Because I had just enough left in the bottle for my nightcap, and I didn't want to spoil that."

Alice noticed the sail boat, and pulled her hand out of my shorts with a grin. "I know that kind of lying, and I can understand it. I don't do it much myself because I find it spooky. Especially when it has to do with the authorities. I have this feeling that the police will come looking for me if I put a foot wrong. You know what I mean? Everything I do has to be clear and above-board. Just in case they come looking for me. To atone. That's what it feels like, anyway, *inside*."

I was staring at the sail boat. "I hope those bastards don't spoil our idyllic little desert island here. They're getting closer."

Alice used her spare towel to cover her middle. "Maybe I could pretend to give you a treatment."

"Why pretend? Leave the towel off. Maybe that will keep them away."

"Take off your pants, then."

"I'm bashful."

"So am I."

"I've got a little dick."

"It's *not*!" she exclaimed. "It's beautiful. Perfect. Just right. Best dick I've ever seen. And it's *mine*!"

I hooked my thumbs under my waistband and pulled down my shorts, kicking them off. "OK, then. My world is your oyster."

IS ALICE?

She squealed with embarrassed delight as she brought one hand to her mouth. "*Really*? I mean, that's *outrageous*! Do you think we should?"

I grinned from behind my sunglasses, my hands behind my head. "It'll be a good demonstration of how you can manipulate the world around you. I'm sure those people have done it themselves, but to *watch* it – or, more importantly – to be *seen* watching it should easily overload their fuses. We can't tell them to go away, the beach is too small. That's unacceptable. However, by our *actions*, we make it uncomfortable for them to be here – even though we will make no contact with them whatsoever when and if they arrive. This then will become *our* beach. They can't land on a rich man's beach. And that's the point. We're rich, too. In our invention. Our insouciance. Our love of life."

With a giggle, she threw off her towel and rolled over, her face towards me. "Should we really? Do you think? Am I mad?"

"Not now, you aren't."

She glanced at my privates. "You don't look very interested."

"That's because I'm nervous. I'm just pretending to be cool. Remember? *Image.*"

She began playing with me, still giggling.

"Marvellous," I said with a sigh.

I was becoming aroused, and our eyes were now locked together. By our rules, I couldn't move my hips or resist in any way. Slowly, I slid towards helplessness.

"Careful," I said softly, warning her that I had a jolt from my loins. Also by our rules, I was not to come unless she made the decision. She paused briefly, then began moving her hand again, and again I warned her to be careful.

Her head blocked out the sun and was framed by an azure halo that seemed to sparkle with little liquid rainbows. Alice was breathing heavily now, bringing me close again and again, the intensity increasing. We forgot about the sailing boat, the sailors, the beach, and Greece. Her eyes seemed to change from hazel to brown, to grey, then green, spiralling inward, towards the depths of her soul.

"Do you want me?" Her voice was low, even and strong. It was no longer taut with tension. Had I heard that voice before? I felt somehow I knew it.

"Yes," I murmured, still held in the tractor beams of her eyes, unable even to move from 'now.' I was trapped by her, trapped *with* her in some timeless metaphor.

"I... can feel your being, Theo." Her voice was lower, more powerful, but still soft and breathy.

Waves of desire crashed in counterpoint with the sea, and it seemed as if my spirit was hovering above my body, seeking hers. Her hand caressed my penis and my thighs, my belly. It was agony, and yet it was also heaven. Then for an instant the blue halo dissolved, and she was a real princess, dressed in white silk, standing regally before me on marble floors, her feet bare. She looked both like and unlike Alice, and the molten lava of love surged through me.

Her hand had stopped moving. She just held me, and we held each other, almost dizzy with the perfume of mystery. The sun stopped overhead, and we levitated in silence, beyond the sound of the waves. I have no idea how long that instant lasted. One second? An hour? A lifetime? Or perhaps it wasn't an instant at all.

"Did you see something?" My voice was sepulchral.

She hadn't moved. "We were so…close."

"You wore a white gown."

"Yes. White room, big."

"Strange. So strange…"

We could hear the sea now, as the sun continued its course across the sky.

"Look!" I said.

She stopped, pulled her hair back from her face, and stared out at the sea. The sailing boat was nowhere to be seen.

"It's gone," she said, turning to me with a wide smile.

"Magic." I said. "You see, we are real magicians. One moment that boat was drawing nearer and nearer, and in the next it vanished. How many magicians do you know who can do that? Make a whole boat disappear from the Mediterranean?"

"It's fantastic," she said as she held me close again, pressing her body against mine. "But...what will they *think*? Those people on the boat? What will they *think* of us?"

"Now, this is important," I whispered to her. "We actually *controlled* what they think. We *made* them do something they didn't want to do. You see? By a better understanding of the world. They wanted to land on our beach, and we made them leave without touching them, without saying a word."

"Yeah," she agreed, "but what do you think they think about *us*. We were scandalous. Nefarious. Probably not even *legal*. What if they call the *police*?"

I laughed. "What are they going to say to the Greek police? In Greek? These are tourists – German, English, French, who knows? They're going to go into a Greek police station and do what? They don't know the Greek for wanking, so what are they going to say? Make motions with their hands? They're the ones who'll be arrested, not us. Going like *this* to the police..."

I did a pumping action with my right fist. "The Greeks will think they're calling them *malakas*."

IS ALICE?

Her body bucked against me. "I shouldn't do these things, Theo. I'm not cut out for them. I didn't think about the police. Oh, *shit*!"

I stroked her hair. "Calm down, sweetie. The police are not a part of the picture. We are not going to be reported, because we *can't* be reported. It would be too embarrassing for *them*."

She looked up. Her face was still filled with concern. "But what if we see them?"

"We don't know what they look like. We never saw them, just their boat."

"But they saw us. What if..."

"They didn't see us close enough, darling. They were still fifty, sixty yards away from the shore. Imagine it yourself. Put yourself in their place. A couple were lying on the beach. A couple. Some couple. Two distant bodies. *But* you could see what they were doing, so the best thing to do was skedaddle."

"What will they be thinking of us?"

"To hell with what they think. Or anybody else. You can never *know* what others think. And remember – you can't even believe what they say when they *tell* you what they think. So it's impossible. All you have is a selection of *stories* in your head about *stories* in their heads. What you're doing is creating a drama with you as a central character in stories you create from nothing."

She hugged me tightly. "I love you."

"That's changing the subject."

"I adore you. I'm sorry I freaked. It was such a special moment. I forgot all about myself, all about…everything. Except us. And that place."]*

CHAPTER THIRTEEN

Tim O'Grady's attack was always smooth. He was in place almost before you knew it, and in the next instant you were in the air. Historically, Hawthorn was vulnerable to *tai-otoshi*, which is a body drop with one bent leg blocking your leading foot. This time, though, he quickly countered by moving his balance to his back foot, and, just as quickly, O'Grady changed to *o-ouchi-gari*, attacking that foot. It was a good combination – one that almost invariably worked for him. Instead of blocking O'Grady, Hawthorn felt something happen to him. He was floating. His whole body just responded to his opponent's minuscule movements, detecting a faint weakness, sliding into it. Hawthorn seldom used 'sacrifice' throws – where you slide to the ground to complete a throw. Before he was even aware of what he was doing, he turned to his left – *sumi-otoshi*, a hand-throw. It was one he never used in *randori*, and O'Grady was beautifully in the air, and, even before he landed smartly on his back, Hawthorn snaked into a *juji-gatame* – arm-lock – as perfect as a posed demonstration. O'Grady tapped the mat twice in submission and rose with his open jaw widening into a big smile.

"Theo, my friend. Where did *that* come from?"

Hawthorn was in a state of deep peace as he held O'Grady's eyes. "I honestly don't know. About eight times out of ten you nail me with that combination, and I've tried to answer you in a number of ways. But I never even thought of that one. Didn't occur to me."

They were both standing now, and O'Grady clapped him on the shoulder. "That was as clean a throw and follow-up... well, I don't know what to say. And I've been thrown by champs whose names would make your hair stand on end..."

Two other club members practising nearby had stopped and approached them. One of them was a stocky 3rd grade black belt who still competed. His dark-red curly hair was in a sweaty tangle, and he had close-set blue eyes. His name was Alan, and Hawthorn sometimes trained with him as well.

"What have you been teaching him, O'Grady?" Alan asked with an impish look in his eye. "Or did you just take a fall?"

O'Grady held up both hands as he shook his head. "Oh, no. I didn't even know what was happening myself. Beautiful." He nodded at Theo. "I think maybe you've got some hidden talents you haven't told me about."

Hawthorn chuckled and shook his head, feeling a little embarrassed now. "It came out of the blue. One of those moments. You know, like turning over your cards in poker and realising you've got four aces. For all I know...it was God."

After practice O'Grady joined him in the pub for a pint of Guinness. They were both in good humour. Hawthorn had continued to be impressive for the rest of the session. Though he never managed anything nearly as inventive, he had thrown his partner cleanly twice more before they finished.

O'Grady was looking at him. "What do you think brought all that on?"

Hawthorn shook his head. "I wish I knew. So I could do it every time. This probably won't make sense to you, Tim, but I felt like somebody else tonight. Just at the moment you dropped into that deadly *tai-otoshi*. I stopped *thinking*. I was complete, together. The Tao was with me. I felt like... like a warrior. A western samurai, maybe."

The Canadian leaned forward and laid his pipe on the table. "For the first time *ever*, I felt the movements of my opponent. They were like colours. Or words. I feel like that sometimes when I'm writing. The words seem to come from another place, and I'm just an amanuensis, writing as fast as I can. I'm taken over. Possessed. Well, tonight I felt possessed – at least when I executed that fucking throw. But all night I was in a groove..."

He stopped, not knowing where to go from there, and took a sip of his cold Guinness. It tasted good.

O'Grady was studying him. "I could say I was feeling off-colour myself, but I won't. I wasn't. Not top of my form maybe, but I was in there. And suddenly you skipped a couple of grades above me..."

Hawthorn laughed and picked up his pipe again. "Ah, don't be silly, Tim."

His partner took a big drink from his glass, taking almost a third of the pint. When he put down his glass, he was still serious. "Grades. Grades aren't really important. Those worried about their grade shouldn't really be in judo. I'm talking about something else. You astonished me tonight. We've been working and working, then suddenly… a giant leap forward."

Hawthorn blew a cloud of smoke at the ceiling. "You know, it might have something to do with a little incident the other night."

He told his friend about the three hoodlums he encountered outside the The Drum.

"One moment I was like a coiled spring, ready to rip into them. Then suddenly I was in control. Their master. On the surface it was nothing to do with judo. Underneath, it had everything to do with it."

O'Grady nodded with a chuckle. "When I started judo – I was about 12, I think – it was all for self-defence. I wanted to toss bullies around…"

"Same here…"

"Then, over time, I became aware of something else going on. There are a few judokas who have this kind of aura. You know who I'm talking about. The old Japanese masters with inscrutable faces, the legends. You grip onto them and feel like you can throw them anyway from Sunday. Then you're in the air. They're like the wind. The technique must be incredible…"

IS ALICE?

"It's not just technique. It's *who* they are. The person. The man. He has a better understanding of who he is and where he is…than you do."

"Is that what you felt tonight?"

Hawthorn thought for a moment. "Immodestly, yes. Like you, I learned judo was more about the human spirit than throwing an opponent. Yet it's both. A paradox. And I like that, because it has the twang of life."

"You think life's a paradox?"

Hawthorn thought for a moment as he re-lit his pipe, then waved it towards the crowded bar. "Look around you. People are living very ordered, mostly boring, lives. They come in here, get a little drunk, go home, maybe have a snack and watch TV, get up in the morning. Most of them go to work at an unchallenging job, worry about finances, wind up back in here in the evenings. A cycle that continues till age drags them down like wolves, then death. At the same time these same people are probably capable of greatness – or moments of greatness. With a little effort they could unlock pleasures they can't even imagine. They could discover what we find in judo. They are blind to the one thing that could emancipate them. Spirit. And all they have to do is raise the lids of their eyes. Just see. I find that paradoxical."

O'Grady looked over his shoulder at the bar. "You can't condemn them. They're following the only path they know."

"I have no power to condemn. Condemnation is a self-inflicted wound. Always."

"I suppose I'm one of them. I run that little antique shop, and I don't do that for love any more. I'm mid-40s now, over the hill, two kids and a wife I barely get on with."

"Why don't you sell up and retire to that little farm you've got in Andalucia?"

O'Grady sunk another third of his pint and pushed back his chair. "A question I ask myself. And I always come up with the same answers. I'd rather do it with someone besides my wife, there wouldn't be enough to live on for more than five years, and, most importantly, I don't know what the fuck I'd do with myself with time on my hands."

Hawthorn grinned. "The last one would solve itself. After a couple of months, you'll wonder how you ever had time enough in the past to work."

"I wish I could believe you. I'd like to back out and raise my kids somewhere quiet like the farm. In London you have to worry about paedophiles, terrorists…"

Hawthorn thrust the mouthpiece of his pipe at his friend. "Ever wonder how you pick up words like 'terrorist'?"

"Newspapers, TV… religious fanatics running around with bombs…"

IS ALICE?

"Let's suppose you and I are big-time gangsters. Competitors. Our territory overlaps. There are confrontations. People get killed. We're both thinking, 'What's the easiest way to win this thing?' What would you do?"

O'Grady laughed. "I don't know. Hire some guys from Newcastle. They'll cut your throat for a bottle of brown ale."

"You know what I'd do?" Hawthorn used his pipe tamper to crush down the ash. "I'd make contributions to a politician. Under the table, over the table. If I were big enough, I'd contribute to a whole political party. Attend dinners, go to the right clubs, make public gifts to charity. Get the politicians crawling up my ass, no problem, convince them I'm in 'property.' In return, I'd lobby them to be more decisive about crime and the *causes* of crime. In no time at all, I'd have you labelled a criminal. Without spilling a drop of my gang's blood, I'd get the police to do the job for me. Hell of a lot cheaper than fighting it out on the streets with you and bombing each other to extinction…"

O'Grady blinked. "What's this got to do with the price of tea? I don't follow you."

"Simple. Exactly the same thing as terrorism. Israel has succeeded in identifying the Palestinians as the terrorists, when they are engaged in exactly the same trade – with a fully equipped army to do the business for them."

His friend waved his hand dismissively. "Ah, politics. I never pay attention to that crap."

"You would if you'd been raised on the West Bank. In fact, you'd see a totally different world. The Israelis have completely succeeded. They're the richest, best-armed, best-trained gang in the neighbourhood, while their foes are a bunch of poor, bewildered rag-heads whose only effective weapon is strapping explosives to their bodies and pulling the wire in the middle of a bus queue. And just look at the luck of the winners. Everybody in the world jumps in on their side to kick shit out of the guy hopelessly trying to defend himself. Just after World War II, the Jews were the terrorists in Palestine. Now they've hung that label on the Arabs, using the same methods I described to you. Lobbying, bribing, spinning to the media, getting the global wealth behind them...."

"Yeah, well, the Middle East..."

"I'm not talking politics so much here, but how the meanings of words are manipulated in very organised and conscious ways. Words are manipulated to manipulate us."

"Ah, Theo, I'm not much of an ideas man."

"Yes, you are. You were speaking meaningfully about judo a moment ago, in a way few people would understand..."

O'Grady thought for a few seconds. "I used to be interested in politics, but it's all gone grey now. What's the difference? Whoever gets elected, you get stung."

IS ALICE?

"You have three main parties here now. Three different masks. Underneath the masks you'll find the same face. You only have one choice, a single party. No competition is tolerated. Not now. That's one of the things that has changed. There used to be some difference. Not much. Some. The three party leaders are just three types of salesmen who work for the same boss. Today that boss is global capital."

"Look, I was an idealist back when, along with a lot of my friends," O'Grady said amiably as he shook his head. "Times have changed. What you say may be true, but what can we do? Nothing. So we just buy all the toys and get deeper in debt. I only need a van, but I run a van and a car with no place to park either of them."

"And are you happy?"

"When I'm away from home, when I'm playing judo, yes. Otherwise, no."

"I think we can do something," Hawthorn said quietly as he put his pipe back into his pocket. "Two things. We can understand what's going on, and we can wait."

"What's the point of understanding? That'll just depress me."

"Change yourself, and you change the world."

O'Grady laughed out loud. "Sorry, but I think that's a load of shit."

"It's something I've tried to explain to Alice, and it's one piece of solid ground for her. It's not *the* world out there. It's *a* world. And the only place it exists is here." He pointed to his head with a forefinger.

His partner snorted. "Try walking in front of a bus, and you'll see where the world is."

Hawthorn shrugged. "Is that because you believe the bus will kill you?"

"I know it will."

"I'm sure you're right, then. It will."

O'Grady leaned forward on his elbows. "Are you telling me that the bus won't kill me when I walk in front of it, if I *believe* it won't?"

"In this particular world that we both seem to know, the bus will kill you every time. In other worlds, it might not. I'm never sure. But we've convinced ourselves that *this* world is true, and I'm discovering that it's not. It's false. There are others closer to the truth. If we find them, this world will collapse. We are living in a fairytale, not a real world."

"Well, it's one that seems to work."

"Does it? How do you know if you don't understand it? For instance, I suspect we are rushing towards global disaster – something we don't *have* to do. Yet we rush on. So long as today is fine, tomorrow will look after itself. Any farmer will tell you that if you gorge yourself on your crop for a month, you won't have enough left for the year."

O'Grady struck his finger on the table. "But you're giving examples from *this* world. Isn't that contradictory?"

"It's the only one where we can communicate. For the moment."

"So this world only exists because I believe in it?"

"That's right. This one depends on our belief and trust to sustain its existence. As my belief is undermined, it changes as we speak. Even a small amount of doubt begins to corrupt the fabric."

O'Grady drew a formless picture in the circle of condensation left by his glass on the table. "So what about everybody else? If *we* see a different world, what about *them*?"

Hawthorn laughed and pointed again to his head. "Everyone else is in here."

O'Grady looked at him with one eye half-closed. "Theo. Personally I think you were better off in the nut house. Look, I should have left half an hour ago. I'm gonna get an earache from the wife now."

He finished his pint with one gulp, got up, offered his hand.

"Great throw tonight. Fantastic moves. Speak with you later…"

After he returned home, Hawthorn grabbed a can of Guinness from the fridge, opened his back window, and stepped out onto the roof. He still had his jacket on, and he zipped it up. It was colder now, as autumn slipped towards winter, but the sky was clear. He drew up his deck chair and sat down. Looking across at the other terrace, the Minx's window was lit, but the curtains remained drawn. Her performances took place only during the summer season when the nights were hot, and he missed them. The flats on that side were probably quick-let and expensive. In fact, they were no doubt communal rooms, not flats at all. The Minx would probably be gone by next summer. Replaced by some pimply boy. He saw her once in the street, and she looked every bit as pretty in a few clothes as she did in her thong. Young, though. All the young had beautiful bodies – it was all so new and fresh, unworn by being dragged backwards through life and stuffed too often with junk food.

He sighed and cracked the can of Guinness. He had already scolded himself for introducing politics into the conversation with O'Grady, but he allowed his exasperation to lure him forward. They weren't really friends yet, just two men comfortable with each other's company, sharing a common interest. He took a long sip of beer, and realised the pint he'd had in the pub was enough. And the taste wasn't the same. He put the can down on the roof, and resisted pulling out his pipe. Instead, he stuffed his hands in his jacket pockets to keep warm.

IS ALICE?

The judo had been magic. He couldn't remember a session like that, ever. There was some phenomenon that occasionally occurred in the human psyche which was so elusive. He knew it existed, because it often happened during periods at the keyboard of his computer. He suspected the mechanistic nature of the social matrix now suppressed what was once – or perhaps *could be* – an expression of godlike ability. How to describe it? At times when writing, he would find his fingers moving at lightening speed, with words flowing onto the monitor like a paste-in from another document. His mind would be still, trance-like, even able to reflect on what was happening with a roving third eye. It was as if he were an open conduit *from* some other place *to* the written page. He could look down and mildly observe the blur of his fingers, and hear the plastic rattle of the keys. In trying to visualise what was happening, it seemed as if a golden radiance entered his body from above, flowing through his body to the clattering keyboard.

It was the same sensation that evening at the dojo. If O'Grady were really making an effort, he had little hope of ever throwing him cleanly. He was about 13 years younger, for a start. And a grade higher, with better early training. O'Grady was a former national and international competitor, and he was personally happy just to be training with such a man. Then – seemingly from nowhere – Hawthorn threw him with an obscure technique as easily and cleanly as he would a beginner, following up with a secure and absolutely fluid arm-lock. Looking back, he *knew* what he was doing at the time it was happening. Something in him opened. All the portals lined up perfectly. Then the golden beam, the flow, the mysterious connection to some other time, space or plane. Genius passed through him, and he suspected that, at that moment, he could have thrown the current world champion. How to *grasp* it, though? How to become a person where that flow was uninterrupted? What a wonderful thing that would be. He had only written a couple of plays where that spirit remained throughout the whole writing process – and even then it was necessary to 'filter in' each time he sat down to work on the pieces. At other times the magic was intermittent. In between those moments, it was hard going. Then, at the end, he had to smooth over the joins technically in the hope that no one would notice. But those plays that came straight from heaven – they were his best.

Hawthorn chuckled gently. Maybe his real quest was simply for wisdom. That odd word, so out-of-place now, so elusive even to define. Yet he knew what it meant, however shapeless it might be. The divine talent of being in harmony with self and world. He was only capable of achieving moments that twinkled like precious stars in a dark sky. *Only*? He laughed again at himself. He was complaining, when he should be overwhelmed with gratitude. What he experienced must be as rare as perfect symmetry. That phrase startled him – *perfect symmetry*. Of course, that's what it was like, the feeling, the sensation. Or the harmonious rumble of the overtone series. It was as if he were at one with all of creation. A natural part of existence. At that point he could become the essential and comfortable conduit from one state to another. A part of being. A whole, instead of opposing particles. Simultaneously he was master and servant.

IS ALICE?

How curiously that thought struck him. Words were dull and primitive tools to try and describe events of the spirit, yet they were his only tools, and he struggled to use them as artfully as he could. It seemed as if he were marooned in time and space on a comic replica of reality, where worthlessness was worthy and real riches were spurned. With every meaningless fart there would be rejoicing throngs of the blind dancing arrhythmically to aimless noise in an increasingly toxic chamber. Could this possibly be Hell? Was he some hapless pilgrim damned to endure a lifetime of nightmarish squalor in a place so potentially beautiful it sucked his breath away?

This time he laughed out loud, a big one that bounced between the sleepy terraces. Oh, no, not damned. It was a further blessing – beyond his dizziest dreams. The wealthy had only money. His gifts couldn't be purchased. Millions scrabbled for gold with crazed eyes and minds twisted by greed. By comparison, Hawthorn was a demi-god. He had some understanding of how the world worked. He was privy to golden moments of creativity – whether at the keyboard, or on the mat, or in bed with his lover – or, indeed, where he was at the moment, sitting under a cloudless cool sky, able to think in abstract parabolas about wisdom and magic and the origins of consciousness.

Year after creative year passed in a life that offered him mighty portions of absolute joy – along with a few mouthfuls of bitter rottenness, a price he paid without complaint. The understanding of consciousness was a lifelong project. A troubled and baffled youth first rebelled and lashed out at the world. Then he was drawn to philosophy, where he could read the words of others as they toiled to explain their theories. Many years ago he became fascinated by the nature of dreams. That led him to other paths, along with the realisation that he no longer needed to read the research of others, because his human legacy gave him his own laboratory for endless experimentation.

Hawthorn closed his eyes, involved with his own thoughts as the people across the terrace relaxed in front of TV sets. He never arrived at a satisfactory explanation of dreaming, but it led him to a plain but amazing discovery. Dreams were stories. It was the simple but ubiquitous *story* that was the fountain head of consciousness. Stories were its DNA building blocks. They were the communicators that carried massive information from person to person, and within every single individual. Without stories consciousness could never exist. This discovery created a ripple effect that led him to the complex nature of the State. Perhaps it also led him to Alice, because it was with her that everything began unfolding in ceaseless multiplicity. Of course he was many times wrong – wrong, wrong and wrong again and again, as with his notion that Alice should strive to bring together the 'two' worlds that haunted her. But being wrong – and knowing it – is an integral part of being right.

Now he applied his detective's magnifying glass to the trail once again, deerstalker set at a jaunty angle, pipe in hand. It seemed obvious that they should never have attempted to bring the two together. Instead of starving the bad wolf, they fed him. Or she fed it, with his encouragement.

IS ALICE?

Part of the mistake was believing the self was a single entity. The self knows what it is. But does it? Hawthorn was not a physicist, but he knew enough to know the brain probably operated on sub-atomic principles where 'here' and 'now' are not easily determined. Matter can be in two places at once, and, most importantly of all, an observer often changes the configuration of the observed. He now suspected one set of stories indicated a self for only a small amount of time before it dissolved into another, different self that could be radically changed – yet, for the self, they were apparently the 'same.'

Was the Hawthorn who tore off his clothes in anger and frustration at the Royal Albert Hall the same as the one now sitting on a roof contemplating the meaning of consciousness? He could easily recall those memories, but, crucially, not all of them. What he remembered was a story that explained *that* self to *this* one and provided a link that gave an impression of some kind of continuity through time. But the memories, the continuity and *now* were all stories that linked together to form his familiar concept of self. Sitting under the October skies, though, he felt that the angry, demented figure in his memory was a grave disappointment. That outrage, the protest at the ticket office, the days in hospital, his demonstration on stage during Alyosha's concert – who was *that* man? Clearly it was him. Now, though, it seemed an alien figure, one which puzzled him slightly. At the other end of the scale, there was the Hawthorn who, that evening, threw O'Grady around the mat like a baby. OK, an exaggeration, he thought quickly. But it made the point. In between those events, how many times had he morphed into different characters, different sets of stories held together sometimes by serpentine matrix linkages? The language of movies occurred to him. Frames of still images moving fast enough to convince the eye that real movement was taking place, all cut together by an editor whose object was to form a narrative. It wasn't an adequate metaphor. The difficulty was that the observer was in a different state in every frame. Therefore there was at least one further dimension. As the 'film' of his life ran from reel to reel, there were as many viewers as there were frames, even though it all took place within the same self. To complicate matters, each one of the 'viewers' constantly constructed and re-constructed the universe, so both the 'outside' and 'inside' were in rapid motion as well. And that helped explain the preposterous power of stories, because they held everything together in what appeared to be a rational enough framework to emerge as his self. The main story of self didn't give anything like a true account of events, but it was plausible enough to seem as if it did. Existence of *things* depended entirely on the awareness of each different observer-self in every passing frame of 'now.' The 'real' was no more than a story that made sense in a remembered context. It struck him suddenly and violently: *consciousness could not exist without a matrix*. It *was* a matrix, a social one, where everything else existed, held together by stories.

With his eyes still closed, Hawthorn was dazzled by the cascade of thoughts and ideas as they sought each other for unity, like a four-dimensional magnetic picture puzzle. There were no final conclusions yet, but he had burst through to a precipice with a view that was outstandingly beautiful. *That* was the meaning of beauty. A harmonious display of imagination, in such a way that it expressed meaning and truth, however baffling. There was something in human consciousness that actively sought the beautiful. It was healing. It united spirit with *something else* by a gossamer thread. It filled the soul with a sense of freedom. And, for a moment at least, it brought together all the selves into one integrated whole that radiated with happiness.

Hawthorn's inner eye turned towards the social matrix. The 'world.' That world was gripped in some nightmarish and savage insanity, yet millions – billions – of people were happy to accept it as 'normality.' They had an obsessive-compulsive disorder, expressing itself in measurement. Land was measured, parcelled, sold – as if you could possibly *sell* land that had remained unsold for billions of years. Quantities were weighed, values agreed. Even future possibilities were traded on stock markets for loot. Time was divided up, bought and sold. Happiness was determined by the degree of wealth, the quantities of possessions, and the number of glittering acquaintances. The rich stole from the nearly rich, who stole from the well-off, and they all stole from the poor, who completed the insane circle by being jailed for stealing from the rich. Accompanying this demonic scene was an ever-increasing wall of noise, the like of which the stately earth has never known. Grinding mechanical sounds, shrill electronic punctuation, throbbing and whining combustions, pneumatic palpitations, rasping abrasive whirling blades, clattering steel against rails, whooshing engines sucking stale air, whistles and bells, the growl of huge jet engines howling above virgin land that has become a thrashed whore as it is de-forested, deflowered, disfigured, quantified and trafficked by pimps in sharp suits who have grand titles and estates and entry into the lower depths of human depravity. Pure mountain water, once clear and clean, stank of shit and chemicals. Humanity is on the swarm, unknowing, uncaring, as they slurp take-aways in front of winking screens, or listen to incessant pop noise through pods in their ears. Vacant eyes seek vacant eyes for brief moments of rutting sex before re-joining the swarm in its hysterical and masochistic pursuit of pain, destruction and personal disintegration, disguised by sanctimonious masks of pleasure and success.

Hawthorn squinted up at the sky. Was that Venus almost touching the roofs of the terrace opposite? He remembered the satellite pictures he saw that were taken of that planet on recent space expeditions. Despite its lovely appearance from his chair, it was a fiery, stormy, sulphuric hell. Was it once an Eden? And did it produce a cancerous swarm of crypto-intelligent animals that ravenously gnawed off every living fibre on its surface? From a distance Venus was as beautiful as the earth, its twin in the solar system.

It was probably fanciful thinking – more of a suspicion than a theory. But it was certainly a possibility. A wise alien visiting the earth could only come to one conclusion. There was an infestation by a suicidal parasite.

On the other hand, if the alien looked more closely, he – or it – would see a tenuous spirit running through the perimeters of the swarm, a faintly-glowing halo not yet extinguished. In this swarm, the wise were pushed to the margins and listened to by few. No, the leaders were dangerous fools, but the potential remained. The potential of what *could be...*

There was another path, one which would make every citizen rich beyond their dreams. With slight relative effort, they could live in peace *and* harmony with nature, their own kind and themselves.

Hawthorn smiled at the thought, because such ideas were, and would be, met by jeers, rather than cheers, by those dementedly crowing that nature was red in tooth and claw. Life was a fight, a life-and-death struggle epitomised by savage aggression and devastating responses to the slightest opposition. He was certain humanity could not live without its imagined 'threats.' Understanding was the last tool reached for when humanity was confronted by a threat.

He had been over these ideas before, but they looked different in another context. Though understanding was nearly always the best tool, it was seldom used by the individual or community. Perhaps that was because understanding was more difficult for those stretched thin by fear and threats. A certain precondition to understanding was courage. Turn with calmness towards a threat, and most often it is a shadow, without substance. If it is a true threat, then meet it with only enough force to neutralise it. Use its own energy to defeat it, not your own. Judo again, with whiffs of Zen. Do not personalise these threats so they immobilise you with fear. 'Winners' and 'losers' are phoney categories, best left to games for kids.

Look at the prize! There is a heaven to be created from that hell! Not a heaven of clouds with angels thrumming lyres. No white robes and sandals. Just a gentle move sideways, in order to see clearly. The right decisions could then follow. If this is a dream, the alternative is a nightmare.

Hawthorn studied the skies for a few more moments, before retiring through the window. Since the very beginning of self-reflection in the human species, so many studiers of the universe seemed to have developed arrogant understandings about how they thought it was all put together – from primitive religions to modern science. All of it could be wrong. Today, the emphasis was on measurement, and he recalled William Blake's suspicion of Urizen. There was something about pure measurement and order that inherently oppressed creativity and passion.

CHAPTER FOURTEEN

Alice was staring out of the small window over the basin where she was washing her tea mug. The scene outside was quite dramatic. Though it was midday, it seemed like dusk. The wind was howling, and the branches of the trees thrashed off their autumn leaves in terrified nudity. Sudden and ghostly light flickered in uneven flashes, followed quickly by an explosion so loud it shook the frame of the window. It was a storm. Several of the other inmates were gazing outside, as quiet as a row of worshippers in church. It was a mighty scene. The lights in the hospital dimmed for a moment, went out, then came on again.

Alice continued to wash the mug, because she did not see the storm at all. It could have been raining frogs or footballs or hot coals and masturbating ballerinas without drawing her attention. For her, the 'outer world' was not being decoded. It was like a TV monitor that was on but unconnected to any station. Snowy dots. The thunder was not 'heard' either, just more static that for a moment drowned out the fizz of water running from the tap, or the hospital noises from the corridors. Alice was in a strange, luminous universe that had been with her since she put down the novel she was reading. She was not self-aware in the sense that she knew the state was unusual. All her attention, her whole being was involved in the story. She was one of the characters, and her name was Allison, and she was living the book in 'real time.' Of course. 'Alice' was so incomplete, so she was now son of Alice, or Alice's sun. Or Allison could be *pregnant with Alice*. Everything tied in, like the weave of a basket.

The day before, she had been accompanied to the shops by one of the nurses. There were several things she needed – some tissues, lip salve, Q-tips, socks, woolly tights. They also stopped in the charity shop where she picked up several books – novels by authors she had never heard of. For her, the cover was everything – or sometimes the title. Most of these books she started but never finished, because the words came through with different meanings, so the stories were only a maze for her. Or else they sparked other thoughts, and she would squeeze through a wormhole into another scenario as the book dropped from her hands. But this one held her attention. It was about a Jewish woman who felt she bore the guilt of her whole family, and even for the awful things that had happened to her race. During a dream or vision the Allison of the story imagines she is the daughter of God, sister of Jesus, born on earth to redeem the sins of man. She is subsequently sectioned to a mental hospital, where she performs 'miracles.' There is ambiguity whether the miracles are 'real' or are imagined from her point of view. Allison falls pregnant, and she is convinced the father is *her* Father, and her son will be in the image of God, the true Redeemer.

Alice poured the boiling water onto the tea bag, then squeezed the bag on the side of her mug with the spoon before throwing it into the bin. After adding the milk, she looked through the window. At first, she saw nothing but meaningless movement. She blinked twice, and at once saw the trees were bowing to her, and it made her feel holy. Very graciously, she returned the bow and walked in a slow, stately manner back to her room. She sat down with her tea in a straight-backed chair, and stared at the white wall. Things were so clear now. All the millions of tiny balls rolled into their little sockets. Peace, at last. She felt she was inside a beautiful halo, the absolute centre of the absolute universe. On the one hand, she was the apogee of evil, the one person responsible for every sin committed by every sinner from the beginning of time, culminating in the Nazi outrage. She was Himmler. She was Hitler. And, as Allison, she was also the daughter of God, put on earth to suffer as the prophet Jesus had once suffered. For what? For *sins*. The book was about *her*. She was chosen to choose *that* book. It was a message. This was her. The meaning of her. Her story. The reason for her existence.

The book ended with Allison pregnant, the whole story wreathed in ambiguity, awaiting... birth. So Allison-here-and-now was pregnant. That, too, had blossoming significance. Her periods were spotty, hardly any blood at all, and her tummy was big. She thought that was because she was fat, but now the real reason was totally clear.

She suddenly paled with nausea. It was the thought of bearing a child, something she had never, ever wanted, because she was too selfish and wanted everything for herself. No screaming children, no burping or changing nappies or dedicating her whole life to...another victim. But now she knew she must give birth. It was God's will, and there was no arguing with that.

An inspiration struck her. Of course. She would die in childbirth, in agony, delivering the Son of God, the Messiah of the Jews. Allison was the vessel, the ripe pod that would burst open with the delivery, then wrinkle and wither, falling to the ground, a mere casing for the new Seed. Would she then be redeemed?

The thought overwhelmed her, and she spilled her tea in her lap. It reminded her to take a drink, and it was not very hot now. *Redemption*!

"No, please, God my Father..." she muttered out loud. "Please, no longer. Let me be the withered husk that falls away from the miracle of Your Son. Give me, please, true blackness, nothingness, real death, a true end, because... because... I have no courage. I am small and weak and fear more pain... so much pain. The squalor of despair. I will somehow... *somehow* give You Your Son. As You command. But then, please, let me go."

She shook her head violently. "Allison! Allison! Always thinking of yourself, just like Alice."

Then she quickly came to her senses. "No, you're *not* Alice. That's blasphemy. I am Allison, daughter of God, mother-to-be of the Son of God. That is my role, and I mustn't forget it..."

She took another sip of her tea, now a little overwhelmed by the significance of it all. Her solar plexus was burning and aching, and her spine felt like an overloaded electrical cable. Her body tingled and trembled as the storm inside shook the world. She realised she was alive in a way she could barely imagine. A tornado tore through her landscape and uprooted everything in sight, then all the objects fell into the places they should have been, the places she *should* have seen before, if she hadn't been so stupid and so closed to the truth. But fortune was with her. Yesterday she discovered The Book – and then her real name and her destiny.

She dropped her mug abruptly, and it shattered on the floor. Alice ignored it as she rose slowly from her chair. Did this... situation make her a Princess? Oh, no, she hadn't thought of that. The Princess of God? The Princess...

She had been a princess, but that was so long ago – light years and night years. There was a palace and slaves. Alice waved both hands, as if swatting at insects crawling on her face. Were they memories? Were they *real*? Had she lived so long? Was she to emerge again after she died in childbirth? It could be the ultimate nightmare, an endless series of Hindu lives as her soul degraded slowly towards the horizon of eternity. She could end up as a moth...

A MOTH!!!

Again she slapped at the air with her hands. Not a moth, please. Those fluttery, furry, whirring insects born from maggot-larvae. She HATED moths.

But now – right now – she was the Princess of God, awaiting a holy birth. Again there were distant memories, like dusty moths. She was mistreating a slave, whipping him, encouraging him to crawl before her, kiss her feet, to draw his tongue from her instep up her leg, inside her thigh as she trembled and writhed in lust. The Whore Princess – who was she? Where had she lived? When? The slave's face – was it Theo? Oh, please let it not be Theo. He had suffered so much for her. Another thought rolled into view like a heavy stone. She would make Theo accompany her through her many lives of the future, until, finally, he mounted her, and she gave birth to thousands of little maggots.

She fell on her knees and didn't feel the pain as a tiny piece of the broken mug embedded itself in her flesh. She clasped both hands in front of her face and looked to heaven.

"Please, Holy God, I ask only to do Your will. But may I also pray that You release Theo from his suffering. He has nothing to do with me! I promise! He does not share my sins, and I pray to you, my Father, that he doesn't share my fate. Please set him free. Set poor Theo free, and I will bear Your Son and all the pain of heaven and hell. Then, dear God, please let me die and return forever to ashes, blown meaninglessly by the wind."

She lowered her head, then murmured, "Your loving daughter, Allison."

* * *

*[Dear Alyosha

I've just returned from the hospital. Alice has been demanding that the hospital staff change her name to

IS ALICE?

Allison Levy. I don't quite know what to make of this. I've never heard her mention anybody by that name. Furthermore – and get this – she is insisting that she is *pregnant*! To be honest, I'm a little worried, because I know that anything can happen on those wards. I talked to the chief nurse, and naturally he waved aside such a suggestion, but I'm insisting that she be tested. Just to eliminate the possibility. In fact, she has been losing weight and is as thin as I can remember seeing her. She is now insisting that she be moved to the maternity ward as soon as possible.

Mad? Yes, of course. However, she incorporates some aspects of 'reality' into her world in unexpected ways. I know that, for a while, she was following one of the male inmates around. She probably thought he could enlighten her or be her guru, I don't know.

No, I don't actually consider Alice *mad*. Ironically, she is as 'normal' as anyone else. She has installed a different matrix. The problem is that her world lacks any form of communication with ours. It's enclosed, complete – *and* completely under her control. In her hands is the ultimate joystick of consciousness – go where you like, do what you want. A story, a play, in which she's always the star. I believe that's the attraction of this place she disappears to. *This* world, the one you and I understand, can appear to many as if it's controlled by others who are capable of inflicting pain or discomfort. Tax demands, parking penalties, financial fluctuations, political decisions, relatives, even traffic problems. We are individual rats trapped in a maze run by and for the benefit of *others*. Alice is free from that world, but the price she pays is high, because it puts too much sea between her island and the main archipelago.

Before we met I had already been skating on the icy slipperiness of the concept of consciousness for many years, and I had begun to develop the idea of stories as the key to understanding it. These investigations first led me to the nature of the State, and several of my earlier plays were devoted to how the stories of consciousness were woven into support for the society in which we lived and by which we were governed. It was the fabric of the weave that was missing, and that is how I came upon the matrix. Alice was the source of my inspiration. As her problem became my own, the perspective changed enough to enlarge details of the panorama.

The matrix is a latticework of tales developed to allow individual consciousnesses to create the living fiction of a social world in all its intricate and infinite detail that exists only in the present. As for the State, it is a separate 'organism' that takes lusty advantage of the matrix without being directly aware of its existence or nature. The State is a parasite of the matrix. It has learned to feed, enrich and extend itself and its meaning by exploiting the inner mechanisms of the matrix. However, it is hugely important to understand that the two are separate but inextricably bound together. Perhaps that is why one obscured my view of the other.

Everyone is political, even (or especially) those who feign no interest in 'politics.' If the matrix were the river in which we swim, the State would be the direction, the order, the speed of movement, the definition of values and interests, and – above all things – the focus of our attention on highlights of its choice. It is necessary to speak of the State as a 'thing,' but in truth it is but a bundle of stories itself - yet one that imposes itself on each instant. The parasite becomes the master, and enslaves the matrix for its own ends without ever being aware of the process through self-knowledge. At the same time, the State senses its self-revelation as dangerous, and constantly develops new technologies to deal with such perilous threats. I admit that I am awed by its sinister beauty at times.

Of course it isn't necessary for the State to be sinister. It simply developed that way as a means for dominant interests to maintain control and direction over the interests of the people governed. It's absolutely logical. It's transparent. Revolutions do occur – in fact revolutions are happening intermittently all the time – but I'll only mention the three main ones in what's known as the West. The English Revolution when Charles I was beheaded, the French Revolution, and the October Revolution in Russia. The first two are more closely related, though they occurred more than a century apart. Very briefly, those two were necessary to allow business control over government, instead of the old landed and royal interests. Of course, this was cloaked in ways to make it appear more of a democratic upheaval, especially the French Revolution. Nevertheless, when the dust cleared, capitalism was legally able to advance and to sweep away any remaining shackles so that it could eventually flourish. The Russian Revolution was the first to have a more truly egalitarian nature.

The enormous wealth created by capitalism was still controlled by relatively few, despite the technological explosion it caused and its apparent distribution of more wealth to the whole of the population. In real terms, the poor remained poor whether they were medieval serfs or urban proletariat. The reverberations of the October Revolution are continuing, even after the dissolution of the USSR. Remember, both the English and French Revolutions had their various 'restorations' as well, even though political and economic reality had changed radically. It remains to be seen whether the last big revolution will follow the pattern, because it is far too early for any definitive clarity.

However, the basic apparatus and mechanisms of the State are ancient and remain valuable to whichever illusionists are manipulating the control levers. To understand the basic format of the State, I'll draw your attention to the Gang. Criminal gangs continue to foment and emerge simply because they are following the basic design that has worked so well for so many over so many centuries.

How do you acquire wealth? The handbook tells us it is by hard work and entrepreneurial skills, along with perhaps a little talent for trading. The reality is different. Or, really, it's not. It's just that the words of the handbook don't mean exactly what they say. It is hard work, and it does help if you have the other skills, too. But the simple truth is that wealth is acquired by stealing. Wealth is important because it gives access to the real crown jewels – status and authority. Power. Power is more intoxicating than any drug. It dazzles. It can reduce the greatest intellect to a corrupt and gangrenous rind of a human being, a parody of spirit. It is infectious and more addictive than heroin. The USSR was not immune.

Gangs – the true criminal firms – are completely illegal in any country I know of, because entry at that level is no longer allowed. It is the door used by our ancestors, and must remain closed to newcomers. Aspirants to wealth must use only nominated avenues, NOT that one. Nevertheless, it is still a successful entry point for candidates as ruthless as those who already have wealth and power and their predecessors.

It is not difficult to discover how kings and rulers evolved in earlier times. Perhaps there are a few exceptions, but it is surely true that nearly every kingdom began with a ruthless gang that was good at thieving. A peasant tills his land. The gang, a heavy bunch of thugs, arrives at his homestead and he is presented with the Basic Deal. The occupier of the land must pay rent or taxes in cash or kind. In return the gang will offer him protection – protection from other gangs and, of course, from themselves. If there is any dispute about the new arrangements, then the occupier loses his land, his family and his life. It's quite simple and easy to understand. The principles remain valid today. In time, the leader of the gang becomes king and his henchmen are given titles and land in return for their continuing oaths of loyalty. A modern gang essentially works the same way, though they deal with traders, rather than landowners.

The Romans were the first to make the breakthrough in administering a really large region, an empire. It is a complex matter, because it involves a great number of people. The Romans demonstrated a genius in developing ideas for control and manipulation of whole populations, and I suspect many of these institutions were borrowed by the new empire builders following the English Revolution. There is certainly a striking similarity, and in my view this was the basis of the Renaissance – or a re-birth of the classical world. How did they do it? The Romans were studied for their expertise in empire administration. How was it to be done – in a modernised way, of course? Some new ideas were simple, based on the old templates. Workers wanted in the cities? Take control of common land through the enclosures. And in the colonies, slavery provided the same economic sense that appealed to the Romans – raw materials could be cheaply provided for the new factories.

Thievery was re-defined by capitalism, as Marx pointed out. Each worker is paid less than the value he creates, thus allowing the accumulation of capital by the owners. This money could then be used as investment in shares of new ventures that opened up further colonies or markets for exploitation. The idea was just... *brilliant*. And like all brilliant ideas, it remained simple. It is easy to understand. Any illiterate peasant could make it out, if he cared to listen. This fact is well-known by the State, and that is the reason so much of the truth is hidden by golden avalanches of words and the magic world of smoke and mirrors. Economics – too difficult. Philosophy – impossible. Political science – what?

When the mechanisms of the State are broken down into their much more elementary parts, one thing that becomes clear is that the people have never come close to the supposedly achieved goal of democracy. Any genuine enquirer is left numb with confusion. *Where is the democracy?*

Where, indeed. Let's continue to keep this simple. Blow away the smoke, put drapes over the mirrors. There are various examples in various countries of so-called representative congresses and parliaments which have been elected by the people. But who has been elected, and how have they been selected for election and presented to the electorate? America is a fine example, as they're the first to wheel out lectures to other countries on democracy. It is still *possible* to stand without money as an 'independent' and win any election there – just like it is *possible* to win a national lottery. But in reality what you need is money and LOTS of it. Personal fortunes are nothing, compared to corporate ones. So, for the ambitious politician, it's best to choose one of the existing parties, as a party itself is an astronomically expensive entity to create and maintain. Furthermore, it is *meant* to be this way. It is part of the design. After all, representatives elected to a congress or parliament need to be *controlled*. By whom? The people?

It's obvious now, isn't it? All the old stage scenery just collapses, and you can see everything that happens backstage. We don't have democracy in modern States, and have never had it. What we have is an illusion, no more than that. It's a hugely expensive, high-energy one, but an illusion nevertheless. The legislative, judicial and executive branches of every nominally democratic country primarily operate in the interests of national and global corporations. The market is king, and the corporate owners and shareholders are the barons.

Here is Nathan de Rothschild, of the British branch of the family:

"The man who controls Britain's money supply controls the British Empire, and I control the British money supply."

Speech may be free, but it's damned hard to highlight anything that may be defamatory of this system. This is exactly the point where the matrix is used with great effect by the State. Of course there is dissent, but it is not, nor can it be, mainstream. Dissent is often reported, but never supported in the media. Newspapers? They are owned by the wealthy and raise much of their finance by advertising. Television is largely the same story. In the case of State-run TV, like the BBC, they are closely monitored for 'bias.' Bias is a tricky word, but it suggests anything that veers far from what might be called a normal consensus. It's this normal consensus that leads again to the social matrix, because the State has been wildly successful in determining exactly what it is. Noam Chomsky has published views which lucidly and spellbindingly dissect exactly what has happened. The manufacture of consent. The vast majority of people believe any 'radical' view is automatically suspect or worthless. Neighbours, peers, friends, fellow workers all have an underlying core belief that the normality of their State is unquestionable.

IS ALICE?

This 'consent' is sold harder than any snake oil or used car. The executive branch of any State consists of salesmen of the highest possible expertise. They are given the social spotlight of quality publicity, and they relentlessly sell the concept of normal consensus under the guise of policies. The reason 'democratic' States have four to five year expiry dates for their governments is not because of fears of permanent party rule. It's because even the finest salesmen on earth look like shop-worn liars after two or, at most, three terms. Hence another election is called, and those salesmen are replaced by newer ones with the same (though slightly varied) message.

The infinitely assorted advertising organs pelt out the message in sophisticated as well as primitive forms. Meanwhile the 'electorate' is increasingly shackled by debt, mortgage and oppressive working conditions. It is no longer easy to complain, or make any impact on what is happening. The people become just a part of the flow determined by the State. It is a contemporary form of slavery, every bit as degrading as any historical example. To protest now or go on strike is to jeopardise the whole way of life that has been finely tuned to the slogan of normality.

In most large States, there was an earlier attempt to break the control of political parties by corporate interests. Unions were born through much struggle, and provided an alternate system of finance for more radical parties formed to oppose the capitalist model. The early success in the creation of these parties was partly based on general western fears of something worse – violent revolution being imported from Russia. But after the collapse of the USSR, any political ground gained by these parties is rapidly being clawed back. In the UK unions have been emasculated by laws enacted by the party their contributions help support, an egregious irony. Unions have been attacked physically, financially and viscerally. Corporate interests smugly discovered unions were not immune to the viruses of authority, status and power, and such corruption is infectious. Retired union executives sit in the House of Lords, or live in sumptuous homes provided by their memberships – rewards for loyal service to the State. Despite fierce internal resistance over the years since its inception, the Labour Party has been systematically hijacked and turned into a parody of the US Democratic Party, itself already a parody. In other words, a faintly liberal wing of the Conservative Party or the Republican Party. Meanwhile union membership is only human. They, too, are drawn by the siren enchantment of normal consensus and all the new avalanche of consumer toys. And naturally they are in debt. Struggle is not as easy as it was before – and it was never easy then. People have been blinded by stories sold by hucksters and gangsters.

These nasty stories woven into the matrix by the State are affixed to the latticework by fear, that powerful and useful emotion. State-sponsored fear has been relatively constant during the course of my life, though it changes rapidly. There was the threat of 'communist takeover' and a white-knuckle dread of nuclear conflict until the disintegration of the USSR, and now there are terrorists under every mobile phone. Additionally, there is fear of financial ruin and failure. Stress from these fears elevates consumption, thus forming a self-perpetuating loop. The cleverness is diabolical. Once the engine is up and running, no fine-tuning is necessary. Now all corporate energies are concentrated into making the phenomenon completely global.

Of course the gangs at the top reflect the nature of the criminal gangs below. They fight among themselves like starving wolves over a fresh kill. It's territorial, and more is never enough. This is true insanity, beyond the abilities of its participants to understand it. It's the creation of a world far wilder and more dangerous than Alice's modest invention, and it threatens to engulf all of humanity. Her demons are nothing compared to those generated by global capitalism. This is not a lunatic running down the street brandishing a samurai sword, either. These are genuine madmen with whole armies under their control – armies equipped with cutting-edge technologies and weapons of mass destruction at their nervous fingertips. Lunacy is far too inadequate a word to describe this seething mass of cancerous protoplasm. Alice's altered state is based on the *addiction* to the energy of her inner stories, and the power it gives her. Likewise, the capitalist world is just as addicted to its own much more insane tales and its sad, predictable destiny. Both worlds are located at the negative polarity of consciousness.

One of the carrots used by the State and its matrix host is the concept of *progress*. Yet the understanding of progress is difficult for even the wisest. All that can honestly be said is that we exchange one set of circumstances for another. We don't necessarily 'progress.' To gain a perceived advantage, we leave behind something that was once seen as a part of normality. It is by no means certain that a historical visitor from earlier times would exchange places with us. He would come from a place unspoiled by noise, fumes, traffic, airplanes, gluttony, electronic invasion and contamination of rivers and seas. Who knows what his choice would be? It is certainly not self-evident, as most people believe. Our skewed understanding of history is no help, as the State ensures a built-in prejudice. Their list in support of progress includes health, when most ancient societies had access to drugs, cures and medicines. Dental work was once carried out with bow-drills, and there is very early evidence of trepanning. I would not be surprised if even infections were dealt with successfully by some social groups. After all, the same ingredients to make antibiotics were available then, and people then were as smart as we are now – or we wouldn't be here.

There are definitely more advances in technologies, more things, a much denser population – that's clear. But what has been swapped in the process? When we gain something, we always lose something else. One of the biggest losses is sensitivity to the rhythms of nature. We are now surrounded by concrete, electric lights, heightened mobility, insulation from weather changes, information provided by machines. We are able to live and work '24/7,' as they say today. For those 'gains,' though, we lose something I believe to be vital – contact with the planet and the environment in which it exists. This could easily be fatal. Not only are we a part of the *process*, we are a continuous part of existence. An earlier fisherman would have known over-fishing would result in future famines, but our world is driven by the obsession to make more wealth in search of the slippery goals of status and power that are our perversions. The last fish would be hooked out of the ocean with glee, if the present fishermen were convinced it would make their fortunes.

In retrospect, this misconception of progress was a profound flaw in the ideas of Lenin, as well as those of Marx. It doesn't emasculate their work, but it was a built-in formula for failure. To embrace the capitalist State's definition of progress was to ensure the collapse of a rebel State competing on those terms. Having said that, though, it would be morbidly naïve to believe a rebel State could have emerged and existed in any other way. The currency used by power is *force*, and it must have been sobering to the point of nausea when, after the end of World War II, the West was mesmerised by the looming bulk of the biggest land army the world had ever seen – poised in the very middle of Europe. The financial and political encouragement given by the so-called democratic governments to the rise of fascism as an alternate lure to the workers had completely backfired. The armies of Hitler swept west, instead of east, giving the USSR time to build an army that would devastate the fascists and threaten the entire existence of the capitalist world. It furthermore united a pre-socialist country that was in virtual disarray. It is not beyond belief that the USSR would have collapsed 30 years earlier, if it had not been for WWII. Such an irony is absolutely lost on mainstream historians as well as politicians.

There is a need for a further big revolution. This one needs to be in a totally different category from those of other centuries. Essentially, the State needs to be shaken loose from the matrix and its connections scrutinised carefully. Radical changes must take place before it is re-attached. Honest people must sit down and think about what kind of world they want, because it is ours – and theirs – to change, create and establish. That must be done first, and we must know what we are doing and be clear about why we are doing it. Fanciful? No, not at all. It is a necessity. It is clear that capitalism must be assassinated and buried. It is now time – past time – for a socialism that is ruthless but humane. Of primary importance is the dissection of the idea of progress. We must establish what we want and what we are willing to exchange for it. That has never been done, and it must be done. I echo Lenin here. That which is beneath the surface must rise to the surface to be seen by all. Leadership is still necessary, but this time it must be honourable, transparent and wise. It is too late to make many more mistakes.

These leaders must be capable of questioning themselves as closely as they question their motives and their direction. Every treaty, every agreement, every important meeting must be available for all who want to see. After all, what is there to *hide*? Lying now is so commonplace that truth is hard to imagine. Nonetheless, it is possible to have this REAL revolution, a turning through the complete 360 degrees *of the way we look at things*. If not, it seems probable that we will lie our way to complete self-destruction, so that our bones lie alongside those of Neanderthal and other evolutionary cul-de-sacs. And what a loss it will be! The arts spring to mind even before the sciences. What beauty, what balance and harmony we are capable of, and how we are near to squandering it through mendacity and perfidy. Yes, we are near. We are close to choosing that disaster.

IS ALICE?

Those with their eyes down on the cracks in the pavements under the lash of their owners – those slaves have the power to understand and revolt and demand changes that will turn us away from Armageddon.

No, Alyosha, I'm not being over-dramatic. I have eyes, and I am capable of scanning the horizon. This way is not the way, and if we persist, we are already as good as extinct.

Starting such a revolution is simple. If everyone – or even the majority or a large minority – just stopped working, the whole thing would collapse in weeks, rather than months. But this State is so deeply cemented into the fabric of the matrix that this very simple act is almost impossible. In the first instance, people will not allow themselves to know the problem or the solution or its urgency. In the second, the call to quit would be lost in the colossal dissonance of the sinister symphony of advertising, sport, political lies and fear conducted by the global corporation of the State. Those who believe they are not slaves are utter fools who do the work of Satan and damn *themselves* to hell.

I would not be writing these words if I did not have hope. After all, you and I will be dead before the real chaos begins. Also, this analysis is written in the dialect of the times with evidence from *this* matrix of *this* world. However, I've spoken of manifestations that lead me to believe that other forces may be active. I know that our own matrix is not presenting an accurate landscape of 'reality.' My difficulties arise from the fragmentary nature of the information. My Satoris and visions display something far richer, accompanied by more depth and meaning. But whatever I see is soon shrouded again by mists or vanish like frightened geese at the noise and clatter of the common sense world. My analysis is materialistic because it reflects the values of a materialistic world. My conclusion is that another, far more serious revolution is necessary. Yet I'm aware that *many* other events could take place, with their 'causes' only very dimly understood. Even so, I maintain that revolutionising the matrix is the crucial necessity. Look at Alice. It must happen with her, if she is ever to leave the asylum. Now turn to humanity. It is far more deeply insane than she will ever be. But, like her, humanity has no idea that it has alienated itself from a healthy destiny and the universe itself. Is rescue possible?

Yes, it's possible – *but it's by no means inevitable.* This lunatic is armed, dangerous and obsessively compelled towards the catacombs of doom.]*

IS ALICE?

CHAPTER FIFTEEN

"What is it?" I asked.

She was staring at her hands. "I feel a little wobbly. Porous. That woman at the table. Was she taking the piss?"

I was concerned. We were in Waterlow Park, sitting on a bench together after having a coffee at the café in Lauderdale House. "No. Just making small talk. Look at me." Slowly she raised her eyes. "Keep looking, darling. I love you. You understand?"

"Yes."

"Good. Hold on to it."

"It's still tugging at me. Something she did... said... and I was suddenly wondering why I was there, what she was talking about. Are you sure she wasn't taking the piss?"

"I promise. She was just looking for company or something, making small talk."

She touched my arm with her hand. "I think I'm OK, Theo. Those thoughts are so strong."

"Tell me again. What are they like? It's so difficult to understand."

"Well..." She thought for a moment. "We were talking to her at the café, and I began to wonder if what she was saying was a kind of subtext. Like she knew something I didn't, and was laughing inside about it. And I looked over at you and wondered if you were part of this subtext, too, a part of something I could never understand."

I covered her hand with mine. "That's devilish. How did it occur? What were your feelings, your thoughts?"

Again she paused. "I don't know. I mean I can see now, from this perspective, that she was probably a little nutty herself, just wanted to be friendly..."

"But then, a few moments ago, tell me exactly. If you can."

"It may have been a facial expression, a kind of sign. Or the way she said something and flashed her eyes. That... little combination, probably innocent, completely innocent – I can see it better and better now – and she was just being conversational. I... I was too bubbly, trying to make wisecracks..."

"Yes," I broke in. "That's a common factor, it seems to me. When you're trying to engage someone with humour, be a little lively..."

"But that's how I am. Or how I think of myself."

"I know. This is so difficult. It may be best to try and lay back when you first meet someone, until you get used

to them, watch how they combine expressions with words..."

"I can't," she replied in exasperation. "It rubs against my nature. I get caught up in what's being said, and, naturally, I want to join in the fun. Then I'm in trouble. I only trust you. And my friends. Just a few people on earth I can relax with."

"At least you have a few," I said with a smile, trying always to be 'positive,' but feeling a little meretricious.

"I know, I know. I should be grateful. I am grateful. My god, you've given me everything. Before I met you, I couldn't have hoped for such success. It was all stretching before me, a barren landscape of never-ending fear. Getting ill again, going back to hospital, not knowing whether or not I'd ever get out again, the fear of being hospitalised for life, the despair. Oh, Theo! The horror! I just wanted death. And if anything happens to you, that's what I'll do. But at least it will be in happiness, not in hopelessness. I hope you understand..."

I sighed. "You know, Alice, personally I love life, adore it. I'd leap at the chance to live forever. It's been a wonderful journey. An old reprobate like me, a life full of sexual antics with other women – and now I've been blessed with the greatest bounty I could imagine, the best sex, warmth, love, trust..."

"Oh, Theo..."

"Shut up," I laughed. "I'm not finished. I was going to say, if I had an illness such as yours to look forward to or anticipate endlessly, well, I think... I know I'd consider suicide myself. The fear of enforced nightmares, hospitals, stupid psychiatrists, drugs with toxic side-effects, loneliness, constant anguish... it's too grim even to consider. It's one of the few really good reasons for taking your life."

"And you'll help me find something to use if something happens to you? Maybe find someone who has something I can use? I just can't bear the pain of other methods."

"I've told you already. We'll find someone. I don't have any contacts myself now. There's nothing legal I know of. Maybe there's something on the Internet. I think there's a place in Switzerland where euthanasia is legal..."

She put her head down and clasped her hands. "I can't stand the thought of being without you. Who would look after me in hospital? Who would intercede on my behalf? They would force me to have ECT. I had it, and it left me confused for a couple of months and may even have affected my memory to this day. You stop them from doing that. You make sure my interests are looked after, pay my bills, buy cigarettes, argue with the nurses and doctors..."

Alice trailed off, almost in tears, and Hawthorn sat back on the bench, looping one arm around her. "The scenario I'm pursuing... trying to pursue... is somehow helping to make you well. It would be my dream that, on my death, you could manage to hold your head up, knowing you were free from the threat of illness. Finish your life, maybe with the inspiration of our relationship..."

"...But I couldn't, Theo. You are everything to me..."

I touched the back of her head gently with my hand. "Look how far you've come already. When we first met, you were scattered. Nothing was focused..."

"...like those little dots, none of them joined up."

"Oh, some of them did. And you've joined up more. I can't explain how different you are now. You're more earthed. You know more of yourself."

She paused for thought. "It's true. But you've done it. You've helped me. Without you..."

I shook my head. "No. It was you, Alice. No one but you can join up those dots. If I could do it, I would. But I can't."

"It is you. You give me hope. A reason to try."

With his arm he pulled her close to him, and she turned her face up to his. They kissed. He spoke softly. "We can't predict the future. It's opaque. We have to continue. One step at a time. You anticipate too much. Concentrate on your inner balance. Then, in a crisis, you will have a reservoir of strength. Whatever comes, you can face it. Fear adds coals to the fires of pain..."

* * *

Hawthorn lay on his bed, propped up by pillows, and blinked away a memory of an incident in Waterlow Park. A glass of whisky stood on the bedside table, and the second movement of the Schubert B-flat Sonata was just beginning. It was the recording by Aleksei Cherkasov, and it never failed to move him deeply. He listened to the music, as remembered scenes flickered through his consciousness. So often he and Alice had listened to it together, eyes closed, holding hands perhaps. He returned again and again to memories of their long talks or little social crises. Or sex. He realised he was – somehow – going to have to change the way he thought. The common sense world, the social matrix, had too strong a pull, an irresistible gravity, and he knew the answers would never emerge if he continued picking at the questions with a rational axe. You couldn't get it out of your head – that was the deadly thing about this world. The temptation to measure and weigh everything, find reasons that, when examined, were no reasons at all. The reverie he just experienced was like that. His responses to Alice seemed so mechanical in retrospect, so pedestrian. He knew there were two separate aspects of her illnesses. First, there was understanding it, but the second was even harder – doing something about it. Much of the time he felt on the brink of the understanding, just lacking one or two degrees of fine adjustment. He could see so much of it, yet the pieces did not fit into a whole. He avoided conventional psychology, determined that he would proceed with his own intuition and judgement, unclouded by the observations of others. Frustrated by rationality, he turned to visions and spirituality, instinctiveness, the art of *knowing*. However, that was a process that evolved in its own time and space and didn't necessarily result in 'answers,' either. Nevertheless, he realised they were more likely to lead to understanding. Afterwards he would have to address the hard part – how, actively, to help her. The process was now an obsession.

He took another sip of delicious, cold whisky, then closed his eyes again. Agitation and desire were insistent voices at the margins of thought.

* * *

The curtains were drawn, candles were lit, and little clouds of frankincense emerged from the top of the bureau in the corner. I was lying on the bed, but it felt like I was sliding slowly downward and inward. Though I had had nothing to drink, I was tipsy from unrelenting desire. It was no longer possible for thoughts to entrap me as I slipped into complete immediacy. All of me was in the moment, without memories, without a future – and the moment was vibrant with muted colour, fragrance and the impossible tilt of passion. Alice re-entered the bedroom wearing a diaphanous dress that only vaguely disguised wispy underwear, and, as I turned my head slowly to look at her I smelled only the perfume of her existence as it saturated and inflamed my loins. She was smiling as she slowly lay down beside me, and I felt her touch again, as delicate as the fabric of her dress. She pressed herself against me, as I lay there helpless and static, and my arousal was too much to bear. I felt her hand and fingers tracing little arabesques on my belly, around my thighs. The whisper of her voice was hypnotic.

"We are together now, once again. You are where you are, and I am here. We are on a journey, Theo, and the sea is calm and fresh. You are the ship, and I am your north star."

She placed her hand around my penis and moved it gently, rhythmically. Emotionally I exploded, but my body did not move or even shudder. On instinct she paused just at the point of no return and waited a moment before continuing. I felt her leg snake over mine, warm in its slippery stocking.

Her mouth was at my ear now. "You cannot move, Theo. As much as you want, as much as you try, it is not possible. You are sailing towards my star, towards me, beyond all that you know. Your will is my will..."

The walls of the room were rubbery, as if alive, and it felt as if the bed were moving. I was a ship. On the sea. And those were the heavens above me. I felt a sudden gust of wind as her hand left me. Alice was moving herself on top of my boat, now straddling the mast. Slowly and unbearably she lowered herself until she was touching the tip. Then, like velvet night, she enveloped me into her and sat there atop me. I could feel the heat of her bottom and the furnace within her.

"Theo," she sighed. "My god."

"I feel too close, going towards the edge..."

IS ALICE?

"No," she said gently. "Not yet."

I felt her slowly raise herself, leaving me wet and naked, before she settled again in front of the mast and leaned back slowly against it.

The wave had almost engulfed me, but now I felt it slowly ebbing away before rising again at the touch of her bottom. She lay down on me, her mouth now close to mine.

"Not today, Theo." She was breathing heavily, almost orgasmically. "Tomorrow, maybe. Or tomorrow. Or tomorrow."

It was agony but ecstasy, too. The polarities connected with electric flashes. I could feel her thoughts within me, and I knew she could feel my own, as she moved her body slowly upward, allowing her thighs to trap the mast for a moment before moving again. Her belly was smothering me first, before I was overwhelmed by the scent of Eden before the Fall. We stayed like that, then, her hips convulsing slightly above my head, her breath quickening. All was darkness now, and her filmy dress was like the touch of fairy fingers around my shoulders. It was Eternity, and we were the universe – not cold, but warm from the heat of a billion suns

.

* * *

The reverie was so clear and so warm that he felt he was nearly there again. Their sexual lives had become a magic garden, and their creativity seemed to push it further and further from anything he had ever known before. They invented space and travelled through that space and beyond it into other places too intoxicating to be called 'places.' Each weekend – and sometimes during the week – they would travel together, each entwining the other at atomic levels, so close that they were one being. He could feel the indescribable membrane of her consciousness as they moved beyond all that they had known, together, indivisible.

* * *

Hawthorn realised he might be a little drunk – either on the whisky or the memories. As their play became more intricate and inventive, their relationship subtly changed. They became closer, more intimate, more trusting. There were times when fragments of her illness would intrude, and her deep anxiety would have to be addressed. But they would eventually return to their play with intensity increased rather than diminished.

He knew also that they were experimenting with a crucial mechanism of consciousness. Nevertheless, he couldn't deny the overwhelming attraction of the sexual percussion. Never had he known such devastating desire, nor had she. Consummation was delayed again and again over days, then weeks, occasionally months. They would lie together as she brought him again and again and again to the point of ejaculation. He would warn her every time he neared orgasm. She would stop, then start again, relentlessly. Finally, both of them would cross an invisible barrier, and the pellicle of self would dissolve. They would become two parts of a whole that was subtly different from the selves they knew. Double-thinking and reflection were impossible,

IS ALICE?

and thought was confined to the infinity of the moment. They merged and migrated to strange and undulating places where there was neither darkness nor light.

It was agonising for Hawthorn to think of these events, yet he couldn't help himself. As he lay back down, he sighed. His love was unlike anything he could remember, a fusion in wonder. Beyond explanation.

* * *

I held her close to me after it was over. She had allowed me to come after weeks of tantalising scenes beyond the edge of the experiential horizon. I lay on my back as her hands brought me continuously to the brink for more than an hour. Or it seemed like an hour, if time must be measured. She talked to me confidently in a whisper at my ear.

"I think it's time," she said. "I feel it is. Something moves inside me."

"Thank you," I murmured. I was lying still as her hands moved.

Like a silky python, she moved on top of me before guiding me into her with excruciating slowness. "Come," she breathed. "Come…"

I realised what the earth must feel as its largest volcano erupts from its bowels and blows square miles of rock and soil into the atmosphere, dimming even the mighty sun. Red skies pulsated, humid with condensation, as the fire blasted into the air and molten lava foamed from tormented entrails. Light struck open the doors of darkness, illuminating old corpses of memory, and swept clean the space. Now pulsed towards eternity, scattering fragments of past and future into the throbbing horizon of being. Forces beyond those ever imagined severed time like a maddened snake, and the duality writhed and squirmed for unity once more. It was rapture.

We lay together then, arms and bodies entwined. Her breathing was heavy, the world remained unstructured.

"I still feel you," I heard myself whisper. "We're together still."

"I know," she gasped. "It's strange and wonderful..."

"Pieces of me are scattered round the universe embracing morsels of you..."

"Magic," she murmured. "A magic spell. I wish it could last forever."

"I think it has. It will. The whole of our session I was with you. Right from the beginning..."

"We were dancing," she continued with words I was going to speak myself. "You're a sorcerer."

"No. A sorcerer's apprentice." I looked into her eyes as she kissed me and smiled, before she kissed me again, pulling away, kissing and smiling. "I just wish I could do for you what you do for me..."

IS ALICE?

She laid a soft finger over my lips. "I feel everything, know everything..."

"Those fucking drugs you take now, since..."

"Shhhhhh... It's all right. I don't need it. In a sense I feel it so much more..."

"But it's a sin that psychiatry is so insouciant about the medications they give out like candy. And I don't even think they work..."

"I have to have them, Theo. Just in case they do work. When they changed my medication recently, I found I had this problem, as you know. Side-effects are impossible to predict. I don't want... I don't want to take even the slightest risk, the horror. Listen. I'm happy. So happy..."

I looked into her eyes again. "But darling, I've just exploded and scattered myself through starry skies. I want you..."

"I was with you, Theo. I felt everything. It was...unexplainable. A wonder."

Strands of her blonde hair stuck to her cheek, and I smoothed them away with my hand. My leg was between hers, trapped in the warm nylon cushions of her thighs. My hand idled down her bare shoulder, brushed her breast and stopped briefly at her waist before roving onto her hip. The gauze of her skirt thrilled me as my hand slipped down to her soft, round bottom. As I caressed her, my loins jolted again. Her knickers were nothing but sheer film.

"I can't tell you how much I wanted you. Still want you. I've known many women – some beautiful, some not so beautiful – but they are dwarves by comparison. Two dimensional. Partly formed..."

She squeezed against me, thrusting her hips madly. "Do you really mean that? Truly?"

"I thought I knew the meaning of sex, and now I'm not sure if I even know how to define it any more. What happened today...it was a transfiguration! Since I first knew you, we have been on a constant upward spiral that doesn't seem to have an end. Though all things seem to end. Now... maybe... everything is in a state of becoming. Or at least we are. I'm going to have to re-jig my metaphysical underpinnings..."

"Metaphysical wot?" She was giggling and lurched against my body.

"I'm gonna drive one underpin into you to stabilise my system!"

"You're not! Not until I say so!"

"But I'm sorely tempted."

"Theo. I can't describe my happiness any more. These things were never for me. Others, maybe. I was the odd duckling – the ugly duckling – they all ushered me

toward the margins. Normality was not for me, never, never, never..."

I let go of her and reached for my pipe as she turned over and lit a cigarette. "I don't think you can call this normality, Alice. Not even super-normality. Or hyper-normality. I can't help but think that we found each other after a long search..."

"You found me."

"Maybe. I don't know. Causality falls apart when you move this far from the frontiers."

"Before you," she said, "I was nothing. This was not my world, not one I knew or recognised. It wasn't anything I could understand. I couldn't bear the thought of living it all the way to the end. Everywhere I looked the flowers wilted. The earth was blighted, dull, meaningless, painful. Hateful. With you, I've seen a few magic blossoms, the sky, the sea. Laughter. Oh, my god, Theo!"

She squeezed my hand and wouldn't let go.

* * *

Hawthorn studied the picture of his mother hanging on the wall across from his bed. The Schubert sonata had finished a few minutes ago, but he had stopped listening as his memories unfolded. They re-ignited his hunger for sex. No, he thought, that was wrong. His hunger was for Alice. Just 'sex' was no longer good enough, and masturbation gave him no pleasure now. He played with himself idly for a few moments, then swore in frustration before throwing off the duvet and walking to the toilet for a last piss. When he came back, he had his glass of water in his hand. After shaking out a sleeping tablet, he threw it in his mouth and washed it down with the last mouthful of whisky. Then he pushed in his wax earplugs, turned off the hi-fi and light, and pulled the duvet around his body. He felt really tired, and dragged one of his pillows to cradle closely in his arms. He guessed the habit dated back to the time his dad made him throw away his teddy bear when he was about eight.

* * *

He was on a dark street, and his sense of fear was overpowering. It was necessary to walk down that street to get to the place where he parked his motorcycle. He was already late for rehearsals, and it was getting later. Maybe too late already. And they were depending on him being there. There were re-writes, and tonight was the opening performance.

He had seen this street before, and dread seeped through him like inky, toxic, icy treacle, chilling his blood. There was a figure in the shadows of a doorway, and he could only see the white teeth of his grin. Someone else moved on the other side of the street, cutting off his escape. Two others sitting on a doorstep turned slowly to stare at him. He was trapped, and now he could actually taste the dry bile of terror. The man in the shadows stepped out. He had hairy, thick arms, one forearm tattooed with an anchor.

"Hey. You."

IS ALICE?

Hawthorn backed away from the man, his shirt now clammy with sweat. The two men at the end got up and spaced themselves aggressively. One of them pulled a flick-knife from his pocket. It snicked open, revealing a slender, deadly blade. His thoughts became chaotic, without form, boiling in a fierce whirlwind, out of control. He knew he was going to die, and he felt he was also going to cry like a baby, pleading with them to spare his life, begging on his knees...

"Shit," Hawthorn said, as his eyelids snapped open. He threw off the duvet. He was hot, but his whole body was shaking. It was an awful dream. He couldn't remember such a sense of visceral panic. His hands were shaking, but he grabbed his teddy-bear pillow and held it tight as he closed his eyes again. He didn't want to return to the dream, but at the same time he was gripped by the suction of compulsion. His resistance crumbled as he was drawn by the magnetism of inner disaster. *The street was there, the men were still staring at him. There were two men behind him now – one from the doorway and someone else – as well as the two in front. No way out. An avalanche of thoughts cascaded through him too quickly for him to grasp. Run? No, impossible. Try and break through? Too dangerous. Too dangerous also to stay where he was. He was already crying now, baby-like, and calling for help. That made all the men laugh as they slowly closed in on him. He turned first towards the ones behind. One of them now had an axe. An axe! How could you fight against an axe? He just wanted OUT OF THERE!*

Again he woke. His heart was pounding, and now he was cold, shivering. His legs, his feet. His hands were clammy. Hawthorn had never imagined such an avalanche of fear, and it was drawing him in again! It mustn't happen. It was a dream. He knew it was a dream. But it was also extremely vivid, inside his head. Knowing it was a dream didn't ward it off, like garlic in the face of a vampire. No, he thought, no, I don't want to go there again. His whole nervous system was alive, throbbing electrically, and he realised his breathing was desperately shallow.

"No," he said out loud. "NO!" He grabbed the duvet again to cover himself, looking for warmth, seeking comfort, reassurance. Yet he was instantly into the dream again. He realised he even *wanted* to return to it. To see it through. To see what happened. And especially, to witness his shame as he dissolved into weak and useless pleas to his imminent murderers. He knew there was a way out, an escape, but was astonished that he did not *want* out. He wanted *more*. Greed bloated his thoughts, as he sought ultimate humiliation before mutilation and awful death. *He was on his knees before them now, but they decided on torture as they taunted him to resist. But he couldn't, as he spasmed in agony...*

Hawthorn woke up, completely terrified now. His body was hot again, burning. He thought of turning on the lights, and dismissed it. He wriggled out of the duvet and fought it, as his eyes were forced to close once more. It seemed inevitable now. He had no choice but to descend again into the nightmare...

IS ALICE?

They were dragging off his trousers now, laughing, their ugly faces close to his. One of them spat in his mouth as he cried. Someone held his arms, someone else his feet. They grabbed his genitals, and the man with the flick knife leaned over as the blade caught some ghostly light. He began cutting, sawing at the base of his penis....

This time Hawthorn sat up in bed and turned on the light.

"Motherfucker!" he said out loud. "What the *fuck* is going on?"

He leapt out of bed, shaking himself, then began doing stretching exercises he did before judo practice. Spreading his legs, he touched the floor three times, stood up and bent backwards, then repeated the movement. Then he rotated his arms before shaking his hands loosely and rolling his head round his shoulders. He sat down cross-legged, keeping his back straight, closed his eyes and breathed – slowly in, slowly out – centring himself, pushing everything back towards the edges of consciousness, refusing any corporeal thought. Breathing. Just breathing. In and out. Slowly. Nothing, nothing, nothing.

After a few minutes he was calm. He imagined a big tap root growing from beneath him, going deep into the earth, drawing up nutrients, gathering together the oneness of body, mind, spirit. A golden beam of healing radiance touched the top of his head, then filled his body as it cleansed him.

When he opened his eyes, he immediately realised what had happened to him. It was in fact some kind of awkward gift, but he would wait until tomorrow to think it through. Meanwhile, he knew how to dispel the nightmare. It was a tool he often used when confronted by bad dreams in the middle of the night. He lay down on the bed, stretching on his back. Then he closed his eyes and conjured up the scene consciously. The moment he did so, he was surprised that it still tugged at him. *Go*, it said to him. *Go to sleep. Come back to me.* He resisted, but now with a strong spirit.

They were there, two on one side, two on the other – he was surprised just how real it was. He glanced at his watch. Still time to make it to the theatre. He took on the axeman first, deflecting the blow with his arm, then executing a perfect seoi-nage shoulder throw. As the man slammed into the tarmac, the axe came away in his hand. He turned smoothly and sank the axe into the forehead of another one. Flick-knife thrust a blade, and Hawthorn easily trapped his arm and dislocated the elbow after pulling him off-balance. The third one was moving forward, and he swept his foot out from under him. When he fell, he dropped with his knee into his victim's neck, snapping it. He was then perfectly placed as the last one charged. Tomoe-nage, stomach throw. The thug slammed with his whole weight into a wall. Hawthorn got up to check the bodies. One was still breathing, so he cracked his spine.

And that was it. He found his motorbike, started it up and headed for the theatre.

IS ALICE?

It always worked, he thought to himself smugly. And it did this time, too.

The next morning Hawthorn sat at his kitchen table, still in his nightshirt, and stared thoughtfully through the blinds. He could see a blue sky. The day was sunny, and he was enjoying his first mug of green tea. He couldn't help being awfully pleased with himself, because he was right. The nightmare was certainly a gift. The provenance was unknown, but it did not matter. It was a demonstration carried out by his own psyche of the mechanism Alice used when she slid helplessly into illness. Of course he was stunned, because he never thought for a moment that he would be vulnerable to such an exotic episode. Above all, it showed how creative *and* fragile human consciousness was. Furthermore, it reinforced his certainty that he was right about the basics of the social matrix. The psyche was *easily* manipulated, despite certain conviction that, somehow, the individual was safe, whatever the social pressures. It was also infinitely inventive.

Mainly his excitement was aroused by the experience itself. So often he had found himself facing gruelling frustration in trying to imagine what *exactly* caused Alice to slip away into her nether world. What did it feel like? How could it possibly take hold against determined resistance? At times he felt exasperated with Alice as she tried to describe her experience. He was tempted to grab her shoulders and say, "*Just try!*" Yes, he knew the pull was irrational, but nevertheless the human will must be able to prevail!

Now, finally, he knew.

So…he knew *what*? Hawthorn put his feet up in the chair opposite and tilted his seat. To hell with the cork tiles, he thought as he had another sip of warm tea. Well, it confirmed what she told him. It *was* irresistible. If his dream had been a state of madness, then the first time he was drawn back into it, he would have been 'gone.' A sense of humility is never a bad place to begin.

But what was this place, and why could anyone be drawn into it? Hawthorn never really liked the idea of an 'unconscious.' It seemed to him too convenient a carpet under which it was easy to sweep puzzling litter. Furthermore, he disliked the concept of one part of the mind working against another. What possible advantage would that give – evolutionarily or otherwise? However, if his reasoning about the social matrix was right, it implied the possibility of creating any number of 'fields' – coherent clusters of stories invented to explain the 'outer' world. Using the electrical metaphor, a 'field' would have *polarities*, and these helped energise the web-strands of a matrix.

His brow furrowed, and he put his feet back on the floor and brought the chair down onto four legs. Did emotions then provide the energy of the 'field'? He wasn't completely convinced by the accuracy of the metaphor, but at least it was in itself a kind of story that allowed him to think about the problem diagrammatically. It would certainly make more sense of mental structures than psychology that used the explanation of the 'unconscious.' Hawthorn wished he knew more about quantum theory, because he had a hunch it might be a useful tool at this point. Well, there was plenty that neither he nor anyone else knew about the world. He would have to continue with the tools he did have.

If the equatorial region of the 'field' could represent 'stability' – in other words, a story that held maximum social feedback and a reasonable interaction with the 'outer' world – then the meridians towards each polar region could express the tension necessary to hold the story in focus. The polar regions themselves needed more thought, but for the moment he visualised bright positive and dark negative poles. There was a similarity between them, though, a kind of mimicry in operation. Something seen clearly at the positive end could be observed only as the shadow of itself at the negative end. Immediately he thought of Plato and the metaphor of the caves – everyone seen as shadows in the cave is illuminated upon exit into the sunlight.

Hawthorn didn't care to theorise any more about the polar regions just yet. It was vital to understand his new model first. And the model was intriguing. A singular 'field' of consciousness hovering within a human body, completely separate from everything, yet, paradoxically, a part of everything. This was so much more harmonious than traditional views. A buzzing hive of stories set inside a bigger story involving self-defined time and space, enhanced by the use of language – a tool to name, structure, manipulate and colour thought. What struck him sharply was how powerfully *creative* such an engine would be. Such a consciousness was alone in some kind of universe of unknown immensity.

What that consciousness historically proceeded to do was to try and find a story to explain the phenomena it found itself reacting with. That story would allow the 'outer' world to have shape and meaning. This was the creation of the social matrix. It would have the illusion of solidity in order to encourage belief. Once believed, it sprang to life. Yet it induced giddiness to realise the fragility of this world. All depends on the stories of perception and agreement on those stories. And there was no way of ever actually knowing what was 'real.' His thoughts swerved round to Kant. From before Plato through to Kant and the phenomenologists, perceptive minds had seen this problem all along.

And what of the compulsive nature of nightmares? Hawthorn believed these new tools using new models could provide an answer. Then he laughed, almost spilling the remains of his tea. There. He was at it himself, imagining solidity where there could be none. Answers? No. No-one could provide answers. They could only seek stories that provided brief glimpses of other stories. Certainty was increasing, though, that consciousness, to exist at all, *must have* a matrix.

He laughed again, and this time wiped his eyes with his hand. Here he was, a lone magnetic field within some kind of world, totally blind, except for his tapping white cane of stories that attempted to make sense of what it touched while he tried to imagine what it really was. Human beings were blinder than bats. Stone blind, in fact. In effect, all they had in order to survive was their *imagination*.

IS ALICE?

Yes! And for *real* imagination every facility was needed. No, not needed, *required*. The maturation of that faculty might even be the ultimate nature of evolution, one of the most powerful stories ever imagined. Hawthorn got up and stretched both hands to heaven. Such ideas inebriated him. He threw down his hands and staggered out of the bright kitchen feeling more alive than he had ever been in his life.

CHAPTER SIXTEEN

*[Ah, my friend – can I call you my friend? With all these instalments I'm sending, I feel I know you well. Right now I imagine you sitting in your dacha in the country. It must be snowing by now, and the fir trees through your window should be crinkling white and heavy with the frozen drool of icicles. I imagine you to be sitting at your desk, reading this letter under the mellow light of a bulb. Do you have another dressing gown besides the one you gave me backstage after I destroyed your performance? And you might be drinking lemon- or clove-flavoured tea from one of those heat-proof glasses in an embossed silver holder. The hot water is heated by an old samovar once owned by your grandparents. The samovar is sitting on a side cabinet reflecting your reading light in brassy elegance. It's easier to use the electric samovar nowadays, I suppose.

I have no idea of your thoughts on what is becoming such a massive manuscript, as I porpoise through this sea of ideas. I have received no answer from you since I began, nor did I really expect one. I have not yet finished my tale. Alice is still in hospital, still refusing to see me, still embedded in her dark and lonely world full of alien and odious times – still confronting the twisting devils of her creation, naked to their hatred. As you are aware, I spend most of my waking hours trying to tease out threads of the Gordian Knot – the elusive nature of a consciousness that has no nature. Perhaps I need Alexander's sword. Paradoxically, I find judo practice is probably more fruitful than pure thought. I've also taken up the game of Go again. At least I've played a few games of Capture on the small board. I crave a different way of looking at things. I think we are all so seduced by the western industrial paradigm, the epic story imposed by our social matrix. Hammer away, chip away, apply the razor of reason, measure, weigh up, judge, prove, consult statistics. It's a blinding blizzard of boundless bullshit. Insight, imagination, invention… are all found elsewhere. The Japanese have always intrigued me – that is, until they began aping the west under the lash of the global economic whip. From an early age I sought courage – you can even still see traces of this in the dark matter of the nightmare I wrote about. I believe it was the main reason for learning judo in the first place. Because of early bullying, I yearned for security from physical attack. Yet I was deaf to my better teachers at first. I saw judo as a mechanism for inflicting grievous damage on an attacker. All you had to do was learn the techniques, perfect them, and you could turn the villain on his head. Well, no. This was wrong. Because I bristled with hostility and aggression, I was still drawing the attention of those I wanted to avoid – making it more, not less, likely that I would have to defend myself. And I never had the confidence (or madness) of an aggressor. So I was also fearful. Displaying fear is like lighting a torch in a dark room. All eyes turn to it. The wrong attention in the wrong way. This attitude was also a barrier to my progression in really learning how to apply the techniques. When the penny began to drop, it was another cave experience – walking out of the darkness into the light. Learning can sometimes be close to ecstasy. As my 'attitude' improved, so did my judo. Nonetheless, my darkness remained with me, and that's as it should be. However, control passed from the darkness to my own control, because, ultimately, I am the creator. I am responsible. The simplicity is fragrant with eastern essence. Simplicity is the most difficult of all things to see. No one frees himself from fear. But you can learn its character.

Fear knocked on the door. Courage answered. There was no one there. An old eastern proverb.

I thought about the nature of what I am writing to you. Naming is irresistible to us, as it is easier then to weave it into our stories. It is not a novel. It is not really a documentary, either. I have to reach out to the Japanese for the right word, because there is none in English. They call it a *shosetsu*. This is not an autobiography or set of memoirs. It is a chronicle which contains elements of fiction. Time and events are occasionally re-ordered or compressed. However, these colourings of 'true' events are meant to help *reveal* the truth rather than embellish it. Many people fail to realise that 'true documentaries' or autobiographies, where all the 'facts' are in chronological order, are themselves highly coloured by the individuals who create them. In addition, the act of writing a biography or documentary, apparently highly honest, is not what it seems. It is devious, and can often be dishonest or downright dishonourable. It is a physical impossibility to re-create *all* the 'facts' about a series of events. Those facts you read or see are *chosen*, and so are their contexts. Indeed, you are presented with a highly subjective version of those events, and invited to give them the status of truth because they happened or are in the right order. Even cameras cannot film everything, including the presence of the cameraman or film unit. They always point in the direction chosen by the operators, leaving us to fill in the wider panorama guided by their words and emotions. Truth is as elusive as the wind, if you try and catch it.

These principles apply also to descriptions of 'the world.' Our attention is drawn to that which is convenient for those who work tirelessly to ensure that we focus only on those things which are illuminated. Just like illusionists. Thus, again, the social matrix. Never forget that this is the prism where we are enchained. This is our cave. It's not necessary to break those chains. Understand them, and they will dissolve before your eyes.

In early years I believed written history was a way to discover the 'past.' After reading Max Weber, though, I began to realise history would always reflect the values of the historian, as well as the times when the history was written. There is no escape from the subjective nature of the observer. The camera is pointed at something by somebody for some reason within some world view. The historian works with – presumably – documented 'facts.' Yet whoever wrote the documentation in the first place was choosing those facts from all the others being presented. Often the lives of kings, queens, popes and so-called nobility are documented, but those of peasants, serfs and the millions of ordinary people are sketchy or ignored. So the historian orders the documentation of the period and attempts to understand the Zeitgeist through evidence. Perhaps he makes every endeavour to re-construct this past world as honestly as possible. Yet his understanding of *that* world depends so much on his understanding of *this* one. In whose interests are the decisions made by past kings, generals and bishops? These interests are almost always hidden, because we can assume that deception is a crucial part of the picture. This goes for the chronicler as well. There are his interests to consider. Turning to the historian, every one of them writes with a political point of view, no matter how 'balanced' he tries to be. Is it a history of the elite, or a history of the oppressed? They will be very different tales. At every point the reader can ask the historian, "Which side are you on?"

And in any case, they are all just possibilities. Possible pasts, created for the present. The present is our infinite tyrant. And we cannot *know* even that.

Histories are stories written about the past, but often they are less helpful than fiction – see Zola or Dickens, for instance. Voltaire said history is the lies we agree on. Therefore, so is the present.

Of course, I'm still talking about the elusiveness of consciousness. At times I feel it's an aimless quest. Hopeless. Can I explain again to you that my love for Alice has much to do with this circuitous, spiral voyage? In truth, self and Alice are inextricably mixed. As they would be. Beneath a ticking clock I feel I must find the key to unlock her cell and set her free. At my centre, I know it is possible, and this knowledge provides my fuel. It is my mission to free my princess in the thinly sliced frames of my present. Forget the rational for the moment. Segue into fairy-fiction. I'm a kind of warrior, lost in space, lost in time, compelled to pursue level after level of realisation towards an unknown goal. There is something in Alice I seem to have known 'before.'

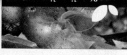

IS ALICE?

Maybe 'I' was her slave in classical Greece, maybe not. But I'm emotionally propelled by the tale. After all, the past may not be anything like we think it is. Remember also that *stories* are involved at the basic structure of consciousness. It is a *story*. And so are the actions of a warrior moving through layers of time, seeking a goal that is somehow eternally important. If I can help unlock Alice's cell, I just *know* something vital will happen.

I'm not speaking just about her illness now. By her 'cell' I mean that thing within her that twists and dampens her self and her being, that thing that draws her down, with the yoke of obsession heavy on her shoulders. The fear, the shadows, the hovering nightmare. It oppresses her spirit and refracts her wholeness into puzzling fragments. I almost want to scream at you – *I can already see it*! It is a part of the incomplete Satori of a warrior struggling against time, fighting forces he does not understand, not knowing what weapons he might need. Moving blindly. Seeking the Tao.

Ah, Alyosha, such extravagance. The common sense world scorns the rainbow arcs of my imagination, but the freer I feel to use so-called metaphor and analogy, spirit-colouring the plumes of liquid fire that lick at the secrets of the heavens, the closer I know I am to the truth. Take the nightmare I described earlier. For me, it delivered a meaning. How could it have been accomplished any better than that? No amount of rational, common sense description could have replaced those images, linking emotion to emotion in a dark little sonata for solo self. It helped me understand something that was almost – but not quite – impossible to understand, probably in the only way I *could* have understood it.

My little fairy tales, my visions and Satori, *also* have meaning. Like the nightmare, it may not be an exact description of what *is*. On the other hand, an exact description of what is, is utterly impossible. Why do we have music? It is to express something that cannot be expressed any other way.

My recurrent flashes of servitude to Alice in ancient Greece would be dismissed by the common sense man as false imagination, unreal, worthy of no further investigation. Thus the common sense man instantly displays the complete bankruptcy of the modern world and the thought that supports it. It proceeds in rank-and-file, marching at a relentless pace towards its own destruction, heedless of those who offer gentler and softer ways that may lead to unimaginable riches. I view this flashback to 'another life' as latent with meaning that will never be picked apart with rational probes simply because it is *harmonious*. On the page, words describing it lie as dead as notes on a symphonic score. But as the scene unfolds in consciousness, it resonates with self in glorious consonant euphony. For the ignorant it is a useless toy to be cast aside. For me it has the importance of another sense, another eye capable of seeing through the debris of 'reality.' Yet it remains a part of a puzzle for the time being. The reason? My instinct tells me I must experience other events, alter my thinking, seek connections that at first may seem irrelevant. Patterns are important, along with shadings. At the very least such stories and visions increase sensitivity to as yet unseen phenomena.

IS ALICE?

Children play. You can't stop them playing – though we try desperately to do so. I'll tell you why they play. It is an instinct even more primary than language, but adding language gives it infinite dimensions. If I were elected a Teacher of Children – an amusing thought – and my remit was to try and help them to be wise, then I would never force them into dark, uncomfortable classrooms. Instead, I would encourage play, freeing it up rather than circumscribing it. I would hope the resulting adults would remain playful the rest of their lives. Each day they would go to play, rather than to work. I can already spy the common sense man shaking his stony head in the shadows. "Airy-fairy. Wouldn't work. We need technicians, managers, organisers and many millions of people willing and capable of carrying out operations..." Etc. No. We have developed a crazed machine that is no longer open to serious questions about its purpose or nature. We are in desperate need of playful people to provide a source of wisdom. Furthermore, they need to be given our full attention.

For example, let's turn to the paradigm partnership. Man and woman. We think we know the functions and limits of such a relationship, but this paradigm is so leaden, boring and – frankly – insolvent that I can feel my eyelids half-close just by visualising such a thing as marriage. I'm sure you are fully aware by now that I am enchanted by women – their movements, their mystery, their core femininity. This is perhaps natural. If not, it should be. When I see a physically or spiritually beautiful woman cross my path, I sometimes shut my eyes first to breathe in the allure of pure oestrogen that begins to transfigure my soul. The *male* is conjured up like a genie – not just genitally, but including that. He has the power of Taurus or Leo and the guile of Reynard. Yet he can be easily or swiftly defeated by a serpentine movement or the cast of an eye. Wonderful magic! The sorceress evokes her spell, at times without a word being spoken. Leo and Taurus deflate to hopping toads as Reynard ruefully repairs his tattered net.

For most marriages, this evocative and priceless magic evaporates in the space of eighteen months or less. Or as soon as sexual appetite wanes. I am personally appalled by the sheer waste of this primal resource. And the solution is so simple, as are most 'solutions.' If the couple were never allowed to play properly, they should begin to learn. I say 'begin,' because there *is* some work to do first. As far as possible, they must not be dishonest with each other, and they must try and find genuine trust within themselves. If you have those two things, and you also have love, you are truly blessed. Therefore it would be a criminal, if not a mortal, SIN not to then *begin to play with each other*!

So. This is the biggest hurdle of all. Trust and honesty. Not surprising in a world buttressed by lies, disguise, dissembling and fakery. THAT is why I want those children to PLAY. Only in that way can they discover their most powerful human resources. Instead we wind up with adults who are retentive, fearful, devious creatures, who are accustomed to venality and illusion as their currencies of exchange. Naturally, disaster is the common result. People live together by habit and in isolation, fearful of troubling superficially still waters. Or else they stagger from one predictable catastrophe to another, in the thin hope of a kind of luck that would make a slot-machine addict look like a conservative investment broker.

It is my conviction that most people simply would not know how to go about installing trust or honesty in a relationship. The first reason is that many risibly believe they already *are* honest and trustworthy. This is, almost always, a lie. The worst kind of lie, the one to self. As proof of this, just start listing all the items that cannot be raised or discussed or oxygenated between you. Can you say *anything*? Can you accept *anything* your partner says with relaxed understanding and good humour? Are you resentful of your partner for any reason? This exercise is designed to enlighten, not to degrade. Just take all those items and lay them end to end. You would be surprised how often they stretch to the horizon. The *shorter* column is the one containing any form of trust and agreement.

And mark this: fear is the polar opposite of trust.

Ah, Alyosha, you and I probably both know the irony of this exercise. To be truly honest, you must begin by being truly honest with *yourself*. A tough one. It returns us to the first square. Play. Lack of play – or lack of the right kind of play – has left these adults brutally handicapped. Too soon they have been herded into atrophying school cages that perform the same functions as cattle-runs to slaughterhouses. Behaviour is standardised, imagination is circumcised, creativity is neutered. Lying is encouraged in epidemic proportions, and discipline is ferociously enforced. Children of spirit become adults of despair. A possibly magical world makes way for a truncated, enervating landscape with little light and less hope. It is, quite starkly, Hell. This particular world is Hell. It is only honest to admit it. It's the first step to understanding.

The work ethic is a killer. If I were some dopey 'guidance councillor,' and I suggested more play in a strained relationship, the first response would be the complaint that *work* took up too much time and left the couple exhausted, with only a little time to do chores before collapsing in front of a TV or diving into bed. My advice would leave me without a job myself, as I would shrug and say, "Give up work, then. At any rate, create some space. Play needs *space*. Plenty of it." Having said that, though, once you realise the importance of play, the space will create itself.

Within the dynamic of a partnership between two people, the prospects are literally endless – as broad as the participants' imagination. They can create any kind of world they want. I smile as I write this, because of the circularity of the idea. You are responsible for your world because it is yours and yours only. Therein lies your emancipation. The definitions are yours, as are all the values. You are *free*. Free to create your prison, or your landscape of infinite interest and compelling originality. If you are living in a turgid, unhealthy, oppressive world, you are the god. You created it, touched it with your finger. Made it live. With some enlightenment, it can be collapsed, too, and another one raised in its place. Any one you choose. Just look at the array of 'goods.' All free. No mortgage. No interest payments.

IS ALICE?

I thought about developing a little scene from a play for you, in order to better illustrate what I mean. But I hate doing that. A play is meant to be performed, not read, and I don't have the means to realise a special performance with lights and sound for your music room.

Sadly, such advice about play is not appropriate for every relationship. There is too much alienation and distrust, fear and mendacity. I can understand that even thinking about it would be terrifying for many. Illumination is frightening for those too accustomed to the dark. It's a bit like political change, isn't it? It's disruptive – and therefore to be avoided, even if it meant a much more enjoyable and meaningful life...]*

* * *

Alice sat in her room and stared at the white wall. She was slumped on her bed. Tears silently ran down her cheeks, as time passed by, sluggish and hushed. She glanced at her watch. The second hand crept around the face. It was a cheap watch, but it kept the time. She had had one before, but threw it in the washing machine and ruined it. Eventually another one appeared. Probably from Theo. It was impossible to keep him away. Against her better judgement, she kept this one running. On her bedside table was the little diary he probably gave her as well. She saw him occasionally from the corner of her eye as she tried to scuttle away, out of his sight, out of his life.

She picked up the diary listlessly. There were entries on many pages, but she didn't bother reading them. She was looking for today's date. The last page. Blank.

October the 25th. She sobbed softly, and more tears warmed her cheeks. How many months? How long had she been here? There was little to do, nowhere to go – just the awful room and the boring place. Alice was sure she would now end her days in this wretched hospital. She was condemned, and this was doom. No way out. *Huis clos.* She furrowed her brow for a moment. Was that the name of a Sartre play? Her memory was terrible.

Alice didn't realise it, but she was beginning to 'surface.' The nightmare was still there, but the demons were depopulating it. Everything was grey, not flickering reds and pinks, or threatening blackness. However, she prevented herself from breaking through the membrane fully, by reminding herself that *the* world was not *her* world. Therein lay the finality of her doom. The other world, *their* world, was too alien, and she lacked the means for communication. In other words, she was still highly paranoid but was now able to visualise self and circumstance – at least in fragments – within the 'other' social matrix.

At the moment she was trying desperately to remember just how long she had been in the hospital. The diary couldn't help, because it only began at the first of October. Other diaries had been thrown away or dumped into the washing machine. It had been summer anyway, she thought, and now it was winter. Glancing at the window she saw it was already dark outside, and only four o'clock. Her birthday soon. Then Christmas. But nothing for her, just a boring daily routine in the same rooms with the same depressing people.

IS ALICE?

It was going to be forever. She was certain of that. Forever and ever. Until she died, however long that took. As if encouraged by the thought, she dug another cigarette from her pack, and lit it. They allowed her to have a lighter, now that close observation was withdrawn. She knew for certain that this damnation was completely unbearable, beyond her means to change or transcend. What were her options?

She took a deep drag on the cigarette, picked up her diary again, and turned to the note section at the back. Heading up a page, she wrote: What To Do? Then she drew a wavy line underneath the question, going over it several times with her pencil for emphasis. There was no one with her to explain encouragingly that what she was doing now was a good thing. Faced with doom, she was making a positive effort to think her way out of it. The sense of doom was still there, and so were the tears and occasional helpless sobs. But something within Alice wanted to live, and just did not have the continuity to put together the sequential steps. Everything was skewed, though it looked normal to her.

After the number (1) she put 'Escape', and underlined it, too. But her pencil paused, and her cigarette burned unnoticed in her other hand as she was suddenly frozen in a sense of failure. Alice Dance *was* a failure. She had tried to escape, and failed. They brought her back, as they always would. It was then that she spotted a single dim light on her horizon. She immediately took a drag on the cigarette and added something after the first option. It now read, 'Escape. And ACT. IMMEDIATELY.' She double-underlined it all. The thought made her shudder, because it meant doing something like throwing herself underneath a bus, or off the Archway Bridge, as soon as she got away from the building. These conundrums always prevented her from successfully committing suicide in the past. There just wasn't anything that was guaranteed to be painless. She vaguely remembered that she had tried twice in her past with overdoses of paracetamol. Both attempts failed, as she vomited in her sleep and woke in A&E after being discovered by her father. Violent death under the wheels of a train was a visual image that jolted her with nausea.

There was now a glow on her horizon, not just a dim light. It illuminated the landscape like an extended, wicked flash of lightening. She realised suddenly that she was her own enemy. "As ever, as ever," she moaned to herself, as she closed her eyes and rocked. She was so scared of death that she condemned herself to life. Her phobia was a form of self-protection, a way of looking after herself, a way to somehow survive. Self-hatred broke through like pale yellow toxins in a wound. She ground out the cigarette butt in her makeshift ashtray, and immediately lit another one. Her thinking was clearer now, though still largely dark. Again she was drawn to the single violet bloom of illumination on her landscape.

"What makes me *work*?" It was a turbulent, renegade thought. It was the kind of question Theo pursued endlessly. "Theo, Theo, oh, my god, Theo…"

With all her will and energy she tried to turn away from the next thought, the one that was always there and which she always avoided. "I love him, I adore him…

my life, my heart, my desire, my treasure, always, always, always..."

It was impossible then to hold back the rush of more tears, as she threw herself back onto her bed in an agonising paroxysm of despair. Her sense of loss was so immense and absolute that it overcame all defences. A tidal wave of misery crashed across her ghostly panorama of self, dashing all her hopes. She threw the diary across the room and didn't even hear it hit the wall, as anger accelerated her pain. The tsunami of emotion was actually forcing her closer to the surface, but Alice Dance thought otherwise. Instead she cursed herself for sheer indulgence in her one secret and sacred thought, the one she tried to bury every day of her existence beneath a giant pyramid, and hermetically seal it forever. It was far worse than the fear or boredom of her daily life. There were now brief memory-glimpses of him sitting on a huge rock on the coast of a Greek island, smoking a cigar as the waves lapped his bare feet, looking back at her with his gentle smile. There was the sensation of his body as he held her. IT WAS TOO MUCH. Far too much. Her weeping turned to wailing as slim, sharp razors slashed her softness into shreds of bloody flesh. It was gone – all gone. The happy dream, the lazy days of rapture beyond all reveries of heaven and earth. At that moment, she would have gladly, giddily rendered her soul to Satan for one last full minute in Theo's arms. That indicating grave and intolerable *weakness*. She was a weak failure through and through, without grace or charity, without even the courage to commit fucking suicide, as she dragged her meaningless carcass through day after dull, tedious day, endlessly. She was a dreary slave chained to a millstone, walking round and round as she tried to slowly wear down the earth deep enough to hang herself by the chain. The sharp razors now became swords, because the wounds were far deeper. They thrust inside her, and she felt the cold impersonality of the steel points seeking turbulent vulnerable organs. The pain became so fierce that she felt she had to stop it. It was no longer humanly bearable.

She got up from her bed, realised she still had the stub of a cigarette in her hands and threw it to the side. Picking up the diary, she looked in panic for her pencil. She must write it down before she forgot it altogether. She must, she *must*.

Immediately she was confused again. Incomprehensible flashes exploded in her visual cortex. Theo was lighting a candle on the chest of drawers in his bedroom, in front of a framed picture of her. He placed two quartz crystals beside it… The image was so brief and so real that she stopped breathing. It was there, then it was gone. She stood like a statue, holding her diary in one hand, timeless, breathless, eyes wide with equal mixtures of awe and terror. She was dizzy, about to fall, and the walls of her room were becoming rubbery before she finally inhaled, gulping air as if she had broken the surface of reality after a deep dive. Dazed, she sat back down on her bed and reached for her pack of cigarettes. Her chest hurt. Her lungs were sore. But she imagined the smoke from the cigarette helped.

Other images overwhelmed her, and she tumbled helplessly. She was astride a galloping horse in a different landscape, a chestnut mare, her hair tied behind her head. She was naked, and felt the weight of her juggling breasts, as she screamed with delight. There were olive groves, and someone was with her, a man, on another horse, laughing. His name was Silenus, of course, and they... Another image flickered in her memory, just a landscape, two suns in the sky, one larger than the other, illuminating a lush plain with unearthly bright light.

She stared at the diary as if she didn't know what it was. The long ash of her cigarette informed her that she hadn't been smoking it. She let it fall on the bed and put the filter to her lips slowly, because she was totally confused.

"Oh, god," she murmured. "Please. Somebody help me..."

She sagged to her knees on the cold floor, and burst pitifully into tears again. The cigarette stub fell from her fingers, and the diary dropped beside her as she sank forward, face down, clawing at the tiles.

"Help me!" Alice Dance began to shout, then scream. "Help me! HELP ME! **HELP...ME!!!**"

She heard laughter as the demons returned, ghoulish giant laughing lips on black insect legs. They danced around her in glee, holding razors and swords, as they mocked her for imagining that she could escape them. They taunted her, as they held the images of her sweet memories overhead. Once again she had dared to hope, even if just for a moment, and they were going to make her pay. She realised she was the lowest, filthiest creature in the universe, and her self-disgust was so viscerally powerful that she felt her bowels began to empty in her pants. She could feel the turd grow, firm and solid, as she rolled and blubbered helplessly.

She reached behind, fumbling desperately and, almost with satisfaction, finally dipped both hands in the shit before smearing it over her face and head.

IS ALICE?

CHAPER SEVENTEEN

Hawthorn stood in a peaceful, beautiful garden. It was small, cloistered by walls on three sides, and it backed onto a bungalow with a low, red-tiled roof. In one corner of the garden were dahlias so vivid it made his eyes ache, and in another was a squat plum tree heavy with fruit. Towards the middle, off-centre and surrounded by individually-placed stones, was a tiny pond, partly covered by water lilies. Beside it stood a little granite bench. The air was clean, and revived him as he breathed slowly and deeply. The fatigue gripping him fell away, and was replaced by a profound sense of calm. He couldn't recall ever being here before, yet there was something familiar about it. Looking up at the sky, he realised the sun was obscured by a faint mist. It was cool, but not cold.

A darting swallowtail butterfly drew his eyes to the sliding back door of the bungalow. It was open, and he began walking toward it without wondering why. He had to duck his head when entering, after leaving his sandals outside the doorway. The deep peace of the garden followed him into the interior of the low-ceilinged house. It was completely silent, without so much as a light breeze to rustle the paper walls of the room to his left. It, too, had a sliding door, decorated with a single vivid maple leaf. This door was half-open, but he hesitated. Suddenly the silence was broken by the loud click of stone on wood – just one, then silence again. Hawthorn stepped forward gently, and turned his body slightly to enter the room.

In the middle was a Japanese man in a black silk kimono, sitting in the seiza position before a magnificent lacquered Go board that appeared to have been cut from the trunk of a large maple or oak. To each side of the board were wooden bowls that held the black and white stones. The man at the board did not look up as he entered the room. He appeared distantly familiar. His age was not easy to assess, but his thinning white hair was pulled tightly to the top of his head and tied in a knot in the manner of the samurai. His back was straight, and his head was tilted only because he was studying the layout of the stones on the board.

Without knowing why, Hawthorn moved opposite the older man and knelt, sitting back comfortably onto his ankles. The Japanese did not acknowledge his presence, and his face was impassive. He was a slight, compact man, and must have been less than five-and-a-half feet tall when standing, yet his presence seemed to fill the sixteen-mat room.

Hawthorn lowered his gaze to the Go board, and felt suddenly frightened with incomprehension. Though he knew a bit about Go, he had played only about 25 games in his life – a rank novice. He did know enough to realise that this was probably the middle game. There must have been nearly 100 stones on the board, and they formed an abstract pattern of black and white snaking lines, thickening in some places, thinning in others. Like the unknown Japanese, his concentration became focused. Somewhere in his being he realised it was a beautiful game. Absolutely beautiful.

IS ALICE?

Go has the simplest of rules but, during play, can develop to the limits of human capacities and beyond. There are 19 x 19 squares on the board, the stones are black and white, and played one stone per move. The aim is to capture the most territory. Black always moves first. Stones whose 'liberties' have been cut off can be removed. Basically, those are the rules. Simplicity. Yet during the course of a high-level game, tactics and strategies become so complex that they are difficult (if not impossible) to unravel using only reason. Certain configurations are said to have balance – and beauty. Truly great play is also said to come from the spirit of the players, rather than from their intellectual capacities.

Hawthorn sat mesmerised by the arrangement of the stones, and minutes became an hour. Neither man moved a muscle. The stones seemed to draw him into their structure, and detach him from awareness of self. From time to time, doubt would grip him treacherously, when he remembered his lack of knowledge, or even any understanding of the situation or this game. Heavy anchors threatened to drag him back to a 'reality' where he was more comfortable. On the other hand, real comfort lay in opening himself to the experience as it unfolded. It was the more-known confronted by the less-known that was the problem.

The tiniest of sounds drew his attention from the board. He glanced up to see an unbelievably ravishing Japanese girl enter from another room. She was dressed formally as a geisha and carried a tea service on a tray of glossy lacquer. Without a word, and with her eyes lowered, she first placed the tray on the tatami, then sat in the seiza position. The tea was poured delicately from the tiny ceramic pot into two small china cups. She stood up, and placed one cup to Hawthorn's right, and one to the right side of his opponent. Collecting the tray and tea pot, she withdrew from the room as silently as she arrived.

After a pause of several minutes, the man opposite him exhaled an audible snort before lifting the cup to his lips. Hawthorn raised his own cup and sipped the aromatic, delicate flavour of the tea. For the first time since he arrived, the Japanese looked at him directly. His gaze was steady, his eyes dark and partially hidden by the folds of his eyelids.

Hawthorn heard himself speak. "Who are you?" he asked in a hushed voice.

The man did not answer. Instead, he lowered his eyes once more to the board. Then he had another sip of tea.

Hawthorn followed his gaze. He knew he was playing black, often a courtesy offered by a stronger player to a weaker one. Carefully he picked up his cup, and allowed himself another sip of the fragrant tea, realising that it was refreshing.

Finally he said, "I have no idea where to play the next stone, Sensei."

The Japanese rose with an abruptness that startled Hawthorn, adjusted his kimono and obi, and walked out of the room. Hawthorn got to his feet and followed him through the small opening of the room door, and out again into the garden. He paused to put on his sandals. When he turned, the Go player was sitting on the little stone bench beside the pond. Hawthorn walked over slowly and stood beside him. He looked reflectively into the still waters of the pond, and waited for the man to speak.

"You forget because you are still inexperienced," the Go player said finally. He spoke in Japanese, but Hawthorn understood him perfectly. "I am enjoying our game, but have to wait long periods of time for you to continue. Your last play was..." He paused to find the right word.

"...very able," he continued after nearly a minute. "It has given me some difficulties."

"I'm puzzled, Sensei, by..." Hawthorn began.

"Don't speak," the Japanese warned in his soft voice. "You are not yet fully present. Even so, I must talk with you before we continue our game."

"Please, Sensei, I don't understand."

A long silence followed. Hawthorn allowed himself to enjoy again the peace of the beautiful little garden. He let the breaking waves of questions roll by, until the water was still again. His mind slowly began to clear.

"No one knows the meaning of the process," the Japanese said finally. "We are a small part of it, but small is never insignificant. One molecule of alcohol changes the nature of a large quantity of water. Errors are made. By us all."

"Us?" Hawthorn queried with a raised eyebrow.

The man held up his hand. "Yes. Even by my own sensei. Errors, if not fatal, are a vital part of learning. We engage powerful forces, and we, too, are strong. But beware. Our strength must never become obvious. If that happens, it will turn our enemies' attention to us before it is time."

The older man paused again. A blackbird rose suddenly from the bamboo leaves, and was gone. The sun was warmer now, and Hawthorn looked upward. The mist had cleared. He studied the back of the seated man, and felt within much warmth, perhaps even love. The body was erect but relaxed, and exuded tranquil nobility.

"You are playing well," he said finally. "When we return to the Go, look at the board again, and it will become less opaque. If you continue like this, you will win. For me, that will be a good thing. I will be happy to see you so strong. Soon you may be able to take your place."

"My place." Hawthorn repeated the phrase, but it was not a question. The meaning had some resonance within him.

The Japanese got up from the stone bench abruptly, and turned towards him. The air was still, and so was the man. They held each other's eyes for a moment, as if in a trance. Neither spoke, and Hawthorn heard the blackbird again.

IS ALICE?

"Remember," the Japanese spoke in a hushed voice. "A really good sword stays in its scabbard."

Without another word, the man turned and walked to the bungalow without another glance, and Hawthorn followed him up the path.

As he was removing his sandals at the door, he reached up absently to smooth his hair, and was completely jolted when he found the top-knot of a samurai. At that moment, he knew who he was and where he was. He eagerly entered the room and sat at the Go board, already anticipating his next move.

* * *

He looked in the mirror critically, turning his head from side to side. His goatee was fully grown now, and actually needed trimming. It was getting a little too bushy. Reaching for the comb and scissors, he made a mental note to buy an electric trimmer when he was out. The beard was completely white, as was most of his hair now. As a young man he had often wondered how his face and shape would change with age. Now he knew. He liked the effect of his goatee, but that was mainly because it hid a double-chin he inherited from his father. Age made the flesh looser. He loathed his father's shape, and was determined to keep as fit as possible. The beard hid some of the obvious reminders of his inheritance.

As he trimmed with the scissors, he turned his head from side to side again. Fundamentally he wasn't unhappy with his appearance. A large head – his father again.

His hair was receding slightly at his forehead and a bit more around the crown, but he could never see that bit. It was a slow recession that began in his early 20s. Someone pointed out a tiny bald spot at the back, about the size of a quarter. In more than 30 years the spot had grown only to the diameter of an orange. Hawthorn shrugged. He wasn't worried about his hair, anyway. Or about his wrinkles, even the ones around his brown eyes. His fair, Celtic skin, though, was obviously a gift from his mother. Her antecedents were mainly Welsh. Some of his old freckles were still visible in his pinkish skin.

He finished clipping, hung up the scissors, then frowned. He was still trying to remember fragments of a dream that must have occurred early that morning, before he woke. There was something compelling about it, but every time he tried to refresh the imagery, it seemed to fade further away. He had been somewhere in Japan, playing a game of Go. At first he dismissed it, because he had recently taken up the game again, only to find he was completely inexperienced and even awkward with the stones. But now he had found someone who could at least teach him a little. He was the son of one of the judoka at his club, and they had already played a few games. Hawthorn lost heavily, but he knew winning and losing weren't as important as in chess. And that was one of the reasons for its attraction.

However, there was something devilish about the dream. It seemed as if it were very important to remember at least the outline of what happened. At first, he lay in bed for over half an hour, trying to piece the thing together. It just wouldn't come at all. A game of Go, a complicated one. A beautiful garden. And a bird that flew from the bamboo. An older Japanese talking to him, something very important.

As he walked towards the kitchen, he stopped suddenly, frowning again. There was a pond, wasn't there? Or maybe he was just filling in the empty spaces. Why was he playing Go beside a pond? What did the other man look like? He had no idea.

He flipped the switch on the electric kettle, and reached for the pot of green tea in the cupboard above. It was an important day. Alice's birthday. November 2nd. She was taking too long to recover. It was unprecedented. At most, during her past, she had only been hospitalised for a maximum of three months. Now it was already five. The thought jarred open the entrance to a long, dark corridor of despair. Hawthorn quickly slammed the door, determined not to allow himself to drift any further down that corridor. He cleared his head and closed his eyes.

"Alice will recover. She will be whole again. There is no doubt," he muttered with determined confidence.

Quickly he poured the boiling water onto the infuser and stirred rapidly, fascinated as the liquid turned slowly to a darker shade of brown. Then he knocked the leaves from the infuser and hung it up on the side of the cupboard.

Dropping onto the sofa in his front room, he sighed and took a sip of tea. At once a dream fragment returned. They were in a room with a Go board, and he recalled the taste of tea. He laughed, and thought about the absurdities inherent in some dreams. First they were playing beside a pond, then they were inside a building. Flit, flit. Dreams had their own logic, their own structure.

Ironically, the study of dreams provided the first success in his struggle to understand consciousness many years ago. He laid out various theories and examined them carefully, before rejecting them as incongruous or absurd. He would only be satisfied if his eyes rested on an idea that resonated honestly with his inner knowledge. It finally occurred to him. Stories. That's all they were, just stories. Being such a simple idea, though, it became immediately more complex. Just like the game of Go. What? Were? Stories?

He tried to begin at the beginning. Stories were obviously vital. He himself was a writer, and spun them as a craftsman. Childhood began with stories. Human existence would be nothing without a history, a written or spoken past. There were religious tales, folk verses and songs, rhymes, poems – and now pictures, videos and movies. Then there were variations, like painting and music. All were fundamentally *stories*. Finally, he turned to thought itself. A few years after he began excavating beneath the foundations of his inner landscape, he met Alice Dance, whereupon his explorations became more focused and intense.

He chuckled as he picked one of the Upshall pipes from the rack, and began to fill his first bowl that day. To be honest, it was always the first bowl he really enjoyed. One day, perhaps he would try and restrict himself just to that. It was one of the disappointments of age. Moderation had to be recalibrated regularly. Less food, fewer drugs, less alcohol, more rest and meditation. He remembered nights or whole weekends he spent drinking and screwing. Six pints – even eight or ten pints – at the pub, with whisky always a necessary nightcap. Different women in his bed, along with accompanying emotional turbulence. Now he was down to one glass of whisky at night. And one woman.

He leaned back on the sofa and relaxed his head, as he puffed joyfully on the pipe. One woman – and one of the best. The *only* one for him. That was a thought he never imagined he would entertain, because the world of flesh heaved with excitement. New bodies, fresh skin, exotic smells and tastes, the sheer heaven of different vaginas writhing beneath him, pinned like butterflies. Drunken gropes in dark hallways as his fingers stroked silken nylon, as some young woman ground her pelvis into his.

He sighed with such delicious memories, but his inner eye fell finally on the warm and luxurious figure of Alice. In the end he had found one who was the essence of all the others, and allowed him into the private chambers of love. Love. In the past he had dreaded that word, and scorned it. Only later did he realise it was because of its social reduction to trivial sexual enigma, and it was the primary buzz word used by advertising scum. It was soiled by overuse, and therefore the meaning was all but lost. It was a word best left to the finest musicians and poets, along with the relative few who were blessed with the serendipity of its comforts. Hawthorn guessed that love was often glimpsed but seldom captured. It was more than 'an emotion.' That was clear. It was an altered state of being, and allowed the human spirit access to unequalled privileges beyond the reach or imagination of the common sense world. Above all else, it had dramatic importance for the success of the human experiment.

Hawthorn raised his head from the pillow rest, and took another sip of tea. Instantly, fragments of the dream recurred, induced by its gentle fragrance. Did the dream also have something to do with love? It was maddeningly frustrating not to be allowed entry into his own memories.

He looked at his watch and sighed heavily. He told the baker he would pick up the cake before noon.

* * *

He opened the white box and showed it to Pan Subarti. They were standing in his hospital office. It was a strawberry, banana and cream cake, and the words were written in dark chocolate. 'Happy Birthday Alice.'

The head nurse smiled and nodded. "She'll like that, Theo. Very pretty."

Hawthorn also gave him the handful of birthday cards from her friends. Along with one from him. "My guess is that she won't want it, Pan. But I had to do it anyway."

Subarti nodded conspiratorially. "She's in the TV room. I'll take it in to her."

IS ALICE?

"I'll have a peek from behind the door. I don't think she'll see me from there. Oh, yeah, and here is another carton of cigarettes. Please make sure she's the only one who gets them."

Subarti put down the cake and cards, took the plastic bag with the cigarettes and put them carefully in the bottom drawer of a filing cabinet. "Oh, don't worry about that. I'll take care of it…"

Hawthorn sighed. He relaxed, and regarded the head nurse with a degree of sympathy. It was the system they served that was intolerably polluted. It demanded the cheapest and easiest forms of control. It imposed order with medication that was chiefly designed to disable patients, make them docile and obedient. Not too unlike the governmental system outside the hospital, he thought wryly. They crush the spirit of patients like others crush the spirit of their children. Pan Subarti was simply a helpless officer spinning out his life in a filthy job so he could pay his rent, eat, and watch soaps and sport.

He peered from behind the door to the TV room. Alice was sitting back in her chair staring vacantly towards the window. The TV was on, but no one in the room seemed to be watching it. There was a half-full mug of tea on the table in front of Alice, and a cigarette smouldered between her fingers. Pan Subarti approached her with the box, and put the cards on the arm of her chair.

"It's your birthday, Alice. Happy birthday," he said in a kindly voice, as he placed the box in front of her and opened the lid.

She stared at the cake for a full minute, then finally put down her cigarette, removed the cake from the box and immediately turned it upside-down on the table. For good measure, she placed her hand on the back of the cake and squashed it, leaving her hand-print in the middle. Then she grasped the cards in both hands and tore them in two, before throwing the pieces onto the top of the cake. The head nurse backed away from her.

"Shame on you, Alice. That cake was bought specially for you. Now you've ruined it."

Hawthorn tried to catch Subarti's eye, vigorously shaking his head and waving his hand. Scolding was the last thing he wanted, the worst thing to do in the circumstances. He knew immediately that Alice was incapable of seeing the meaning of the cake or the birthday. Of course, he had hoped that the gift would catch her at a moment when she had a brief glimpse into normality. At the very least he just wanted to watch her enjoying a taste of it. Strawberry-banana-and-cream was her favourite.

He put his head down and turned back up the corridor. Pan Subarti hurried after him apologetically.

* * *

Hawthorn snapped into the shoulder-throw with a whip-like suddenness. O'Grady's defence held for less than a second. It was a clean throw, right out of the textbook. And, because of his height, it was one he seldom used on anyone shorter than he was. He had to drop his right leg slightly to the side in a variation of the throw, but O'Grady landed solidly on his back.

"Here we go again," O'Grady moaned as he got to his feet. "You're back in the groove."

Hawthorn grinned. "I had one night, about a month ago. Since then I've been rubbish. You've slapped me all over the mat like a wet fish."

Immediately O'Grady attacked with a blinding series of combinations. But Hawthorn felt light on his feet, as if choreographed by unseen hands. Not only did he defend, he began a counter-attack, and suddenly caught his opponent with a beautiful *ko-uchi gari*. It appeared as if O'Grady stepped on a bar of soap, and Hawthorn followed up with a hold-down, a simple *kesa-gatame*. It was perfect, no chance for an escape.

O'Grady shook his head as they got up. "You're hot tonight, squire. I didn't even see where that came from."

Then his partner leaned forward and whispered. "You couldn't have picked a better night for it." He nodded towards Kawabata Sensei, 7th Dan, the highest ranking member of the club who made occasional visits and held teaching sessions.

Hawthorn tilted his head in acknowledgement, but he didn't want to stop. He was in full flow, on a landscape he had only visited once before at the club. He didn't feel himself as an individual, but as a part of something else, a point of power. Repeatedly he threw the man who usually trounced him. Good throws, clean ones – not sloppy, straining efforts, when both contestants lose their balance and fall. Several times he followed through with arm-locks or strangles that were instant and unbreakable.

Several pairs of the other judoka present stopped and watched them. O'Grady was fighting hard, but Hawthorn's movements were so smooth and strong he was barely tiring. Everything just seemed to be working in fluid majesty.

O'Grady was grinning amiably as they finally finished and bowed. As he clapped Hawthorn on the shoulder, they were aware of the approach of Kawabata Sensei. He wasn't a large man – maybe just over five-and-a-half feet tall and eleven stone – but he was lean and wiry. Kawabata was about the same age as Hawthorn, or a little older, perhaps. His black and grey hair was trimmed short, and his face was impassive. He wore the red-and-white belt of his grade.

"Good *waza*," he said to Hawthorn with a slight smile.

"Thank you, Sensei," he replied.

"Would you?" Kawabata indicated the centre of the mat. He was being invited to a *randori* session with a 7th Dan.

Hawthorn followed him, the Japanese turned, and they bowed. He had worked with Kawabata before, mainly in training sessions, and each time the Sensei treated him like a toy, throwing him easily. He was somewhat in awe of the man.

Kawabata's grip was light, his stance erect, and his movements were soft and sure. And Hawthorn was thrown almost immediately with a *tai-otoshi* that was so smooth and rippling he never saw it coming. But as he got to his feet, he felt strangely calm. His fear evaporated. He had found his space again – or it had found him. As they continued, Hawthorn immediately feinted with a foot technique, slightly unsettling the 7th Dan, who moved forward slightly, his legs a little apart. Before even Hawthorn knew what was happening, he was standing over Kawabata after completing the cleanest *uchi-mata* he ever performed. He heard what sounded like a single intake of breath from the judoka watching.

Kawabata rose from the mat as gracefully as a cat. Their eyes met, but nothing was said. The Japanese attacked immediately with a blinding series of movements – forward, backwards, to the side. Hawthorn kept his balance, defending only enough to prevent the throws. Inside he was aware of a glow, a lightness, some connections beyond his comprehension. He made a beautifully-timed *o-ouchi-gari*, followed by his own *tai-otoshi* that staggered the Sensei. He did not fall, though. Instead he whipped into a tight *seoi-nage*. Just on the point of being thrown, Hawthorn entangled his leg with his opponent's, and they both crumpled to the mat. Even before they hit, the Canadian was fighting for his favourite arm-lock, but Kawabata was a serpentine coil of piano wire, and just managed to slip out of it. Hawthorn kept up the pressure with a *shime-waza* – a strangle – executed so quickly he surprised even himself. It was just instantly *there*. Solid. His Sensei almost immediately tapped his arm in submission.

As they both rose from the mat, the enormity of what had happened began to seep underneath Hawthorn's guard as it dissolved his serenity. He was shaken, and watched Kawabata intently. But the 7th Dan only smiled gently as they both bowed. There was spontaneous applause from the watching judoka, and Hawthorn caught sight of O'Grady clapping with his hands over his head, a huge grin on his face.

Kawabata took him by the elbow and led him to the edge of the mat. Both men bowed as they left it, and his Sensei led him into the little office. The desk was against the wall, so Kawabata sat in one armchair, inviting him to sit in the other as he rolled his around to face him.

"So," he said immediately. "What do we have? You are a *nidan*, and you now perform at the eighth level." His English was excellent, though accompanied by a melodious accent.

The tension and embarrassment were too much for him, and he defensively leaned forward, elbows on knees. "I…honestly don't know, Sensei. In fact I'm totally confused. It happened once before with Tim O'Grady, but tonight it was very strong."

Kawabata raised one eyebrow. "An inner wind, perhaps?"

IS ALICE?

Hawthorn smiled. "Something like that. As if it were not really me, but someone else. Someone much more skilled. I'm no longer *thinking*. And I…I react to someone else's energy. Not to them, but…at any rate, I can somehow see clearly. And everything works perfectly. Then…" He held up his hand as his mentor started to speak. "Then the next time I come, I'm awful. Worse than I am normally. Unconnected. Awkward. O'Grady cleans the mat with me. I'm thrown by 1st Dans, once even by a brown belt. At other times I'm back to 'normal.' I don't even know how to describe it."

Kawabata cleared his throat. "In my lifetime I have observed this happening maybe once."

The Japanese paused as he turned and looked at the wall. "You see, when I was a child, I was equally strong in judo and Go. My father taught me Go. He told me I must choose, judo or Go. Not both. You cannot do both and do well in both. From then I trained four days, sometimes five or six, including competitions. That is how you learn good *waza* – if you are fortunate enough to have strong teaching. It becomes part of your life. Inseparable from your life. Many, many people – in Japan as well as the West – only play part of their lives. They may be able, but they will never reach beyond the fourth or fifth rank. There are a few exceptions, of course. Judo today is very different, and we established this club to try and return to early principles of judo. Today they play a corruption of what was once meant. A fine athlete may succeed and become champion without all the years of practice."

He stopped, clearing his throat. "But this – what you did tonight – can happen. Very, very rare. Tell me more about this feeling of 'energy'."

Hawthorn sat up and leaned back in the chair, closing his eyes. "It's difficult to describe in words. It's like talking about ghosts and apparitions, almost. Yet I wonder if it's not more imagination than anything else. On the other hand, I don't think it is. At first, when you invited me to *randori*, I was full of awe and fear, and you threw me straightaway, as you usually do. But then I slipped back into the space I felt with O'Grady. I was not sensing your body. Or mine. I was aware of your core, your energy…I don't know what to call it. *My* energy *understands* it."

Hawthorn stopped to think a moment. "Let me put it another way. What it *feels* like is that my own energy is being manipulated from some other…plane. Some other, perhaps larger, source of energy. Because, Sensei, I know I do not possess the skill to throw you or even to defend properly against you. I can't. I don't have your experience or wisdom."

He stopped again, worried by another thought. "I hope I haven't committed a grave discourtesy by throwing you…"

Kawabata interrupted with a wave of his hand. "Please. No. For some known to me, perhaps it would be a discourtesy… Whatever I may know, I still have much to learn myself. I was surprised by your *uchi-mat*a, but quite defenceless against it, because it emerged so naturally at precisely the right moment. How could a thing of absolute beauty be discourteous?"

The Japanese paused for a moment, thinking. "I know of these energies you speak of. I have even at moments found them in myself."

Hawthorn leaned forward onto his elbows again, frowning. "Perhaps you could advise me how to have access to them. Because I believe they are related to other events that have taken place in my life. I believe I have experienced Satori at other times, but I can never call them up. Or put them together. As it is with my judo. It comes, then it goes, and I can't find it again."

"Satori as well?" Kawabata leaned back and looked at the ceiling. "You see, we live in a world inimical to these extraordinary experiences. It is a mechanical world where things are of more value than ideas or beauty. Look only at judo. A beautiful thing is beautiful no more, except in a few remaining places like this one. Most now is just win-lose, in order to better mirror the world. But to return to your question. You have somehow managed at times to have each foot in two different worlds, yet you live in this one. You cannot be completely of that world while still in this one."

"What is this other one?"

"It is, I believe, more real than this one. Other than that, I cannot say. I'm going to recommend that you be advanced to sandan."

Hawthorn sat up again, alarmed. "No. Please don't."

Kawabata laughed. "Ho. Why not? Most judoka would jump at an advance in grade."

"With the greatest respect, Sensei, I do thank you very much. I would never have expected to reach *sandan*, however much I tried. The truth is that I do not deserve the grade. I'm barely qualified at 2nd Dan, and certainly not a good example. On the whole O'Grady is a much better player, and could beat me in any contest – unless I happened to be lucky and have one of these... moments. So I would be frankly embarrassed to carry a grade I could only occasionally defend. If *ever*. Who knows if I will have the experience again?"

Kawabata picked up a pen on the desk and tapped it. "Think, Theo. You are beyond the age of competitions, as are many of us here. In your youth grading is based on competition. Later, it is on other things. You may advance with confidence, as all will know your capabilities after your *uchi-mata* and *osaekomi-waza* with me tonight. If you are truly modest, you will accept the grading. It is my judgement."

IS ALICE?

CHAPTER EIGHTEEN

*[The wind whines, my Russian friend, it's wet outside, and either dark or sullenly grey. It's December already, and the outer world perfectly reflects the inner man. I haven't written in a while, because I've felt so drained of life, so thwarted and frustrated. Meaninglessness envelops me like a shroud. I've tried all the usual smelling-salts, but nothing seems to revive me, not even Mozart. I'm not joking. Last night I tried to listen to *The Marriage of Figaro* – probably my favourite opera – and found my ears dammed by the incessant circuitry of my own anxieties. Alas, this is one of my Black Dogs. I don't have many of them, and that *is* a blessing, the only one I can find on the bare trophy shelf of my present. To be honest with you, during this Black Dog, I find the thought of living another day agonising. I'm not looking for pity, but would like you to contrast this with my usual headlong optimism and determination to solve a mighty problem and somehow reach the mystical land of wisdom. Yet here I lie, inert as a piece of fly shit on an old melon rind, all that's left of hope.

I'm determined to write my way out of this thing, Alyosha, so prepare yourself for drowsy boredom. Either that, or chuck this part of the manuscript aside, as I probably will. Anyway, it's no help to think that probably everyone is subject to such dark moods, including you, and try and cheer myself up with the observation that I have had so few of them during my life. What is its most universal characteristic? Weakness. I'm speaking of heroic weakness here, even to the point of fading like a monumental ghostly phantom. Nothing works, nothing connects, everything is a beat out of time, and the smallest thing swells to atomic proportions in an instant. At the end of my arms are two left hands complemented by ten thumbs. I pick up a spoon to stir a coffee, and it drops to the floor and slides effortlessly underneath the cooker. When I try and fetch it out, I find it has disappeared completely, and I hit my head on the worktop as I try to arise, spilling the coffee and breaking the mug. That is actually a high point of my day, because something has actually happened – something nearly absurd enough to make me laugh. But not quite. Do you know that border between dreary awkwardness and farce? I've seen plays like that. The comedy is almost there, but the lack of timing leaves the audience embarrassed.

This has been going on for over a week now, as I dread the approach of Christmas. Even in normal times I loathe Christmas. Perhaps it was once a genuine celebration of the winter solstice, as people were filled with a little joy at its passing, with spring to look forward to. I'm peering out of my window right now, past the monitor of my computer. A local resident, muffled against the cold and damp, is loaded with bags and parcels as she skids in patches of snot or dog shit. Her stress is palpable. No doubt she has spent most of her money on presents that will be looked at for a moment, before being cast aside and shortly thereafter thrown away. Or maybe the bags are filled with food, but from the size of her, food is the last thing she needs. Already they are buying for Christmas. At the very apex of this spending holocaust is Satan himself, who gleefully rubs his hands as he says, "So many fools. So little time."

IS ALICE?

Probably the worst thing of all is the evaporation of my social confidence. In company, I observe that I'm now a puny, impotent force, no longer able to move smoothly or effortlessly. It seems arrogant to realise that I used to think of myself as a big presence in a room, able to turn the head of a pretty woman or entertain others with tales and jokes. Well, maybe I did these things, but so what? It means nothing in the end. In a relatively few years I'll be dead, and so will be the world. No memories, not even the awareness of nothing. No self. The world will be the same as it was before I was born. It all happens quickly. Birth, a struggle for the light amid the delusions of happiness and life, then failure and death. Is it inevitable? It must be. It figures, doesn't it? In the end there will be no survivors. In other moments I've imagined mysterious events, and I studied them seriously. Other planes? Experiences in what appear to be other times and other places now seem like no more than mental doodling. Yearning for wisdom is a simple waste of time. I am mortal, and stupidly drunk on my own dreams.

I'm going to bed. Right now I long only for a glass of whisky with which to salute a hopeful few hours of oblivion.

The next day. Or rather the next evening. I write only in the evenings, as I am definitely not a morning person. In the wild, I would no doubt be classified as a nocturnal troglodyte. When eventually I wake up, I much prefer at least an hour luxuriating in the sensual mists of sleep – usually lying on my back to ease the strains and pains from an ageing body subjected to the Judo Centrifuge.

Bill Bailey

With one languid arm I turn on the radio to the classical music station. When I finally get out of bed I stumble to the toilet for a slash, before making my way to the kitchen, where I pour out a portion of oatmeal and milk, ready for the microwave. Then I comb my hair, dress shabbily, turn on the microwave, and weave to the corner shop for a litre of milk and a newspaper. On return I sit and eat my oatmeal, as I take in a little journalistic propaganda. It is then time for a change of location, and I move into the front room and onto the sofa, where I fill and light my first pipe of the day.

In the mornings everything mental – or even cranial – is so slow it must be nearly static at the molecular level. I stare at familiar objects and fail to fathom their meanings. How could I possibly write? I can't even talk. If the phone rings, I let the answerphone take the message, as I couldn't begin to make an intelligent response, especially to an emergency.

To be honest, I had a very good sleep, the first I've had in several nights. The Black Dog is still outside, but he's no longer howling. I'm beginning to get some purchase on the wall with my fingernails. There are even moments of clarity. In this world, addicted to causality, some would say this depression has been triggered by doubts about Alice. I don't think so. I believe doubts about Alice have been used as fuel, as my consciousness moves into the dark polar zone in some seasonal pattern I have yet to understand. I think this dark region is necessary for even the healthiest minds, but some, like Alice, suffer more magnetic and insulting pulls. Also, my own current experience informs me that I've been right about *addiction*. Your struggle is to *stay there*, not to escape. Every action and every creative story is used to darken, not lighten, the atmosphere.

One curiosity I've noted while the Black Dog has been visiting is my intense vulnerability to the obvious mechanisms of the social matrix. For instance, the views and opinions of others shake my foundations like mighty earthquakes. That is to say, my *invented stories* of those incoming judgements begin to affect the core of my being. I'm reminded of my early days as an adolescent, trapped under a cascade of emotion about those around me and what they might be thinking of me. I'm even angry – as I was then – overheated by rebellion, always looking for an opportunity to lash out and hurt those unable to give me the respect I think (or wish) I deserve.

I wrote to you about those extraordinary events at my judo club, when my teacher was so impressed that he offered to recommend me for an advance in grade. Well, since then, I began plummeting, no doubt self-propelled. At the club I'm increasingly self-conscious, overly aware of other eyes judging me, looking for proof that I am really some kind of fake, a grandstander who can't really pull off the deception. As my technique falls apart and I deepen the impression of a clumsy oaf who has lucky moments, I suspect the eyes turned in my direction are filled with pity. Or scorn. Or, worst of all, sniggering contempt. "There he goes, Theo Hawthorn, a so-called 3rd Dan-to-be, not even worthy of wearing a black belt…" I usually train with Tim O'Grady because we get along so well, but now others want a taste of me, younger guys who are current competitors. They seem to get their rocks off banging an old man hard into the mat. Are they secretly laughing with each other as I struggle to my feet? My tactic is to just withdraw, not comment, not say a word – no apology for not being terrific or anything like that. But I *yearn* to throw myself at their feet and beg forgiveness for my failure. Do you understand the depth of this feeling of humiliation? Additionally, I'm feeding the flames with thoughts of these things getting back to Kawabata, I'm dreading him calling me into his office and telling me how he has now changed his mind. I assure you, I don't even *want* to be a 3rd Dan, and…

Ha! So there you are. Don't you see the childishness of all this cut-rate paranoia – particularly after all I've said about the nature of consciousness? From being a steady little boat, I'm reduced to being a rudderless wreck, spinning in the water with the mildest little storm. Today – just today – I'm beginning to see the awesome and very real power of the social matrix, something I underestimate during normal existence. Even knowing, as I do, much about how it works, one little visit from the Black Dog, and I'm helpless – lured into believing two items: first, that the world is solid and second, that what I detect from it is 'real.' The result? I imagine that I lose control and am completely reactive to events beyond my intervention. This is obviously somehow similar to the prison Alice builds for herself. The truth is that I have not 'lost control.' It's an impossibility. I'm in control at all times, whether I like it or not. HOWEVER, during my Black Dog, I have made a connection with the social matrix that is so strong no amount of will-power will destroy the illusion. Is that confusing?

IS ALICE?

OK, I'll try and explain a little further in a brief recapitulation of what I've already written. There is no hope of knowing what anyone else is really thinking. We manufacture stories based on what we observe of their actions (which are themselves interpretive stories), and confirm or question these by continual feedback and internal judgement. The story of the stage where all this takes place has already been created by our history, which we always carry with us in the present. This is the matrix, where our social being 'connects' with others in the story of a shared world. However, each of us is wholly responsible for the make-up and *meaning* of this connection. It is all done within our own consciousnesses, by our own thoughts. The *magic* of it all is that most of us believe that what we observe exists in its own right, independent of us. And therein lies its power.

I have been uncomfortable at the judo club since the evening of my luminous performance with Sensei Kawabata. I am carrying an old story within my history, that I am incapable of genuine achievement. It has been with me at least from adolescence, and normally does not trouble me at all. It was drummed into me by my father with little metal hammers, no doubt because he felt the same way about himself. This has remained a little trap for me during incidents when my confidence drains, and becomes a full-fledged, child-frightening hairy troll during the rare times when the Black Dog re-visits his old lair. Even as I write, I externalise by metaphor, accusing the Black Dog with shades of colour I add from my own inner palette with which I paint my world. Perhaps a key to understanding Alice is in discovering how this *desire* comes to pass, this wish to go to The Inferno and stay there. There would be no Black Dog if I did not actively desire its snarl and its hostile familiarity. And yet I also sense there would be no illuminating and creative moments without the existence of the Black Dog in my landscape. This is my current insane conundrum.

It is easy enough to see some of the mechanisms. The 'high' of the dramatic events one night at judo triggers its shadow 'low' carried in my historical baggage. That I do not deserve to be 3rd Dan, is something I genuinely believe, yet it is not through lack of self-esteem. I realise something expressed itself *through* me that evening. That is my healthy and honest assessment, because I simply have not spent the time and effort someone like Kawabata has spent learning the skills necessary to maintain that level of genius. I even tried to explain to him the other factors that may be involved, and he appeared to understand them.

The trouble is, the thesis of my very real achievements have their antithesis in a locked, solipsistic cycle, expressing itself as the knowledge that I'm unable and unworthy of any achievement at all. So, is the 'normality' of my existence the *synthesis*? I beg your pardon for this cod-Hegelian theorem. Also, I don't think it's right. However, there is a certain resonance that might lead to something that is relevant. It is interesting that both states attract a high emotional content. Well, emotion. Heh, heh. That's a word that transfers a known meaning. Or does it? My guess is that it is misleading, because 'emotion' refers to a general area which all seem to understand. As I turn my attention, though, to emotion itself, I see immediately that there are profound differences between what I feel during a 'high' moment and what I feel at a 'low' one. Think of 'consonance' and 'dissonance.' They are definitely related in sound, and not exactly in terms of opposites, either. No music since the Middle Ages would be complete without the two. We understand that they give both depth and breadth to musical expression.

I don't want to make too much of the analogy, but just wish to draw your attention to it. In my desire to create a story that better reflects what might be happening, I return to my search by listening for the tinkle of little bells that may lead to the well-struck, shuddering tam-tam.

I'm already feeling better and better. I swore I would write myself out of this, and it looks like I am. I have a little better control of the Black Dog. I invented him, and he barks only at my bidding.

It occurs to me that 'forces need to be gathered' for either state, high or low. So Alice is involved, too – or thoughts of her are. Despite all my efforts to the contrary, doubts creep in beneath my defences like little invertebrate wriggling worms. Is she now *permanently* mad? Is there no hope at all? Will she spend the rest of her days in some hideous institution in a hermetically sealed hell? That is her eternal fear, and that may indeed be another key.

Vertigo. The fear of falling *incorporates* a desire to fall. I have vertigo, even on my back roof, as I try and tend my plants with watering cans. Not only do I imagine a skid or stumble, I dwell on the imagery of each delicious/repellent moment, especially the ones I imagine during free-fall after leaving the roof. The thoughts that would go through my head briefly during the fall are intense – magnified by the certainty of death or very serious injuries. The thud. The finality. The meaninglessness of it all. Above all, perhaps, the humiliation. It would rank with the demise of Tennessee Williams, who choked to death on a bottle top.

There I go again. You see how many references about the seeming solidity of the social matrix creep into innocent narrative? Why should the question of what an abstract 'other' may feel about the situation of my death be of any interest to me? Yet those are the ones that spiral towards me, propelled by the explosion of fear. In truth, if I fell from my roof, fear would be the most likely assassin. And we all know that fear is surely the warden of Alice's prison.

Is fear an emotion? Can it be grouped together with joy, elation, love, or maybe even boredom? I think fear is an anti-emotion, because it destroys other emotions. It is the master of catastrophe, and fundamentally disables human consciousness. I'm not speaking of useful fears – fear of fire, or even heights. But at some point fear becomes a conflagration, a raging inferno, a panic, out of control and capable of breeding complete chaos. In its grip, the human being is compelled to make the worst decisions by default. If fleeing is the right course, an individual is statuesquely frozen. If stillness is required, flight is instantaneous.

At times I can feel the fork in the road in the flash of a visual instant. If someone were to attack me in the streets, I could either be panic-stricken or watch more closely as the situation unfolds and react to it, seeking a natural way of diverting the threat. That I'm more likely to choose the second option is due to years of training and study, both of myself and judo. Nevertheless, I know that panic is hovering there in the initial moment. If I've got the Black Dog's jaw clamped to my leg, I could easily jump the wrong way, dragging it with me. If I were to allow myself to panic, I would be propelled down old pathways towards the absolute terror I felt as a boy when bullies threatened me – those old stories I dutifully still carry in my luggage. I felt a hatred of this fear back then, but hatred doesn't help to excise it. If anything, it's reinforced and magnified. Slowly, gradually, I changed – and, naturally, the world changed with me. Fear and hatred became secondary instincts, not primary ones. Other people's attitudes consequently altered, and this strengthened the feedback. It was clearly a better way to engage with the social matrix because it broadened and deepened my vision. More briefly, I began to *trust* – not fear – myself.

Of course when you first met me, I was filled with anger. Anger is another heavy tool, but sometimes it is called for. Its use can be very dangerous and is often unwise. On the other hand, in this case anger broke through another pathway, when I could find nothing else that worked for me at the time. I met you, and this has reverberated in my life and in my present. I have a feeling it is significant.

It seems to me that Alice, like her namesake in Wonderland, has fallen through a rabbit hole that has become a continuous wall of fear that obliterates all other emotion, except perhaps anger. She can feel no joy, no trust or love, no sense of beauty, and hope is replaced by absolute fatalism. To make sense of what she sees, she creates a universe – a kind of negative matrix – that is as logical as possible – though part of her problem is mistakenly visualising her lack of understanding as stupidity. Even that is logical; she can't know how things fit together, ergo, she must be stupid. Others do, thus they must have 'higher powers.' Her creativity doesn't fail her – it damns her to perpetual loneliness, without contact or warmth from another soul.

I struggle for some overall concept of consciousness, an imaginable model, but this is as yet frustratingly vague. Whatever form it may take, it has to be in a state of temporal flux. The consciousness we have inherited is not the end result. It must have advantages and handicaps. Do you know the Jesuit philosopher Teilhard de Chardin? An interesting man, despite his Catholicism. Somehow he combined his scientific interests with religion, and came up with an intriguing vision of what he called an Omega Point somewhere in the abstract future. At the Omega Point, consciousness will evolve as godly. Presuming mankind does not fall at an early hurdle – and this is a big assumption – then evolution will surely propel us *somewhere*, given enough time. My hunch is that some of us already carry experimental 'capsules.' That would provide some explanation for the strange polar oppositions that create such dramatic swings, incorporating the beatific as well as the satanic.

Though I'm not an author of predictions, one thing is certain. If we are allowed to evolve, then we will eventually be little like what we are now. Nor – and

IS ALICE?

here's the important point – will the 'outer world' look the same. Those who insist it will are egregious fools. What we can see is only what we can see at this brief moment. It is not what *is*. The present human expression is just as barbaric as any in our history. We are little more than brutal savages. Accepting just that little element of self-knowledge would represent a faltering first step towards civilisation. The degree of delusion now is far deeper than any Alice is experiencing. Technology has far outrun the wisdom to use it. Matches have been given to a baby sitting in a room full of gunpowder. The State is using all its mischievous power to ensure that we are herded into a story so phoney it is tragically risible. Maybe you could call it *réalité concrèt*. It is set in concrete. There is no alternative. Even the Soviet experiment was no real alternative, because it incorporated the insidious poison of *progress*.

The stories I've been speaking of relentlessly are emphatically *not* interpretable in a so-called common sense – or concrete – way. There are many different types of stories – how many, I don't know. Some carry logic, others eschew it. Sleep stories and waking stories are different and, more importantly, vary widely in meaning and genre within themselves. Before us we have dozens, maybe even hundreds, of different tools, but insist on using only one or two. Who, then, is really mad?

I'm sure I would attract social scorn, or even wrath, if I tried seriously to debate the meanings of my dreams and visions – yet none are without meaning. They are just not necessarily all literal. They are ways of describing things that can't be expressed 'literally.' I ignore them and their meanings at my personal and spiritual peril. Spirituality is anathema in these times. Could you imagine an advertising executive working the word into his sales patter as he garnishes a product for its shareholders? Spirit is dismissed to the same glum realm as religion, with neither of them understood, because understanding them would undermine *réalité concrèt*. Though I am nominally an atheist, I'm very selective about when I apply it. I'm an atheist when it comes to definitive godliness and, especially, to the use of religion as an instrument of the social matrix as it is applied in developing power over people. The strength of religion is that it allows a broader interpretation of the nature of stories.

God? Gods? The one thing I distrust most is certainty, and that goes for death itself as well. The moment anyone speaks with absolute certainty is usually the very moment I lose complete trust in them. There is something I'll call 'local certainty' – a craftsman speaking about his craft, for instance. That's OK. But universal certainty is the sure sign of verbal hoodwinking. This is the organ ground by the generals, the bishops, the salesmen, the politicians and the scientists.

There is a god. There is no god. These are two faces of the same positivist coin. This doesn't automatically make me an agnostic, either. I'm simply unenlightened about most of 'reality.' So, too, are all the others, however certain they may be. Some of my experiences may be better explained by a presumption of a god, but they may have an explanation in other shimmering ways as well. Besides which, explanation is not a certain way to decide matters. I'm not searching for clues with a deerstalker and magnifying glass, in the classic tradition of modern investigation. If a god should speak to me, then that's a story that I will need to unravel and fit into the tale I'm making now, if I am able. So, agnostic? No. Call me a deeply limited atheist.

Where does my Black Dog differ from Alice's madness, then? Obviously, hers is infinitely more intense, but let's say they are nevertheless related, as I believe they are. I've made it clear that, whatever our state, we are fully responsible for it, and ultimately in control of it. Control? How can Alice be in control now, and how can I be, when the Black Dog is standing on my chest and drooling into my face, revealing his yellow teeth in a snarl? It is because something interesting happens to the 'I.' In fact, the 'I' is restless, never really still. In a temporal sense, the 'I' can never be captured and held in one moment. It is fleeting and ephemeral, yet there are enough similar states to be able to 'know' ourselves as integral personalities. Especially, there is a state that we consider to be normal, when we can interact with the social matrix without the jagged interruption of constant self-awareness during the process. But if we are *in control* of the stories we use to support consciousness, then why can I not decide to kick the Black Dog out the back door and slam it? Because it does not work that way. The levers of 'control' are not located in the rational headquarters. A few are there, and perhaps more can be added, probably by re-defining the nature of rationality. Rationality is limited and, importantly, limits itself by creating a sector we call the Will. And we all know the Will disintegrates instantly on contact with raging fear. I believe my Black Dog and Alice's madness share the common ground of what Sartre called *mauvais foi* – bad faith. Naturally he doesn't mean 'bad' in any moral sense. He means the mind's attempts to relinquish its fundamentally free nature and bind itself to a self-created 'external' force. This exercise is doomed. Or rather, it dooms us to the consequences of the exercise. Alice's world and my Black Dog both appear to be self-limiting prisons. We make the rules and abide by them under the main commandment that *no other rules are possible*. Now, even when my Black Dog is at his most aggressive, I still have a distant but distinct awareness that it is limited. It has come, and it will go. If I put one foot in front of the other for long enough, it will pass. I can also do what I'm doing – write myself out of it. Which means I slowly bring my focus onto other matters, and that will help guide me from a place where control is impossible to a place that is not so oppressive.

I know Alice's world does not contain the slightest awareness that what she is experiencing is temporary – thus her hopelessness. She is attempting to seal her tomb *forever*. But I know her well enough that, however hard she tries, she cannot completely excise her control.

We think our love is unusual, and that its uniqueness gives it great strength. Perhaps it does, but it is powerless against the engines of her fear. That much is clear. Even though she is mad, she hasn't lost her intelligence. Which is why she has succeeded in preventing me from seeing her. I'm sure she senses that I present a threat to the structure of her world, thus she weaves an intricate story to remove this threat – and, strangely, this is perfectly normal. It is the way we all rearrange the furniture so that it is consistent with our rules and beliefs. She strongly thinks that she is helping to free me from the millstone of herself, an act of love on her part. And that story has succeeded in its *real* objective, which is removing a weakness in her defence. She is smart enough to know that the more she sees of me, the more likely she is one day to present a 'weakness' that will draw her back into the 'false' world where she can be fooled and tricked.

That is how stories work, Alyosha. It is truly a thing of stunning beauty, the whole panorama. The self vanishing and being reborn each instant, constituted and re-constituted by a flickering and changing landscape of at least four dimensions (but likely more than that). This ephemeral self is the ultimate composer and conductor of this gigantic squirming orchestra of reality. It's god-like, really. Let There Be Light. And there it glitters in its fragile vulnerability, a sprite in a fairyland. As I sit here contemplating it, I realise suddenly there are no limits to discovery. At the same time, this rude leprechaun of life is hunted down, captured and imprisoned by forces within the social matrix antithetical to its spirit. A beautiful being is transformed into a common carthorse that aspires only to fatten at the same trough as its masters. It's obscenity.

As I wrote these words, Alyosha, I had a bizarre little vision – brief but as clear as my hand in front of my face. I was struggling with metaphor, coming to the end of this letter, wondering if I should stop it just there. 'It's obscenity.' Or further back. 'Let There Be Light.'

In this vision – it only lasted a few instants – I witnessed a great battle taking place. It was clear the time was now, but the place… ? It seemed to be all around me, *here*, but not to be seen – real, but invisible to a common sense eye. There was much activity, but it was noiseless. It was a magical scenario, and figures were moving through the air, or maybe they were standing on unseen ground. Sets of figures were in two different dimensions. Demons and angels? Hell, these are just words to give you a taste of what I experienced. I suppose you could say they were extreme opponents struggling to gain an advantage or a goal that would mean defeat for one side or the other.

Am I being lured by madness, or is the social matrix itself demented, as it madly churns its stories in an effort to produce a reality so distorted it no longer has integral meaning?]*

IS ALICE?

CHAPTER NINETEEN

Christmas day. Theo Hawthorn leaned back in his desk chair and re-lit his pipe, after checking his email. Nothing but spam. Earlier he had been playing Bach's *Christmas Oratorio*, but all three CDs were finished now, and he had hardly noticed. He didn't listen to music like he did in earlier years when he used to lie back, close his eyes and let the sound envelop him. Now he listened while he did other things – or rather he mostly didn't listen. Nevertheless, he played music almost constantly while he was awake. It was comforting. It was also a little profane.

As for 'celebrating' Christmas, it was something he really enjoyed *not* doing. Everyone knew he neither gave nor received presents, though a cousin in Canada always sent him a fruit cake in the post. During his last marriage his wife made a big event of the day – the tree, trimmings, everything, including an arduous meal. He found it absolutely soul-destroying, and now he enjoyed pulling right out of the whole seasonal farce. He kept off the streets by buying in enough food to last him for ten days or so. Just ordinary food, though. That evening he planned to cook himself a hamburger.

When Alice was with him, they did a little more, but not much. She was Jewish, and their family never made it a big event. Sometimes they had a duck or goose, but seldom a turkey. To his great relief they exchanged no presents, either. This Christmas there was also no Alice.

And all through the flat, not a creature was stirring, not even a bat. As a kid, Christmas was the main event of the winter, a time of delight and wonder. He must have been ten years old before he found out about Santa Claus, very late even in North America. That was because he didn't want to know he wasn't real. Other kids would tell him, and he would angrily debate with certainty that it was true. As always, certainty could be so misleading. On each night before Christmas he would curl up under the covers, tingling with expectation. Would it be a bicycle or BB gun or a train set? He made sure he always left Santa a bite to eat and a Coke, along with his wish list. In the morning he would awake to the slow, magical realisation that *this was it*. Check the clock. Was it too early? The brightness of the curtains told him it was daylight, and surely that made it all right to go and look under the tree. Warm feet on the cold floor, the sound of his father snoring, as he crept into the sitting room. What was it? Was it *really* a bicycle! Joy. Wonder. Elation beyond imagination. And there was now a whole day of unwrapping presents, feasting, visiting his friend across the street, and his cousins a little further away, to compare booty. And he always wanted books, lots of books to read. Different stories from other worlds far away across the seas. Apart from the bicycle, BB gun and train, books were always his favourite gifts. Luckily his mother always made sure there were several, carefully wrapped underneath the tree.

After he found out there was no Santa after all, it wasn't the same. It was a step towards being an adult he never wanted to take. It was still a fun time for many years, but as he learned more of the illusion he withdrew from what now seemed to be phoney warmth and cheer, a plot to extract maximum money from people who could ill afford it, and that included his own parents. It was a winter bonanza for business.

Hawthorn certainly wasn't grumpy about Christmas – he simply ignored it, as he ignored so much else he disliked in the world. He just disengaged. Indeed, if he had the money, he would book a long holiday somewhere in a non-Christian country near the equator. From the beginning of December until the second week of January. Six weeks of hot sun, warm seas, fish, exotic food, Arabic pastries, thick, sweet coffee. No doubt it would make him intolerably smug as well. His only cheap weapon was non-participation.

Nevertheless, this particular day he was melancholy, and this was related directly to his thoughts of Alice, which seemed to fill the flat with wistful wisp-like smoke from her cigarette. The 25th of December, almost the New Year, and she remained deeply psychotic. From his point of view there had been some ironic improvement. Alice finally succeeded in excluding him from the ward completely, so he was refused admission at reception. This had been the situation for the last two weeks. It was actually a relief for him, because seeing her on the ward – usually accidental sightings – caused visceral agony. He saw the form of her without the content, and her eyes revealed another person cryptically configured. Such encounters drained him, so he was secretly glad when he was forbidden entry to the ward. The only thing that worried him was the damn cigarettes. They were her only relief, however harmful they might be to her body, and either the staff or other patients would steal them unless he kept a keen eye on them. Alice also had an account she could draw on when she was allowed to go shopping with one of the nurses, but he could monitor that at Reception.

Perhaps he was selfish, but he wasn't dreading his trip to the hospital that afternoon as much as he would if he had to actually see her. He wrapped an extra carton of cigarettes in some pretty foil paper he had saved behind his filing cabinet. Although it was a short trip to the hospital on his bicycle, the hill was steep. On the other hand, it was an easy and quick return, gliding back down. The roads were wet but not icy.

He sighed and got up from his desk, thinking he'd better get it over with, get it done, let it pass. Christmas was just another day. He put on his coat, hat and scarf and inserted the 'present' into a plastic bag he could dangle from his handlebars. He stuffed his gloves in his pocket. He didn't like to wear gloves because they made his hands so bulky.

The old man at Reception was a gentle soul, originally from one of the Caribbean islands, and Hawthorn smiled warmly as he was buzzed through the glass doors.

"Christmas duty, eh?"

The old man smiled and nodded as Hawthorn handed him the plastic bag.

"Do me a favour," Hawthorn said. "Make sure Pan Subarti gets these. More cigarettes for Alice. So many of them go missing."

IS ALICE?

The receptionist studied him for a moment. "Do you want to go up and see her?"

Hawthorn cocked his head, puzzled. "I didn't think I was allowed on the ward any more."

"No, no. You're not," he agreed. "But I think you should go up anyway. And I'm going to let you through…"

Hawthorn was on guard. "Is anything wrong?"

"A little trouble," he replied gently.

"What kind of trouble?"

"I think you should just go up and talk to them…"

Hawthorn put his hands on the ledge and leaned forward, concerned. "Is she OK? Is she hurt?"

The old man shook his head. "She's OK. You go up. You'll see. I think you should be there. Forget about the rules this time."

Hawthorn turned towards the lifts. "Thank you. Thank you very much."

He heard her even before he rang the bell at the ward doors. Alice was wailing and screaming. It was a piteous and elemental sound that broke his heart. With tears accumulating in his eyes he rang the bell again, twice, impatiently. When they finally opened, he rushed in past the nurses' station and saw her crumpled on the floor. She was slumped forward, and her near-bald head hung down miserably as she shook it from side to side. Tears dropped on the tiled floor, and her face was smeared with snot. No one paid her the slightest attention. One nurse sat in a chair looking bored as he glanced up at Hawthorn. Another one lounged inside the nurses' station reading a copy of the *Sun*.

He knew he shouldn't touch her, but he placed one hand on her shoulder as he knelt down beside her, resisting a huge impulse to try and hold her poor head to his chest.

"What's wrong, babe?" he asked in a quiet voice.

"They won't let me go out," she wailed.

"It's not true," the bored nurse said behind my back. "It's too late now."

Alice was still talking to the floor. "They wouldn't let me go out yesterday, and they wouldn't let me go out today. It's Christmas, and I've got to do some shopping. It's *Christmas*, and they won't let me…"

"I'll take you out," he said firmly, delighted she was actually talking to him.

"They won't let you! They won't let me! I'm here for the rest of my life. In this building. Nowhere to go!"

"I'll get you out. I promise."

"No, you can't! *You can't!*"

IS ALICE?

Hawthorn rose and ignored the bored nurse. He leaned into the station door and smiled. "Is Pan on duty?"

The nurse put down her newspaper and looked at him blankly. "No. We just emergency staff today. Nobody to go with her."

"I'll go with her," he said, trying to be as charming as possible. "She'll be safe with me."

"There be no shops open today anyway."

"Oh, we'll find something. An Asian shop. I saw a couple open on the way up here."

"She can't go," the woman said firmly.

"I *told you*!" Alice cried from the hallway. "*I told you*!"

Hawthorn remained calm. "Don't you think that attitude is a little unnecessary, especially since it's Christmas Day? That woman over there is a human being. You might not know it from seeing her like this, but she's intelligent, warm, articulate and very special. You're causing a heap of grief, and it isn't necessary."

"Nobody to go with her."

"I'll go with her."

"No doctor on ward to say so."

"I've taken her out before, months ago. She's perfectly safe. I'm a big, strong man, and I know how to get her safely back here. I know her very, very well."

The nurse sighed. Her English was poor. "We too busy here. Everybody want something. Christmas Day. All shops closed down. She scream and cry, 'take me, take me…' Nobody to take. No place to go…"

He had an idea and turned to Alice. "Would you like to go down to the garden, get out, breathe a little air?"

"*They won't let me!*" she sobbed. "I already asked. 'No, stay here, stay here, stay here, stay here, stay here, stay here…'"

He turned back to the nurse. "I'll take her down to the garden for a while, just to get her out of this stifling atmosphere…"

The nurse was being impossible. She shook her head defiantly. No.

Hawthorn sighed and leaned towards her, speaking softly. "You are being unreasonable. The garden is completely safe. There is a chain-link fence around it, a high one. We will go down in the lift, all locked corridors. Totally safe. No problem. And you will have managed to give one human being a little joy on a day that is supposed to be joyful. You will feel better. Alice will feel better, and I will feel better. With no trouble for you…"

IS ALICE?

The nurse was unpleasantly negative and shook her head again, determined now. Alice's cries were a siren, peaking and falling mournfully.

"If you don't allow this," Hawthorn continued quietly and firmly, "I'll tell you what I'm going to do. I'm going to go take Alice by the arm and lead her to that door. Then I'm going to kick it open, break the lock and take her down to the garden. I'm going to stay down there for as long as she likes, then I'm going to bring her back up here. Then if you call the police, I'll tell them exactly what happened and why. They will call the doctor, and I will tell him the same thing. And you know what? I think they'll be on my side. Alternatively, you can open the door for us, and you can peacefully finish reading your newspaper."

He didn't wait for an answer, turned away and walked past Alice and down the corridor. He found her room and saw her coat and scarf thrown onto the bed. After gathering them up, Hawthorn returned to the crumpled figure of Alice. He leaned down and gently took her arm. "Let's go down to the garden."

She turned her face towards his. Her eyes were swollen, still crazed in their scarlet slits, and her face was red and wet. Her voice was soft now. "They won't let us."

"They'll let us. Trust me."

She got to her feet slowly, leaning a little on his hand. Hawthorn was almost holding his breath now. He helped her on with her coat and wrapped the scarf around her neck as gently as he would for a beloved daughter. She zipped up the coat herself and dug in the pockets for a dry tissue.

When they got to the door, he heard the buzzer that opened the lock, and they passed out of the ward without further incident. Neither of them spoke as he pressed the button for the lift. Hawthorn's heart was still pounding – not because of the confrontation with the nurses, but because Alice was responding to him. It was the first time in months that she had actually spoken to him. He did not dare to hope for anything else, but her words to him were so sweet. In a moment of utter despair and spiritual destitution, she had dropped her guard and let him through. He found himself forming an involuntary and silent prayer.

Downstairs, the corridors were lit with emergency lighting. They passed wordlessly through the darkened canteen, and Hawthorn opened the garden door and held it as she went outside. She walked straight to a bench next to the wall and sat down, staring into the middle distance. He sat down beside her, still silently murmuring his little prayer to some phantom deity.

The view from the bench was eerie and blasted with bleakness. It was only three o'clock, but the thick clouds were low, and it was almost dark. The small inadequate 'garden' was little more than a postage-stamp of flattened green clumps in trampled mud. The chain-link fence must have been 20 feet high, and it was topped with razor wire. Beyond the fence were the trees, but today they were bare and threatening, raising witches' arms to the muscular grey-dark clouds. There was only a slight breeze, but it was cold. The damp stone bench was already numbing his backside.

They sat together in silence before he spoke. Alice did not move or look at him.

"You see," he said finally. "I got you out."

She didn't answer. She was still staring towards the ground and, unusually, was not acknowledging the cold. Her bare hands lay inert on top of her trousers. Both feet were flat on the ground.

Hawthorn decided to continue. "If I had known you wanted to go shopping, I would have arranged to take you out. Those nurses are a sad bunch. They must have drafted in the dregs for Christmas Day. Agency staff on double-time, counting the minutes before they go home…"

He couldn't resist it any more. "Alice. Can you hear me? Can you talk?"

She didn't move. She was as still as a poet contemplating the next line of a sonnet.

"Would you look at me?" he ventured quietly.

Slowly she reached into her pocket and pulled out a damp, squeezed and torn tissue, opened it out as much as she could, then blew her nose before wiping it carefully and dabbing at her eyes.

Then she looked at him. Hawthorn's hopes began to crumple. Those eyes. They iced his heart quicker than the damp freezing wind. They were so hard to describe. Her hazel irises seemed to glitter dully, like little windows to a wounded, confused animal. The flesh on her once pretty face hung lifelessly, and her lips were white with compression. The Alice he knew was not there.

He felt hope melting away, and was about to slide down the oily and familiar slope of failure. But then he thought he heard the bracing sound of trumpets somewhere in the dim twilight of his existence. No! His denial echoed into the deep canyon of his consciousness. He would never give in – *ever*! The real Alice was still beautiful, and he looked again at her small, heart-shaped face. She was there. Somewhere. He had heard her upstairs in the ward when she spoke to him, breaking through the barricades of her own defences.

"I love you," he said simply, strongly, quietly, still looking into those crazed eyes. "I'm telling the truth, Alice. I am not lying. It is not fake. It is real. I am here."

She continued to stare at him. Time exhaled and escaped like a gas, as the moment bloated into a sinuous, stately pavane, pausing for a long, low bow. The tree-witches leaned imperceptibly forward, as if to listen. It was as still as death without a single pulse of sound. The moment continued to billow out, as if it were endless, infinite.

IS ALICE?

There was no motion in Hawthorn's thoughts now. All were poised like ephemeral statuary, frozen, but alert to the slightest molecular flicker. Whatever that singularity might have been called, it was surely purpled by love. Nothing was happening, and something was happening.

"Are you a policeman?" she asked finally, breaking the long, profound silence.

"No," he answered softly.

"Are you telling the truth?"

"I am. I would never lie to you, Alice. Never."

"Are you speaking in codes?"

"No. What I say is what I mean."

"When you blinked just now. Did that mean anything... secret?"

He shook his head slowly, struggling to check his excitement by pulling on the reins as hard as he could. "No."

"You're not lying to me. You're telling me the truth. The real truth. You wouldn't lie. You wouldn't do that, would you?"

"No. I promise with all my heart. On my mother's grave. I promise."

He could tell. The eyes were changing, and Alice was emerging like a long-held breath of life from a tomb. The gates broke open, and the barricades were scattered in an explosion of birth and light.

"Oh, Theo!" she screamed in ecstatic agony as she threw herself forward, her arms around his neck. "Oh, god, Theo! How I missed you! How I love you! Please hold me, hard and tight. Hold me, hold me!"

He rocked her in his arms. She felt as if she might burst and consume them both. Tears warmed his cheeks.

She stopped suddenly, pulled back and looked at him, her eyes wide as scallop shells. "It's true, isn't it? Don't lie, please. You aren't a policeman. You're real... you're... you're THEO. No, no, please, only the truth. You have to tell me. I have to know. This can't be a cruel joke, no, don't let it be that, not a cruel joke, not now..."

Alice's face contorted as she burst into tears. Theo took her again gently into his arms, his right hand passing over the stubble on her head, so glad to feel her body against his, so deliriously happy to hear her voice.

"There are no lies, my darling. No jokes, no lies, no policemen, no codes, no more horror now. You'll be laughing soon. And happy, too. We'll go out together to a Chinese restaurant. Or to Maison Bertaux in Soho for tea and cakes..."

"Oh, Theo, Theo, Theo... how I love that name on my lips. It's been *so long*!" She broke away again, and again her face was contorted with suffering. "So *long*! How long? How long have I been here? In this hateful, awful hell of a place. I hate it. *HATE* it! And now, they'll keep me here forever, won't they? Oh, no... oh, Theo. When will we be able to... go out, get away? If I relapse, what'll happen? They'll keep me here forever and ever. The nutter in the loony bin! Oh, no, I can't even think about it..."

"Stop," he cautioned quietly, and held a forefinger to her lips. "Listen to me carefully, and trust me. I give you my promise. Tomorrow we will go out. It's Boxing Day, there may be only a few places open. But we'll go out tomorrow and hold hands, walk around, browse the shops..."

"Tomorrow! Oh, no, you won't be able to. And what if... No, please don't let me relapse again, not into that, not there. No more. Enough." She turned, doubt flooding into her eyes again. "And they'll keep me here, Theo. They won't let me go. I can't bear it, the thought of it. I can't tell you."

He drew her to him again, and pressed her head against his chest. "You have to be well. You must get through tonight alone, here in the hospital, alone with your scattered being. But you can do it. Remember the prize. Get through the night. Be well tomorrow when I come..."

"Oh, come early! Please come early!"

"I will. If you hold on tonight, and you are well tomorrow, then I'll get you out of this hospital in one week. That is a promise. One week."

"You can't." She was sobbing again. "Not in a *week*. It'll be *ages*. I'll be here. Locked in, lonely, alone, forever..."

"One week, beautiful Alice. Just one week, and you will be discharged. Completely. Out of here. And we will be together. Forever."

"It's not true! You must be lying!"

"No!" he almost shouted. "I'm *not* lying. Listen to me. Tomorrow we will go out, just like I said. The day after, when I can get in touch with the doctor, he will let you come to my flat for an overnight visit. Just imagine! All night in my bed. No more nights at the hospital..."

"It's too much," she cried. "You can't do that. Nobody can..."

"I can do it, I *will* do it, my darling. But you have the hardest part. You have to stay sane tonight and tomorrow night. After than, no more hospital. You'll visit at home with me, in my care, and after a week you will be completely discharged. It will be done, even if I have to psychically *levitate* this hospital off the ground. Do you understand?"

She was shaking her head. "It's so hard... I can't believe you. I *want* to, but, Theo, it's been so long, such a long time. Night after night, day after day. The same things, the same food, the same place. And inside, I've just been… oh, my god, it's just too horrible to put into words. I don't even want to think about it…"

He linked his arm with hers and squeezed her hand. "I know a little something of what you've been through. I can barely imagine the horror. But I need to make you listen very closely to me now, every word I say…"

She turned her eyes up to him, and he marvelled again at the new brightness and intelligence. It had been so quick. "You have not finished yet. You have to survive the night. Survive tonight, and you will be free. Do you know the old vampire movies? Where the priest holds up a crucifix to back off the undead human bat? That's what you have to do. When you are lured by those shadows within you, hold up your crucifix…"

"I don't have a crucifix," she said innocently. "Would a Magan David do just as well?"

Hawthorn laughed out loud. "I'm talking about love. With you and me, it's the strongest weapon we have. That's your Magan David. Hold it up and say, 'Begone!' Make it turn the monster to ashes and scurry back to the shadows of your soul. Let it *begone* forever. It's important that you *act*. It's something I can't do for you."

She leaned her shaven head on his shoulder, tearful again. "Oh, Theo, I can't tell you how I dread it. Going back upstairs. Back to my room. Back to the noises, those nurses, the screams. It's like the deepest damp rising and chilling my blood."

He stroked her head again. "Whatever it may be, you must be stronger. I don't want to arrive here tomorrow to find you have disappeared behind those baffled, trembling, unseeing eyes. I want to find the warm, beautiful Alice, the one I love so much."

She clutched at the lapel of his coat. "Do you *really* love me? How *can* you after all this time, after seeing me like this… after, after…?"

"That's the love I'm talking about. The one so strong it will carry you through tonight. You must survive!"

"What happened with Aleksei Cherkasov?" she asked suddenly.

"We'll talk about all that later. It's a long story."

"A bad story?"

"No, a good one. You'll enjoy it. But you have to be well tomorrow. Do you think you can?"

There was a long pause. "I don't know, Theo. I honestly don't know. I'll *try*."

"Don't try weakly. Try strongly. You have strength. Use it. Don't let it whistle out of you like air."

Without warning, she threw her arms around him and kissed him deeply, sexily. When she finally broke away, she spoke with unbridled passion. "I *love* you. *I love you so much!*"

IS ALICE?

"Good," he whispered in her ear. "That's what you need. That kind of love. It will help you get through tonight. And tomorrow night. You have your job, and I have mine. Mine is getting you the hell out of here as soon as I possibly can. You survive two nights, and you're out. One week, you're discharged FOR GOOD."

"Oh, no, it's too much. I can't believe you. I want to believe, but I can't. It'll be months and months..."

"Days," he said. "Two days and the rest of one week. You remember that."

"Oh, I want to, I want to, but I can't. They won't let me..."

He pulled back and grinned. "Then you just watch the Hawthorn performance. Sit back and enjoy it. Meanwhile, you'll be back at home with me. Tomorrow, all day. Tomorrow night here. Then – FREEDOM. Finally. Forever. I *promise*."

When they finally returned to the ward it was well past visiting hours. Hawthorn's arm was resting on Alice's shoulder, and hers was around his waist. They stopped at the nurses' station. The nurse had finished reading her newspaper and was tapping out a text message on her mobile phone with a bored expression on her face.

"Look," he said to her gently. "A well woman for the first time in six months. Thank you for letting us be together tonight."

The nurse glanced up at the clock. "You here past time now, you know."

Hawthorn smiled. "I don't think you heard me. Alice is OK. She's fine. I'm coming tomorrow to take her out to the shops."

"No. The doctor won't be on duty till after Boxing Day…"

Alice squeezed his hand hard, trembling.

Hawthorn leaned forward, his head now inside the doorway. "Have you ever wondered why you obey rules? Or ever wondered about the purpose of rules? We have here a human being who has risen from the grave like Lazarus, and you give me rules as your response. That's not a very healing, sensitive way to deal with your patients. Are you on duty tomorrow morning?"

The nurse suppressed a yawn and glanced again at her mobile. She shook her head wearily.

"I know you're tired. You want to go home. It's Christmas for you, too. Someone else will be dealing with this tomorrow while you're having a well-deserved sleep. But neither they nor you nor all the king's men nor all the police in London will stop us leaving this hospital tomorrow. You can make a note to your colleague, if you want. If necessary, we will contact the doctor, even if he's at his favourite brothel after snorting up a gram of coke."

IS ALICE?

The nurse was tapping again at her mobile as they turned away towards the corridor that led to Alice's room, thereby breaking more rules. Once they were out of sight, she stopped, then hugged him with both arms. Then she looked up, glowing, her cheeks rosy from the cold garden.

"You're right, of course," she giggled out loud. "Your performance is worth watching. Mr Cool himself. *Brothel*! Can't you just see Dr Pincer in a brothel!"

Hawthorn was laughing, too. "Maybe I should have said a gay leather bar, but I didn't want to be unkind."

She buried her face in his chest to muffle her laughter. "Oh, Theo. I don't deserve you. How could someone like you love a nobody like me?"

"Nobody? Listen, you are my Princess, and starting tomorrow we will be setting out on a long, beautiful voyage of inner discovery. Together. I want to show you the beauty of the world and, in it, you will find your own priceless beauty. Soon it'll be clear I'm the worthless one, not you."

"Yes!" she hissed excitedly. "Tomorrow! I can't wait! Sex tomorrow, yes?"

"Yes," he whispered. "Lots and lots, more than you can imagine. Days of it next week and weeks of it next month. We'll go back to our journey, but we don't have to begin again. We'll start where we left off."

"Oh!" she exclaimed. "But what if… what if I… oh, I don't know if I can face it tonight. I don't want you to go. I wish you could stay. Oh, please stay…"

They walked on slowly. Another patient passed them in her pyjamas, lighting a cigarette with trembling fingers.

He held up his hand, smiling, as he nodded towards the patient. "Look there. You haven't smoked one cigarette since you came round."

"Ha!" she said, scrabbling in her coat pockets. "I knew something was wrong. That's the longest time I've given up in 20 years."

She lit up as they arrived at the door to her room, then turned to him. "Theo, listen. Seriously. How am I going to sleep tonight? What if I can't? What if it all comes back, the nightmare…?"

He took out a small bottle of tablets and shook it in her face. "Dr Hawthorn has brought his little bottle of medicine. I have it with me, right here."

"What did you bring?" she squealed.

"Listen, sweetie. I know they won't give you anything to help you sleep, when sleep is your kindest friend. I've begged them to make sleeping tablets a required bedtime medicine. But they won't. Instead they overload you with drugs that leave you plastered to the ceiling. So I always carry a few of my Valium with me in case I get a chance to give you a bit of relief. I just leave the bottle in my coat pocket all the time"

IS ALICE?

"I can't believe it," she replied.

He shook out two tablets. "Dr Hawthorn prescribes 10 milligrams for tonight. So you'll be well tomorrow when I get here. A good night's sleep."

She took the tablets and gave him a big hug. "Wouldn't Dr Hawthorn like a nice blow job before he leaves?"

"Gagging for it. But I think we've broken enough rules for one night. We've got more to break tomorrow."

She looked up at him. "Aren't you worried about it?"

"No. Looking forward to it. Just let them try to stop us. Because Dr Hawthorn is also a master of prestidigitation, illusion and nurse-hypnosis. The black bag I carry is full of tricks. Or is it dicks? Pick a dick. Any dick."

"The only dick I want is yours."

"Ah, Dr Hawthorn *comes* with *that* dick!"

"Oh, very funny."

"At your cervix, as usual."

"Theo. Theo. How I've missed you. I've never stopped loving you, you know. Never. Deep inside. That's one thing I could not kill, however hard I tried. Beneath all those putrid layers of shit you were my only darling. Untainted. Untarnished. I yearned for you, missed you, longed for your touch, the sound of your voice. But I knew I was too unworthy, and you loathed me really but were somehow forced to be with me, despite being nauseated by…"

"Enough. We've got all the time in the world now. You're free. Now just stay free tonight. Be well tomorrow. Don't allow yourself to be dragged back into the cave by those demons."

"I'll *try*."

"No. You'll *do*. Trying isn't good enough. You can do it, Alice. You have great strength that you've never discovered. But it's there. I can feel it even now. The strong Alice is hungry, starving. Feed her. Let her eat like a glutton. Pull your eyes off the floor. Hold up your head proudly. No one can hurt you except you, yourself. Remember that. You have played the devil. It is now time to play the god. The goddess. You can do it. You must do it. You *will* do it."

Hawthorn put all his passion into his words, caught again in the moment as they stood together in the corridor of that alien, industrial burlesque of an asylum that was shorn of any evidence of warmth or humanity or care. There were no excuses. The resources were available. The intelligence could be supplied. Yet, as they stood there embracing, he knew no efforts would be made to relieve the suffering or to help those trapped in disaffected worlds, writhing in anguish. The hospital was the result of gestures throbbing with lies, but sold as healing human concern. It echoed. It was cold. It was indifferent to everything but trouble for the staff. Doctors scorned Hippocrates by harming patients with their biological interventions that deepened their agony.

IS ALICE?

Hawthorn looked down the hallway as he held Alice's head to his chest. A middle-aged woman stood outside her door, lonely and confused, lost, terrified, humiliated beyond despair. There was no one for her, even on Christmas Day, as so many people sat round their tables laden with food, surrounded by gifts, drinking and laughing. For *those* people, *these* people were being looked after but were not a part of their world any more. Given the choice of what humanity *could* do, if it had a mind to do so, it was such a savage act to lock them into such a loveless, lifeless, chilly and destructive place.

Even the straggly plants on the window ledges died from lack of care. An idiot could see these people needed kindness and patience more than powerful, unsettling drugs, electro-convulsive therapy or psycho-surgery. He wished he could tear aside the veils so the hospital staff could see *what was real*. They were little better than torturers. Ignorant, vain, self-important and – so sadly – convinced they were doing something *good*. That was the ultimate irony. Where was the Christ they believed in – or the Mohammed, come to that? Would those two have created such a despicable place as this? Would they have administered electricity or scalpels to human brains? Or dosed them with any drug to keep them quiet? It is said that god is love. But these patients received nothing but contempt. They were ignored as liars. They were no longer worth the effort of understanding. They were excluded from even the simplest of joys, and had only their cigarettes for comfort.

What a lot could be done with so little effort and just a little kindness. A residence in beautiful countryside or by the sea. Staff who treated every patient with the same respect and dignity they demanded for themselves. Doctors humble enough to admit they knew fuck-all, but were capable of listening and learning – and doctors who would never give a patient treatment they would not happily administer to themselves. Is that too much to ask from a society dripping in wealth?

"Mr Hawthorn!" The nurse was shouting at him from the top of the corridor.

He pulled away from Alice. Both had tears in their eyes. He laid a forefinger to her lips.

"Tomorrow, my love. Promise me now that you will hold on."

"I promise I'll try my best," she said softly.

He wiped away her tears before pulling his sleeve across his own eyes. Then he kissed her and turned to walk resolutely towards the angry nurse.

CHAPTER TWENTY

Hawthorn held the telephone in his hand, gripping it like an oar on a lifeboat. Alice finally answered.

"Tell me right away. How are you?"

"I don't know," she mumbled. "I'm confused, Theo…"

"Did you sleep well?"

"Yes. Yes, I did. Very well. I was OK this morning. Then… this hospital, old memories. Come up. Come quick. It's all coming back to me…"

"Alice. Listen carefully. I'm practically on my way. I just phoned because I had a hunch, that's all… that you needed to talk to someone right now. It's a matter of minutes, and I'll be there. You have to promise again to *hold on*. Think of us. Think of getting out of there…"

She was beginning to cry. "It's so hopeless. I'm here forever. This place… it's closing in around me. It doesn't want me to go…"

"Alice. I'm ending the conversation right now, because I've got to get up there to you, and there's not a minute to waste. Hold on. *Hold on*. I love you."

He put down the phone and hurtled to the hallway to get his coat, his mobile, his wallet and his cap. Then he flung open the door, letting it slam after him, for once not caring whom he woke, because he was already halfway down the stairs. He passed by the bicycle, because today he was determined and sure. Her car was parked just outside his door, a little blue Renault Clio. He hadn't used it much, except for shopping, but this was the day. He would bring her back in it, and that was all there was to it.

The old receptionist was there again, and just gave him a kindly smile as he let him through both sets of doors. He went straight to the lift, looking up at the coloured circles to see where it was, counting the seconds. The doors finally opened, and he pressed the button for her ward impatiently two or three times. As the lift moved sluggishly, he began to lecture himself.

"Expect nothing. Be calm. Breathe deeply. Be ready to move in any direction. There is no such thing as failure, as time displaces time. Find your balance, your *ki*. That is your strength. Fear nothing."

The improvised mantra settled him immediately, and he realised her first words on the telephone had frightened him. Her tone was lifeless. It contradicted all his feelings and intuition. She was *going* to be well. They were *going* to leave the hospital *today*. Together. The fear crept up on him from behind. Never mind her tone. If she had fallen back into the fires of Hades, he would guide her back across the Styx like Orpheus.

As the lift doors slid open, he cleared his mind and relaxed his back and shoulders. He buzzed the ward door.

IS ALICE?

She was sitting in a chair opposite the nurses' station, staring into space. She didn't look at him or acknowledge his presence. Theo knew instantly that she was again trapped, even before looking into her eyes. Still… she was there. Waiting for him. So the struggle was not over yet.

He turned to the on-duty nurse, who was sitting in the office chair staring at a folder on the desk. "Could you open the door to the conference room for me, please?"

She looked up at him, and he recognised her, but had forgotten her name. "It's very early for visitors, Mr Hawthorn."

"This is important, and I need your help. Alice came round last night for the first time in six months. When I called ten minutes ago, she was still well but very much on the edge. It's vital we move decisively here. Give me a chance alone with her, and I will get her back round again. But you must hurry. Please."

The nurse didn't say anything, but stared at him for a moment. He held her eyes but said nothing more.

She got up, felt in her pocket for the ring of keys. "Come on, then."

He walked over to Alice, who was now gazing absently at the pattern of tiles on the floor. He gently raised her from the chair by her arm and smiled. "We're going to the conference room, darling. We can be alone there."

The nurse left them and closed the door quietly. They sat side by side. The old piano was still there, its lid still safely locked in case anyone wanted to enjoy themselves by playing it.

Hawthorn turned to her. "How do you feel?"

She remained mute. She had allowed herself to be led to the room, but it was as if she were blind or senseless. Hawthorn gathered all his strength. He could feel his centre radiate with power. There was no fear.

"I called you a few minutes ago, Alice. We talked. I know you remember, but now I think you are trying to close me out. You think I may be in the land of the codes, but I want you to believe me once more. Just one more time. This is important. Very important. Look at me. Please. Just once."

He ignored the craziness in her eyes as she turned towards him slowly. "You want out of this hospital. I will get you out. Now. That is my promise to you. Out. Now. All day. Tomorrow, you will be able to go home with me, stay all night, the next day and night…and the next. In one week you will be discharged for good. Do you hear me? Don't worry about what I'm doing with my eyes or hands. I'm not using code. I'm speaking the truth. Listen. Find your love for me and listen. Find it, Alice. You said it last night. You can't kill or change it. It's there, inside. Use it. Like a Magan David. Hold it up in front of you and push back the evil spirits. They will crumble into dust before your eyes, and you will have freedom. Only you can do it. You. Alice. And you *will* do it…"

IS ALICE?

He had made his voice intentionally hypnotic, speaking softly, clearly and slowly. The only added ingredient was the intense focus of his inner power, where his balance was acute. There were no other thoughts. He was concentrated but relaxed, firm and gentle.

"… You have only disappeared for a moment. You survived the whole night here, and only this morning did you weaken a little. But it's not for long. You're coming back to me. You're going to walk away from this filthy place today. With me. There is no alternative."

He stopped speaking, but held her eyes as they desperately searched his face, darting in micro-movements, almost like an ocular tremor. Suddenly he felt a distant connection being created. It was not his imagination. He was dancing with her, and they were both moving slowly, uncertainly. It was a stately, formal dance at first, as they mirrored each other across a large ballroom. There was a rhythm, stronger than a heartbeat. It was a thread that held them together, gossamer-thin but strong and taut. If he had been self-reflective at that moment, it would also have resonated with sexual desire and longing. It was becoming as enchanted as the descent into their erotic world of perfumed magic. Hawthorn knew that this time – contrary to the legend – Orpheus must not break eye contact with Eurydice as the ferryman rowed them slowly back across the Styx.

"Are you a policeman?" she finally whispered.

Hawthorn allowed his lungs to fill with gusts of radiant triumph. The questions were beginning again, very similar to the ones she asked the day before. Hesitantly at first, her clouded eyes began to clear. Then she was there. Safely on the other side, she again lunged into his arms.

"Theo, Theo... oh, so close. I was gone again, and I thought it was for good. I was sure this was all a set-up, that you weren't real, that I was somehow manipulating you, forcing you to come and get me, and I was determined this time that I was going to stay forever where I was condemned for eternity. It was my destiny. Your love was just a trick, and I was falling for it. Right after your call, I spun away like a dervish. Mocking laughter echoed down the shaft as I fell, the walls plastered with faces scoffing at me. It was so dramatic. I was gone, *gone*, never to return. Oh, Theo, I love you... I found something somehow, something more compelling than the mockery. I was so far away, so far, so far..."

She was talking fast in his ear, and her grip was as strong as the coil of an anaconda. It was a cascade unleashed like a fireworks display, exploding brightly with pops of delight. She wasn't crying this time, but was carried away by her own words and imagery. She shot forth from her purgatory like a ball from a cannon. He listened more to the torrent of emotion rather than the actual words, the sound and colour, the incredible orchestral harmonies. As finally she began to wind down, he pushed her away and held her at arm's length.

"Now," he said firmly. "Let's get the fuck outta here."

IS ALICE?

Her mouth fell open, then snapped shut. "How?"

He shrugged with a comic smile. "How should I know how? Come on. Time's a-wastin'."

They both got up and, with the same idea, kissed lovingly – holding, caressing.

"Go get your coat, hat, whatever you're going to wear, while I talk to the nurse."

"What are you going to say?"

"I don't know yet."

They left the conference room and strode gaily down the corridor towards the nurses' station. Alice almost ran towards her room.

Hawthorn grinned at the nurse. "OK. We did it. She's up and out, this time for good."

The nurse gave him a clinical smile. "I'm happy to hear that."

"Now," Hawthorn continued gravely. "We've got an important problem here that we have to solve in the right way. When she comes back, have a little talk with her to reassure yourself that she's now got all her marbles back. Then we have to contact the doctor – or I assume we do, unless Pan is here to make a decision. Because it is now vital that she be allowed to leave in my custody just for the day. I'll return her here by 9pm tonight. If she's still OK tomorrow – and she will be – I will be asking for overnight leave for her."

The nurse looked dubious. "I…"

Hawthorn interrupted her with his forefinger. "I can't stress too strongly how important it is for us to leave… for her to leave. Now. She's hauled herself from the darkest, deepest hole – not just once, but twice. The only reason she relapsed *today* was because of this *hospital*. I'm being honest, I'm being straight with you, because I know you will understand. Furthermore I know you have her interests at heart…"

He was ladling it on, surprised at the articulate flow of his words. "You know how long she's been here, how bad it's been for her. This…" He leaned closer, dropping his forefinger. "…*this* is a moment of drama, and you have it in your power to help someone who desperately needs your help. I'm not overstating things here. It's the truth. I'm sure the doctor will be as pleased as you and I are that she is well. I'm also certain he will want to ensure this behaviour is reinforced as soon as possible."

Hawthorn glanced behind him, and Alice was standing there, listening to him.

"Now," he said to her. "It's your turn. Talk to the nurse."

The nurse gave her a tentative smile. "Hello Alice."

IS ALICE?

She stepped into the office with confidence. "Well. Here I am. Back. Finally. I'm OK. I heard some of what Theo said to you, and I want to reassure you that I've got all my wits in one basket. It's just so wonderful, and I'm looking forward to today…"

The nurse nodded. "You sound much better, and you were talking earlier this morning after I came on duty. I mean, I'd like to, but I don't have the authority to let you go. You are still under Section."

"You have to call Dr Pincer," Hawthorn said firmly. "I'm sure he won't mind in a case like this. Please. Do it for us. It can't do any harm."

The nurse thought for a moment, looking down at the case notes in front of her. Then, slowly, after consulting a notebook, she tapped a number into her mobile phone. When the party answered, she turned away from them and spoke quietly, then listened.

She turned to Hawthorn, holding her hand over the mouthpiece. "It's Dr Pincer. He'll speak with you."

Gratefully he grabbed the mobile. "Dr Pincer. It's Theo Hawthorn here, and I apologise for bothering you during the holiday, but Alice has rather dramatically come around. I believe it's important that she is allowed out of the hospital in my care for the day…"

Pincer was a little petulant and certainly not happy that he was being pushed so hard, but finally he agreed to speak with Alice. They talked softly for over a minute.

Then Alice handed the phone to the nurse. She spoke briefly, then ended the call.

"It's fine. I hope you enjoy yourselves."

"Back at 9.00?"

"No later."

As they were buzzed through to the reception area downstairs, the old man was smiling so broadly Hawthorn could see one gold tooth.

"Good to see you, Alice," he said.

She smiled at him. "It's been a long, long time."

"Bless you both."

They stepped out into the cold morning, and Alice put her hand to her mouth. "How are we going to get home?"

Hawthorn pointed to her car parked in one of the visitors' bays. "Other days I used the bicycle, but today was only going to have one outcome. You were going to be well, and you were coming back with me. So I brought the car."

"You're so sure of yourself…and me!"

He stopped her halfway to the car. "Now mark it. Two parts of the promise have been fulfilled. I got you out to the garden yesterday and out of the hospital today." He

436

turned and gestured towards the doors. "One more week, and you'll never have to come here again."

They embraced as the winter wind whipped icily through the car park. "I want to go to my flat first, my hero," she said. "I want to see my flat."

Alice's flat was just across the street from his. Hers was on the top floor. When they opened the flat door, it was obvious it wasn't anything like Hawthorn's. It was clean and tidy, neatly carpeted. Green trailing plants hung down the stairwell opposite a huge Picasso print. There was a smell of newness and femininity. Everything was in its proper place. There was a sense of stillness as they passed wordlessly from room to room. The oak desk in the bedroom still held her laptop computer that she seldom used. The bed was covered with a bright yellow-checked duvet with matching pillows, and opposite were built-in Italian wardrobes. Over the bed, shelves were crammed with books. Alice was always a great reader. A make-up table and mirror completed the ensemble.

The sitting room faced the south-west, like his bedroom. A big expensive leather sofa dominated, facing the windows. There were more bookshelves on the party wall, with a neat cabinet holding a small TV and hi-fi unit. There was a Chinese carved coffee table between the two windows and a smaller glass-topped one covered in seashells and rough gemstones. Above the sofa was a beautiful Hockney print.

"I brought some of the plants in here to make the watering easier," Hawthorn said as they entered the kitchen. Her kitchen was in total contrast to his own, though both had cork floor tiles. Hers were laid professionally and were immaculate. There were luxury built-in cabinets, a clean modern cooker and a fridge-freezer, washing machine and dryer.

She leaned against the cooker and looked up at him. "It's so emotional. Being here. I never thought I'd see it again, ever."

"I haven't hoovered or dusted, but it doesn't look bad."

She felt her head with her hand. "Should I get a wig?"

"Do you think you need one?"

"Do you?"

"No. It'll grow out."

She looked up with a mischievous grin. "I know what. Let's go to Chinatown."

"What? Now? Chinatown?"

"Oh, Theo, yes! Let's do something I haven't been able to do for so long. It's Boxing Day – free parking – and they don't close for Christmas at all. And then there's Maison Bertaux. Oh, yes! Please!"

He lowered his head in a little bow. "You're in command. Anything you say."

"Anything?" She moved across the kitchen, held him and caressed his groin.

IS ALICE?

"Always."

"And have you behaved yourself?"

"Always."

She gave his penis a firm squeeze. "We'll see to that later. Now, Chinatown!"

There was little traffic as they drove to the West End, but it was still difficult to park in Soho. They finally found a place after their third circuit of Soho Square. The streets were bustling as they walked towards Gerrard Street. Soon they smelled the crispy duck and heard the shouts of the Chinese porters. There were people everywhere, clumps at corners, singles and couples crossing and criss-crossing the cobbles, idly or with burning purpose. Many were chattering into mobile phones with nasal, incomprehensible excitement. The greengrocers were open with displays of durian fruit, pak choi, eggplant and persimmons. Red banners waved above.

One of their favourite shops sold exotic gemstones in the basement. As they went downstairs Hawthorn couldn't remember being so relaxed, so at ease with himself and the world. He watched as Alice carefully examined the cases of stones. Along the walls were more souvenirs and lots of calligraphy paraphernalia – pens of varying sizes, inks and paper. He followed Alice, examining the gems himself. At the back of the shop he spotted a Chinese kite in the form of a falcon. It was quite delicate, with a fierce-looking head with about a four-foot wingspan. He asked the assistant the price and immediately bought one of them, thinking it would look great hanging from the ceiling in his front room. Alice was delighted, too, and chose a different colour for herself.

When they left the shop, they wandered slowly down Gerrard Street, stopping occasionally to read a menu, or window-shop. They didn't talk much. It was enough for them just to be close once more. They linked arms or held hands, squeezing or hugging. He realised his high spirits were fuelled by the delight in her face – the animation, the spontaneity, the energy. He couldn't take his eyes off her, and when she caught his gaze, she beamed with such pleasure it almost made him shout.

It was to be a day neither of them would ever forget, and maybe that was because of its pure aimlessness. They were flâneurs – that lovely French word used to describe those who wandered without business or purpose, purely for the pleasure of the next little discovery or unmissable view. It was an un-modern word, not needed for all those people who thought pleasure was intricate or only possible with money.

When they rounded the corner at the top of Gerrard Street, they headed towards Shaftesbury Avenue – because, secretly, they *did* have a purpose, or at least a destination. So they turned right on the Avenue to tour the remaining Chinese shops on their way to Maison Bertaux. There was one they had never noticed before. It was the tiniest of them all, barely bigger than a cupboard. It had a small display window in a narrow recess in front of the door. Hawthorn looked up at the sign as Alice examined the window. Mr Chan, Watches & Jewellery.

"Theo. Look."

He squeezed into the narrow passage and peered over her shoulder.

"Isn't that a *beautiful* watch?" she asked.

She was pointing at a round-faced Swiss watch set among several older Rolexes, Breitlings and Omegas. He looked closely, his nose almost pressed against the glass. It was a Le Cheminant Master Mariner. He'd never heard of the company, but it was a striking timepiece – a round face in chrome or stainless with what looked like a 1960s expandable strap.

"It's uncanny," Hawthorn muttered. "It looks like one I wore as a student at UBC. I love that shape. You don't see it any more. Simple, uncluttered, a clear date."

"I'd love to have it," she said, pushing in for a closer look.

"So would I," he agreed. "But look at the price. There. On the tag. Two hundred and sixty five pounds. I don't think I ever paid over twenty for any watch I ever owned."

They both peered into the minuscule shop. The interior was dark, and there were no customers. A shadowy young Chinese man stood at the back, his head down, working.

Hawthorn pulled out his pen and found a scrap of paper in his pocket. "I'll write down the name of it. Maybe we can find a cheaper one on the Internet…"

Reluctantly they left the little jeweller and made their way to Greek Street and Maison Bertaux. It was the atmosphere that made it so special. The walls were undecorated, with exposed pipework and the old black and white photographs. A furled French flag hung on the wall. The two tables were still outside, even in the winter. The interior was not much bigger than Mr Chan's, but they chose their expensive cakes, ordered tea-for-two and climbed the narrow, steep stairs to the floor above. The place was almost full – as always – with bohemian students and a few tourists, along with several Chinese. A couple were just leaving their favourite table beside the window where Hawthorn could smoke his pipe.

He squeezed his large frame onto the little bench, and Alice sat opposite. She immediately began stacking the plates and cups left by the departing couple on the edge of the table. Using a napkin, she then wiped the space clean.

"You do spend a lot of your life making things tidy," he smiled.

"Well," she replied, "You can put your elbows on the table now."

"I can't believe we got this seat today. Perfect."

IS ALICE?

"Yes," she beamed, as she planted her elbows in front of her. "And I love you. I *adore* you. And we got our place. It's wonderful. You're wonderful."

To celebrate, she dug out a cigarette and lit it. "Now tell me about Aleksei Cherkasov. Did he really come to the hospital and play, or is that a part of one of my many memory-illusions?"

"Yes, he was there. He played the Schubert sonata again, just for you."

"*How on earth* did you manage that! He came especially to play for *me*?"

Hawthorn leaned back into the wall. "Alice, it's a long story. I'll go through it briefly, but at home I have a whole manuscript of letters I've written to him during your illness. He asked me to tell him everything, so I've been sitting at my computer, printing off hundreds of pages, letter after letter. Never received a reply, never expected any. He's such a warm and gentle man."

Alice spread her hands excitedly. "But *how*....?"

He laughed, then compressed the whole tale into about thirty minutes, interrupted by the delivery of his lemon tart and her strawberry and cream cake. When he finished, they were both on their second cup of tea. She waited until the end, mesmerised.

"You were in the hospital as a *patient*! That so confused me, Theo. I couldn't understand why you were there. I was sure you must be working with *them* – the others, the other world. I thought you were taking the piss, pretending to be ill. Then you got yourself out, and you got *me* out. And you went naked on stage? Oh, how incredible!"

She hid her eyes with her hands, giggling. "I can't even imagine it."

"I could have found another way, a much better way" he said seriously as he picked up his cold pipe and re-lit it. "But I was full of anger and a sense of injustice. On the other hand, the result was that I made acquaintance with the greatest pianist of the 20th Century, and my life unfolded in a slightly different way. You can never tell what the 'right' action may be. You just have to try and maintain your balance as you struggle to find the entrance or exit. There are times – not many, but some – when patience is wrong, and attack is right…"

"Theo!" She smacked her palm on the table, rattling the tea service. "I'm going to buy you that watch!"

He held up both hands, laughing. "Hey, hey. Stop it. I'm not letting you splash out your money on the spur of the moment like this. Anyway, *you* wanted it, too. Buy it for yourself, if you want."

"No! You're going to have it. It's a man's watch, and it'll look beautiful on your wrist, and we'll always remember this time. *Watch, time* – you see? I mean it, Theo. We're going there right now, and I'm going to buy it, so just shut up, OK? After all you've done, you deserve it."

"I've done nothing!" he exclaimed. He glanced at his pipe and put it down. "Brought you a few cigarettes, watered your plants – nothing."

"Don't be stupid. You know what I'm talking about."

"Alice, stop it. It's too much money…"

"Don't tell me what's too much money! I haven't spent a penny in six months. We're going now, now, now, and I'm not hearing any more about it."

"I…" he began.

"Stop!" She held up her hand as she put her cigarettes and lighter into her coat pocket. "It's what I want to do, and it's what I'm going to do. No more argument…"

When they arrived again at Mr Chan's, they both instinctively checked to see if the watch was still there before pressing the buzzer. The young Chinese man was smiling as they entered. Two customers were examining some jade on the counter.

The young man's name was Andrew, and he told them that he and his uncle, who owned the shop, were only interested in old, classic Swiss watches, not new ones. Andrew was infectiously enthusiastic. He opened a small window to the outside display and fetched out the Master Mariner as the other two customers nodded to him and left.

"This watch? This the one you mean?"

They both held their breath.

"Yes," Alice said finally. "That one."

Andrew held it lovingly for them to examine. "This watch is about 1970. They don't do the design any more. It's automatic, no battery, just winds from movement of arm."

"I've always wanted an automatic," Hawthorn muttered.

"Good movement. Twenty-three jewel. This watch is fine one. Not Rolex, but good company, good name. One of my uncle's favourite. Look, this is original strap. Expandable, but won't catch hairs on arm, you know? Made properly. Try on."

Hawthorn took it gingerly, mesmerised by its simple beauty. When he put it on, the fit was perfect. It looked good. He couldn't believe it was almost his.

"Let's see," Alice said, her voice soft as she held his wrist to look at the watch. "Yes, it's wonderful, gorgeous. Looks perfect on you."

She turned to Andrew. "How much?"

"Two hundred sixty-five pounds," he replied, beaming.

"I'll give you two-forty," she said.

Andrew suddenly looked as if his mother had been cursed. "Ah, no. No, I cannot do that. My uncle restore that watch, very hard to find the parts, much hard work.

IS ALICE?

Look, is only one small shop we have. We make a price that is fair, we cannot bargain. I wish we could. But no."

"Two-fifty?" Alice inquired, raising an eyebrow.

"Ah, no," Andrew shook his head again sadly. Then he brightened. "I tell you what! I make it two-sixty. Two-sixty! You see! I bargain. Special. For you. Make exception."

Alice finally laughed with good humour. "OK. Two-sixty it is. We can't resist the watch."

"Awww, is good watch! Fine watch! You bring here if it goes wrong, we fix it for free. You no pay. We do not sell rubbish. Watch stop, you bring back, any time, year from now, five year from now. My uncle make it run, no charge. I tell you, this watch, they do not make it any more. New watch good, but old, fine Swiss, made a lot by hand. You know, feel this watch. You can sometime feel the man who made it, each one a little, tiny bit different. Now, everything by machine."

He picked up Hawthorn's old watch lying on the counter. "This one cheap watch." He raised his eyebrows under his short, black hair. "But keep perfect time, you bet, run by battery, but it has no…no…"

"Character?" Hawthorn guessed.

Andrew brightened. "Ah. Yes. Character! This cheap watch the same, they make thousands. *That* watch special made. All a little different. That's why uncle likes to work on them."

Alice paid with her card, and, as they were leaving Mr Chan's, she hugged his arm. "I'm so glad I did that. It feels right. It looks right. Now. Is this still my day?"

Hawthorn grinned. "It's pretty much looking like *my* day. Thank you so much, darling. I don't know what else to say."

She stood on her toes and kissed him on the lips, ignoring the other pedestrians. "It gives me so much pleasure. And if it really is still my day, let's choose a Chinese restaurant for dinner."

He looked at his new watch. "Bit early for dinner, late for lunch. Are you sure you're hungry, after the cake?"

"Starving. Haven't eaten out for – how long? – six months? Anyway, I want a proper meal. No prison mush."

"You've lost weight, you know."

"Well, let's go put it back where it belongs. Come on, let's stroll along and look at the menus outside."

It was classic Alice Dance. They made at least three circuits of all the restaurants on Gerrard Street, trying to decide. Some places smelled nice but didn't look right inside. Others were perfect, but the menu was boring. She finally decided on one called the Dumpling Inn because she liked the nice, white tablecloths. Also, they both fancied dumplings.

It was only mid-afternoon, but the highly competitive Chinese restaurants seemed to serve all day, and two or three tables were already occupied. They sat down, studied the menu in infinite detail, and finally ordered more than they could possibly eat.

Hawthorn leaned back in his chair. Alice's face was glowing. She was bubbling with happiness. "Do you feel like talking about your ordeal, or is this the wrong time?"

She turned away suddenly. "Oh, it's too close, Theo. It's still there. Like a voice calling me, telling me I'm wrong, I'm being tricked."

"But you know you're not."

"Oh, yes. I'm not going back now. I can't. I'm too excited, too joyful about being away from it. But I catch myself wondering…"

"You know, it's so strange how quickly you emerge. It's uncanny. Like a toggle-switch. It's only like a minute – maybe two or three minutes at the most – and you move from total psychosis to so-called normality. Does it feel like that to you?"

"I don't know." She shook her head and frowned, thinking. "I latch on to something. Or something catches my attention…"

"Your attention. Yeah. That's the problem. When you're immersed in the dark world, there's no communication at all."

"Yes, I know. I'm watching something else, trying my best to understand. But I just think I'm too stupid. I look at your gestures. I'm desperately *trying*, Theo. I do hear the words, too. I just don't understand them properly. Let me think. A lot of it is sexual. If you say something like 'semantic,' I think it probably means 'semen tic.' I have a facial tic from too much oral sex, or something. Or you're feeding me 'dump lings,' little balls of shit. It… it's mad. So I can never get the real sense of what you're saying."

"Then something happens. Like yesterday and this morning. It inevitably begins the same way, you asking simple questions."

"It's always been like that when I'm coming round. I honestly don't know what it is, just something strikes me. I can't tell you any more than that."

He chuckled. "And the first question is, 'Are you a policeman?' Why a policeman? Do I look like a cop?"

"No, no. I think you're coming to arrest me for something I've done, some bad thing. A lot of times when I see you in the hospital, I believe you're there to kill me, poison me. When you offer to take me out to the shops or the park, I'm sure it's so you can murder me."

IS ALICE?

"Ironic. Seems like you would leap at the chance, as you spend so much time trying to kill yourself. Or praying for your death."

"No." She was adamant. "It's different if somebody wants to kill you. It… it would be horrific, being strangled or knifed."

The waitress arrived with the first of several covered steamers of dumplings. She re-arranged the table, then hurried away. After two more trips, the table was covered with food partially obscured by a fog of steam. Alice was immediately busy peeking under covers, at a loss where to begin until she found the rice. She spooned some onto both plates. Then, carefully, she began dividing up the dumplings, taking a couple from each steamer so the rest would stay hot. Hawthorn watched her and decided she was getting steadier, safer. There was no way of really knowing, because of the quicksilver oddness of her illness, but over the years he had developed a sixth sense. He realised she was in a bright, florid stage at this point, flooded with the delights she had missed in the world. Her energy level was high, but it was nothing remotely manic.

She ate quickly and with relish. He wasn't that hungry. His main pleasure was in watching her eat and enjoy her food. He thought it must be awakening every taste sense in her mouth, after such a long time on institutional grub.

She caught him looking at her and grinned between mouthfuls. "I'll soon put all the weight back on this way. Be fat again."

"You were never fat! Ever!" he scoffed. "You were always just right. The way I like 'em. Nice big tits. Plump thighs."

"Yeah. Too plump."

"No. Just-fucking-right, like I said in the first place."

"You didn't say 'fucking'."

"Speaking of fucking…"

She grinned. "You still interested in a bald, mad glutton?"

"Is a pig's ass pork?"

"Here," she said quickly. "Try another one of these pig's ass dumplings. They're de*licious*!"

CHAPTER TWENTY-ONE

The next day when Hawthorn arrived at the hospital, he found Alice fine but distressed about staying the night there. Again, he had telephoned her first.

"It's schizophrenogenic," she exclaimed on the phone. "If you weren't mad in the first place…"

"I know," he replied. "I was there myself. It's worse than the Middle Ages, with a thin varnish of 'civilisation.' I'll be there in a jiffy. I just wanted to tell you I was on my way."

"Hurry!" she almost shouted.

Pan Subarti was on duty, as was a locum psychiatrist. Hawthorn fidgeted as he waited for the locum to arrive in the conference room. Alice was packing her bags, and he had advised her that it was probably best if he talked to the doctor alone.

Finally a fairly young woman entered the room. He had never seen her on the ward before.

"Hello. I'm Doctor Masterson. How can I help?"

"Theo Hawthorn, Alice Dance's partner. She's been well for two days now, and I am seeking release for home leave, under my care…"

She was already shaking her head as she interrupted. "Alice can't leave the hospital yet on overnight leave."

Hawthorn red-flagged his anger, relaxed himself and leaned back in his chair. "I'm sure you'll find that's not the policy of this ward. The senior psychiatric nurse is on duty, and I'm confident he'll back me up. He knows us both very well…"

She broke in again. "I'm sure we can arrange for Alice to be released after the holidays when things are back to normal."

"Back to normal. Is that a joke?"

"I don't joke." She pulled her thin lips back in a grimace-smile.

"You'd find yourself a lot healthier, if you did," he said.

"I don't see…"

This time he interrupted her, but with an engaging smile. "Let me just explain a little something for your consideration. Alice and I were out all day yesterday with Dr Pincer's permission. I called him at home, and we also discussed home leave for her today, if all went well. Which it did. So I reckon I already have permission to leave this hospital with Alice…"

"…I must advise you that, without specific permission…"

Both were speaking at the same time, but Hawthorn raised the decibel octane and prevailed. "…and we are shortly going to depart through the front door waving goodbye to the staff – you, included, if you like. Alice Dance has been incarcerated in this hospital for six months, and if she stays one more day a relapse is almost certain. Whereas, if we are allowed to go now, her complete recovery is equally certain. If you should have the poor judgement to try and stop us, think about what you'll have to endure first. Please. The last thing in the world I'd want is to embarrass you. Either you'll have to call Dr Pincer or the police. If you call the police, *they* will call Dr Pincer on my insistence. Because he is the one who knows this patient's history, and she is directly under his care."

He rose from his chair and extended his hand. "Now, Dr Masterson, I don't want to keep Alice waiting. She's very much looking forward to leaving here today. If you want any further reassurances, please speak to Pan Subarti. He's very much up-to-speed on the matter. So nice to have met you."

She did not take his hand, but her lips were contorting as anger struggled with reason. He opened the door and left the room.

Alice was waiting at the nurses' station. Her face glittered with happiness and anticipation, and her bag hung from her shoulder.

"How did it go?" she asked.

"Fine, no problem. Let's skedaddle before they try to re-Section *me*."

"Why?" she asked as they approached the door and the buzzer opened the lock.

He pushed the door open, and they walked toward the lift. "Alice, the world we live in is so strange, I often get lost in its corridors myself. It's no wonder you have difficulties and duck out to another one that's probably more rational. Let's just get the fuck out of here."

It was another energy-extravagant day. First they went to his flat where she was going to stay for the week so he could keep an eye on her. Hawthorn made her a cup of tea as she opened a new pack of cigarettes and got on the telephone to call her friends and her family. He went to the computer and continued to work on what was to be his last letter to Aleksei Cherkasov, telling him the wonderful news.

It must have been over an hour before Alice was finished with her calls. Then she wanted to go to the Boxing Day sales. He managed to talk her out of a long trip to Brent Cross shopping centre, as he just didn't think he could cope with the sales-maddened crowds. But she was perfectly satisfied to visit the Nag's Head, just down the Holloway Road.

The Nag's Head was named after a pub that no longer existed, but it was once located on the corner of Seven Sisters Road. It was an area where all the deprived sink estate people shopped. He had heard them described as riff-raff, and it was hard not to think of them that way. The streets were crowded and dirty, heaving with the unemployed, or those who worked at no-hope jobs at the shitty end of the employment digestive system. Dickens would have loved it. Instead of gin palaces, though, there were smelly burger emporiums and cheap kebab joints where people fed the same kind of hunger they used to try and suppress with gin. There were plenty of drunks, too, but they were mostly bellied aside by the fat, the gross and the repellent. Albanians and Kurds hawked counterfeit cigarettes and tobacco on the corners. They would appear like ghostly forest mushrooms and disappear with hummingbird swiftness at the sight of a police uniform. The Nag's Head Market smelled of decaying wet fish, and the cheap trinket stalls were doing good business. Recent rain made the pavements a little treacherous as the water loosened the body fluids and rancid oils, flattened chips and burger parts. There was no longer so much dog shit, probably because there seemed to be fewer dogs, except for the Staffordshire bull terriers used by the crack dealers to take out the police Alsatian sniffer dogs. Cotton and wool were as scarce as fresh flowers. Pedestrians insulated themselves with bri-nylon, synthetic fleeces, baseball caps with American athletic logos, Arsenal football strip, and Chinese trainers bearing advertising for Italian products. Young girls were briefly pretty between adolescence and maternity, after which their hips began oozing from the tops of their polyester track bottoms. The pretty ones tended to gaggle around the drug dealers, dressed in plastic high heels and heavy make-up, talking into their mobile phones. Or else they promenaded their territories in search of the excitement that would turn them into mothers seeking hostel accommodation.

It was grim and only superficially festive. There was spray-on snow in the windows, ropes of gaily-coloured bunting, incessant flashing of fairy lights that hadn't burned out, moulded plastic Santas dangling on string. Santa Claus was a true saint of modern commerce, imported with so much else from America. The old British Father Christmas was elbowed aside by the new imagery, and updated tales spun in the Madison Avenue advertising abattoir. The coarse and savage vulgarity of it all provided a sticky-sweet coating for the depraved hypocrisy. This couldn't be civilisation. The lives of these people had been turned with rat-like addiction to squalid, spiritually empty graveyards of the soul. The bell rang 'Boxing Day Sales,' and the hyperactive zombies came in their thousands to feast on the ghoulish delights of modern commerce. Alice danced among them, free at last to get her dose of sugary products after her enforced absence. Hawthorn wasn't critical – of them or of her. On the contrary, he gorged himself on her sheer pleasure as she dashed from shop to shop, examining 'bargains' and tossing them aside to find another shop that had better ones. He was quite content to hold the bags and parcels and just watch her enjoying herself.

She held up her wrist. "What do you think?"

It was a new watch. Her old one had been tossed into the hospital washing machine. The new one wasn't expensive, but it suited her. Bold numerals set in a round face with a magnified date.

"I think mine is better," he replied with pride as he hugged her. "But yours is on a much prettier arm."

IS ALICE?

"Yours would look better on a prettier arm, too. So what about giving it back? No? OK, then," she said, "we're both prepared for the New Time now. Between us. Two new watches. But seriously, Theo, let it not happen again. Let us not be separated. Ever."

"Amen," he murmured as he hugged her.

She bought a new pair of boots and some silver earrings to dangle from her pierced ears. She searched for a new handbag, but unsurprisingly couldn't find one that suited her. In the Nag's Head, anything that smelled of leather was probably enhanced by the chemical skills of perfumers in New Jersey.

Their last stop was Argos. Inside it looked like a bear-baiting contest had just finished. People were milling around with glazed eyes. Leaflets and flyers formed a muddy carpet on the tiles, and punters stood at the catalogue pedestals, madly looking through the pages for what they thought they wanted or needed. Parents snarled at their kids who wanted more of something they couldn't name – just more, another one, something else, this-not-that, buy, acquire, possess, it didn't matter. The queue at the order desk was long and surly. Staff were staggering under big boxes brought from lifts at the back – camping equipment, garden awnings, microwave ovens, toy tricycles, cake mixers, coffee makers. Most of the customers were fingering mobile phones or talking animatedly into them, providing disjointed conversations in a scene that made surrealism seem mild and understated. One old woman was trying to get out, and could barely see round the box she was carrying. An advertising flyer was stuck to the bottom of her shoe by chewing gum, and her walking stick was hooked over her arm. Children ran around screaming to punctuate the heavy-beat muzak playing on store speakers. A young man struggled to push his hand down the back of his girlfriend's tight, low-slung jeans, his fingers tangled in her whale-tail thong.

It was too much even for Alice. She turned to him. "Let's get the hell out of here. I wouldn't stand in that queue even if they were giving away twenty pound notes."

* * *

When Hawthorn first introduced Alice to alternative sexual adventure, she was a little dubious – not because she wasn't interested, though. She simply felt uncomfortable with playing 'roles.' He explained that they weren't really roles. They were pathways into the self, and you created a persona from elements of that self. There was no pretence. What you felt and what you did were real. You used your basic creative functions to fabricate an alternative universe with different factors of highlighted personality. It all sounded to her like an intellectual landscape that would not work, but as she began to play, she realised her own energies were mushrooming. She scaled high, bright cliff walls that gave her dazzling views and moments of thrilling passion.

Negotiation was always an integral part of the process. Some experiments failed to live up to their imagined thrill, but others led them through apertures beyond her experience. For her, love and trust were the most important features, and the heat of their flames could rise to the stars, fuelled by sexual desire. They borrowed from some known ideas, and invented their own sacred, secret chambers where they brewed the old with the new. The concept of tantric sex was important – extending desire unremittingly, beyond even what they imagined was possible. His hand and her hand guided the magic wand that presented a land of visions and dreams. The two pillars of love and trust supported the stairway that led them upwards.

Change was important. Hawthorn was always gently insistent about this, though he preferred to think of it as metamorphosis. To become static was to invite decay. Yet there was no programme to their movement, and it was never rapid. One state or stage slowly evolved to another one, and from there they went somewhere else.

Deferred gratification had the effect of maintaining his focus and anticipation, so they could more easily expand their sessions, and even develop them into playful episodes of their daily lives. To his delight, Hawthorn realised he could extend prolonged sexual arousal and daily interest, even though he was nearing the age of sixty. In effect he felt a much younger man, able to achieve spontaneous and prolonged erections. His sex life had always been important to him, as he swam through shoals of women like a playful porpoise in earlier years. He loved younger women, and he loved the older ones – their fragrance, the way they moved, the taste of their flesh, their soft curves, the hidden mysteries and the enticing flirtatiousness of endless wandering eyes.

For Alice Dance it was somewhat different. Hawthorn was really her first and only love. Perhaps previous lovers withdrew as they learned of her psychological problems. After meeting him, she found her life profoundly changed. She was presented with a world she never dared to imagine she would inherit. And as she changed, her love ripened and deepened. Sexually, she began by simply wanting to please him, yet she was slowly but powerfully drawn into its mysteries. The side effects of her medication eventually put a stop to complete orgasm, but now that no longer mattered. It was the intense closeness that was most arousing, along with the unaccustomed feeling of control – the effect she had on him, the way she could entice his body and soul to peaks of mindless longing. Then there were the mystical connections…

Alice lowered her head closer to his, so their temples were touching. "I feel you…"

She was caressing him, gently moving her hand around his penis in little wispy circles as he lay helpless on his back.

"I'm inside you," he gasped in a whisper. His mind was inflamed with the torment of desire, and the intensity broke open the perimeter of consciousness. She was there. It was not imagination. He was interacting with her being, abstract but not shapeless. It was like pushing inside a warm, giant gas planet. New atmospheres swirled in muted pastels as their molecular mix was wafted and sucked by secret, sinuous currents. There were no images or words, but there was difference and strangeness. Dimly coloured clouds shrouded any landscape of shapes. Nonetheless, Hawthorn knew it was Alice, and Alice knew she was with him. Neither of them thought any thoughts, because the intensity of emotion swept them away before anything could form. Strangest of all was the sense of time – or, more accurately, the absence of it. They stood still together in the same space and, incongruently, in some other space where time slipped off the restraint of measurement. Nothing became everything.

Hawthorn witnessed little subliminal flickers. Princess Elena in a white gown, Silenus painting the toenails of a delicate porcelain foot. In another moment there were two other creatures – human, but not human – embracing as they embraced now. Then there was a figure like the Flying Dutchman on the deck of a ghost ship, searching, searching again, after losing the thread of love. Suddenly, a lone samurai on the point of drawing his blade flashed and faded. These images were too brief to be visions, and they did not interrupt or disturb the two figures lying together on the bed. Alice's soft fingers were slowly circling the tip of his prick, but it seemed their breathing had slowed down to a shallow rhythm. Hawthorn could hear her breath in his ear and feel the humid air on his cheek.

"Careful," he said softly. "Careful…"

It was the warning he gave when he was close to orgasm. The movement of her hand stopped briefly, only to resume a few moments later, sensing the peak had passed in him. Seconds later there was another surge and another whispered warning. The cycles seemed endless. She would stop, then start again, guiding him further and further into frontiers he no longer recognised. He could not move or resist her. He was helpless but safe in her hands.

Later, as they lay a little apart on the bed smoking, Hawthorn was aware of nothing but absolute happiness and the slowly retreating throb in his loins. She had not brought him to orgasm yet, and he was inwardly glad, because it helped to hold the vigour of their intimacy intact. It was late in the afternoon, their first exotic sexual encounter since she emerged from the hospital.

It was dark outside, and the room was lit only by a small lamp against the opposite wall and two large candles. Incense burned between the candles. Hawthorn put his pipe aside and rose in a cloud of smoke to search the shelves of CDs above the bed. He found what he was looking for and put it in the player. As he turned back to her, he was filled again with a longing too profound to describe. She lay there in a black diaphanous dress, white stockings hazily outlined underneath and the nipples of her breasts dimly visible.

Hawthorn lay back on the bed and pulled himself close to her. She raised her arm as he placed his head on her chest. He caressed her through the gauze of her erotic dress. The piano had just begun to play.

"It's the Schubert," she sighed.

"Aleksei."

"I love it," she said. "Do you really see me in it?"

"Yes. Especially. I always see women I love in certain pieces of music. Very romantic."

"Oh," she smiled. "So I'm just one of a collection."

"The most special one of all. The final one."

She pulled him closer. "Really?"

"Yes. Forever."

"That was so powerful, wasn't it? We haven't lost it. Oh, I'm so happy we haven't lost it!"

"Alice, I have never had such an experience with anyone else. Not even close. I have this huge intuitive feeling that we found each other after such a long, long time."

"We were together, weren't we? I mean… mingling. I don't know what to call it."

"I don't know what happens or how. It seems even stronger now, but that might be because it has been six months since we were this close. I know I'm with you, a part of your consciousness. There's an overlap. We both know it. That's enough. No proof necessary. But it's an exquisite, priceless experience."

The music was swelling as the beautiful theme of the long first movement was played again and again in variations. They lay together just listening for a while, and it seemed the music helped open them again to an overlap of consciousness. Alice had stubbed out her cigarette, and they were motionless. The bed was floating on a calm, warm sea, like a raft, under a dark protective sky. There was much to say, but already they had said most of it with their bodies.

"Feeling your beard is strange," she said finally.

"Yep. I imagine it feels something like your head." They both laughed.

"You know," she said softly, "when I was in hospital, and I noticed your beard, I thought you were telling me something about my pubic hair, mocking me. I thought you were sending me a coded message."

"That's roughly the shape of my beard, I suppose," he said, "but if there was a message, it was more like, 'I'm missing you...'"

"Did you really miss me?"

"Yes. Like some vital part of my body."

"I missed you *so* much, and I felt so guilty about that, as I tried to get it out of my head. I knew I couldn't have you, that you were a part of another race, and you had some awful imposed duty so that you had to be with me, even though you hated and detested me. I thought I was helping you by keeping away..."

"I know that. I knew it. You explained it to me after your last illness."

"Oh," she moaned. "Does it have to happen again? And again? I can't bear it, Theo."

IS ALICE?

"I think I may be able to help you. All the time you've been in hospital, I've been struggling to find an answer. I'm on the right path, but I don't quite understand it all myself. I need to put it together…"

"Can we start tomorrow?"

"Start what?"

"Helping me. Talk to me. Let's talk together. Tell me your ideas, give me some picture of what you've been thinking. Then maybe I can understand. I just can't go on like this. The fear, the anxiety. I'm no good with other people…"

"You are. You have your friends. You feel safe with them."

"I mean *other* people. That's what happened, isn't it? That ticket business at the Royal Albert Hall. Something in the way it occurred, the way people were looking at me contemptuously. Then I was gone. I couldn't even tell you. I mean, I can't go out on the streets these days. All this new technology – CCTV cameras, voice recorders, iris scans. I was terrified in hospital. *Terrified.* I thought there were cameras and microphones everywhere, looking at me, gathering evidence, recording my obscene inner thoughts…"

He rolled over onto his pillow, grabbed his pipe and re-lit it. "OK, tomorrow we'll talk about it all. A lot has been happening. And I'll go through the joint account with you. I've kept all the withdrawal slips, and I've made sure all your bills were paid. Oh, yeah. I did take ten pounds a week for myself. Every Friday evening I went down to the old Pasta House at Tufnell Park and had a fish dinner. Couldn't afford it myself, but I thought you wouldn't mind."

"Oh, you should have taken more than that. That's what I set up the account for – just what's happened to me."

"I didn't need more than that. And thanks. Listen. This is the last movement of the sonata. I like it almost as much as the first."

Holding hands, they listened till the end of the piece. Then she lit another cigarette and turned to him.

"I can't imagine that you really love me. How can you? It's beyond my comprehension. I have disgusting thoughts…"

"We all have dark thoughts, disgusting ones. Everybody. I see those thoughts, but I also see *you*. You are warm and gentle. Thoughtful. Kind. During all the time we've been together, we've never quarrelled. We respect each other. You give way, or I give way, when there's a problem. Or else we enter our little world – a delight to both of us."

He put his pipe away and turned on his side to admire her. "Look at your life since we met. Perhaps even this illness, however horrible it has been for you, is positive in the whole panorama of our lives. We can't know. But we can *act* as if it is. Look at what we just experienced. If anything, it's stronger than it was before. Our closeness, our contact, our love. Maybe it was necessary to take three steps away before moving four steps closer. We define the things that happen to us. Meaning doesn't come wrapped in parcels as gifts from the 'outer world'."

"I'm so happy to be here. Out of the hospital," she said after a long pause. "It's like a re-birth, a resuscitation, a miracle. I adore you. I don't deserve you…"

"Oh, please," he begged. "Do millionaires deserve their millions? Do hordes of people deserve to die of starvation and neglect? Anyway, I'm nothing special, and that's not modesty speaking. I'm only a thoughtful human being, as you are. We found each other. 'Deserve' doesn't have anything to do with it. 'Deserve' has something to do with justice, and you won't find that justice is a major feature of this world. You've got me, therefore you deserve me. End of story."

She started to cry, then stopped herself and turned to face him. "You did all those things for me while I was inside. Paid my bills, watered my plants, took care of my car…"

"Wouldn't you do the same for me?"

"Of course. But…"

"So not that unusual, then?"

"But I'm… not worth it…"

"Here we are back into 'deserve'."

She bit her lip. "I mean, who am I? A nutcase, just out of the nut house, full of foul thoughts about people, a physical wreck. I shouldn't even be wearing these clothes. I mean, look at my face. Have you seen my face? It's haggard. I look sixty at least. Now I'm prancing around in this sexy gear, and I'm about as sexy as stale matzo balls. The only good thing is I've lost a little weight. So I'm ugly, I'm a nasty person…"

Hawthorn stopped her with a warning hand and a smile. "For whom – please note my grammar – do you want to be sexy? Or beautiful? For everyone? Or me?"

"You, naturally," she said a little petulantly. "I don't care about anyone else."

"Exactly. And for me, you are the most gorgeous woman I've ever known. OK, you could use a little more hair, but that'll come…"

"I'll get a wig!"

"I was *joking*! If you believe I tell the truth, then what more do you need? You are beautiful for *me*. You are perfect. I adore every part of your body. Look at those tits, those legs, that ass. Twinkly little eyes set in an oval-heart face full of humanity and honesty. You're short, too. I love that. I've always loved shorter women, makes me feel more of a brute, so I can pin you down like a butterfly or bounce you on my knee like Santa Claus…"

IS ALICE?

"Sanity clause? You can't kid me. You know there ain't no sanity clause."

"Ha, ha. Marx Brothers, right? You're full of laughs today."

Her face lit up. "I know what. Tomorrow...no, not tomorrow, because we're talking. The next day, yeah, the next day I'm going to book a full-body beauty treatment – face, leg wax, everything. The works. Maybe even see if I can do something with what's left of my hair. Maybe I'll look at wigs. OK, OK, you don't want a wig. Anyway, I'll be better, much better..."

"You're great as you are. Perfect."

She pulled herself closer to him. "Do you really, *really* think those things about me? I can't believe you. You're crazy, crazier than I am. How can you find me beautiful? That's beyond me. I was looking at my face in the mirror today, and I almost cried. The lines, the dark circles, the sad, sad eyes. You want somebody younger, nice fresh skin, beautiful hair..."

"I want you. Nobody else will do."

"Mad. Mad."

"Listen. If you don't care about being beautiful for anyone but me – and you certainly *are* – then you are *beautiful*. Is there anything complex about that? Why do you want more?"

She made a mock pout with her lips. "I want to *feel* beautiful."

"Then look in my eyes, my darling."

She looked at him. The seconds ticked by. "I covered myself with shit in the hospital, wiped it all over myself."

She waited for him to answer before continuing. "I ate shit, too. *Ate* it."

"Why?" he asked quietly. "Do you remember?"

"I thought I was killing people with passive smoking, so I had to try and stop. But I couldn't. I tried to stop, everything I could think of. Finally I scooped up one of my turds and poked cigarette butts into it. I was crying. It was horrible. Made myself eat it, gagging…"

Hawthorn stopped her gently with his hand and embraced her, holding her body against him. "You're not there now. You're here. It's over, forever."

She squirmed against him. "Oh, I hope so! Oh, let it be! I just can't bear to think of going back. Ever! EVER!"

"You are going to be well. From now on."

"Oh, Theo. I *love* you!"

He sniffed her lips playfully. "I do hope you brushed your teeth."

IS ALICE?

She laughed heartily and pushed at his chest. "You are gross! Ugh. Oh, god, it makes me remember it. I am gross. How can you love such a gross person, a mad shit-eater?"

"It's not gross," he said seriously. "It's deeply sad. It breaks my fucking heart. Thinking of you in there. With me standing impotently outside a thick glass window, unable to make you hear me, believe me, be with me. Not being able to help, just watching and hoping."

"Yes. It must have been awful for you, Theo. I can't bear to think about it…"

"Pah. It was nothing, compared to what you were going through. For me, it was bad. For you, it was beyond description, the absolute depths of horror that any human being can plumb. Endless hell without even a glimmer of hope. It says something about your strength to even be able to endure it, survive it, manage to walk away…"

"It was you who helped me, my darling. You. I would still be there…"

"Shhhh. Maybe, maybe not. We're not gods who have the power to tell."

"No, no, no. I'm not having that. You must believe me. If it weren't for you, I'd still be there. Probably forever. Tell me, Theo. Who would have done what you did? Who would have fought those despicable nurses and doctors? Who would have known I was on the way up when I started asking questions? Who guided me?"

"It was not 'who' but 'what.' It was love. And I'll say it again. You would have done the same for me, so my value is no higher than yours. You would probably even have handled it better than I did. In fact, I'm sure you would."

"Rubbish."

"Let's not argue over it. I'm just trying to give you a better perspective. Of course I was going to help, do everything I could. The same as you would have done. I watched over you as best I could. I could have done more."

She looked at him and took his head in both her hands. "Let me tell you something. I could not have done it as well, because I don't have your amazing optimism. Your determination against all forces ranged against you. Your courage…"

"I quote: '*rubbish*'."

"Well, it's what I think."

"I'll make a deal with you," he said as he reached again for his pipe. "I'll believe you, if you believe me."

"And what about all this other work you did while I was ill? These thoughts about philosophy, how to work out a way to help me by thinking?"

"We'll come to that tomorrow."

"If anybody can help me, it's you."

"If that's what you think, then we're one step in the right direction. I haven't solved the whole problem of consciousness, partly because I'm a part of the process I'm trying to examine. But I know more than I did. I may even know enough to start helping you out of your maze. Though it's a complex subject, the central issue may be pretty simple. What you need to understand. How you can act and what to do. It's very much your own choice, a question of whether or not you are determined to re-arrange the furniture of existence."

"I can't wait," she said with excitement. "Meanwhile, back in our moment – our beautiful moment – why don't we get our clothes on and go out to eat. I'm hungry."

"That's back in our moment? Eating?"

"Sure! Sitting opposite the dream of my life in a nice restaurant. Delicious food, only you to share it with, forget the other people. Please, Theo, let's do it. Let's eat out every night this week."

His forefinger shot into the air. "You *deserve* it!"

"Exactly! I'll pay."

"Music to my ears. And you are music to my eyes. What more could I ask for?"

She grabbed him as he started to swing off the bed to get his clothes. "Oh, Theo, I'm so happy I'm out. It's so wonderful. So much...so MUCH I was missing!"

CHAPTER TWENTY-TWO

Hawthorn's prediction was wrong by two days. Alice's discharge from Section and from the hospital was the day after the first of January. However, she insisted it was absolutely accurate, completely consistent with his prognostication. The meeting with Dr Pincer, Pan Subarti and an administrator was relaxed and relatively brief. They simply sat around talking informally for 30 minutes, and then it was all over. Alice was free.

For the whole week in between Christmas and New Year, they spent talking endlessly, eating out and teasing the cunning serpent of sex. Anticipating the release, Hawthorn finished his final letter to Aleksei Cherkasov with an added note from Alice, thanking him for his hospital performance and his kindness towards them both.

It surprised him how keen she was for him to talk about his ideas. At first she was just puzzled and asked endless questions, so he had to go back over the points again and again. It was good for him, too. He was forced to create metaphors and allegories, then give examples from his own struggles with understanding. One thing was clear, though. The intensity of her keenness demonstrated the depth of her determination to finally grapple with the demons at the core of her being. She suggested that at least once a week they devote an hour to confronting her problems.

"Not the fifty-minute hour?" he quipped.

"Full hour," she laughed. "I've had too many unfulfilled fifty-minute ones."

"So long as you realise I'm no psychologist. I don't pretend to be, and I don't want to be one. I'm just a friendly human being who might or might not be able to help. That's all. If you want, we'll just talk together. But you'll have to do a little work in between sessions – think of what you want to talk over and, most importantly, try to work on your own mechanisms, your way of thinking and how it may be possible to change."

"Is it possible to change, though? Really."

"Yes. Short answer – long list of reasons. I've already talked about them. We'll talk more, don't worry…"

The sessions became important for both of them. In fact, they weren't really sessions. Their original target was one hour once or twice a week, but the subject emerged at other times or when Alice felt especially anxious. It didn't matter. Both of them found it a compelling journey of discovery.

"It helps," Hawthorn said, "if you forget everything you ever learned about psychology. Not that all of it is bunk – it's just too cosy and taken-for-granted. I believe the effort is important, because it gives you the *intention* of a fresh beginning. You need to acquire access to your own inner knowledge that has so long been manipulated by the social matrix. I'm convinced you *know* your problem, and you know *how* to deal with it. The main difficulty is clearing away the rubbish that is obscuring it. Whether or not I can help in doing that, I don't know."

She leaned forward. "But you *are*. I never even thought of the social matrix. For me, that was just how the world *was*. It's an incredible idea that the whole framework is held together in our own consciousnesses. We are manipulated, but we can adapt and change it, when we are more aware of what's happening. It's almost like a hive, isn't it?"

"Yes. It is a hive – but even more sophisticated than that of bees, because it incorporates vocal language which gives us the decisive extra dimension of time. A story of our past, as well as a concept of our future. There are lots more tools as well. Most important of all, language allows us to infinitely alter the nature of the world self-reflectively. The successful matrix illusion is that the way it *appears* to be is the only way it *can* be. Just like the beehive is to the bee."

"Which would mean you are trapped."

"Exactly. If you are truly trapped, then there is no alternative but to accept the values on offer, behave yourself and be a worthy citizen."

"That's what I feel," she replied as she lit another cigarette and leaned back on the sofa. "Defined. Other people define what I am and my worth. Which is nothing, less than nothing."

Hawthorn sat in the big chair by his desk. It was a small room, and sitting there created a conversational space.

IS ALICE?

"Listen carefully. *All the definitions are your own.* You – and only you – define everything in the space of your world. You may allow other definitions to prevail – ones you think come from other people – but ultimately they're yours. You create them, but tag them with labels. 'From other people.' Or 'real.' Nonetheless, they're entirely yours. Unless you can tell me some method of discovering exactly what someone else is thinking. You have only this. You have what they say in the context of how they're saying it, and you have the tool of focus. After all, there's much happening out there. *Which* things do you notice? *Which* ones do you incorporate? And why those ones and not other ones?"

"When I'm anxious – and I'm anxious now – I'm just overwhelmed by discrete worries…"

"For instance?"

"Well, I've been worrying about the CCTV cameras they have installed at the hospital now – and probably microphones as well. They're in the street, too, everywhere. It sparks my sense of paranoia. Everyone knows what I'm doing, where I'm going and when."

Hawthorn leaned back in his chair and pushed away the thought of re-lighting his pipe. He was smoking too much recently. "I think the first thing you've got to do is try and understand something about the nature of the State. Use reason. It's a good tool, too. For a start, they do not have the manpower resources to examine all the footage of all the CCTV cameras. When they look at recordings, they are searching for specific events. Crack dealers. Whores. Robberies, muggings, car theft. Don't you think the authorities have *enough* to do just to keep up with the poor breaking the law to make a living in order to buy the trinkets dangled in front of them? Why would they be interested in some bird – a beautiful one, though – going into the corner shop to buy a newspaper?"

"I just don't *trust* them…"

"Trust is such a key element of the psyche. The first humans in contact with a child are probably the parents, in most cases the mother. Trust is not immediate. It grows only with time and connective experience. Consciousness, like even the lowly plant, needs more than one watering. Consistency is of primary importance as the child associates discrete actions and – later – the relationship of actions to words. If actions are inconsistent or belie the words, the child will be incapable of establishing full trust either in the 'world' or in its interpretation of crucial elements of its expanding social matrix."

She thought about this for a moment and shook her head sadly. "I never knew – ever – when either Mum or Dad were telling the truth. I was always confused…"

"The polar opposite of trust is not suspicion. It is fear. That which cannot be trusted will be feared, a natural response. In this respect, fear is not a bad thing in itself – it can assist a child in primitive protection. Animals, too, fear what they do not trust, as do adult human beings. As an essential emotional tool, fear is more than just handy."

IS ALICE?

Alice thoughtfully lit another cigarette. "I know what fear is. I've just been through six months of it."

He leaned forward on his elbows, buried in thought. "If fear is allowed to displace trust in the early phases in the development of consciousness, then this would be disruptive to consciousness in later years. The child is incapable of deciphering conflict, or of understanding it. If it receives contradictory information, trust in that exchange will be undermined, and there is a real danger that the necessary trust will be replaced by fear."

She pulled her legs up underneath her and moved the ashtray closer. "I wish you'd write this down, Theo. It sounds good, but I can never remember..."

Hawthorn sensed a shaft of inner illumination, and the words tumbled out. "I'll write it. I'll try. I've written a lot to Alyosha, and you can read that. Existentially, what happens is that consciousness loses faith in its own ability to make sound judgements. It does not trust *itself*. This is one of the most dangerous states that can be invoked. This is why it is so essential to establish strong threads of trust in the very beginning. If consciousness cannot trust itself, the world as it's held in the social matrix becomes fragile and precarious. Again, it is not the components of the world that can't be trusted, it's the individual's perception that has suddenly been emptied of trust. It is 'inside,' not 'outside.' When interior trust collapses like this, it is replaced instantly by fear. If the fear becomes intense, all rational facilities are profoundly useless. Fear is not just mental, it is physical – as it is with you. It is as total as trust needs to be. Paranoia can be more fully comprehensible if it is viewed in this context, as can aspects of so-called schizophrenia. What is an individual trapped in this landscape to do? There are no longer any tools at hand for escape. Where does consciousness go? What resources does it have? Well, the final resort is its fundamental resource of story-telling – because all of its world is nothing more than a complex series of stories. Fear has reduced consciousness to its own foetal position, eyes closed or clouded by tunnel vision, hearing and touch no longer reliable. All it is able to do is create its own matrix, because consciousness cannot exist without a matrix…"

He was totally engrossed now, and waved his pipe at the paper falcon hanging from his ceiling. "When the more mature mind is grappling with the complexities of relationships and values, early injury to trust destabilises the integrity of the 'world' and creates an undertow beneath the waves. Ordinary social intercourse is naturally made up of a witches' brew of truth and lies. Which are the lies of politeness, and which are malicious? Is a compliment true, or is it ironic or sarcastic? Essentially, are you faced with friend or foe? Innumerable judgements are made every day by anyone moving about in the modern world in a society no longer based on community – a handful of people, all of whom are known to some degree. In a city there are strangers everywhere, except in the retreat of a home. And even the home is invaded by the technology of TV and computers. It takes an extraordinarily steady hand on the tiller to navigate the rivers of life, and a steady hand will only be possible if the individual can summon deep self-worthiness."

IS ALICE?

* * *

"...fear is a thread woven throughout the social fabric, because it is so fucking useful. Fear causes the *hoi polloi* to turn to confident voices – authority. Fear is unsettling. It helps fuel commercial obsession – buying something will seem like a kind of balm, when it's just the opposite. Fear of poverty keeps you at your meaningless job, as does fear of losing your house. Spiritually you pick up on this fear, and it exacerbates your anxiety. It's like fire alarms going off in every room, and you can't turn them off. There's no smoke, no fire – just alarms. What I'm trying to show you is that fear is self-generated."

They were lying on their backs in bed, and a CD just finished playing. It was quiet.

"But you just said that I was picking up the threads of fear from the matrix."

"You are," he explained. "Then you are automatically making them your own. That's when the fear becomes *real* for you. You do the translation. And with you, it's dangerous. Fear of CCTV or fear of insects, fear of authority. This develops into paranoia, and you transfer the responsibility *outside* of you. *They* are out to get you. The persona, the value, is *out there*, where you have no control over it..."

"I've got to stop you there, Theo. It makes sense, but, like you say, it's *rational*. Of course I can see what's happening, but I have no time to think about it when it happens. I can't stop myself and say, 'I'm doing this.

It's me. I'm projecting my fears and rejecting my responsibility.' But my problem is that I'm already *in* it. Fear is reverberating every nerve of my body, like a tuning fork. Somehow I need to anticipate my reactions, but I don't know how."

He thought for a moment. "We're looking for a fountain head, and, if there is one, it lies in what you really want. Your initial view of yourself. What seems to be happening is that you are too far along the pathway before you realise it's the wrong one. Then it's too late. I've undergone change myself, and it helped to visualise the beginning of the path, then look down the trail I've been making all my life. That's when I have to ask myself an important question. 'Do I really want this? Or do I really want to change?' I then remind myself that, if I change, I change the world. The next thing is to realise that it is possible."

She shook her head. "I can't honestly do that. I'm not sure I believe that I can."

He smiled and took her hand in his. "All you have to do is look back over the story of your life. You never realised you could have this kind of life with a lover…"

She squeezed his hand. "No. You're right. I never would have imagined it. Ever. If I'd known it could exist, I would never have thought it was for me."

"When I first rode with you in your car, you fought for position, cursed other drivers when they cut you up…"

She turned to him and laughed. "But that was you. You told me I wasn't doing anything at all to the other drivers. I was making myself miserable. I saw it in an instant. Here I was, driving along, fighting all the way. It didn't have the slightest effect on other drivers, but it was guaranteed to wind me up into a frenzy on the way home."

"Exactly. You modified your values, and your world changed. Now you just drive along calmly, ignoring all the 'injustice' from other drivers. That's just one example. There are hundreds of others. The point is, you *can* change. The question then is whether you deeply want to. At first it's a huge nuisance, because it means re-arranging all the furniture…"

* * *

They were sitting in the front room, and Alice was still wearing her filmy dress. She had kicked off her high-heel mules, and her feet were tucked to her side as she leaned on the arm of the sofa smoking a cigarette. Theo rocked back in the big desk chair. He had on the dressing gown given to him by Aleksei Cherkasov, and his feet were bare. It was Sunday, and they had been playing all afternoon. Both were still flushed with the tingling scent of their secret journey. Normally Alice changed clothes immediately to be more comfortable, but their conversation drifted into 'therapy' again.

"You know," she mused, "I often wonder if I would have any chance of success if it weren't for our spiritual and physical closeness. It's a world I want so much."

He remained quiet, waiting, listening.

"It's a connection, isn't it?" she continued. "We talk and talk. Sometimes every day. Try this. Think this way. Look at things that way. Change perspective and focus. Write it down, turn it around, talk again. But you know…"

She took a drag on her cigarette and leaned forward to reach her tea mug. She took a sip and put the mug on the arm of the sofa. "…you know, I don't think I could do it if I didn't want *this* so much. *Us*. What happened today? Do you know?"

"I'm still recovering my senses."

"How can we be so close? Seemingly playing roles. But they aren't roles. They're us, a part of us… sacred, really. I change. And it's not a change, really. It's there. It's really me. And you. I control you and speak with a voice I never had, quietly, firmly. You respond, give yourself to me. There's a connection, a mystery. Something *is*… and *is not*. It's a masquerade, yet it's as real as anything in our daily lives. We move like two spirit worlds, separate but mingling. It makes me shiver to think about it."

He grabbed his pipe, glad it was still over half full of tobacco. As he lit it he looked at Alice. She was so beautiful and sexy it made his loins tingle. He had not had an orgasm, so he was still full of desire denied.

"We don't know what *is*, what exists. We're off the conventional path, though we use some conventional means because we don't know any other way. We are human, therefore we talk. But there's much more to being human – being *alive* – than that. Here in this room we're surrounded by familiar objects. Outdoors is familiar, too, and we expect familiar things and find them. What our senses expect is what the social matrix delivers. It is not what *is*. At most it is only a possibility."

He stopped to think, pulling at his pipe. "With our sexuality – our spirituality – we peel back the expected and create another matrix, an alternative one. I've told you of my visions and recurring imagery. You and I as lovers in the past. And then I'm some kind of weird warrior. I can't determine their reality, nor can I deny it. But the meaning is, for the moment, hidden because it has no context..."

"No fixed matrix."

"Exactly. Rationality can't be avoided when we talk, but it's of little use when we try and understand the spiritual area we have stumbled upon. That depends more on making connections and discovering the right horizon to display them on."

He stopped again to scratch his beard, then he waved his hand. "All these familiar objects here in this room would be baffling without our ability to focus and display them in the context of the social matrix we have learned since birth. Interactions with other people would be impossible. My strong suspicion is that there are many other matrices 'out there.' Somewhere."

"Like a dream?" she asked.

"Well, a dream *is* a different matrix. Which is why people find it so difficult to understand them. They are trying to translate them into *this* one."

"I'd kill for a cup of tea." She pretended to swoon.

"I'll get you one. I need to turn some lights on."

He rose, took the mug and went to the kitchen. When he returned, he placed the hot tea carefully on the coffee table within her reach.

She smiled up at him and touched his arm. "It's strange, isn't it? This trust between us."

He sat on the sofa beside her, and she moved her legs to make room for him. The rustle and zip of nylon were like the whispers of an insistent siren who lured him viscerally. He felt the beginnings of an erection. He could not resist placing his hand on her thigh.

"The magic," he said, "is when play becomes real. Years ago when we began, both of us were uncomfortable – at times anyway. I could see myself doing things because they were exciting. Now, you're right. It's different. We're both swept along by the wind and the throb of the dance."

She smiled, almost shyly. "But all the uncertainty goes when we're riding the wave."

IS ALICE?

Hawthorn shrugged. "Most people don't understand the dynamics in our play"

"Well, no. I don't think so. Taking the active part *gives* me strength. It's not my normal way. Normally I'm uncertain."

The warmth of her thigh and the thrilling gauze of her dress were distracting him. Reluctantly he withdrew his hand. "You see, we've constructed a world shared only by us. The references and values are different. They're infused with our intentions. In this world you have authority – we desire that to be, and so it is."

She leaned over and grasped his hand. "But love is so important. I couldn't do this with someone I didn't love. And I've never loved anyone but you…"

"It proves that, on the right nourishment, you can thrive and grow, continue becoming, open like a beautiful flower. For too long you have planted yourself in a desert – too much sun and no water, nothing but sand. Look around you now. It's a Garden of Eden, an oasis. There's a waterfall, and when you look above you can see shafts of light through the canopy of trees. Food is plentiful on the branches. Throw seeds on the earth, and they grow. *All things* are possible. Nothing is pre-determined. We are free to splash colour on the world, and 'out there' is a world of slaves who define their own slavery. If they discovered they had eyes, they would pluck them out in order to remain blind. They exchange charity for savagery, justice for cruelty and – most important – pleasure for pain! What paradox. With all their infinite choices, they've created a world of misery and greed."

He stopped, threw his head back and laughed. "I'm beginning to sound like an evangelist, and I'm far too much of a sybarite for that."

She looked at him and squeezed his hand again, holding her grip. "I love you."

* * *

They stood on the long, sandy beach at Walberswick under grey skies as the waves danced like white-capped demons, whipped by a sharp wind.

Hawthorn spotted a possibility, walked over and picked it up. It was a tiny, perfectly formed seashell. He went down to the water's edge and washed it. There was just a hint of pink at the opening of the shell.

"This one's not bad," he said, handing it to Alice.

"Best one yet." She smiled at him warmly as she examined it carefully before putting it in her pocket.

They beachcombed, and, as usual, found little gifts for each other. They had to be exactly the right thing, and most were rejected. Occasionally they were perfect. Those were lovingly collected by both of them in little boxes – smooth or eccentric stones and shells with a meaning hidden from all but them. They formed an archipelago of memories, more precious than diamonds.

IS ALICE?

Alice began to hunt desperately. She was falling behind, as Theo had been lucky that afternoon. In no time she bent forward to pick up a stone. She handed it to him.

"Rubbish," he said, tossing it away. "You'll have to do better than that."

They were both giggling like school kids. Alice danced ahead of him, trying to spot good choices first. She stopped several times, made an inspection, then dropped it. Theo was smiling, so pleased to see her happy. Her hair was growing now, and already she had it coloured with blonde highlights. Her red scarf had worked its way out of her coat, and one end was trailing on the sand. Her cheeks were flushed, and her eyes sparkled.

Suddenly she pounced on a small stone, examined it like a jeweller, then rushed back to him, nearly tripping on her scarf. She held it up between her thumb and forefinger like a precious ruby.

"There," she exclaimed. "And if you don't want it, I'll have it!"

He took it in his hand. The stone was almost black and shaped like a doughnut, with a perfect hole in the middle. There was a small moon of white on one side.

"I think this is the winning number here," he murmured as he turned it over with his fingers. "You're back in pole position, and I'll take it, thank you very much."

She re-tied her scarf, and they walked on, holding hands now. The beach was completely deserted. Even the proverbial lone man with his dog was not to be seen. There was the wreckage of an old pier, and Hawthorn eased himself onto the top of one of the shattered pilings. She sat beside him, nestling close.

"Enjoying yourself?" he smiled.

"Immensely!" she said. Her cheeks almost matched the colour of her scarf now.

Hawthorn put his arm around her shoulders, and they both gazed out at the wildness of the ocean. "Do you remember the last time we were here when we offered a prayer to Poseidon?"

She cocked her head. "It was when I was nearly ill, and you helped me. I was so astonished that you wanted to pray to an ancient Greek god."

"Looking out at the sea, one of my thoughts was that Poseidon must be in a frisky mood today. Not necessarily angry, though. Shall we offer another prayer?"

"Why?"

He hugged her. "Despite the materialism of the age, I've noted that so many of the people on earth have insisted on praying for innumerable millennia to various gods, that there must be something in it. I do it as well, did you know?"

"I think you mentioned it. If you find a deserted chapel…"

"Or a cathedral, even better. I slide into one of the pews to enjoy the silence and peace. Almost immediately I find myself meditating. Relaxing. I don't pray to a god. I have something I call my guardian. That's all I know about this entity. I see it as my guardian, so I can have someone to talk to."

"What do you ask for, mostly?"

"Wisdom," he said without a thought. "Wisdom above all, and I can't imagine anyone wishing for anything else. What more could you have? Riches? Fame? Illusions. Eternal life? Maybe – but useless without the wisdom."

"I think you *are* wise."

He wagged his finger. "Don't say it. It's profane. I believe wisdom is possible, but I know I don't have it. I wonder if I ever will, despite my pleas to my guardian. At times I think I'm close, only to realise later that it's a mirage."

"You do have wisdom, Theo. You *do*."

"Nonsense. Now what about our prayer to Poseidon?"

"What do I pray?"

"What you like, ninny. Clear your mind, and pray from your heart."

They sat together on the ancient pilings and faced the sea. Hawthorn relaxed himself and focused on the patterns of white caps, and the sound-suppressing roar. For a few minutes there was nothing. Then, like clouds forming faces, he began to see the outline of Alice's face. Her blonde, shoulder-length hair billowed out and haloed her spirited face, free of troubles, in full balance. She was of the sea, of the earth, radiant, full, complete.

"Let her be well, mighty Poseidon," he said silently to himself. "And guide me, please, to help guide her…"

"What did you pray for?" Alice asked, finally breaking the long silence.

He pressed her close to him. "I shouldn't tell. But I prayed for you…"

"Oh, Theo. I'm so moved I can hardly speak. Really? Oh, I adore you!"

"And you?"

She looked up at him. "I prayed for your wisdom."

He felt an overpowering surge of sentiment and touched her face. "We prayed for each other. It's typical. I think it would be difficult for anyone else to understand…"

"It was a strange feeling, sending a prayer out to sea. Appealing to Poseidon. Again. But I felt moved beyond words. By my serenity, mainly. And awe."

IS ALICE?

"I think prayer is a good thing," he said. "I can think of reasons, but I don't really know why. There is something that compels us to find a special spiritual space within from which to make an appeal. To what? To whom? My guess is that it is something inherent in the human being that reaches right back to our origins. Thus it must have importance. Rationalists would propose easy answers, and they don't convince me. To be honest, I'm not convinced by gods, either – though I leave myself open to that possibility, simply because I think the universe is so improbably strange. So different from what we are programmed to see or believe. We are missing the form, and therefore we are missing the meaning. Perhaps we see some of the letters, but not the words – and certainly not the verses."

"You know," she said after a few moments, "this spirituality I experience with you is as important to me as our therapy sessions. I can sometimes sense a feeling of wholeness, something that's completely alien to me, let me tell you. Those glimpses are so *precious*. Because they reveal possibilities I was unaware of. A landscape where I could walk with comfort! Can you imagine? It allows me to believe a different existence might be possible, that change might be possible. Without that... little peek into... a window in the dense undergrowth, I don't think I could actually overcome the inertia – or maybe reach the velocity to escape. Does that make sense, Theo? It gives me hope."

He thought quietly for a moment. "And play. We can play together. Not just the sexual scenes. But on the beach together, back in London, anywhere we are."

"Oh, yes, play. It's such a wonderful feeling. I lose the inner observer and just pelt along the playground, doing or saying anything I want, knowing I won't be judged or damned, watching you laughing. Then you're impish, and it just delights me. Do you know something? Never once – not *once* – have you ever raised your voice to me."

"Why should I?"

"No heavy hammers of criticism if I get something wrong. If I'm a klutz, you laugh. It just fills my heart with... love. I so desperately want to be with you. Forever. Until the end of time, and beyond even that. I dread anything happening to you. Or to us."

"Never let dread of the future distort the present. The present is all we ever have, and it's harmful to drag scenes of an imagined future into it. They say nothing is inevitable but death, and who really has the wisdom to confirm even that? I think I will die..."

She put her hand over his mouth. "Don't say it. Please don't say that."

He pulled her hand away gently. "Shhh. Don't get excited. Perhaps that will be the absolute end – then again, maybe instead there will be some kind of transfiguration. I can't say. No one can. There are no authorities on this. You can turn to no one but yourself, your world and what you know of it. Priests, scientists, thinkers, psychologists – all are totally worthless when it comes to matters of destiny..."

IS ALICE?

His oration slowly came to a close. He was aware that Alice's hand had worked itself under his jacket and was slowly pulling down the zipper of his flies.

* * *

The parcel arrived not long after Hawthorn rose from his bed, just after noon. Alice had been up for several hours already and was sitting opposite him at the table in the kitchen. He was just getting up to wash his porridge bowl after breakfast, still sluggish with sleep. At that moment the doorbell rang.

Theo turned it over in his hands as he slowly mounted the stairs. He examined the stamp with its Cyrillic lettering. The handwriting on the front was spidery and elegant, as if copied from an exercise manual. His brow was furrowed as he walked back into the kitchen.

"It's from Alyosha," he said, holding it up.

"Let's see," she said excitedly.

He passed the parcel to her, and she examined it as carefully as he had done. She squinted at the customs declaration, but it, too, was in Cyrillic.

"I wonder what it is."

Hawthorn was stunned by a sudden image. "I think I know. It couldn't be anything else."

"What? What?"

"Go on," he said. "Open it. I'll tell you the truth if I'm not right. But I know I'm right. And I'm staggered."

Alice dug at the tape, found an edge and delicately opened it. Inside was a very elegant-looking red satin box. She slowly opened it, then stared.

"It's the Order of Lenin, isn't it," he whispered.

"I don't know," she answered after a pause. She handed the opened box to him.

He looked down at it. "Yes. It is. It had to be. It's so moving I'm about to cry…"

Her eyes were wide. "What? Why?"

"You see, he wore this to the concert. Afterwards, when we talked, he told me why he now wore it. Excuse me, I've got to have a cup of tea, settle myself a little, fill a pipe. Then I'll tell you."

They sat together on the sofa in the front room. Hawthorn lit his pipe, got it stoked up, and then even allowed a little smoke into his lungs. He picked up the box with his other hand, put down the pipe and took out the medal. He held it up for her to see.

"Gold and platinum, I think. I'll have to look it up. Doesn't matter what it's made of, though." He handed it to Alice.

"It's a nice picture of Lenin," she murmured. "Beautiful. Gorgeous."

IS ALICE?

"He told me he never – or rarely – wore it during the Soviet period. After the collapse of the USSR, he always had it on his jacket when performing. Do you know why? Because he wanted to celebrate a great idea, something mighty that had happened, something that had been skewed by manifold later events. But the idea is everything, he said. The struggle by so many for so much against impossible odds had faded into history. Now the Augean Stables must be cleansed again, and this time the idea may be fully realised. If not, then the next time. Or the next. The idea will not die. Human beings could seek their destiny, even if they were never to know what it might finally be…"

Hawthorn realised his voice was breaking, so he grabbed his pipe and re-lit it, only to put it aside again nervously.

His voice was steadier now. "Humanity can change, just as you can change, my darling. It has gone mad. Madder than you'll ever be. I think this incredible gift is for both of us. Did you see? On the parcel? It was addressed to Mr and Mrs Theodore Hawthorn."

"I know," she whispered. "I thought it was a mistake."

"No," he said softly. "No mistake." He sat motionless, his mind a formless lazy haze. Emotion overpowered him. He turned to her and held her eyes.

"Will you marry me?"

NOTE

Bill captures in a magical and inspired fictional flourish the flavour of a hellish psychic anguish, revealing his own tender, loving, and creative compassion. It's rare to find stories that make a serious attempt to portray the workings of the mind of a mad person. This may be because of a widespread belief, often promoted by the psychiatric profession, that such a mentality has no logic. But I think that sense, if not of a conventional kind, can be made of these phenomenologies. He creates a story of a miraculous love affair, located within the political and social context, out of which madness springs, and illuminates the nature of consciousness, the mind and the emotional being.

Bill is an alchemist and a dreamweaver.

Bill's Loving Partner

Printed in the United Kingdom by
Lightning Source UK Ltd., Milton Keynes
138960UK00001B/1/P